MW01030202

MARIAH'S QUEST

DAUGHTERS OF HARWOOD HOUSE
Book Two

SALLY LAITY AND DIANNA CRAWFORD

BARBOUR
PUBLISHING

© 2012 by Sally Laity and Dianna Crawford

Print ISBN 978-1-61626-553-3

eBook Editions:
Adobe Digital Edition (.epub) 978-1-62029-006-4
Kindle and MobiPocket Edition (.prc) 978-1-62029-007-1

All scripture quotations are taken from the King James Version of the Bible.

This book is a work of fiction. Names, characters, places, and incidents are either products of the author's imagination or used fictitiously. Any similarity to actual people, organizations, and/or events is purely coincidental.

Cover credit: Studio Gearbox, www.studiogearbox.com

Published by Barbour Publishing, Inc., P.O. Box 719, Uhrichsville, OH 44683, www.barbourbooks.com

Our mission is to publish and distribute inspirational products offering exceptional value and biblical encouragement to the masses.

 Member of the
Evangelical Christian
Publishers Association

Printed in the United States of America.

DEDICATION

For their infinite patience, encouragement, and tireless support during the writing of this story, we lovingly dedicate this book to our families. May the Lord's richest blessings be always upon them.

ACKNOWLEDGMENTS

The authors gratefully acknowledge the generous assistance provided by:
Elaine McHale
Fairfax Regional Library
Fairfax, VA

Her help in gathering necessary period data and maps
and in sharing her knowledge of various settings
and prominent figures who played a part in colonial America's
fascinating history was most sincerely appreciated.

Special thanks to:
Delia Latham
Robin Tomlinson

Their excellent help in critiquing the manuscript along the way,
proofreading, and adding polish was truly valuable.
May God bless them both.

Chapter 1

Baltimore, Maryland, 1753

"Gentlemen! As I promised, I've saved the choicest for last."

Zachariah Durning, captain of the *Seaford Lady*, resembled an overstuffed goose in his ill-fitting dress uniform and powdered wig as he addressed the crowd of buyers on the Baltimore dock. His gold buttons threatened to pop when he puffed out his chest.

Mariah Harwood's heart pounded with excitement. . .and a mixture of dread and anxiety. She and her two sisters were about to be auctioned off as if they were no more than horses or cattle. But to whom?

For the past seven weeks aboard the huge ocean vessel, Mariah had held fast to the dream that some rich and stunningly handsome colonist would sweep her up in his arms and take her on a great adventure. Yet, standing on display before this assemblage of tradesmen like a flag on a flagpole, she knew she'd most likely be purchased by some uncouth man and end up scrubbing floors in a mean wife's kitchen for the next four years. Four crucial years. By the time she served out her indenturement, she'd be an old maid with rough, red hands.

She could not let that happen. She *would* not. After all, bearing a strong resemblance to her late mother, had she not always been considered the beauty of the family with her violet-blue eyes and black curls? And had she not turned down all of three marriage proposals in the recent past? She grimaced. If only she'd known then of the dire financial straits that would so unexpectedly befall her family and shatter all hopes of snaring a wealthy suitor.

"These three young lasses have been schooled in all the social graces, as well as the art of fine cooking," Captain Durning hollered for all to hear. "They can also read and do sums. Any one of 'em would make an ideal lady's companion or children's governess."

"Put up the one in blue," a fat man with bushy side-whiskers hollered. A gap in his waistcoat revealed a missing button, and the fingernails on his pudgy hands were chipped and dirty. "I'll bid on her."

Mariah gazed down at the fancy taffeta gown she'd donned that morning and swallowed. *I'm the one wearing blue!* What a stupid, romantic fool she'd been to deliberately sell herself into servitude for the inane reason that her chances of making a profitable match here in the colonies were likely to be far better than they'd been back home in England.

The captain reached down and hauled Mariah up onto the auctioneer's platform. "I'll expect a starting bid of no less than twenty-five pounds for this one."

Her heart in her throat, Mariah scanned the crowd sweltering beneath the June sunshine. Surely there must be a few, far more pleasing bidders than the sloppy old man who'd spoken up, men of higher quality—and hopefully far more attractive to the eye.

"Captain Durning!" she heard her older sister, Rose, challenge in her no-nonsense tone. "You agreed to sell us as a family." Determination glinted in the expressive, azure eyes she leveled on the commander of the ship, her fists planted on her slender hips.

Hope sprang anew inside Mariah. As forthright as Rose was in that sensible, nut-brown gown, she'd put an end to this travesty. Surely she would. She'd always done her utmost to look after the family to the best of her ability, putting their welfare far above her own.

But Durning didn't even bother to acknowledge honey-haired Rose. "What do I hear for the first bid?"

"I'll give ye twenty pounds." The paunchy onlooker raised a finger high. "Not a pence more."

Gritting her teeth, Mariah resumed her desperate search for a more promising individual.

"Twenty-one," came a voice at the back of the gathering.

Mariah turned her attention in the direction of that rich voice and caught a glimpse of a younger gentleman astride a long-legged bay. Her pulse skipped a beat. There he was! Just like in her dreams. Tanned and raven haired, and attired in a loose shirt and fitted breeches tucked into tall boots, he locked his dark eyes with hers. Entranced and enthralled by the fine figure he made atop his mount, Mariah willed him to outbid any others. *Please. . .please. . .*

"Twenty-two," she heard on the fringes of her consciousness as she continued to stare at the man she prayed would rescue her.

His mouth quirked into a half grin. "Twenty-three."

Trying to contain her hopeful smile, Mariah nibbled her lip.

"Mister Durning!" Rose interrupted more sternly. "I shall be forced to call the authorities if you do not honor the agreement you made with our father." A frown marred her otherwise feminine features but somehow only added to a beauty that radiated from within.

Mariah felt her smile wilt at the edges. Would the young gentleman part with enough funds for her *and* her sisters? The starting bid asked for her alone was far more than the captain had paid their father for all three of them.

"We have no written contract, wench," Durning spat, his florid complexion darkening as he glared down at Rose. "I'll thank ye to keep yer mouth shut."

"And I'll thank you to honor your word as a gentleman, sir." Rose had never been one to give up easily.

Mariah glanced again at the handsome rider at the rear of the crowd. He'd pushed his tricornered hat back, exposing features so stunningly perfect as to have been fashioned by an accomplished sculptor. His grin widened as his gaze remained focused on her alone. Her smile regained its strength. Perhaps there was hope, after all.

Nevertheless, the confrontation between the captain and her older sister continued. "What we have, shrew, is yer name on a legal document that says I have the right to sell the three of ye to whomever I please." Durning puffed out his bulging chest again. "And if ye don't keep quiet, I'll have ye locked in the hold of me ship until I complete the rest of me business."

"Not before I summon the port authorities." Rose whirled around, her expression rife with purpose.

The last thing Mariah wanted was to be parted from her sisters. . .but she could ill afford to lose her ardent bidder, either.

"Good sirs." The captain nodded to some men in the front. "Lay hold of this baggage and hold her whilst I fetch my men."

The insufferable cur actually intends to lock poor Rose in the hold? Mariah felt her own anger coming to the fore. The man's insensitivity was not to be borne.

One of the onlookers laughed as he and another fellow grabbed Rose's arms. "Don't fret, Cap'n. We'll see the lass stays put."

Trying to wrench free, but to no avail, Rose turned her fury on the two ruffians. "And I'll see you and your manhandling cohorts brought up before the magistrate."

Outraged at the injustice of seeing her sister being treated so roughly and held against her will, Mariah started forward to aid her, but the captain caught her arm and held her fast.

Their youngest sister, Lily, flaxen-haired and delicately formed, edged next to Rose and tugged on her ruffled half sleeve. "Please, Rose. Don't say anything more. They'll take you away." At a tender fourteen, Lily was too young and innocent to lose the sister who had mothered her since she was three years of age. Shy by nature, a flush on her fair cheeks matched the pale pink of her gown and accented the sprinkling of freckles across the bridge of her pert nose.

Rose's taut body slumped in defeat as the fight left her.

Mariah swung her attention back to her dream man and sighed her gratitude. He was still there, beholding her.

"I'll bid thirty pounds on the beauty in the blue frock." He tipped his head slightly in her direction.

Thirty pounds! No one had to tell Mariah that was an exorbitant amount to pay for four years of service.

"Thirty-one," came another voice on the opposite side of the crowd.

With every fiber of her being, she willed her hero to bid more.

His grin widening with confidence, the young man hooked his leg over the pommel of his saddle, a sure sign he was prepared to stay as long as it took to win the bid. "Forty."

A murmur swept the crowd.

Such a high bid! And all for her. Truly he was her knight of the realm.

A long pause ensued. When no further bid was forthcoming, the captain gave a decisive nod. "Sold! To the gentleman on the fine stallion."

The handsome rider gave a triumphant laugh and nudged his mount forward, weaving through the crowd until he reached the platform. He reached out to Mariah.

With a nervous giggle, she moved to the edge and allowed him to pull her and her voluminous skirts onto the bay steed. His arms encircled her, and the scent of his bay rum cologne blended with the smell from the baking houses that provided bread and rolls to seagoing vessels. The man smelled every bit as good as he looked.

But leave it to Rose to ruin the moment. Marching right up to the two of them, she snatched a handful of Mariah's blue taffeta hem. "Come down from there this instant."

"Miss Harwood does have a point." Captain Durning nodded.

Mariah's breath caught. Surely he hadn't changed his mind about the sale.

"Ye'll not be taking that lass anywhere until there's hard cash in me hand and ye put yer signature on the indenturement." With a smug look, Durning turned to Rose. "Everything proper and legal."

Her lips in a grim line as she glared at the captain, Rose yanked on Mariah's skirt again.

Mariah had no recourse but to offer her new owner an apologetic smile and permit him to lower her to the ground, which he did, but ever so slowly. He then dismounted and came to stand beside her, enveloping her hand in his. Mariah sensed from the dedication in his expression that he would have paid whatever amount of money it took to purchase her. It was a heady notion.

Then a rather unsettling and unwelcome thought intruded, bringing her back to earth. This powerfully built man, however handsome and charming he appeared, did happen to be a total stranger. Why had he bought her? What exactly were his plans for her? For all she knew, he could be an abuser of women. Or worse!

As she tried to absorb the fact that she had no idea why a complete stranger would offer good money to purchase her papers, she felt Rose latch on to her arm and tug her away to stand between her and Lily. Now that her hand was no longer tucked inside her new owner's, Mariah missed the comforting warmth his grasp had provided.

She glanced over her shoulder to find him standing directly behind her. His dark brown eyes gazed down on her with a sympathetic smile. This man was not someone to be feared. Surely he had stepped wondrously, magically right out of her dearest dreams. She allowed herself a moment to admire his manly features.

So caught up was she in the moment, she scarcely noticed when her baby sister Lily was put on the block for sale and stood with head bowed, trying to be invisible. Nor did she feel concern that Rose was again acting like a mother hen and causing a humiliating fuss, arguing with Captain Durning. As the two events made their way into her consciousness, however, Mariah decided to use them to her advantage. With Rose otherwise occupied, she turned once more toward her gentleman. She certainly didn't want him to entertain second thoughts about the exorbitant bid he'd made. But the captain's voice drew her back to the moment.

"Sold to the fine gentleman in the front."

Mariah searched the crowd to find the individual who'd bought Lily.

Appearing to be in his late twenties, and attired in coarse, homespun clothing, the man was no gentleman of wealth. With dark brown hair and eyes of soft blue, he did have a kind face, though, and a tall, lean build similar to their own father's. More important, Rose seemed pleased, and so did Lily. At least a modicum of the younger girl's trepidation seemed to have eased.

"Hie thyself up here, wench." A sour scowl accompanied the captain's command, and Rose's smile lost its luster as the two ruffians who'd stayed her earlier bumped past Mariah and hoisted Rose onto the platform with boisterous laughter.

With all her older sister's discordant protests, Mariah knew Rose had made a spectacle of herself. This became even more evident when guffaws and a round of applause resounded from several quarters. How mortifying!

She checked to see her owner's reaction but saw that he was pre-occupied with toying with the wispy plume of her bonnet.

He came alongside her, now that Rose no longer hovered, and took her hand in his with a gentlemanly bow. "Allow me to introduce myself. My name is Colin. Colin Barclay, of Barclay's Bay Plantation."

Mariah smiled and gave a sweeping curtsy. "Pleased to meet you. I'm Mariah Harwood, daughter of the finest goldsmith and jeweler in Bath, at your service." As the irony of her statement dawned on her, she flashed a wry grin. "Quite literally, it would seem."

"And I yours." Colin accented his grand gesture by lifting her hand and brushing it softly with his lips.

Remembering Rose, Mariah shot a guilty glance up at her.

Her older sister had other worries at the moment. She stood rigidly beside the captain as he raised his voice again.

"Now, if ye want a full day's labor for yer money, this spinster here's the one yer lookin' fer. The female's five and twenty. In her prime. She's run an entire household since she was thirteen. Raised her four siblings, including two brothers, and ye've seen how the lasses here turned out." The reprobate cocked a self-satisfied brow.

Rose looked utterly devastated. Mariah's heart went out to her. In reality, Rose had been far more to her and the rest of the family than Captain Durning had expounded. The very selling of herself into servitude had been a desperate measure she'd taken upon herself to save their father from debtor's prison. She had intended only to sell herself, but Mariah and Lily had volunteered to accompany her for their own personal reasons, no matter how altruistic they'd considered themselves. Young Lily hadn't wanted to be parted from the only mother she could remember. And as for herself, well. . . Mariah turned another admiring look back at her handsome new owner.

"The wench's sisters may have virtues enough," someone yelled, "but this one's got the tongue of a fishwife!"

Laughter at poor Rose's expense again rang out. These unfeeling men were making cruel sport of her. . .even if the last remark did happen to be funny. Mariah couldn't squelch the smile that twitched her lips.

And Rose saw it.

Chagrined, Mariah quickly covered her mouth with her free hand as warmth climbed her cheeks.

Durning quieted the crowd with a raised arm and continued. "The woman's only actin' the way of any mother hen worth its feathers. She's tryin' to keep her little chicks tucked beneath her wings. Of the three of 'em, she's by far the most experienced worker."

Mariah was glad that the captain, the real deceiver, finally defended Rose.

The haggling started up in earnest but was interspersed with paltry comments. Someone said her hands looked soft; another said she and her sisters' clothes looked too fine. "Mayhap the lasses are more used to givin' orders than takin' 'em," one finally suggested. Mariah rolled her eyes.

By this time, even Durning himself appeared weary of the process. He hiked his pretentious bulk up and scowled at the speaker. " 'Tis true, the Harwood sisters come from excellent stock on t'other side of the water. To see any of 'em put to work as simple scrubwomen would be a pure waste. This one in particular is accomplished at preparin' tasty foods. She can put every spice ever brought to the British Isles to proper use."

That remark accelerated the bidding to such a pace Mariah couldn't discern the source of each offer as they rose a pound at a time to nineteen.

Then from the rear came a piercing high voice. "Did ye say the lass is a good cook?"

"Aye."

"I'll gi' ye fifty pound fer her."

"Sold!"

Astounded murmurings swept through the gathering, and Mariah swung to see who'd offered such an unheard-of price without so much as a second's hesitation. Her mouth dropped open in shock.

The buyer climbing down from a loaded wagon was by no means a fine gentleman. His clothing and floppy hat looked soiled and disheveled. As his scuffed boots reached the decking and he turned to face forward, she saw that he was a squat older man who couldn't possibly have bathed in months. In a deplorably smudged and droopy ruffled shirt, he kneaded his frizzled beard and headed straight for the platform.

And straight for Rose.

Following the captain as he stepped down to meet the unkempt man, Lily rushed to Rose's side. "What are we to do, Rose? You cannot go with that nasty lout. He's horrid."

In complete agreement with Lily, Mariah drew close to her sisters. "We must not allow that disgusting creature to take you off to heaven knows where. I shall have Colin speak to Captain Durning on your behalf."

Despite her own unbelievable turn of fate, Rose's brows dipped into a frown at Mariah's words. "Colin is it? And I suppose *Colin* is already addressing you by your given name, as well."

Mariah's hackles went up. "Upon my word, Rose. This is not the time for such trivial nonsense." She whirled away to fetch her own stylish buyer.

Right on her heels, Rose caught up with her and wrapped a staying arm around her as they approached Colin Barclay. She spoke to him in her forceful tone. "Sir, before you sign my sister's papers, I'll thank you to relate exactly what duties will be expected of her in your employ."

What a crude thing to imply. Mariah felt her face grow hot with embarrassment. She lowered her gaze to the splintery planks of the dock. Embarrassed or not, she wanted to hear his answer, to set her own mind at rest.

"To be quite truthful, Miss Harwood," he said, his voice smooth and unperturbed, "I have no duties in mind for her whatsoever."

At his odd reply, Mariah peered up from beneath her bonnet's brim to see his relaxed and smiling face as he continued.

"But I assure you, my mother shall be most pleased at my finding someone of your sister's refined qualities to be her companion."

What a perfect response to Rose's impudent inquiry, Mariah mused, marveling inwardly.

Her older sister looked stunned. "You. . .you bought her for your mother?"

"Why, yes. Of course. Surely you didn't think me the sort to have something else in mind for the lass." He arched his brows in pure innocence.

Mariah had a hard time keeping her mirth to herself.

Rose, however, was unimpressed. "Then I'm sure you'll not mind pledging to see my dear, virtuous sister placed into your mother's watchcare before the sun sets this day. And you'll see to her religious instruction as well."

That was beyond rude. *"Rose."*

Colin placed a calming hand on Mariah's arm as he met Rose's eyes. "You have my most solemn word, miss."

Somewhat mollified, Rose withdrew a shard of lead and a scrap of paper from her pocket. "Might I ask where I might post my sisterly correspondence? I should hate to lose touch with one of the only two relatives I possess on this continent."

"Of course. Send it to Barclay's Bay Plantation."

Mariah swelled with pleasure as the conversation receded into the background. Colin Barclay must be the owner of one of those sprawling, prosperous farms she'd heard that so many of the British aristocracy had come to America to establish. Why, he could quite possibly be related to a lord, or even the king!

A sudden gasp from Rose interrupted her musings. *"A day's ride?"*

Letting out an impatient breath at having missed some pertinent details, Mariah suddenly recalled her older sister's impending dire fate.

She turned to Colin. "Pray, sir, forgive me, but I'm afraid my sister and I have a matter of much deeper concern. We must not allow that swarthy old man to take her away. Would you please speak to the captain? Implore him to withdraw those proceedings."

For the first time, Colin's expression turned grave. "My dear Mariah, the man bid fifty pounds."

"Yes, we're aware of that." She offered her most pleading smile. "However, if you would just try."

He gave a sad shake of his head. "I regret to say all closing bids are final. I do find it rather astounding, though, that one so unkempt should have that amount of ready cash on hand. One can only wonder how he came by such funds."

So nothing could be done. Mariah caught Rose's hand and gave it an empathetic squeeze. Still, she could not bear to think the worst, especially after exchanging addresses with her sisters and learning that correspondence to Rose could be sent to the Virginia and Ohio Company in Alexandria. From what Colin had told them, that was a town not far from his plantation. "We shall keep in close touch," she assured Rose. "Everything will be just fine." It would. It had to be.

Mariah's optimism prevailed as the moneys were paid and signatures recorded, as she again was lifted up to Colin on his finely bred horse, and as she waved a fond farewell to her two forlorn-looking sisters. Her spirits continued to stay high as she rode through Baltimore with Colin pointing out the many mercantiles and shops of what appeared to be a very prosperous city. Truly it proved to be far beyond her own expectations.

But once they passed by the last sprinkling of buildings in the bright midmorning sunlight and she found herself enshrouded by eerie, shadowed woods and totally alone with this strange man, she came to her senses.

As glib as Colin Barclay—if that was even his true name—had been as he'd reassured Rose of his good intentions, Mariah could now imagine any lie might roll as sweetly and smoothly from this charmer's lips—this man who now held her captive within his arms.

Who was he? Where exactly was he taking her? And for what purpose?

Unable to imagine what uncertainties awaited her when they reached their destination, Mariah's fears raced ahead of her through the primeval forest in this unknown land.

Chapter 2

M ariah. . .that is a beautiful name."

They'd ridden through the dim woods in silence for a time. No sounds accompanied the steady *clop-clop* of the horse's hooves other than the rush of wind through the treetops and the trilling of birds, so Colin Barclay's richly modulated voice startled Mariah. He had a sort of lazy-sounding accent she found quite pleasant to the ear. She struggled to maintain a calm demeanor before answering. "So I've been told."

Neither spoke for another quiet span, until Mariah decided that conversing might help to dispel some of her unease, particularly if she selected the topic. "My father chose to call my other sisters by rather fanciful biblical names—Rose of Sharon and Lily of the Valley. But because I favored one of my late aunts, I was named after her."

"It suits you perfectly." His mouth was so close to her ear, she felt the warmth of his breath. "Mariah. . . Your name fairly floats on the breeze like a will-o'-the-wisp."

She answered cheerily, hoping to keep the moment light. "My, but aren't you the poetic one. Speaking of families—"

"I didn't know I was." His breath feathered across her ear again.

"Speaking of families," Mariah repeated evenly as she sat up straighter, "I've got two brothers at home in Bath. Have you any brothers or sisters?"

She heard him inhale, and the leather saddle creaked as he adjusted his position. "I'm the only surviving son. I do have three younger sisters, however. The youngest is eight, and the oldest is fifteen."

Mariah gave a small nod. "As you must have concluded from the speech that dreadful Captain Durning gave regarding the three of us, our mother went to be with the Lord more than a decade ago, rest her soul. Are both your parents still living?"

"Yes." A low chuckle rumbled from his chest. "They're both very much alive."

"Then you are truly blessed." With that third reference to her family's faith, Mariah hoped to quell any untoward plans Colin Barclay might have. Though she was by no means as ardent as Rose in her religious beliefs, Mariah did retain certain standards, and she knew her actions on the auction platform had stretched propriety more than a little.

Gazing forward, she noticed they were about to break out of the trees, into the safer light of day. She spotted a river just ahead of them on the wagon-rutted road and saw a ferry dock jutting out at the bottom of the bank. A light wind stirred shallow whitecaps here and there among the current. "Will we be crossing to the other side?"

"Aye, as a matter of fact, we will. We'll cross this river along with several others before we reach my place."

"So many?" Mariah frowned. Just how far away was this place of his? And would the daylight hold out until they reached their destination?

"Yes. Quite a few. We'll dismount for the ride over, give Paladin a chance to rest. It'll take us almost the entire day to reach the plantation at the leisurely pace we've been travelin'," he drawled. "Since we're ridin' double, I don't want to put too much on the boy." He leaned harder against Mariah to administer a pat to the bay's muscled dark brown neck. "He's bred for speed. I've won some pretty pennies with him."

"He certainly is a fine-looking animal." Mariah deftly tilted forward to keep at least the semblance of a proper distance between her and her owner. So the man was a gambler. How many other vices did he have?

As if taking her subtle hint, Colin straightened his posture. "Yes, we're quite proud of our stable."

We? Was the blighter married? He couldn't possibly be, could he? But then it was entirely feasible there may not be a mother, either. It might be advantageous to plan some sort of hasty escape, should one become necessary. He'd reported that Alexandria, where Rose was headed, was a short distance from his plantation. She might be able to seek a safe haven there with her older sister. In any case, Mariah knew she would need her luggage. "With such a distance to your plantation, do you think my trunks will arrive by wagon before the morrow?"

"Of course. I gave the driver a generous tip. He's probably not more than a mile or so behind us." He paused. "Speaking of those trunks—if the gowns they contain are even remotely as fashionable as the one you're wearin', you could have sold them and paid your own fare to Baltimore, thereby avoidin' an indenturement entirely. Not that I'm complainin' at all."

Picking up on the eager note in his tone, Mariah decided she'd be relieved when they were able to dismount so she could see his face and discern his true merit. She tried for a bright lilt when she spoke. "Surely you know a young gentlewoman could not possibly present herself in public without an adequate wardrobe." Then, recalling the way Rose had ravaged all their best frocks, she couldn't help a moment's grousing. "I do grieve, however, that my sister felt compelled to sell my two most elegant evening gowns."

"Hmm. If you don't mind my askin'," Colin said as they started down the bank, "what dire calamity befell your family that necessitated your having to sail across the ocean? I believe you said your father is a goldsmith and that you resided in a most fashionable resort, did you not?"

"Ah, yes. The calamity." Mariah shook her head, feeling her blood heat at the memory. "The cause was the untimely death of a rapscallion young nobleman. The young lord had purchased dozens of very expensive brooches on account for his many lady friends, for which my father was never reimbursed. After the scoundrel's death, his uppity skinflint uncle refused to honor his nephew's enormous debt. In turn, my father was not able to pay his."

"I see. Say no more for the moment," Colin spoke quietly as they reached the dock. "Ferry operators have the loosest tongues in the colonies."

As Colin swung down from the stallion, Mariah eyed the wiry ferrymen, one at the mule-drawn wheel and the other opening the front gate of the docked flatboat. She wished she could question them, learn from their lips who exactly her handsome owner was. But as he took his time lifting her down, then wrapped an arm about her waist before leading the horse onto the raft, she doubted she'd have the chance to question anyone.

Mariah had to admit that Colin Barclay had not lied about the distance, at least. They'd passed numerous plantations containing miles of rolling, cultivated farmland and several charming hamlets brimming with a veritable symphony of flowers that took her breath away with their brilliant hues. The colonists appeared every bit as industrious as the folks back home in Britain. She suppressed a weary sigh when Colin finally suggested they stop at a roadside inn to rest the horse and partake of a meal. The horse wasn't the only one who needed a rest. Hours of bumping her bottom against the hard leather saddle had taken its own toll. Would she be able to manage anything akin to a ladylike walk once her feet touched solid ground?

Colin reined their mount onto a gravel-lined drive that fronted a two-story fieldstone building with royal-blue shutters and double doors. A sign hanging from a signpost read KNIGHT'S REST INN. He swung down to the ground and reached up to assist Mariah. The weakness in her legs did make it difficult to stand, momentarily, and she more than appreciated the way he steadied her with a strong arm.

A freckle-faced lad came running from around the side of the inn, his floppy cloth cap almost tumbling from his copper hair with each footfall. "Mr. Barclay! Back already?" Then, spying Mariah, he slowed to a stop and gawked at her. "Oh. Uh. . .I better see to your horse."

Grinning, Colin flipped him a coin. "I'd appreciate that, Billy."

Even outside the structure, Mariah could detect a delicious mixture of food smells emanating from within, and her stomach came close to rumbling. Thank heaven it wouldn't be another moldy shipboard meal awaiting her here! And the boy had called Colin by name, so surely that had to be her owner's true identity. Mayhap everything else he'd told her would prove to be true, as well. Perhaps he actually did have a mother to whom he would deliver her.

As he opened one of the blue doors and escorted Mariah inside, she determined that by the time the meal was over, she'd learn whether or not he had a wife, or her name wasn't Mariah Harwood.

~

"Good day, Mr. Barclay." The exuberant greeting came from a flaxen-haired serving girl balancing a tray of soiled dishes against her shapely hip as Colin escorted Mariah across the inn's low-ceilinged common room. The girl's gaze then swung to the beauty on his arm, and her smile flattened.

The server had every reason to be envious, Colin conceded. Any woman who entered Mariah Harwood's sphere would place a distant second. Long lashes framed her stunning violet eyes under tapered brows, and beneath her straw bonnet, silky brown-black curls caressed her slender shoulders. He could hardly keep his eyes from focusing on the soft, rosebud lips that turned up at the corners. The English beauty was as much a champion as Paladin. "Where would you like us to sit, Peggy?"

Her attention returned to Colin, and she flopped her free hand in a casual gesture. "Anywheres. We ain't too busy this time of day. Will you be wantin' a meal?"

"Yes. And some cool cider, if you please."

The ruffle on her mobcap bobbed with her nod as she carted the soiled dishes to the kitchen.

Colin figured that if they chose to sit at one of the long wooden tables occupying the center of the room, some bloke might scoot in next to his lovely companion. Wanting to keep her all to himself, he seated Mariah at a small square table by a window, then took the opposite chair while she settled her skirts about her. Only a sprinkling of other patrons talked among themselves as they enjoyed their food. None seemed to pay Colin and Mariah any mind.

"I hope I don't reek of horse too much," Mariah commented, wrinkling her nose. "That serving girl, Peg, didn't seem too pleased with me."

Colin chuckled. "My dear Mariah! You are a star that outshines all other young maidens. I would imagine you'd be used to that sort of reaction by now."

The small ivory plume on her bonnet dipped as she gifted him with a coy tilt of her head. "La, but you do flatter me."

"Truth is not flattery."

"That may be so. However, my sister Rose never ceases to remind me that true beauty is not outward but comes from within."

He sat back and grinned. "Ah, yes. The valiant Rose. She makes quite the impression on one."

Mariah's tapered brows knitted closer as her expression filled with dismay. "Dear Rose. Having to go with that grimy oaf who bought her. I cannot believe she's bonded to someone like that awful man. I do hope she will fare all right."

Reaching across the table, Colin covered Mariah's smaller hand with his. "Don't fret. Your sister seems to be a stalwart sort. And I'm sure we saw that fellow at his worst. Since he works for a fur company, he most likely just arrived from the wilderness. Once he reaches home, his missus will no doubt make sure that he's scrubbed down good and proper."

"Oh, my." Mariah sighed with longing. "I've not had a real soak in a tub since we departed England." Twin spots of color suddenly sprang to life on her cheeks. She jerked her hand from beneath his and covered her mouth, her eyes wide with shock. "I cannot believe I uttered something so unseemly in the presence of a gentleman. Pray, do forget my rash words."

"Never fear, my dear Mariah," he said gently. "Unseemly or not, I'll see that you have your wish the moment we arrive at home."

His remark seemed to aid the return of her composure, as she visibly relaxed. "Bless you." She paused. "I certainly wouldn't want to cause your wife undue inconvenience."

Colin couldn't help but chuckle at her not-so-subtle attempt to gain personal information. "I have no wife, I'm sorry to say. . .nor even a betrothed, much to the dismay of my matchmaking mother."

He caught the barest hint of a smile playing with a corner of Mariah's rosy lips just as Peggy arrived. The serving girl bore a platter loaded with tall glasses of cider and plates heaping with shepherd's pie, along with generous chunks of crusty bread. Setting it down, she distributed the various items without meeting either of their eyes and quickly swung away, her serviceable indigo skirt flaring with her movements.

Mariah seemed oblivious to the girl as she immediately picked up her fork and speared a bit of meat. Obviously her ladyship wasn't too coy to reveal she was as hungry as he was. Suddenly, however, she stopped, her fork posed midair. "Do forgive me. I was so caught up in the delicious scent of real food after the sorry ship's fare we were forced to endure that I completely forgot my manners. You must think me a heathen, not waiting for you to bless our food."

She expected him to pray aloud? In this public place? A quick glance around revealed that the other customers didn't even know he and Mariah were there, but from the corner of his eye he could see Peggy observing them. Still, he couldn't allow this lovely Englishwoman to think a Virginia gentleman was any less a Christian than she. "Shall we bow our heads?" Even as he said the words, he felt heat climbing his neck. "Father in heaven, we thank You for this hearty meal. And thank You," he tacked on for good measure, "for Mariah Harwood's safe arrival to our shores. We know it had to be Your providence that brought me to the Baltimore wharf at the very moment she was most in need. In Jesus' name. Amen."

"Amen." After her echoing whisper, Mariah met his eyes, her own filled with questions. "May I ask what brought you to the docks so far from your home?" She sliced a bit of the pie's potato crust.

"Horses. I delivered a mare and her foal to a man about to embark by ship to Bermuda. I made certain the animals were safely aboard and then left. . .and that's when I saw you in your lovely blue gown and bonnet."

"I see." With a smile, she lifted her food to her mouth.

Colin slathered butter on a chunk of bread and took a bite, wondering how his father would take the news that forty pounds of the horse money had been spent to purchase a bond servant they didn't need. Then he realized his father was the least of his worries. The biggest challenge ahead was how to get Mariah into the house past his mother. A slow smirk tickled his lips. Of course, he could rent her a room across the river in Georgetown. Digging into his slice of shepherd's pie, he glanced up at the stunningly beautiful, but rather prim, young lady across from him. No. No matter how much she'd flirted with him from upon the auction block, she'd actually stiffened whenever he'd moved too close to her during their ride here. No doubt she'd balk at the very idea of being his mistress. . .delicious though the notion might be.

He had no other choice. He had to take her home with him to the plantation. Taking a sip of cider, he mulled over the story he'd concocted for Mariah's sister, how he'd bought her for his mother. The more he thought about it, the more he surmised that perhaps it was just the ticket.

"Mariah," he ventured after a few more thought-filled swallows of his drink, "I noticed when you signed your name to the bond that you had lovely penmanship. Did you, by chance, handle any business correspondence for your father?"

She blotted her lips on her napkin. "Why, yes. I did. And because of my handwriting, I also answered the various invitations our family received to social engagements."

Excellent. "And I'm sure you possess many other accomplishments, as well. The art of stitchery, perhaps."

A frown creased her smooth brow. "Stitchery. Such a tedious endeavor. I'll allow I can do it adequately, if I must, but I much prefer playing music for others to stitch by."

Good. Good. "You play an instrument, then."

"I play two, in fact. The flute and the harpsichord. I can also play the cello and violin a bit, if need be."

Even better!

"But alas, Rose sold my flute when she sold my prettiest frocks, as well as forfeited my dowry." Her lips thinned to an angry line; then with a sigh, she relaxed and mustered a weak smile. "No sense crying over spilt milk, as they say. I must learn to embrace whatever the Good Lord has in store for me."

Colin reached an empathetic hand across the table to cover hers again. "Be assured I will do all in my power to make your introduction to our fair land as enjoyable as possible." He had to admit it did sound good and was easy to say. But getting Mariah past his formidable mother and comfortably ensconced in their home would take far more effort and ingenuity. . .if it were even possible.

Chapter 3

Colin felt Mariah inhale deeply and knew she was about to speak.

"Since we took leave of Baltimore, we've passed through quite a few farms and plantations surrounded by forest, and a scant number of small villages. Is Alexandria merely another hamlet, or is it, perchance, a city?"

He reveled in her British accent and liked listening to her lyrical voice. . .almost as much as he enjoyed holding her within his arms. He only wished he'd been able to hold her close during the numerous ferry rides, particularly the last one, across the Potomac. They had arrived in Virginia at last. "Alexandria isn't a city like Baltimore, but it does boast a fine little string of shops. I'm afraid we won't be traveling into the town this evening, however. The crossroad just ahead runs alongside the river and edges our plantation."

"And how much farther do we still have to go?" she asked over her shoulder.

Colin sensed her weariness. A ride on horseback from the port of Baltimore was a challenging distance for even an experienced rider, and added to her ordeal on the auction block and the ensuing parting with her sisters; she'd had a long, trying day. "Less than an hour." He glanced at the sinking sun. "We should arrive home in time for supper. I'm honored to report that our cook happens to be one of the best in the county."

A slight tip of her head acknowledged the information.

Much of his uneasiness over having purchased Mariah had dispelled during the hours since leaving the roadside inn in Blandensburg. Now as they turned east onto the river road, he mentally tallied the reasons for his confidence. The young Englishwoman was a perfect fit for his family. Besides the excellence of her education, her every mannerism was grace itself. His sisters could learn a lot about being accomplished young ladies from Mariah. And best of all, she spoke with the cultured accent his mother continually tried to instill in the rest of the family.

He smiled to himself. Coming from a Boston merchant background, his mother considered the more relaxed drawl of a Virginian quite common. "*Quite common, indeed,*" she'd told them all hundreds of times. He and his pa strove to speak properly whenever they were in her presence. She was certain to appreciate having Mariah around.

Tilting his head a bit, he studied the delicate curve of Mariah's very tempting neck. Even if it weren't so tempting, four years' secretary and tutor service for a paltry forty pounds sterling was an astounding bargain. Besides, he was a grown man. He'd be twenty-five in a few months. High time he stopped allowing Mother to question his every decision.

"If I might ask, how do you plantation folk pass leisure time, living so far from a city?" Mariah asked, the musical lilt in her voice pleasuring him yet again.

Colin recognized that, as a stranger in a strange land, she needed to be put at ease. He gave a light chuckle. "You won't be bored, I can assure you. We have parties and afternoon teas and do almost everything our more sophisticated town dwellers do. If there happens to be an interesting play or musicale in one of the larger cities, we don't find the distance overly daunting. We go downriver to the port and catch one of the coastal packets that ply the waters between our cultural centers." For a moment he envisioned himself having this lovely Englishwoman on his arm wherever an activity might take them, a delightful possibility.

Mariah nodded, then straightened her spine. "There's a rider coming toward us. I think he's trying to get your attention."

Leaning to peer around her, Colin spied Dennis Tucker, his lifelong chum from the neighboring plantation, waving an arm. He groaned inwardly at the bad timing. With the young man's golden-boy looks and natural charm, the two of them were forever in competition when it came to the local belles, and Tuck would definitely be interested in Mariah.

As his friend rode up to intercept them, Colin raised a reluctant hand in acknowledgment. "I'd hoped to keep you to myself a bit longer," he said under his breath near Mariah's ear, "but. . ."

As expected, Dennis wasted no time in filling his hooded hazel eyes with the sight of the English beauty. "Thought you'd be in Baltimore a few more days, Colin." His lips quirked into a teasing grin. "I say. Looks like you spent your last farthing, too." With his focus still on Mariah, he reached up and removed the plantation hat from his sun-streaked blond hair. "Good afternoon, milady. Dennis Tucker at your service. And it appears you are in serious need."

"What do you mean by that?" Colin interjected before Mariah could respond to the interloper and instruct him in the art of proper introductions.

"It's obvious, isn't it?" A smirk added a glint to his eyes as he edged his mount closer. "For someone who set out with a wealth of horses the last time I saw him, you somehow managed to lose all but one. Why else would a damsel with the face of an angel be crowded onto Paladin with a man so unworthy of her undeniable beauty?"

Colin ground his teeth in irritation. "Tuck, allow me to introduce you to Miss Harwood, our houseguest. And now if you'll excuse us, we're in a bit of a hurry and must be on our way. You know how Eloise gets in a tizzy whenever a family member is late for supper."

Reaching for Mariah's hand, Dennis swept it up and brought it to his mouth. "Miss Harwood. The pleasure is all mine."

Colin reined his mount away, forcing his friend to release his hold.

"Till we meet again, miss," Dennis said with a gallant tip of his head. Replacing his hat, he shifted his gaze to Colin. "Before you rush off, I was wondering if you'd heard anything significant regarding that business up north—about those French soldiers heading down into the Ohio Valley. You'd think Governor Clinton in New York would assume his duty and do something to stop them." His attention drifted back to Mariah. "After all, we have our womenfolk to think of. . .especially our very loveliest ones."

Mariah swiveled toward Colin with a puzzled expression. "Are the French on the verge of an invasion? We had no word of this in England."

"It's nothing to trouble yourself about. Dennis is referring to some turmoil brewing hundreds of miles from here over trading rights with the Indian tribes."

She relaxed and turned forward again.

Dennis flashed a sheepish smile. "I must apologize, miss. I wouldn't dream of causing such a lovely lady a second's distress. In fact—"

"In fact," Colin interrupted, taking a firmer grip on Paladin's reins, "any more delay and we'll surely be late for supper. We must press on. No doubt you have an appointment to keep yourself, since you're headin' toward town."

"Indeed. I was on my way to the Pattersons' for dinner and cards. Lexie and Mary Ann invited me yesterday after church." He continued to ogle Mariah. "I'd venture to say they'd be pleased if you two would join us. You know the Pattersons always put on a generous spread."

"Another time, Tuck." Colin nudged his mount into motion. "We're expected at home."

"I'll drop by tomorrow, then, to hear the latest from Baltimore," his friend persisted.

Colin suppressed a groan and spurred Paladin to a faster pace.

⸻

The setting sun had turned the river into a glorious amber ribbon by the time the horse veered onto a rambling lane shaded by towering oak trees. Observing the sprawling fields on either side, Mariah studied the large, brownish-green leaves of the crop Colin had told her was tobacco. Until this moment, the only tobacco she'd seen had been in small pouches Papa had used to fill his pipe.

As her gaze drifted ahead, she saw a magnificent, two-story white house with black shutters, sitting like a jewel amid stately trees and gardens. Pristine round columns fronted a porch that extended across the anterior. Her heart swelled with joy. This beautifully situated mansion was to be her new home!

Colin had spoken only the truth. He had not lied about his name or where he lived. This incredibly handsome man truly was her Prince Charming. . .everything a girl could want. And he was attracted to *her*.

As the horse picked up its pace, obviously eager to reach the stable, Mariah couldn't help but smile. The animal was no more eager than she was.

"We're almost there," Colin announced, taking a firmer hold on the reins to keep Paladin from breaking into a trot. "I do hope my home pleases you."

"It does. Very much. It is breathtakingly lovely." But even as she uttered the words, a disturbing thought spoiled the moment. As an indentured servant, how much of the grace and comforts of this elegant home would she be permitted to enjoy? Thus far, Colin had treated her like an honored guest, not a bonded worker. *Dear Father in heaven*, she finally remembered to pray, *I quite forgot to place myself in Your care. Please make my dearest dream come true. Amen.* With a twinge of guilt, she imagined Rose would view such a prayer as a selfish request. But surely the Lord wanted good things for His children, didn't He?

Mariah filled her eyes with the splendor of the flower-bedecked fountain gracing the center of the circle drive as they neared the mansion.

On their approach, a young girl sprang up from one of the chairs on the veranda and ran through the open doorway. "Mother! Poppy! Come and look! Colin's back, and he's bringin' a woman with him!"

Behind Mariah, Colin emptied his lungs with a grunt. "That was Amy, our little snitch. I vow, she's worse than a town crier."

Before Mariah could respond, people started pouring out of the house. A tall, distinguished, bearded man and two girls—one who appeared about Lily's age and one a bit younger. The threesome stood staring in surprise from the edge of the porch.

Surprised, but not dismayed, Mariah hoped with bated breath.

Then a slender, gracefully elegant, and handsome woman attired in rich turquoise brocade stepped outside. Mariah knew immediately where Colin had inherited his good looks, from his raven hair to his dark brown eyes. Truly the woman would have been the belle of the ball in her younger years—the belle of *any* ball.

As the girl Colin called Amy came alongside her mother, Mariah realized that all three daughters had inherited their father's complexion. Each of them had varying shades of golden blond hair, while his held a smattering of silver among the strands.

"Colin, my dear," the woman said as she started down the wide gray steps, "we didn't expect you home for several more days." Her gaze then centered on Mariah, and she offered a decidedly practiced smile, more polite than warm.

The extra tension Mariah felt in Colin's arms as he assisted her to the ground added to her renewed trepidation. She hurriedly smoothed down her hopelessly wrinkled skirt. Undoubtedly it smelled of horse. She swallowed as Colin dismounted.

As the rest of the family continued to watch from atop the stairs, Mistress Barclay reached the landing and stepped toward Mariah with a hand outstretched in a gesture of greeting. "Welcome, my dear. This is a pleasant surprise."

Mariah curtsied the best she could, considering her wobbly, saddle-weary legs. "Thank you, madam. 'Tis my pleasure."

The older woman tilted her intricately coifed head in question. "I do not believe you are one of our local gentry, are you?"

"No, Mistress Barclay. I was born in Bath, England. I've only just arrived in the colonies."

"How delightful." Her smile widened. She turned to her family as they came to join them. "I should like you to meet my husband, Eldon. And these are our lovely daughters, Victoria, Heather, and our youngest, Amanda." Each of the girls bobbed a curtsy in turn.

"I'm very pleased to meet all of you," Mariah said, offering a smile.

"But everyone calls me Amy," the youngest drawled, crowding in front of the others.

"Or Brat," Victoria, the oldest, added, rolling her eyes.

As Amy pursed her lips and turned to retort, Mariah interceded. "Which do you prefer, Amy or Amanda?"

The youngster looked up at her. "The way it sounds when you say it, either would be real fine."

"*Really* fine," her mother corrected.

The girl flicked a swift, irritated glance in her mother's direction. "Either name is *splendidly* fine." She fluttered a hand in a theatrical flare.

Mariah had to admit the child was a bit of an imp.

Colin moved alongside her just then. "Mother, Father, I'd like to present Miss Mariah Harwood. She and her family are recent arrivals to our fair land."

"Harwood." Mistress Barclay turned to her husband. "My dear, I don't believe you've mentioned a new family in the neighborhood by that name."

Mariah moistened her lips, intending to clear up the misunderstanding, but an African slave stepped out of the front door just then. Her dark head, swathed in red calico, nodded to Colin's mother. "Mistress Barclay," she announced in a drawl more pronounced than Amy's, "suppa' is served."

"Thank you, Pansy. And we'll be needing two more place settings."

"Yessum." She switched her expressive dusky gaze to Colin. "Welcome home, Masta Colin. We wasn't 'spectin' y'all back so soon."

As the servant returned inside, Colin's father kneaded his trim Van Dyke beard and addressed him. "That's true, son. We weren't. Did the transfer go as planned?"

"Yes, sir."

"We'll have no business talk for now." Colin's mother threaded her arm through Mariah's and started for the steps. "I should like to get further acquainted with our lovely guest."

Mariah gulped in dismay. Guest! They had no idea she was actually purchased help. This would not do at all. "Mistress Barclay, I don't think I should—"

"Miss Harwood is concerned that she smells a touch horsey," Colin piped in, speaking over her.

His mother chuckled softly. "I'm afraid she'll find that's quite normal around here. We can, however, remedy the situation." Releasing her hold on Mariah, she turned back to her oldest daughter. "Victoria, dear, would you please show our guest upstairs so she can freshen up a bit? We'll delay dinner a few minutes. And Colin, you don't exactly smell like a rose, yourself."

He laughed and ushered Mariah and his sister inside.

Entering the marble-floored foyer and noting the exquisite crystal chandelier overhead as they approached a grand, graceful walnut staircase, Mariah turned and shot him a meaningful look. Wasn't he ever going to tell his family what she truly was? To her dismay, he and Victoria ignored her and exchanged casual comments while mounting the stairs.

As she reached the top landing, Mariah forgot everything except what lay before her eyes. These people were wealthy beyond all expectation. A delightful sitting area overlooked the tastefully appointed foyer below, where huge urns of fragrant summer flowers topped mahogany pedestals situated between gilt-framed family portraits. Her assessment of the splendor was interrupted as Colin took his leave and strode into one of the rooms down the hall.

"This way," Victoria said pleasantly and led her into a bedroom easily twice the size as the one Mariah and Lily had shared back home.

Mariah barely concealed her awe as she beheld the utterly feminine bedchamber obviously belonging to the two older sisters. Matching brass beds with frilly canopies, one done up in pale pink, the other in soft lavender, were separated by a carved washstand. A pair of armoires faced each other across the expanse of the room, dark spots against the floral wallpaper.

Victoria led her to the commode, bearing a hand-painted pitcher and bowl. Lace-edged white cloths for washing and drying hung on either side of a large oval looking glass. "I'll help you out of that gown so you can refresh yourself."

"Thank you." Mariah observed Colin's sister's reflection as the girl gently undid the lacing in the back of her gown. Such sweet features housed those enormous azure eyes. A yellow ribbon that matched her flounced day gown held thick golden curls off her face as she met Mariah's gaze in the glass.

"I must say, your gown is quite stylish," Victoria admitted. "Is it what they're wearing in England this season?"

Mariah nodded. "It's one of my newer frocks. But I'm afraid that for now a good brushing will have to disburse all the travel dust. My trunks won't arrive until later this evening."

"Not at all. You can wear something of mine—that is, if you don't mind wearing one not quite so up to date."

"How kind of you, Victoria. I'm sure whatever you loan me will do nicely."

Dipping one of the washing cloths into the bowl, Mariah squeezed out most of the water and placed the cool dampness to her throat.

"Do people really go to Bath just to take baths?" a childlike voice asked.

Mariah caught reflections of the two younger girls in the mirror. They had come in without her notice. She grinned at them, then continued her ablutions. "The baths are large indoor pools where a number of people can benefit from them all at one time. The waters come hot out of the ground and contain healing minerals that attract older folk with aching joints. In season, the city is filled with music and dramas, and young maidens stroll about with their friends, hoping to catch the eye of dashing young gentlemen who will then invite them to dance at the evening ball."

Heather, the middle daughter, scrunched up her face. "That sounds a bit silly, if you ask me." She flicked a strand of nearly straight blond hair out of her face.

"Well, I don't think it sounds silly at all," Victoria breathed, her beautiful eyes gleaming as she looked over Mariah's shoulder. "You children will understand when you're older, I'm sure."

Heather snorted. "You're scarcely two-and-a-half years older than me, you know."

"A very important two-and-a-half years," her older sister said, arching her brows. She began working on the corset that had been one of the causes of Mariah's discomfort that day. "Heather, would you fetch my lavender gown out of my armoire? I think that would look nice on Miss Harwood."

"You may call me Mariah, if you wish." She felt someone tug on her arm.

"Are all those people naked in the baths?" Amy wanted to know. Questions filled the blue eyes in her heart-shaped face.

Victoria and Heather both gasped, but Mariah burst out laughing. This was like being with sisters back at home in her own room. She swung around and gave Amy a hug. "No, little one. They wear bathing costumes. It's all perfectly respectable."

A thought came to her as she stepped out of the dress pooled at her feet. How delightful it would be if she were a real guest in this happy and wealthy home. . .or perhaps, someday in the future, the mistress. . . .

⁓

Colin washed, changed, and brushed his hair before rushing out of his room and down the hall, the envelope of money in his pocket. He needed to speak to his family before Mariah came down.

As he reached the stairs, he slowed. What exactly would he say? *Lord, please give me the right words. You know how much I want her to stay.* With a last glance at the room where the girls had taken Mariah, he descended the steps at a deliberately slow pace. If he did not appear calm, how could he expect his parents to be?

Voices drifted from the parlor, so he joined them there.

"You look much better," Mother said with a smile as she looked up from her embroidery. "I've been wondering, Colin, dear, where exactly it was that you met the lovely Miss Harwood. How did you happen to bring her home unannounced?" She set the needlework aside on the lamp table next to her Queen Anne chair.

Not even a moment's grace? He swallowed.

His father rose from the brocade couch. "Cora, my love, do allow us to take care of the horse business before you start the inquisition."

With a slight frown, she opened her mouth to protest, then sighed.

"As you wish. First business, then the inquisition."

"Did Lindsay try to get away with paying less than we agreed upon?" Father asked, as he and Colin strode past the massive unlit fireplace to an open window overlooking the flower garden.

Colin smiled. "He tried, but once he examined the animals, he stopped attempting to negotiate." Removing the envelope containing the contract and banknotes, he felt his heart pounding. "Pa, I'm afraid you'll find it forty pounds shy."

His father frowned. "But you said—"

Giving the older man's arm a squeeze, Colin edged him farther away from Mother.

Too late. She tossed aside the hooped material she'd resumed working on and came to her feet. "What did I just hear? Forty pounds is missing? What on earth have you been up to?"

Chapter 4

I'd appreciate it, Mother, if you didn't speak until I've finished," Colin requested with all the confidence he could muster. "I'm sure you'll appreciate what I have to say by the time you've heard the entire story. First, however, let's all sit down." Not wanting to earn a disapproving glare from her, he concentrated on using proper diction.

As they took seats, Colin noticed his father didn't appear quite as suspicious as his mother. But then, the older man had always been harder to read.

"To begin with, I had just finalized stabling the horses aboard ship when I happened to notice this lovely young woman in very fashionable blue standing on the city's auction block."

"An auction block!" From the look on Mother's face as she glanced out to the grand staircase, one would think he'd said Mariah had come straight off a prison ship.

He shook his head. "You must stop leaping to wrong conclusions. Miss Harwood's being there was actually quite heroic."

She tucked her chin in disbelief and opened her mouth to respond, but Father placed a hand over hers. "Cora, love, let's hear the lad out. I'm sure there's more to the story."

"Thank you." Colin gave his father a grateful nod. "As I was saying, there she stood with a ship's blubbery captain touting what a highly educated gentlewoman Mariah was, how she played several musical instruments. He also reported that she'd sacrificed her own opportunities to willingly accompany her sister—or rather, two sisters—here to the colonies."

"Aha!" Mother gasped. "So she and *two* sisters, no less, could actually be infamous criminals." A note of triumph rang in her voice.

"No, Mother. Wrong again." Colin fought to squelch his mounting irritation with her. "Miss Harwood's sister Rose learned that their father, Bath's finest goldsmith, would be put in debtor's prison because a young lord met an untimely death before he could pay a huge debt he owed the man. Therefore, Mr. Harwood was unable to meet his own expenses. Without consulting her father, Rose packed up most of their furnishings and sold them on the Bristol docks to satisfy her father's creditors. She even used her sisters' dowries. But she was unable to raise the full amount, so she contracted an indenturement with a ship's captain."

"A reputable father wouldn't allow such action," Pa interjected.

"I'm sure he wouldn't had he known of her intent. But it was too late. She'd already paid out the money. Upon learning of her deed, her two sisters were loathe to have her sail to this foreign land alone. Out of their love for her, they also contracted with the same captain. The crafty man made a solemn promise to sell them together, but upon arriving in Baltimore he reneged and sold them separately."

"I know the kind," his mother admitted. "Always profiting from others' misfortunes."

At that moment, their slave, Pansy, stopped at the doorway and rapped softly on the jamb. "Mistress, Eloise be wantin' to know how much longer y'all wants her to hold suppa?"

"Just a few minutes more," Mother answered, then turned back to Colin.

"Considering that these highly accomplished sisters were not the usual bond servants," Colin went on, "and considering our Miss Harwood's remarkable beauty, I was appalled to see a number of unsavory types intent on bidding for her. They made no attempt to disguise their vulgar reasons for wanting her contract. I simply couldn't allow her to fall into any of their despicable hands."

His father nodded and sat back with a knowing grin.

His mother, however, pursed her lips and huffed. "So, my gallant son, you had to charge right in and save the fair maiden. . .with your father's money. Just tell me, what possible use do we have for another servant? All our needs are already being met." One of her brows rose slightly higher. "Or can it be that, like those other men, you decided to buy her to meet some personal, might I add baser, need of your own?"

"Mother! I cannot believe you would think such a thing of me, much less speak those words aloud." He purposefully sat straighter. "To be quite honest, my thoughts were of you. You and the girls. Not only does Mariah have exquisite penmanship for writing letters and invitations, she's been educated in all that finishing school nonsense, and—"

"It's that finishing school nonsense," she inserted, elevating her chin, "that turns a clumsy girl into a marriageable wife and mother."

Colin realized with a measure of relief that she'd fallen right into his plan. *Splendid!* "Well, you and Pa are planning to send Victoria off to that ladies' academy in Williamsburg this fall, are you not? And at substantial expense, even though she doesn't want to go. Now you won't have to send her away. Mariah will be here for the next four years, long enough to turn all three girls into simpering, British-accented gentlewomen, and for a fraction of the cost you expected to lay out. Plus, she plays four instruments, and having just arrived from a fashionable resort city in England, you'll have the advantage over other ladies on the latest styles. Think about it."

She tapped an impatient finger on the armrest of her chair. "Well, I can see she's certainly made a believer out of you, at least." Mother's doubtful tone attested that she remained unconvinced.

What more does she want? Colin elaborated further. "I had the opportunity of meeting both her other sisters. In fact, the eldest one insisted we were not to neglect Mariah's religious instruction. She made me promise to deliver—as she so aptly put it—her 'virtuous sister' to you before nightfall."

That information put a grin on his mother's face. "You don't say." Releasing a sigh, she tipped her head to one side in thought. "Very well. I suppose we can give Mariah a try. I did not fail to notice, however, that you have already begun calling her by her given name. That's far too familiar for such a brief acquaintance, to be sure. And should I ever catch you two in any sort of dalliance, I promise you this: we will sell her at once."

By the time Mariah left Victoria's room with the other two girls in tow, she looked and felt much improved in a clean frock, with her hair restyled. Even with her corset laced so tightly she could scarcely breathe, she found the bodice more than a little snug, but the strategic placement of a lace handkerchief helped alleviate the problem. She knew the gown's lavender hue, her own favorite color, was quite flattering and brought out the hint of violet in her eyes.

In addition, the girls seemed delightfully eager to get to know her, though they continued to address her formally, as their mother wished. As they reached the top of the graceful staircase, Mariah hoped the dinner with their parents would go equally well.

Her confidence faded on the descent. Detecting a decided strain in the voices coming from what must be the parlor, she sensed that Colin had most likely told his parents about her. *Please, dear Lord, give me just this one perfect night.*

Halfway down, she saw her rescuer and his parents exit the room. Colin and Mr. Barclay smiled up at her. Mistress Barclay did not.

What exactly had he said to them? How she wished she could get him aside and ask. But of course, that would be impossible at the moment. She made a concerted effort not to falter as she continued down. "I do hope I haven't kept you all waiting overly long," she ventured cheerily.

"No. Not at all." Mr. Barclay inclined his head. "You look lovely, my dear." He turned back to his stony-faced wife and offered his arm. "Shall we go in to supper, Cora, my love?"

The girls trailed after their parents, three sunny blossoms in their blue, green, and yellow pastels.

Colin offered his arm to Mariah. "Everything is fine," he whispered, pulling her arm within his. "And Pa is right."

"About what?"

"You look lovely. Exceptionally so."

She relaxed a little. "Thank you, kind sir." Releasing a pent-up breath, she gazed up at her handsome knight of the realm. Once again, he'd made everything right. On the other hand, if everything was right, why was his mother not smiling?

The dining room, Mariah noticed upon entering, fit in perfectly with the other beautiful accoutrements in the mansion. White wainscoting lined the lower portion of the walls, with pale blue, flocked wallpaper above. A slightly smaller chandelier above the long, lace-covered table sent rainbow prisms dancing over the gleaming china and crystal goblets set before each place. Colin drew out one of the mahogany chairs in the center for Mariah and took a seat next to her.

Lively Amy scooted onto the chair on her other side, while her sisters took their places across from them.

On the edge of her vision, Mariah could see Colin's parents occupying the head and foot of the table. She casually adjusted her position just enough to avoid Mistress Barclay's brittle stare.

A half door swung open, and the maid, Pansy, entered the room. Attired in a serviceable black dress with a crisp white apron, she carried in a tureen of a delicious-smelling soup and began ladling it out.

Mariah's stomach crimped. She'd thought the fare at the roadside inn had smelled enticing, but this was pure heaven. Colin had not exaggerated about his family's excellent cook. She sighed as she waited for her soup. Hopefully, his mother would keep any unpleasantness she might have planned until after the meal.

Once Pansy had dished out Mariah's portion of the creamy chicken soup, Mariah was about to pluck up her soupspoon when she remembered her napkin. She unfolded it and placed it on her lap as a lady should.

It was that precise action that saved her further embarrassment, because before she could reach for her spoon again, Mr. Barclay cleared his throat. "Let us bow for prayer."

Of course. Mariah cringed. How easily she had forgotten her manners.

"Our Father in heaven, we do thank You for continually showering us with such bounty. I pray we never take Your blessings for granted. And Lord, I especially want to thank You for bringing Miss Harwood to our home to tutor our girls. Because of her, my precious daughters will not have to be sent away to school. I would miss them terribly. We pray this in the name of our Lord Jesus. Amen."

A definite stirring from across the table could be heard even before the man concluded his prayer. Mariah opened her eyes to see a grin dancing across Victoria's face. "Do you mean it, Poppy? I don't have to go to that awful school? Becky Sue absolutely hated it there. She was forever sharing horror stories about the dreadful headmistress."

"Yes, dear," her mother replied, "but what a marvelous improvement that school has made in Rebecca. She's so much more graceful and mannerly since enrolling there." She turned to Colin. "Wouldn't you agree, son?"

He drew his attention from Mariah and focused on his mother. "I can't say I noticed, myself."

"Me neither," Amy piped in. "She only acts stiff and snooty and ever so proper when old people are around. The rest of the time she's her regular old self."

Her sisters giggled along with her, making it all the harder for Mariah to keep a face as straight as their disapproving mother's.

The mistress shifted her sharp stare to Mariah. "Well, now that we'll have a tutor right here at home, I'll know from the start if we're getting our money's worth."

Would she ever. A woman with her sharp eye would never miss a thing. Just observing the elegant lady of the manor delicately fill her spoon and lift it to her mouth, Mariah had no doubt the woman would fit right in were she dining with royalty.

Carefully raising her own spoon to her lips, Mariah assured herself she'd do her best in the task of tutoring. She'd been an apt student herself.

No one had to tell her that catching a man of any consequence required diligent effort. And for now, as an educator, she'd surely be given a room in the manor and take her meals with the family—and Colin—every day. That certainly beat having to scrub floors as she'd feared she'd be forced to do as a bond servant. Yes. In her quest for Colin, she'd be diligent. Extremely diligent. After all, as her instructress, Miss Simkins, loved to remind her, Rose, and Lily, *"A man has no need to buy a cow if he can get the milk for free."*

She stifled a smile. Things were working out quite well. If only Mistress Barclay would smile, even once.

Chapter 5

Colin exhaled a slow breath of relief when his mother finally relaxed enough to sip at her soup. The meal continued in silence for a short span, until the soup bowls were taken away and the main courses served.

Cutting into a slice of roast pork, Father looked up, his expression pensive. "Son, I was wondering if you'd heard anything of consequence regarding that business out in New York's backcountry." He forked the meat to his mouth.

The change of subject could not have come at a more opportune time. "Not much." Colin bit a chunk of his buttered bread and chewed it before elaborating. "The Six Nations are asking Governor Clinton to take action."

"The Iroquois tribes?" The older man left his fork suspended in the air. "What difference could it possibly make to them? No matter which nation sends traders in, they'll still be able to exchange their furs for trade goods."

"Perhaps." Colin cocked his head. "But they claim it's tearing their tribal alliances apart." He paused and took another bite.

"Likely they're just hoping to arrange a better deal, get more presents from the powers that be."

"I wouldn't be too sure of that." He toyed with the fresh collard greens on his dish. "According to the word floating around, it sounds a bit more serious. The main chiefs made agreements to trade exclusively with the British as long as our soldiers will ally with them against their enemies—the northern tribes who made treaties with the French. Seems some of the more remote Iroquois villages feel it's better to go with French strength and the northern tribes than to stick with English weakness." He speared a chunk of meat and rested his hand beside his plate while he spoke. "They're very aware of the French invasion into their territory. So rather than be overrun, they are aligning themselves with the French and the tribes that used to be their own sworn enemies."

"I see." His father reached for another slice of bread and tore it in half before buttering it. "Sounds like there's much more to the situation than I thought. If England wants to maintain that flourishing trade with the Indians, they'd better make a forceful showing of their own."

"Speaking of a flourishing trade," Colin said, glancing down at Mariah, "the man who purchased Miss Harwood's sister is in the fur business."

That got Mariah's attention. Eyes wide, she returned his gaze while reaching for her water goblet.

"The man made one astounding bid for her. Fifty pounds." He switched his focus to his father. "Fifty pounds, without the blink of an eye. It silenced the rest of the bidding at once. Perhaps we went into the wrong business, Pa."

The older man chuckled. "That may very well be. But don't forget, European fashions change every few years, and—"

"Every season, Papa," Victoria corrected airily.

He gave his daughter a fatherly smile. "Even if fur muffs and hats never go out of fashion, the frontier may one day be trapped out, just as our coastal counties are. And as your mother likes to remind us, ships and goods may sink, but our land will still be here. Right, Cora?" He tipped his head toward her.

She smiled in her superior way, but Pansy's arrival with a laden tea tray precluded a response. "Pansy, dear, I believe we'll have our tea and this evening's dessert in the parlor." She then turned to Mariah. "We had a harpsichord shipped from London a few months ago but as yet have not had the privilege of hearing it played well. I'm afraid too many years without an instrument have diminished my already limited skill. Perhaps you'd be so gracious as to treat us with a sampling more pleasing to the ear."

" 'Twould be my honor, Mistress Barclay."

Colin held his breath. His mother was testing Mariah's honesty. Was she truly accomplished in music, or had everything she'd said thus far been fabricated?

Moments later, escorting Mariah through the wide double doorway leading into the parlor, he didn't sense any trepidation in her. But his steps slowed as they drew near the large, intricate-looking instrument with dual keyboards.

She smiled up at him, then patted his hand before moving away to smooth her palm across the polished wood surface. Turning back to his mother, who had taken a seat nearby, she dipped her head. "May I?" Without waiting for an answer, she dropped onto the harpsichord's stool and adjusted her skirts around her. She poised her fingers above the keys, then looked up at the family. "It has been awhile for me, as well. But I shall do my best."

Colin cringed. That was not what he wanted to hear her say. Still, he remained near the instrument for support. Or possibly, her protection.

Mariah ran her fingers up and down the keyboards as if she knew what she was doing, then stopped and looked over her shoulder at the others.

What now?

"I must say, it has lovely tone and seems to be in tune."

"Yes," Mother replied. "I hired a man who came all the way from Philadelphia to set it to rights after it arrived."

"Philadelphia," Mariah breathed. "And how far away is that? I have yet to learn where the various cities in the colonies are located."

She was stalling. Colin had no doubt.

"He took a coastal packet," his mother answered. "I can't say how far it is overland."

"We have a map in our schoolroom," Amy piped in. "You can look at that and see."

Colin stopped breathing. That's right, a diversion. Probably just what Mariah was hoping for.

"I shall look forward to checking the map," Mariah said and rested her fingers on the keys again. Smiling, she began to play—beautifully play—a charming, lyrical tune unfamiliar to Colin.

He drew his first real breath since entering the parlor.

⌐

The family took their time enjoying their raspberries with coddled cream as a welcome evening breeze filtered through the lace curtains of the parlor's open windows.

"Miss Harwood?" Heather inquired in an airy voice.

"What is it, dear?" Mariah interrupted her slow perusal of the room's elegant furnishings and turned her attention to the quietest of Colin's three sisters.

"Would you please teach me to play the harpsichord like you do? I've never heard anything so beautiful in my life."

"Once you're older," Victoria cut in, "you'll hear even prettier music. Last winter at the Christmas ball, the Tuckers hired a string quartet. They played wonderfully well. It was quite. . .romantic." She closed her eyes with a dreamy smile.

Colin removed his arm from where it rested against the fireplace mantel, his movement drawing Mariah's gaze. "I agree with Heather. I've never heard our instrument played more beautifully."

"Why, thank you, Mr. Barclay," Mariah said lightly, making sure she used his formal name, since his mother was watching them both closely. She raised her teacup and turned back to the girls. "Actually, I think it would be lovely if we were to create our own musical ensemble as my sisters and I did. One or two of you might also want to lend your talents to the violin or cello, or possibly the flute."

Excitement brightened Heather's expressive blue eyes as she swung toward her parents. "Oh, Mother, could we?"

For the first time, Mariah glimpsed the elegant older woman's expression soften with a warm smile. "You'll have to ask your father, dear. Musical instruments tend to be quite costly."

"Papa?" Heather pleaded.

His demeanor also gentled as he smiled at his charming middle daughter. "Of course, Heather, my sweet. Since I'll be riding in to Alexandria tomorrow on tobacco business, I'll stop by the music seller's and see what I can find."

"Oh, thank you. Thank you." Leaping to her feet, she went to her father and gave him a big hug.

Never one to be outdone, Amy followed suit. "I want an instrument, too."

He laughed and included her in the embrace. Watching as he kissed the giggling girls, Mariah felt a pang of homesickness. Would she ever get another hug from her own papa? She hadn't begun to realize until now the full price of leaving her homeland.

"One for each of you," Mr. Barclay said, his gaze including Victoria in the group. He then peered over his daughters' heads. "Colin, I would appreciate your company on the morrow. It always helps to put forth a united front when dealing with buyers."

Colin shot a quick glance at Mariah before answering. "Of course. I'd like to challenge Quince Sherwood to a race, anyway. I think their filly Brighton Rose is ready for the test."

"I agree." His father gave a nod.

Colin will be gone all day tomorrow. Mariah's uneasiness returned with the realization that she'd be left alone here with his mother. For the entire day.

Outside, several plantation dogs began barking in chorus, adding to her distress.

Colin strode to the open window and looked out into the dark, then turned back to Mariah. "I forgot. That must be the wagon bringing your trunks."

"Trunks?" His mother put her teacup aside and came to her feet. "How many trunks does the girl have?"

"Three."

"So many?"

"Yes. Which room shall we put them in?"

The lady of the house paused no more than a second. "Put them in the room adjacent to Amy's."

Colin tucked his chin in disbelief and stared at her. "You're delegating Mariah—Miss Harwood—to the room with the brat?"

"Yes." She smiled quite triumphantly and sat back. Taking up her tea once again, she lifted the cup to her lips and took a sip. "It's the perfect place for her."

Something was different. Mariah came awake to an unaccustomed stillness. Raising her lashes, she realized she was no longer at sea in a rolling, creaking ocean vessel, sharing a cramped cabin with several others. She had her own private bedchamber. She sighed and stretched languorously.

No doubt this personal haven of hers was far more sequestered than Colin might have hoped. His very clever mother had placed her in a room that could only be reached by passing through Amy's. And Amy's door faced her parents' room, with naught but a small second-floor sitting area separating them.

So much for any untoward dalliances with the son and heir. If what Colin had said regarding his youngest sister proved to be true—that she was the family snitch—he would find a venture through the girl's room to reach Mariah's door much too intimidating. Yes, Mistress Barclay had been clever indeed.

Mistress Barclay!

Mariah sprang up to a sitting position. She was supposed to meet the woman downstairs first thing this morning. And just how *first thing* was it? Throwing back the covers, she padded over the braided rug to the window and moved aside a sheer curtain panel to check the angle of the sun.

It had barely risen. Mariah sighed with relief. In the fragile morning light, she gazed down to dew-kissed fields of leafy plants and on to a line of trees edging the distant river that already reflected the sky's growing brightness. Such a delightful change after weeks of viewing nothing but the vast expanse of the dark Atlantic, and before then, a city crowded with stone buildings and cottages that blocked the sight of the surrounding countryside.

How pleasant it would be to simply wander outside and stroll the grounds in the cool of the morning, but alas, that was not to be. Turning back, Mariah grimaced at the sight of three overflowing clothing trunks that occupied so much of the limited space in her small room. They would have to stay there. The room lacked a wardrobe for her use. Since it had once housed a slave nanny when Amy had been an infant, the room was nowhere near as fancy as the family bedchambers. It contained only one small chest of drawers, which also served as her commode, and a wall rack with three hooks. Dreadfully inadequate for storing the contents of her trunks. Nevertheless, walls painted a soft green kept it from feeling gloomy, as did cheerful, apple-green calico curtains and a colorful counterpane. Accommodations could have been much worse, to be sure.

Mariah poured water into her washbasin and made swift work of her morning toilette before rummaging through her things to find a no-nonsense, unembellished gown a tutoress might wear. Every one of her frocks sported an abundance of wrinkles, since she'd unfolded them last evening to show all her gowns to Victoria.

Discarding several that appeared too grand, she wished for the first time in her life that she'd had a measure of Rose's more sedate taste in clothing. Finally she chose a deep rose gown with front lacings. It would have to do. Besides, she could dress in it without assistance.

After struggling into her layers of clothing, she brushed out her hair, then snatched it up and twisted the thick curls into a rather severe bun.

Colin wasn't the person she needed to impress today. Remaining here depended entirely upon his suspicious mother.

La, how she wished Colin had been master of his own house.

⁓

Amy remained sound asleep as Mariah tiptoed through the young girl's large, pink-and-white bedroom and opened the outer door, hoping she'd risen before Mistress Barclay. Alas, the door across the sitting area stood wide open. Both of Colin's parents must already be downstairs. And since Colin planned to leave with his father for Alexandria shortly, he must likely be up and about himself.

The last thing Mariah wanted was to be abandoned by him on her first day in the household, but there was little hope of his changing his mind and staying behind. Naturally he'd want to live up to his responsibilities. Scooping up her skirts, she hurried to the staircase and descended, praying all the way down that some miracle would cause Colin to remain at home. *If not, Lord, please make Mistress Barclay decide to allow me to stay here for the duration of my indenturement.*

Just as she reached the bottom landing, the older woman strolled from the parlor into the foyer looking exceptionally regal, even in her dressing gown of pale-blue *peau de soie*, her dark hair in a long, loose braid down her back. "Mariah. Come with me to the dining room. We can discuss matters over breakfast." No smile softened the invitation.

Mariah tamped down her unease. At least Colin's mother planned to feed her. Not to be outdone by the matron, she straightened her own posture. After all, Colin would also be there.

He was not.

The long sideboard held a variety of foods and a tea service. Mariah noticed that some of the artfully arranged fare had already been removed. Obviously the men had enjoyed an early breakfast before leaving for their jaunt to the city.

Without a word, the mistress served herself, so Mariah did the same. Then the older woman took her place from the night before and motioned for Mariah to take a nearby seat. Once they were both settled

SALLY LAITY AND DIANNA CRAWFORD

and Mariah lifted her cup to her mouth, Mistress Barclay leveled a pointed stare at her. "Shall we ask the Lord's blessing?"

Humiliated yet again by her out-of-practice manners, Mariah closed her eyes for a brief second, then returned the delicate teacup to its saucer and bowed her head.

"Our most gracious Father," the woman began, "we thank You once more for Your wondrous bounty and ask Your blessing upon it. Amen." She then sat back and took up her own cup as she studied Mariah, causing her great uneasiness. Finally, she spoke. "I want you to know I am no fool."

Mariah cut a swift glance at her. How should one respond after such a comment?

A knowing smirk twitched a corner of the matron's lips. "I know exactly why my son bought your papers, so let us not dance around the issue. The fact is, you are here, and while you are part of this household, I shall be charitable and give you a trial period, though I have serious doubts that you will work out."

Making an effort to remain composed, Mariah swallowed and met her gaze. "Madam, I assure you, I shall put forth my very best effort to educate your daughters in all the graces. You will not be disappointed. And if the current quality of their penmanship is not a credit to this fine home now, I promise it will be shortly."

Mistress Barclay dismissed the remark with a wave of one hand. "Indeed. Well, that can be hired. What I'm more interested in is a marked improvement in their diction. I cannot abide the lazy sliding of words so common in this area. My girls must be able to mingle successfully with those of the Bay states as well as those of British society."

Confident that she had no lack of expertise in those elements, Mariah formulated an apt round of praise for her abilities, but the woman gave her no opportunity to utter a word in her defense.

"My husband and I are adamant that our daughters marry respected merchants or men of other successful enterprises. I myself would not be adverse to a man of the cloth, as long as he happens to be well placed."

"I see."

"No, I don't believe you do. City dwellers are more interested in monetary dowries than those which include land, and we do not plan to sacrifice even an acre of our property for the purpose of securing advantageous marriages for our daughters." She spread marmalade on a triangle of toasted bread and nibbled a corner of it.

"As mentioned in the conversation around the table last eve," Mariah inserted, "the land is here to stay. And lovely land it is, I must avow."

The older woman's expression hardened. "Let me be clear on this. My husband married me against his family's wishes. I brought no land to the family, you see, only the profit from a ship in my father's merchant fleet. After only a few years, the vessel sank in a storm. You, of course, do not possess even that much. I will not allow a marriage between you and Colin, no matter what. Not even should you turn up with child."

Mariah gasped, lurching to her feet.

Mistress Barclay caught her hand. "Do sit down again, my dear. I do apologize for being so. . .blunt. However, it is imperative that you understand how serious I am about this." She paused briefly. "Your main duty, while you are here, will of course be tutoring the girls in their lessons. You will have one day off each week. I think that should be Sunday—after you have attended services with us."

Under any other circumstance, Mariah would have left the table and stormed out the door. But where could she go? All her worldly belongings were upstairs, and by law the Barclays did own her services for the next four years. Four years. She drew a defeated breath and sank back down on her chair. "The girls' speech. I suppose if you want them to be accepted everywhere, they'll need to know at least a smattering of French. Have they had any instruction in that language?"

"No, they have not."

Mariah let out a humorless chuckle. "Then, it appears I have my work cut out for me."

Surprising Mariah, the stern matron smiled. "Perhaps you will turn out to be worth the money my son paid for you after all." Then the smile vanished. "But make no mistake. If you betray me in the slightest way, I will sell you to the first old wretch I see."

Chapter 6

Early morning light added translucent beauty to the verdant countryside on the way to Alexandria, sprinkling dewy diamonds over wildflowers and among the tall grasses dancing on the breeze. Riding beside his father's dapple gray stallion, Colin tried to compose in his mind the perfect words that would secure the older man's commitment to the cause. . .that of convincing Mother to retain Mariah's services for the next four years. He discarded idea after idea as weak and sought a better approach to the subject.

An unexpected laugh broke his concentration. He raised his gaze to the fair-haired man at his side, who shook his head, still chuckling. "You've certainly managed to make things challenging for our little Amy."

What a strange comment. Colin reined Paladin closer to his father's mount. "Whatever do you mean?"

"That lass you brought home." His shrewd blue eyes focused on Colin. "What could Amy possibly bring home that could top a new bond servant?"

Colin frowned. "I don't understand."

"You know as well as I do, son, that the little squirt makes it her life's ambition to try and outdo you, outrun you, outrace you on horseback, even outeat you—"

"Only if the food is somethin' she particularly likes," Colin inserted on a chuckle of his own. "But I do catch your meanin'. I hope Mother doesn't find out that the little imp jumped off the edge of the waterfall into the creek last week. It seems that Old Samuel, our horse groomer, told her I'd done it when I was her age."

His pa nodded thoughtfully as the two mounts plodded along. "I've always been careful not to let Amy get wind of all the critters you used to tote home, especially after the opossum she sneaked into the house last month. In its frenzy to escape, that varmint shredded one of the drapes in my study. Needless to say, your mother was in high dudgeon over that episode."

"Our little snitch does manage to get herself into piles of trouble, that's for sure." Grinning as a few of Amy's escapades came to mind, Colin felt his humor wane, and he turned serious. "The difference is, I did not bring Mariah home on a mere whim."

Pa shot him a look of disbelief—one that made Colin reiterate his position.

"Well, perhaps it was a whim at first. I'll readily admit it. But as she and I conversed during the journey home, I began to see what a perfect fit she is."

"You mean, *felt* her perfect fit, I daresay. Otherwise you would've done the logical thing and had her ride on the wagon with her luggage."

Colin cut him a sidelong glance. "If you were my age and that had been Mother, would you have consigned her to a tediously long, bumpy wagon ride?"

His father thought for a moment. "That's not a fair question. However, since you brought up the subject, I certainly would not have taken such liberties with a woman like your mother unless I'd planned to wed her— even if that Puritan blood of hers would have permitted such action." He eyed Colin. "May I ask if that is your intention for this young, penniless English maiden? This indentured servant you've thrust upon us?"

"Well, I—" A low-hanging branch necessitated Colin's having to duck beneath it, a most welcome diversion. He was nowhere near ready to answer his father's query. He watched a squirrel scamper up a tree as they passed by.

"I suggest you give the matter some serious thought, son. You know your mother will fight you tooth and nail, should that be the case. Even worse, she'll send the girl packing someplace where you'll never be able to find her. She's that determined for you to marry one of our local belles—hopefully, one with her own strict religious upbringing. Constance Montclaire, for example." A chuckle rumbled from his chest.

Colin had no doubt his father adored his mother, despite all her rigid New Englander ideas. And Colin would settle for no less than that kind of affection himself. "Constance may be Mother's choice, but she's not mine. I'd rather remain a bachelor all my days than marry without love."

Abruptly, Father reined his horse to a stop, prompting Colin to do the same. "You couldn't possibly be in love with Miss Harwood after just one day. The very idea would be absurd."

Pa had really put him on the spot. "Correct me if I'm wrong, but it seems I recall you telling us all that you fell in love with Mother the first time you laid eyes on her."

"That was different. She and I met at a Christmas ball in Baltimore. She'd come down from Boston to visit a cousin. Her very clothing attested to her family's wealth."

Not to be dissuaded, Colin pressed on. "I also considered Mariah's attire to be exquisite. She was elegance itself, not only in her appearance but her bearing, as well."

"Perhaps, my boy, but my lady was standing in the ballroom of a fine manse. Your young woman was perched on an auction block. Forgive me if I point out the obvious difference."

"I understand what you're saying, sir. All I ask is that you make certain Mother gives Mariah a fair chance to prove herself. If you'd met her sister Rose—she could have been Mother, the way she pinned me down with her questions and her insistence that Mariah continue her religious instruction."

"So she believes the girl still needs some instruction, then."

Colin let out a weary breath. "No. It wasn't like that at all. Rose Harwood was deeply worried about handing her sister over to a man she'd never met. She had no way of knowing my true character, my motives. She was concerned for her sister's welfare."

"No doubt." After a moment's pause, Father relaxed his tight lips and nudged his mount forward again. "Very well. You've made a good case. I'll do my best to corral your mother. We'll take it one day at a time. Let's just hope Miss Harwood doesn't say or do anything to make your mother determined to sell her to the first reasonable bidder before we get home."

Deriving encouragement from the older man's response, Colin breathed a bit easier. "Thank you. I'll appreciate having your help with Mother, sir. That's all I can ask." For a moment he was tempted to add that it was his name on the indenturement papers, not his mother's. Neither she nor his father could legally sign off on the documents. But Colin wasn't ready to offer any kind of ultimatum just yet, or draw a line in the sand over a lass he'd barely met. Still, at this very minute he wished Mariah was sitting on Paladin in front of him with that silly feather flopping in his face and that he was smelling the delicious, slightly briny *eau de Mariah*.

He exhaled a long breath and changed the subject. "How do you feel about posting a letter to your friend Yarnell Lewis in Williamsburg after Quince Sherwood and I set a date for a race? I heard his horse made a good showing last month in Charles Town."

～

Mariah spent most of the day in the schoolroom at the end of the upstairs hall, assessing the education her three charges had acquired and compiling a list of the various texts she would need in the months to come. Mistress Barclay popped in numerous times doing her own assessing—of Mariah. It was very unnerving, since the only time Mariah had done anything akin to teaching school was when she'd helped her younger siblings, Lily and Tommy, with their reading and sums before they set off to Master Gleason's classes.

Now, thank goodness, the school day was over. Mariah had scarcely announced that fact before Amy raced madly out of the house and down to the stables, her mother's reprimands trailing after her to no avail.

But most gratifying, the mistress of the house had seemed pleased by what she'd seen. She almost smiled when she entered the schoolroom as the other girls took their leave. "That seems to have gone well." She glanced down at Mariah's desk. "I assume that is a list of the supplies and books the girls will be needing."

"Yes, mistress." A slight pause. "However, there is one thing in particular that I need, if I may be so bold."

"And it is. . . ?"

"I've not had a bath since I set foot on that ship, only a few basins of seawater to freshen up with on occasion. If it is not too much trouble, would it be possible—"

The older woman blanched. "I have been remiss. I should have thought of that myself. I shall have Lizzie and Ivy see to it at once."

"Thank you most kindly."

An hour later, feeling more refreshed than she had in weeks, Mariah found herself in Victoria's room demonstrating a new hairstyle on Heather's smooth, golden tresses. "Watch, Victoria. The hair has to be brought up to the very top of her head, quite high, or it will begin to sag."

The fifteen-year-old stepped nearer for a better view as her sister sat at the dressing table, watching their reflection in the large oval mirror.

"Now, twist it round and round but not too tight," Mariah said, exaggerating her movements a bit so the procedure could easily be observed. "When it's all twisted, except for the last eight or ten inches— which I'll thread through to the center and curl—it must be secured with pins and a pretty comb. Like this."

"Even if Ah do all that, Ah vow it shan't look like yers," Victoria said in a slow drawl.

"*I* vow it shan't look like *yours*," Mariah echoed, more crisply.

Heather giggled. "You are as bad as Mother!"

"And I shall continue to be until the two of you start speaking like the proper young ladies you are." Suddenly feeling she sounded more like Rose than herself, Mariah drew a surprised breath before returning her attention to Heather's hair. "Once I have everything secure, I shall very carefully catch a few tendrils here and there to bring down in curls to tease the back of her neck. And of course, I'll do the same in front of her ears to soften the look around her lovely face."

"I don't have a lovely face." Heather spoke barely above a whisper and lowered her lashes.

Mariah reached out and lifted the girl's chin with the edge of her index finger. "Now, how can you possibly say such a thing? Take a good look at yourself—those gorgeous azure eyes, those rosebud lips, and exquisite cheekbones. In just a few years, they'll definitely be finer than mine—and finer than a lot of other girls' your age."

"Do you really think so?" The twelve-year-old met Mariah's gaze in the mirror.

"Absolutely. In fact, I daresay your father will have to hold the young men off with a brace of pistols—"

Heather giggled.

"Just as I'm sure he's doing for Victoria right now."

The humor in Victoria's face evaporated. "I hardly think so. The one person I wish would admire me still thinks of me as a little girl."

"I know who that is," Heather singsonged.

"Hush!" Her sister silenced her with a frown.

"It's Tuck. Don't try to deny it."

Mariah made a mental note of the information. Ah yes, the dashing young gentleman she and Colin had met on the road yesterday—the one on his way to visit another young lady.

Victoria averted her blushing face but managed an angry retort. "I said, hush! Or I'll tell about you know what."

With an exasperated sigh, Mariah rolled her eyes. "And I, for one, care very little how much you girls argue, as long as you do it with precise diction."

"I say bravo to that." Their mother swept into the room, already dressed for the supper hour. She looked more elegant than ever in a sapphire taffeta gown with a ruffle at the hem. The sleeves of her gown dripped with lace at the elbows.

"Miss Harwood is showing us how to create the latest hairstyles from England," Victoria blurted, obviously hoping to distract her mother from whatever she might have overheard.

The lady of the house moved closer and eyed Mariah's work. "Yes, that is quite nice, Heather. It makes you appear six months older, at least." A teasing smile tugged at her lips.

"Does she not?" Mariah piped in as she continued pinning. "Back home, my sister Lily and I spent hours and hours practicing hairstyles on each other."

"Oh?" Mistress Barclay arched her slender brows. "You did not have a maid who dressed you?"

Mariah could see no reason for anything other than the truth. Lies were too hard to keep track of. "No, ma'am. We had only a housekeeper. But anytime we needed help with some little thing, she was kind enough to assist us."

The older woman offered one of her polite yet humorless smiles. "Well, you might be happy to learn we have two upstairs maids and two downstairs, plus Eloise our cook, and of course, Benjamin, the butler."

"You are truly blessed." Mariah flashed an equally practiced smile, then turned to Victoria. "Would you please fetch the curling iron from the brazier?"

The three Barclays watched as Mariah deftly curled Heather's top locks and the scattering of tendrils, making them as springy as Victoria's natural curls with the aid of the heated iron. Heather bobbed her head back and forth, a huge grin displaying her perfect teeth. "I do look older, don't I? And not just by six months."

Mistress Barclay's smile softened. "Yes, my darling. You shall be the belle of the evening." She turned to Mariah. "Do instruct Lizzie on the latest styles. I'm having some neighborhood ladies over for tea in a few days, and it would be great fun to show off a bit."

"Of course. I'd be pleased to."

"Oh, and do hurry, girls. The men arrived home a few minutes ago, and Eloise will be serving supper promptly at seven." Mistress Barclay's normally pursed lips twitched into a tiny smile. "The cook declared, with a shake of that finger of hers, 'Ah don't wants no repeat o' las' night, neithah.' " That said, the lady of the manor turned and sashayed out of the room.

The girls bubbled into laughter, and Mariah joined in. She couldn't believe the perfect southern accent the mistress had mimicked, considering her dislike of a lazy drawl. The elegant lady of the house actually had a sense of humor.

The day had gone so much better than she'd believed possible this morning. Now Colin was back. Who knew what wonders the evening might hold?

"Victoria, do take Heather's place. And Heather, be a dear and set the curling iron to cool. Victoria's curls need very little help. We've got to hurry."

Chapter 7

Colin would have given his right arm to know how Mariah had fared with his mother during the day. Calling on every ounce of self-control he possessed, he somehow managed to effect an air of disinterest as he, Amy, and his parents waited in the parlor for the English beauty and his other sisters to come downstairs.

Mother let out a huff. "Amy, do stop fidgeting with your hair bow. It's quite annoying."

"It's too tight," the wiggle worm replied.

"That, young lady, is your fault. You should have returned from the stables sooner." She rose from the settee and walked behind her daughter's chair to retie the blue ribbon.

With his mother's attention diverted, Colin took the opportunity to step away from the mantel and move closer to the doorway, where he had a better view of the staircase.

"Eldon, dear, how did things go in town today? You didn't mention the results of your trip."

His father drew a deep breath, obviously enjoying the delectable aromas emanating from the dining room, where large, covered serving dishes of hot food lined the sideboard, awaiting the arrival of the family at the table. "Fine. It appears we'll be getting a good price for both the tobacco and the grain."

"Splendid. And you planned to go to the music seller's. Were you able to find any instruments for the girls while you were there?"

He opened his mouth to answer but closed it again as the rapid patter of footsteps sounded on the stairs. He stood from his chair and followed Colin out into the foyer.

Heather flew into their father's arms first, breathless with excitement. "Papa! Did you buy me a violin or a flute?"

"We'll talk about music over supper, my darling."

Victoria descended at a more sedate pace, followed by Mariah, who met Colin's gaze with a radiant smile.

She looked as pleased to see him as he was to see her. Attired in peach taffeta adorned with delicate lace, her hair drawn back in a cluster of dark curls, the young woman's incredible beauty never ceased to amaze and enthrall him. Returning her smile, he took several steps toward the stairs.

Suddenly her smile lost its luster as she darted a glance beyond him.

Colin didn't need to turn to know his mother had made an appearance. He saw it in Mariah's stilted expression. Sensing they were being watched, he veered slightly and reached a hand up to Victoria. "You look very pretty this evening, little sis."

She beamed. "Do you think so? Mariah fixed my hair. She says it's one of the latest styles the ladies in England are wearing."

"Papa!" Heather cut in, latching on to her father's arm. "Please. I can't wait. I need to know now."

He chuckled and drew her into a hug. "Of course, my sweet. I surrender. I bought an instrument for each of you." He gave her a peck on the cheek. "I was unable to find a flute, as you hoped, but the seller did have two violins and a cello. I hope that will please you."

"What do you say, Mariah?" Heather swiveled in her father's embrace and turned to her. "Will they do?"

A light laugh accompanied Mariah's nod. "I should say those

instruments will do very nicely, dear. Perhaps once you've mastered those, your father can see about adding a flute at some future date."

The older man shifted his attention to Mariah. "As a matter of fact, I've already done so. I asked Mr. Smith, the music seller, to inquire hither and yon for a flute. I'm confident one will turn up before long."

"Oh, Papa! You are wonderful!" Normally shy Heather threw her arms about him and gave him a big hug. "Where have you put our instruments? I must see them."

"Why, upstairs, of course. In the farthest reaches of the house."

"In the schoolroom?"

"Yes. The three of you can go up there and start screeching the bows across the strings to your heart's content. After supper." He softened the remark with a playful wink.

Watching the loving exchange, Colin's gaze once again gravitated to Mariah, and he wished he could give her a playful hug. . .or any kind of hug. In one short day she had brought new life into the household. How could anyone not see that and adore her as much as he did? Well, perhaps not quite so much, he amended, aware of his mother again. He turned to find her intense brown eyes narrowed and focused on him. He flashed his most charming smile. "How was your day, Mother, dear?"

"Productive." The curt answer gave indication that she would not be so easily swayed.

Colin was spared further placation of the lady of the house when the brass knocker banged against the entry door. The butler, Benjamin, appeared out of nowhere and opened it wide to allow the visitor to enter.

Pa stepped forward. "Why, Dennis Tucker. I must say, this is an odd time for you to come calling. To what do we owe this unexpected pleasure?"

Colin stared at the interloper who stood resplendent in a fine navy frock coat and gray breeches, his ruffled white shirt accenting his tanned complexion, and he rolled his eyes.

Dennis swept off his three-cornered hat and handed it to the butler. "Didn't Colin tell you to expect me?" His gaze roved the gathering, stopping on Mariah. He gave a polite bow of his head. "Miss Harwood.

Delightful to see you again." His gaze lingered briefly, then he returned his attention to the man of the house. "I didn't mean to intrude. Perhaps another time."

"Nonsense, my boy." Pa said. "You know you're always welcome here."

"Why, of course." Mother swept toward him. "You're most welcome. Amy, go tell Eloise there'll be one more for supper, and ask Pansy to set another place." She flicked a glance at Mariah and back to Tuck, a scheming glint in her eye. "We're delighted to have you join us. Shall we all go to supper?" Taking Father's arm, she strolled through the parlor toward the dining room.

Colin cringed at his mother's sugary sweet graciousness and turned on his heel to escort Mariah, but Tuck was already offering the young beauty his arm. It would have been gratifying to wipe that satisfied smirk off his pal's face, but Colin could not afford to make a scene, could not reveal the depth of the feelings he already had for Mariah. He'd never before been so drawn to a woman.

Fortunately, Victoria moved beside him and threaded her arm through his. Something about the soft light in her eyes and her sweet smile revealed that she understood.

He filled his lungs and manufactured a grin as he patted her hand before starting after the others. "Shall we?" He'd just been outflanked on two sides, but the battle for Mariah Harwood had barely begun.

This is not good. Strolling into the dining room on Dennis Tucker's arm, Mariah managed to govern her emotions admirably. There was no denying Mistress Barclay's pleasure in having someone other than Colin show interest in her, and it wouldn't hurt Colin to have a little competition to increase his regard...but one look at Victoria, and Mariah could see the girl's heartache. That was really not good. The last thing she wanted was for Victoria to decide she'd rather be sent away to school than stand by and watch her tutoress steal her secret love's affections. But what could be done? Mariah had no idea how to keep both mother and daughter happy when their desires were at such odds.

Her thoughts in a muddle as she allowed Tuck to seat her, Mariah decided avoidance of the whole drama might be the most prudent tactic. She turned to Heather, being seated on her other side by Tuck. "Heather, dear, have you given thought to which instrument you'd prefer to learn first, the violin or the cello?"

The girl looked at her in all innocence, unaware of the tension surrounding Mariah, and her face brightened. "May I try both of them before I decide?"

"Of course." Only wishing Victoria looked as happy as her sister, Mariah felt added despair as Tuck positioned himself so closely that his arm brushed hers.

Across the table from Heather, Amy leaned forward and addressed her father at the head. "Poppy, I wish you only bought two instruments. I can't abide stayin' inside all day every day. I'm already spendin' hours and hours practicin' readin' and writin' and cipherin', how to walk and how to talk. And now music, too?" The last phrase ended on a high-pitched whine.

"Please speak properly, child." Her mother wagged her head. "The study of music is for your own good, and you did request an instrument of your own. It's time you stopped spending so many hours down at the stables. Whenever you return to the house, you smell like an old horse blanket, for pity's sake."

"Oh, Mother."

Mariah surmised that if Amy had been standing, she'd have emphasized her last protest with a stomp of her foot. She made an attempt to smooth the child's ruffled feathers. "You know, Amy, I've heard so much about your stable of Thoroughbreds, but I've yet to see them. If you promise to work at your music studies, I'd be honored to have you introduce me to every horse on this farm."

Amy brightened a bit. "Can we do it tomorrow?"

"If your mother approves." Mariah tipped her head at Mistress Barclay.

The lady of the manor smiled slightly as she eyed her daughter. "Only if you apply yourself to music for at least one hour."

"A whole hour?" The child's shoulders sagged. Then, with a look of resolve she perked up. "Oh, very well. One hour at music and one hour showin' Miss Harwood the stables."

A chuckle rumbled from her father's chest. "Colin, my boy, perhaps you and I should take Amy along with us the next time we deal with the tobacco buyers. She drives a hard bargain."

Mariah chanced a quick glance at Colin and saw him looking at her with a satisfied grin, even as he answered his father. "As you wish. If anyone could wear those thieves down, it would be our little squirt, for sure."

Mulling over the thought of touring the stables with the youngster on the morrow, Mariah had little doubt that Colin would somehow manage to be there at the same time. How hard could it be to distract an eight-year-old so they could steal a little privacy? A few moments would be enough to whet his interest, while not so much time that his mother would be alerted. Yes. A few sweet stolen moments. . .

"Shall we bow our heads?" Mister Barclay offered a simple blessing, and directly after the *Amens*, the tall African butler brought the first serving bowls to the table. Dressed in crisp black and white like the other house slaves, Benjamin moved quietly and efficiently without being obtrusive, as did Pansy and shy little Ivy as they assisted him.

Victoria was the first to start the conversation. She offered their guest a tentative smile. "Tuck, we're so happy to have our Miss Harwood here as our own private tutoress. Colin graciously bought—"

Though Mariah was impressed by the girl's diction as she spoke in the rather cultured accent she'd been practicing, the word *bought* hit a sour note. Mariah was grateful when Colin's voice overrode his sister's gentle tones.

"Yes, Tuck. I was extremely fortunate to find such an accomplished instructress for my sisters and hired her on the spot. Now Victoria—and hopefully the other girls—will never have to be sent away to school. They made no secret of their dislike of the idea."

For a split second, Mariah feared the mistress would finish what her daughter started by mentioning that she was actually here as an indentured servant. Then she realized it wouldn't be in her employer's best interest.

The woman wanted Tuck to think Mariah was a worthy conquest.

Apparently the young man did just that, as he tilted a dimpled cheek toward Mariah and smiled. "Beauty and education. What more could one ask?" A spark of humor lit his hazel eyes.

Remembering Victoria, Mariah shot a glance across to see if her jealous young charge would finish telling Dennis Tucker what she'd started saying a moment ago. But the girl was filling her plate as if nothing were amiss, which unnerved Mariah all the more. At any moment the lass so chose, she could blithely blurt out that Mariah was nothing but a bond slave—no matter how much she tried to pretend she wasn't.

A subject change was again in order. She turned to Colin. "Mr. Barclay, while you and your father were in Alexandria, were you successful in arranging the horse race you were hoping to schedule?"

He blotted his lips on his napkin and met her eyes. "Please call me Colin. Otherwise I'll think you're addressing my father. And yes, our friend Quince Sherwood is going to invite a few other horsemen he knows to participate. We thought it would be grand to make a festive day of it. Games, a picnic, that sort of thing."

Secretly reveling in the intensity of his gaze, Mariah had a fairly good idea what he meant by a *festive day*.

Tuck whacked his leg. "I say, old man, that sounds like great fun." He then tilted his head toward Mariah. "Miss Harwood, I'd be honored if you'd accompany me to the festivities."

Her spirits sank. Would this day never end? "Actually," she fibbed, "I promised the girls I'd accompany them to all social gatherings. Didn't I, Victoria?" She waited for what seemed forever for the lass to answer, hoping, hoping. . .

"Why, yes, she did." Victoria feigned a note of regret in her voice. "But, Tuck, you'd be most welcome to join us, of course." She offered him a bright smile.

Mariah stifled a sigh of relief.

"Now that that's settled," the lady of the house announced, "I suggest we finish our meal before it gets cold."

For the second time, Mariah felt utterly grateful to her mistress.

Perhaps she'd survive the evening after all. She relaxed and took another spoonful of her venison stew.

The conversation then centered on an upcoming wedding at a neighboring plantation, guests who were expected to attend, and the gala celebration afterward. Mariah gave it little attention, since she didn't know anyone mentioned. She was glad when Pansy brought in the dessert.

"Oh, I almost forgot," Tuck drawled.

Everyone looked up from their bowl of peach cobbler to him.

Mariah stiffened, wondering if she would be the topic yet again.

But the young man turned his attention to Colin. "I originally came by to find out if you'd learned anything new about that French force marching down toward the Ohio River. You didn't have a chance to elaborate when we met on the road yesterday."

Mariah breathed more easily. Men and politics. She only half listened as Colin related to his friend the same information he'd given his father the evening before.

Tuck shook his sandy head. "When I was at the Patterson Plantation last night, the men there were talkin' about it. If New York's governor doesn't raise a militia to stop 'em, Mr. Patterson says Governor Dinwiddie will. He said the Virginia Colony ain't about to hand over the Ohio Valley to the Frenchies. There's too much wealth in the fur trade. Patterson said Dinwiddie won't wait months for word to get to England and orders to come back. By then the French could have all the tribes bought off, and the whole territory would be lost to us."

Mr. Barclay shook his head, a worried expression drawing his brows together. "Let's just pray that Governor Clinton will send his Indian agent, that Johnson fellow from up in the Mohawk Valley, to meet with the tribes loyal to the Crown. From what I hear, he has great influence with them. He even married one of them. If he can keep the Indians from siding with the French, they'll just have to traipse on back to Canada again."

"Right." Colin nodded. "That'll probably be the end of it." He then glanced across the table at Mariah. "As Pa and I mentioned last night concerning your sister, there's nothing to worry about."

"It would be a sorry shame if nothing came of the affair." Tuck flashed a strange grin. "I, for one, would love a chance for some high adventure, ridin' off into the great unknown. Wouldn't you, old man?" He eyed Colin.

Mistress Barclay let out a weary breath. "Enough politics for one evening. We have a special treat for you this evening, Dennis. If Miss Harwood would favor us with a few pieces on the harpsichord. I think you will be pleasantly surprised."

Bravo! Mistress Barclay outmaneuvered everyone again and returned us to her agenda, pairing me with Dennis Tucker. Mariah squelched the snide thought. But one thing was certain. Quite the expert manipulator, the lady of the manor was a woman to be admired. . .and watched—closely watched.

Chapter 8

Colin looked at his timepiece. He'd been at the stables for more than an hour and was running out of things to check on. He gazed up at the big house. How much longer would Mariah hold class before she dismissed the girls?

Noticing the furtive glances between Old Samuel, the Negro horse groomer, and redheaded Geoffrey Scott, the trainer, Colin knew they were puzzled at his puttering around with nonessentials.

At last he spotted movement on the covered office porch, where bright afternoon light played over flouncy skirts. Mariah and Amy had finally come outside and would reach the stables in moments.

He turned to Geoff. "When my sister and Miss Harwood arrive here shortly, I'd appreciate bein' able to have some time alone with the tutor. See if you can come up with somethin' to divert Amy's attention elsewhere. You know the child's tendency to. . .exaggerate." Tattle was closer to the truth.

Geoff nodded with understanding and flicked his green eyes in the direction of the girls. "So that's the beautiful Miss Harwood the little gal's been telling us about, the bond servant you brought home from Baltimore."

Colin turned and saw that Mariah and Amy had already passed the rose garden. Even from this distance he was caught by the Englishwoman's matchless beauty. He switched his attention back to the horse trainer. "Yes. But she's not to be treated like a servant. I expect you to show her the utmost respect." Even as he spoke, he realized coming to her defense was becoming a habit.

Geoff eyed Colin straight on. "I would hope the lass will be treated with respect by one and all."

Knowing the trainer to be a zealous Presbyterian, Colin surmised the man's "one and all" referred to more than just the hired help. "That goes without saying. Miss Harwood is a real lady."

With the barest hint of a smile, Geoff glanced beyond him. "Then I'll trust you to be a true gentleman yourself."

"Of course." It appeared Colin would find no ally in the horse trainer. Added to that, he could hear lanky-framed Old Samuel chuckling as he mucked out the stall beside him. Ignoring the white-haired slave, Colin cleared his throat. "If you'll excuse me, I'll go fetch the young ladies."

This balmy afternoon was the first time Mariah had been outside the manse since her arrival at the plantation, and she was truly in awe of the beautiful grounds she could now observe close-up. The plants in the kitchen plot teemed with life, emitting a healthy freshness that blended with the sweet perfume from the rose garden, where blooms in varied hues stirred on the breeze. She breathed in the mixture of scents as she and Amy headed for the stables and pastures that lay downwind of the big house.

Mariah discovered the vast farm had buildings, sheds, and cabins enough to be its own small village. Beyond the structures, she could see a goodly number of slaves out in the fields, cutting leaves from the long rows of lush tobacco plants and stacking them in neat piles.

"Look, there's Colin." Amy pointed toward the stables and grabbed

Mariah by the hand. "He's there with Mister Scott and Old Samuel. You'll like both of 'em."

Being tugged along by the girl, Mariah had trouble dismissing the sight of so many African slaves laboring in the hot sun. As a bond servant, she had only a few more rights than those fieldworkers. Mistress Barclay had the legal entitlement to order her out in the fields alongside the slaves at any time, should she so choose.

"Blast!" Amy huffed. "Here comes that bossy brother of mine. Colin always has to butt in. I wanted to be the one to show you the stables myself."

"And you shall." Mariah gave the child's hand an encouraging squeeze. But she could no more hold back the smile already dancing across her lips at the sight of the strikingly handsome son and heir than she could stop the sun from shining.

"Go away, Colin." Amy folded her arms and pouted. "I'm going to show Miss Harwood the horses."

"As you wish, squirt." He grinned. "I won't say a word. . .except good afternoon to you lovely ladies."

"Such drivel," his sister groused, as if she'd just been insulted.

Colin stopped in front of them. "Why do you say that, little sis?"

"Because I'm not some simpering 'lovely lady.' That's why."

Still having problems containing her smile, Mariah patted Amy's shoulder. "Ah, but someday you'll be the belle of the county. Wait and see."

"Oh, pshaw!" She rolled her blue eyes. "I wish I was born a boy. I want to race horses like Colin. But nobody will let me ride anything but my stupid ol' pony."

Colin gave one of her braids a gentle tug. "I wouldn't call Patches stupid. He was my very best friend when I was your age."

"Hmph. And I bet they let you go out ridin' all by yourself, even when you were a lad. But they won't let me. I always have to wait around and wait around till somebody has time to go with me."

Mariah glanced at Colin, wondering how he would respond to that. The child seemed to be quite a handful no matter where she was.

He didn't bother to answer and changed the subject entirely. "So which horses are you going to introduce Mariah to?"

"All of them, of course." She flipped a braid behind her spindly shoulder. "I'll start with the ones in the paddocks, then show her the ones in the pastures."

Nodding, his gaze lingered for a second on Mariah. "Well, if you don't mind too much, I'd like to tag along. I promise to stay out of the way and let you do all the talking."

The child cut him a shrewd glance. "Oh, all right—even though I know you're only here so's you can be with Miss Harwood where Mother can't see the two of you."

Mariah had to fake a cough to keep from laughing out loud. Amy hadn't been fooled for a second.

Colin grunted, then gestured broadly, a grin lighting his eyes. "Well, now that we all know why we're here, lead the way, *mademoiselle*. After you. . ."

As the child immediately set out for the paddocks, Colin moved next to Mariah and reached for her hand.

She sidestepped him and clasped her fingers behind her back. "What are you doing? You'll get me sold out of here!" she hissed in a fierce whisper. "Your mother is probably watching us from a window this very second."

He released a weary breath and relented, and they walked on in companionable silence.

⁓

Having been guided through the well-ordered stables and out to pastures framed by tidy, white fences that stretched on forever, Mariah was impressed by the magnificent animals and surroundings. Why, this horse farm would equal that of any earl or viscount back in England. People in Britain had no idea how very prosperous the colonies had become. If only this plantation could belong to her and Colin one day. . . . She glanced up and locked gazes with him. If only. . .

Colin gave a meaningful lift of his brow. "I do believe our trainer is in the tack room." He turned to his sister. "Don't you think our lady should meet him, Amy?"

The child's expressive blue eyes sparkled with excitement. "And Ol' Samuel, our groom. They're lucky, Miss Harwood. They get to live out here by the horses." She snatched Mariah's hand. "This way."

They ambled to the far end of the stables and stepped through an open doorway into a spacious room that smelled of leather. Rope, harnesses, and bridles draped its sidewalls, and in the middle, a series of wooden sawhorses held gleaming saddles ready to be plunked atop horses at a moment's notice. At the end, a wiry, white man of medium build and a lanky Negro with frizzled white hair stood before a long workbench cutting leather strips.

"We're here!" Amy's proud announcement rang in the quiet.

The workers turned around, their tools still in their hands.

The slave's snowy head dipped politely.

Mariah gave an answering nod.

"This here's Miss Harwood, the bond slave I've been tellin' you about," Amy said.

Bond slave. Mariah seethed. The imp could have talked all day without uttering those words.

The other man lay aside his strange-looking knife and stepped forward, nodding a somber greeting. "How do you do, Miss Harwood. I'm Geoffrey Scott, the horse trainer." A multitude of freckles stood out against his fair skin as his lips slid into a smile, putting her more at ease.

"I'm very pleased to meet you. Both of you." Her gaze included the groom.

"Amy tells us you've come to turn our young girls into proper ladies." Mr. Scott's tone indicated a measure of disbelief as a teasing glint sparked in his green eyes.

Mariah laughed lightly and shot a glance to the child. "That is the goal."

He studied her without wavering. "Then I trust they'll be receiving spiritual instruction also. Along with Bible reading." His stern gaze moved to Colin.

"Why, yes. They will." Raising her chin a notch, Mariah attempted her own austere expression. "Grace and humility are vital attributes every individual must endeavor to seek."

Colin cleared his throat and directed his attention to the trainer. "I understand Patches has been off his feed for the last few days."

"What did you say?" Amy looked up at her brother, her eyes wide with worry. "Is he sick?"

Mariah wondered the same thing. Amy had proudly pointed out the adorable white Shetland pony with its large brown spots and commented on his gentle nature. He hadn't seemed to be ailing.

"Oh, there's probably nothing we need to be worried about." Mr. Scott patted Amy's blond head in assurance. "He might not be having a good day, is all." Something about the man's soothing tone confirmed Mariah's suspicion that the suggestion of a sudden malady was a ploy.

"Even so, you will check him for any odd swellings or carbuncles, won't you?" Colin asked.

The man cut another hard glare at him. "Aye. One can't be too cautious."

"Amy." Colin tipped his head at his sister. "Why don't you go with Geoff and help him. After all, Patches is your pony."

She swung a glance between him and Mariah and back, then clamped her teeth tight. "Oh, all right. I'll go check on Patches. For five minutes."

"Ten," Colin blurted.

"All right, but you'll owe me a lot for ten." Amy latched on to the trainer's hand and tossed a smirk over her shoulder. "Come on, Mr. Scott. Those two want to be alone." She rolled her eyes with the emphasis on the last word.

A chuckle rumbled from the redhead's chest. "Ten minutes, you say." Unhooking the chain of a pocket watch, he handed it to Amy. "I'll let you keep track of the time, little lady."

⌒

"Let's stroll outside, away from the smell of the stables, shall we?" Colin tucked Mariah's arm within the crook of his elbow and led her out the back entrance, out of sight from the house.

"As you wish, milord." But once in the open air, Mariah let out a nervous giggle that bubbled into laughter.

Colin found it infectious. Despite his irritation at his sister and the trainer, he echoed her merriment.

Still laughing, she made a wide gesture with her free hand, and he realized that a number of slaves and their overseer stood a short distance away, staring at them. His humor died. Was there no place on this blasted plantation where someone wasn't watching?

"I'm sorry, Mariah," he said, growing serious as he turned her to face him. "I've been hopin' for an opportunity to get you alone."

"I know." She took a handkerchief from her ruffled sleeve and dabbed at tears her laughter had caused. "Though 'tis very unwise, as you well know."

He drew her farther away from the building, away from the unwelcome stares. "I must confess, I had no idea Mother would do everything in her power to keep me from you. The way she's been guardin' that house, one would think she's on sentry duty."

"Quite." Mariah's sad smile crimped his heart.

Leaning closer, he searched her face. "I've been remembering the time we spent together on the road from Baltimore. It was rather enjoyable, and I've missed it. I'd hoped you had, as well."

"Of course I have," she murmured, gazing up at him with those gorgeous, alluring violet eyes. "I appreciated the way you pointed out various settlements and landmarks along the way. And I liked hearing about your family and your home. You were very kind to me."

His heart throbbed double time.

"Nevertheless, you must understand that your mother made her position deadly clear. She will not abide any dalliance between us." She averted her gaze. "Or participation in any other activities I'm too ashamed to mention. I am to remember my place."

"I'm so sorry. Mother can be a touch blunt at times. She's quite set in her ways." He attempted to draw Mariah closer.

She shook her head and backed away, looking in both directions, then warded off any further advances with a hand. "Please, Colin, we

SALLY LAITY AND DIANNA CRAWFORD

must not." Still gazing at him, her worried expression dissolved into one of tenderness. "But since we do have this short moment together—which is all that is allotted to us just now—I want you to know I think very, very highly of you. I do. But—"

"Say no more, my lady." He paused. "I believe I've come up with an idea. A plan, really." *Yes, a perfect plan.* Satisfied with its brilliance, he offered her a reassuring smile. "Just leave everything to me." He gestured for her to follow as he turned and started toward the stables again. "So, tell me, how did our little snitch's first music lesson go?"

Humor returned to Mariah's beautiful face as they headed back inside to collect Amy. "You really don't want to know."

Chapter 9

During the next two days, Colin's statement about having a plan kept Mariah wondering as she worked with his sisters on their school subjects and music lessons. She spent a good deal of time mulling over those mysterious words in her mind even as she demonstrated to the girls how to subtly draw attention while strolling about a room. She illustrated how to flirt with the eyes just enough to intrigue a man without being overly blatant, how to use the fan and parasol to spark interest, and how to *accidentally* allow a bit of ankle to show amid a flurry of skirts and petticoats. The two younger sisters quickly tired of that sort of playacting.

Victoria, however, was particularly eager to learn and did her best to mimic Mariah's movements as gracefully as possible. "Is this the way?" she would ask. "Please show me once more."

Mariah showered Tori's efforts with profuse praise while the other girls were absorbed in laboring over their sums. "I'm sure you shall have no difficulty capturing Dennis Tucker's affections. . .and we'll be sure to invite him to join us as often as you wish."

"Oh, I do hope he starts noticing me," the fifteen-year-old breathed on a sigh. "After all, I'm not a child anymore." She toyed with one of her honey-colored ringlets.

"That is true. However, your mother has set a lot of store by your marrying a prosperous merchant, you know." Mariah softened the reminder with a smile. "She does feel she has your best interests at heart. She wants you to have a successful future." *Just as I wish for myself.*

A dreamy glow filled Victoria's azure eyes. "Mother has a whole list of wants, I'm sure. And so have I." With a flutter of her long lashes, she snapped her parasol open and made a ladylike circuit of the room, bestowing condescending smiles and nods on her younger sisters as she passed.

Mariah couldn't help but smile at Victoria's determination.

A light tap sounded on the door, and Lizzie opened it and leaned her mobcapped head into the room, her smile bright against *café au lait* skin. "Tea is bein' served on the veranda, missy."

The words scarcely left the slave's mouth before books and parasols slammed shut and the three young ladies flew out of the room to the top-stair landing, where they came to a sudden stop, hiked their chins, and paraded down the steps at a more sedate pace, with Mariah trailing after them. A smiling Victoria hopped over the final two steps in front of Heather, as if she somehow expected her charming Tuck to come calling.

As the little group emerged from the front entrance to join the rest of the family out on the veranda, Mariah reveled in the welcome breeze wafting up from the river. Today was by far the warmest since her arrival. The heat compelled her to remove all but one thin petticoat beneath her dimity gown adorned with multihued pastel flowers. Its short sleeves allowed the breeze to cool her arms.

Colin and his parents already occupied some of the wicker chairs surrounding the cloth-covered table as Amy dashed to a vacant seat beside her mother. The two older girls and Mariah bobbed into quick curtsies. If anything, Mariah decided, this family tended toward too much formality.

"Be seated, girls." The mistress directed a cool smile at them. "The ice is melting in the limeade."

Mariah immediately headed for the prudent seat on the sharp-eyed woman's other side, noting the heavenly sight of moisture coursing down the glasses at each place setting in the heat of the day. Just as she was about to pull out the empty chair, Colin reached from close behind her and drew it back, then seated her. She did her best not to react to his nearness, even when his arm inadvertently brushed against hers, causing a delicious tingle.

"Do hurry up, everybody." Amy ogled the platter of small sandwiches, tea cakes, and sugared raspberries, her blue eyes wide.

"Oh my." Mariah turned to Mistress Barclay while Colin returned to his place across from her. "The drinks look especially delightful on such a warm afternoon." Even more delightful, Mariah would be able to slip an unnoticed glance at Colin on occasion from this vantage point. Hopefully he would also be discreet.

Over the persistent drone of cicadas proclaiming the arrival of sultry weather, Mr. Barclay offered a brief blessing for the food. The second he finished, Amy's hand snaked out and snatched a cucumber and watercress sandwich. The child always seemed quick and full of energy no matter the time or temperature.

Mariah's preference lay in the frosty drink. Enjoying the feel of the cool, slippery glass as she raised it to her lips, she took a long sip, letting the refreshing ice chips brush her lips.

Beside her, the lady of the house, slightly flushed from the heat, in a gown of ecru linen, took a draught from her limeade, then blotted her lips on her napkin. Across from the mistress, Mr. Barclay and Colin fared a bit better in thin white shirts with the top buttons open. Mariah turned her attention to the older man. "Sir, may I ask how you managed to supply this glorious ice in such hot weather?"

Setting down his drink, he flashed a friendly smile. "There's a nice little cove not far below the falls where the ice gets quite thick in the winter. We cut ice blocks there, wrap them in burlap, and cart them by wagon to our icehouse near the creek."

"Falls? I didn't know there was a waterfall nearby."

Colin entered the conversation. "It's not exactly nearby. It's a fair ride from here, actually. And it's not just a mere little fall but quite a spectacular series of cascades. Perhaps some day next week—after classes, of course—we could take a ride up to see them."

The mistress stiffened, but Amy all but jumped out of her seat. "Me, too! I love the falls."

"Of course, squirt. We wouldn't dream of going there without you." But her brother's lackluster tone belied his cheerful words.

"Can we go tomorrow? Please?"

"No." Her mother caught Amy's chin and turned it toward her. "Tomorrow is the Sabbath. And as you know, the Reverend Mr. Hopkins and his family will be here for Sunday dinner. Hannah Grace will want to visit with you."

"Oh, I forgot." The child slumped back in her chair, then popped forward again. "Then how about—"

"No, not Monday, either," Colin interjected. "I have to go into Alexandria to meet with Quince Sherwood about the horse race Saturday after next. Soon as I find out how many others will be competing, I must have the announcements printed up and pay a couple of lads to distribute them throughout the area. Once word gets around, folks from all over will show up with their picnic baskets and set up games for the children. And of course the tinkers will be there as well, hawking their so-called miracle remedies. Heaven forbid there should ever happen to be an affair where they fail to make the most of it."

Victoria set her partially eaten sandwich on her plate. "Oh, Mother. I simply must have a new summer frock made, and a matching parasol." She shot a merry glance at Mariah, obviously hoping to test her new attention-getting techniques on Tuck.

"You already have a selection of very nice gowns, dear," her mother reminded her.

"But not in the latest fashion." She looked at the mistress with a pleading expression. "I want a gown similar to Miss Harwood's. The dimity is ever so pretty. I'd be the envy of every girl in attendance. Please?" She scrunched up her face for added measure.

Mistress Barclay perused Mariah's frock as she nibbled a piece of tea cake in thought, her expression gradually losing its resolve. "Monday is not possible. I've invited the neighbor ladies for a light lunch that day, as you well know."

"But Mama, any later and there won't be time to have my dress properly made."

Appreciating Victoria's use of the more familial *Mama* in the same sentence with the word *properly*, Mariah realized the girl was no amateur at begging.

Her mother sighed, obviously growing weary of the topic. "Colin said he has quite a lot of business to take care of in Alexandria. Unless your father is able to go with you, you won't have a chaperone. Eldon?" She swept a questioning look at her husband.

"I'm afraid not." Mr. Barclay gave a slow shake of his head. "Cora, my love, Patterson and Clark will be here while their wives are lunching with you. We'll be occupied in my study."

She arched a brow. "Oh yes. . .you men and your private card games."

"Then Miss Harwood could come with me," Victoria quickly inserted. "In fact, I'd truly like her to come. She could assist me in selecting the perfect fabric and prettiest trims like the fashionable ladies in England are wearing."

Aha. So this must be the plan Colin had hinted at. Mariah reached for a slice of cake. This was getting interesting.

"What about me, Mother?" Heather jumped into the fray. "If Tori gets a new frock, I should have one, too."

Mercy me, a fly in the ointment.

An unexpected smile moved across Mistress Barclay's lips. "You're quite right. And Amy shall go as well. You shall all have new party frocks for the event." She plucked a raspberry from her plate and placed it in her mouth as she switched her attention to Mariah. "In fact, I would like you, Mariah, to have Mistress Henderson make you at least two new dresses. Plain ones. There's no need for you to walk about looking like a fashion plate while you're tutoring the girls." She paused, narrowing her dark brown eyes in added contemplation as she tapped her index finger against her bottom lip. "I think black would be too austere. Perhaps gray would be more suitable. Yes, gray will do admirably well. And have her send two mobcaps along. Those lovely curls need protection from the summer sun."

The cake turned to sawdust in Mariah's mouth. The message was clear.

Amy, however, folded her arms and pouted. "I don't wanna waste a whole day bein' fitted for no new day gown. I have enough dresses."

"*Being* fitted for *any* new day gown," Mariah heard herself blurt out, the tutor in her rising to the occasion despite the growing ache in her heart.

The child leveled a glare at her. "And *being* corrected all the way to town and back again, no doubt." She shook her head.

At that, a round of laughter erupted, lightening the moment. But Mariah couldn't help noticing Colin's deflated expression at having his plan go awry. Her heart went out to him. . .even though the sad turn of events was probably for the best. There was still time. Four years of time. Nothing had to work out just yet. She averted her gaze to the tall oaks lining the drive and watched the lush branches swaying on the summer wind, trying to envision herself looking bland as a turtledove.

Mistress Barclay's voice brought her back to the moment as she caught her daughter's hand in hers. "Amy, dear, how about this? Colin will take all of you girls with him when he leaves for Alexandria early Monday morning. By the time you've all been fitted for new gowns, your brother should have concluded his business affairs. Then you can return home for a quick lunch, after which you can all ride up to visit the falls and spend the rest of the afternoon there. Make a whole day of it. Wouldn't that be jolly fun?"

Amy's bottom lip made an appearance, and her forehead crinkled with a frown. "But why can't I just wait at home for the rest of them to get back from town? Why do I have to go there at all?"

"Because that is the only way I will permit you to go to the falls. That is my decision."

The child mulled the concept over in her mind then, accepting her fate, stood from her chair and flung her arms around her mother's neck.

"Oh well. At least I'll have a whole day with no lessons."

Mariah saw disturbed glances pass between Colin and Victoria, and she took another sip from her tall glass. Another of Colin's plans to get her alone may have been squashed. More's the pity. But it played right into Mariah's own scheme—keeping her desirable self always dangling before him but just out of reach. . .even if she would look a bit on the plain side most of the time. That little Amy surely did come in handy.

With any luck at all, years from now, when she and Colin were wed with children of their own, Mariah would be sure to thank both his everwatchful mother and the snitch for the excellent maneuvers that would help two people in love get together. Properly.

No matter how many obstacles were thrown in the path.

Chapter 10

On her first Day of Rest in the new land, Mariah rode in a gleaming black landau carriage, a completely new experience for her. In this luxurious conveyance, she and the wealthy Barclay family could see and be seen by everyone they passed. She smiled on a wave of pleasure. Her pious sisters, Rose and Lily, must be keeping her in their daily prayers, because Providence had definitely smiled upon her.

The open carriage had room for only six passengers, so Colin sat up top with the immaculately dressed driver, who guided a matched set of beautiful white-stocking bays at a sedate pace. Facing the rear in the deeply cushioned leather seat with Victoria and Heather, Mariah sensed Colin's presence behind her on the box bench. . .so close. Yet with her parasol shading her, there was no way he could view her.

She'd chosen her prettiest gown for the occasion, tiered lavender silk accented with delicate snowy lace, and taken extra care styling her hair. The upstairs maids, Lizzie and Celie, had done wonders with the girls, and in their summer pastels, each one could pass for an exquisite doll, as could their elegant mother. Even the men—and Colin, in particular—

drew attention in their brocade waistcoats and vests and tall silk hats. Surely the assemblage looked like royalty as they rolled smartly along the graveled road in the cool of the morning.

Sitting across from her with his wife and Amy, Mr. Barclay tipped his head at Mariah. "You're most fortunate on your first Sabbath with us to have a formal church service to attend."

Her brows dipped in question. "I don't understand."

"Our Reverend Mr. Hopkins shepherds two other flocks in Truro Parish. He must travel to a different one each week. But because our prospering port is gaining in population, he hopes to remain in Alexandria permanently in the not too distant future."

"I see." The information came as a surprise. So this village they were heading to lacked a full-time minister. Obviously Colin had exaggerated the town's attributes.

The distinguished Barclay patriarch turned to his wife with an affectionate smile. "On the other Sundays, Cora selects scripture readings for us, and we have private family worship at home."

The mistress eyed Mariah. "If you'd care to, we should like you to choose the section to read sometime. Next week, perhaps. And jot down a few questions for us to discuss, as well. It's important for the girls not only to know the scriptures but to understand their meaning and purpose also, so it can be applied to life."

Me? Prepare a Bible lesson? Mariah hoped she didn't betray her shock. On the other hand, she'd sat through innumerable tiresome sermons throughout her life. Surely she could dredge a bit of one of them from the recesses of her mind. "As you wish." Would the woman never stop testing her?

Mr. Barclay, seemingly unaware of the undercurrent, chuckled. "You'll soon learn, child, that my lady was not raised in the less demanding Church of England. She's a Massachusetts Puritan, a Congregationalist. And a particular follower of the famous Reverend Jonathan Edwards."

Having never heard of the man, Mariah leaned forward. "I'm afraid I must admit I'm not familiar with the name."

"I'm sure you wouldn't have heard of him," Mistress Barclay said in her husband's stead. "He's one of New England's more impressive ministers. Through his preaching and writings, he's garnered quite a dedicated following in the colonies. They call themselves 'New Lights.'"

"New Lights." Mariah cocked her bonneted head back and forth beneath her parasol. "That does sound rather interesting." Hopefully that would placate the woman.

"I'm glad you feel that way." The mistress brightened. "Then I shall loan you a copy or two of his writings to study. And later we shall discuss them."

"I should like that, madam." Aware she'd just spoken an untruth on the Sabbath, of all days, Mariah deftly switched the topic. "Mr. Barclay, I've noticed how very lush the fields of tobacco appear. They're quite different from plantings in southern England. The other day, I watched as your workers cut leaves and stacked them with utmost care. Why is that?" She already knew the answer but wanted a diversion from the previous, less than welcome topic.

It did the trick. The rest of the drive to Alexandria, the plantation owner expounded at length about tobacco and the other crops and workings of his vast enterprise. On Mariah's either side, his daughters emitted occasional sighs of boredom. Once, however, as they passed a lane leading to a manse that appeared as large as the Barclays', Victoria jabbed her gently in the ribs. "Tuck's place," she whispered. Mariah surveyed the attractive grounds and smiled.

Soon homes and trades shops began to appear along the road. After passing a few cross streets, the driver guided the landau onto one just ahead. The street lacked any hint of prosperity, so Mariah couldn't help but wonder if the main part of the town spread in some other direction, especially when the red-spoked carriage pulled onto a dirt lot. Peering down the road, she decided it looked even less settled and turned quietly to Victoria. "Is this the center of Alexandria?"

The girl smiled and wagged her head, sending honey-gold ringlets dancing before and behind her slim shoulders. "Not at all. The market square is farther down the Royal Road, and there's also a lot of business down on the quay."

That news came as a relief, particularly when their carriage came to a stop beside two others equally grand. A quick glance of assessment revealed that, although the other carriages were pretentious, the church building itself was far from it. Only Mrs. Barclay's gift for veiled assaults kept Mariah from commenting on the meagerness of the simple clapboard structure.

She and the older girls waited politely for the elder Barclays and Amy to exit the vehicle. Then Mariah and the two budding maidens rose, filling the interior of the carriage with their bevy of ruffled skirts. Mariah waited for the girls to precede her, hoping that if Colin helped her last, he would naturally escort her into the chapel. After all, how much safer and more proper could she be in his company than while they were attending service in church?

"Milady." Looking up at her with an expectant grin dancing in his eyes, the handsome son and heir extended a gloved hand.

She tilted her parasol to shield her face from his parents' view, then gifted him with a slightly mischievous smile of her own.

As they strolled toward the entrance, Victoria slowed ahead of them and waited while Mariah and Colin came up beside her, then tipped her head slightly with a flick of the eyes toward the church.

Mariah shot a glance forward and saw Dennis Tucker on the top landing, watching them approach.

A tiny frown on Victoria's smooth brow reminded Mariah of the promise she'd made the previous evening, that should Tuck happen to be at church this morning, she would invite the young man to come on tomorrow's outing. The promise wouldn't exactly further her own pursuit of Colin, at least not at this moment. Nevertheless, a promise was a promise. She suppressed a huff of disappointment and thought of a way to snag the young man's attention.

Walking alongside Colin, Mariah came to an abrupt stop. "Oh, la. I've a stone in my slipper." She bent to remove the shoe, surmising that Colin would lean down to assist her. When he did, she whispered into his ear. "Your sister Victoria is quite smitten with Dennis. Ask him to join us tomorrow."

"But—" He frowned.

"Please. We need her allegiance." Straightening, she spoke in a louder voice. "There, the stone is out. Thank you, kind sir."

"You're most welcome." Though offered politely, the remark lacked his usual jovial grin. He did, however, give her a meaningful nod as he took her hand and placed it within his arm. "Shall we go greet my friend Tuck?"

The sun was high in the sky when the landau rolled to a stop at the rear of the Barclays' home.

"Hurry, girls." The mistress shooed her daughters out of the carriage with an impatient wave of her hand. "Go fetch the food and drink from the springhouse. And don't get yourselves dirty. The Reverend Hopkins and his family will be here shortly."

Watching her charges clamber to the ground without waiting for assistance, Mariah frowned, wondering why they were being asked to do servants' work.

Mistress Barclay directed her attention to Mariah. "We keep the Sabbath as best we can. Once our house slaves have completed their necessary morning duties, they are free to spend the rest of the day as they wish."

"How very gracious of you. If there's anything I can do to assist with the meal, I'm happy to do so." It never hurt to act helpful, even if Sunday was supposed to be her free day after service as well. Mariah waited for the older woman to precede her down to Colin's waiting hand.

"Thank you, child. But Reverend Hopkins assured me he and his good wife are quite interested in becoming better acquainted with you. I'd appreciate it if you'd entertain them until dinner is served."

Mariah halted on the bottom carriage step. Entertain the minister? Her? And be asked all sorts of questions?

Waiting below for her to step down, Colin took her hand and gave it an encouraging squeeze, then turned to his mother. "And of course there'll be no mention of the fact we hold Mariah's indenturement papers." He spoke with finality.

"Of course not, dear." She gave him a small smile, but there was no accompanying sparkle in the woman's eyes. She took her husband's arm and started toward the house.

Not today, anyway. Mariah stared after the haughty woman. She then gave Colin a half smile and mouthed her thanks as her foot reached the gravel drive.

"It's been some time since the good reverend and his wife honored us with a visit." He tucked Mariah's arm in his. "Let's wait on the veranda for their arrival."

His mother turned back. Her forced smile had vanished.

Mariah gulped. "Perhaps I should help your mother prepare a tray of cool drinks for our guests, this being such a warm day."

To her relief, the woman's smile returned. "Yes. I would appreciate that."

Now her son's congenial expression faded.

Mercy me, but this endeavoring to keep everybody happy is proving to be very trying, indeed.

To Colin's relief, the Hopkins family took longer than expected to arrive, so Mariah was spared the minister's inquisition before the meal. And when everyone finally sat down at the table, Colin and his eager sisters made certain the conversation focused on the upcoming race day, rather than on Mariah and how she happened to become part of the household. Still, from the blatant stares he'd caught from thin-as-a-rail and bespectacled Reverend Hopkins and his short, plump wife, Colin could tell the pair were desperate to question her.

After the meal of cold meats and crisp salad reached its conclusion, Colin, his father, and besieged Mariah accompanied the couple out on the veranda while Victoria and Heather remained inside to help their mother clear the table. Amy wasted no time at all in taking off for the stables with the minister's daughter, Hannah Grace, and her younger brother, Jamie. Colin knew the man of the cloth would suspend his curiosity no longer. . .nor would his wife.

"You were right. It is much cooler out here," Reverend Hopkins declared. Removing his somber ministerial frock coat, he hooked it over one of the cushioned wicker chairs, then seated his wife and took the empty chair next to her. "You folks have a fine home and plantation."

"Thank you." Father followed his guest's suit and gestured to Colin, and they both shed their heavy outerwear, then took seats on either side of Mariah. "We rather enjoy our life here."

"Miss Harwood." The thin-faced man swung his attention to her before she'd even settled her skirts about her. "My good wife tells me you hail from Bath, England."

"That is correct, sir."

"Marvelous. I attended college at Oxford and spent several holidays in your fair city. By the by, which church did you attend?"

Colin sat back in his chair, surprised how quickly the clergyman moved from small talk to the inquest.

Mariah appeared relaxed as she met the man's gaze. "All of my family are members of Vicar Nielson's congregation. Perhaps you yourself attended St. John's while visiting Bath."

"My, yes. A fine church that is. Handsome building, as well."

"Indeed. We've always enjoyed it." She hiked her chin a notch, adding to her air of dignity.

Mistress Hopkins pursed her full lips, plumping out the apple-dumpling cheeks beneath her salt-and-pepper upsweep. "How is it that you happened to take leave of such a popular resort to travel across the water for a position as tutoress?"

Leaning forward, Colin answered the nosy woman. "Miss Harwood came here to be close to family."

"You don't say." Nudging his spectacles a bit higher on his nose, the minister cut her a shrewd glance, then slid it to Colin. "What family might that be? Perhaps I'm acquainted with them, since I shepherd three separate flocks in the area."

"Her older sister is with an associate of the Virginia and Ohio Fur Company. I'll be inquiring after them on the morrow, when I conduct some business in town."

The minister's wife arched a skeptical brow. "With an associate, you say."

Colin was swiftly growing irritated with the presumptive biddy and fought to keep his tone even. "As Miss Harwood is in our employ, her sister is also respectably employed."

"But of course," the woman demurred. "There is no shame in honest labor."

No shame, but no honor either. Colin noted the woman's satisfied smirk. How dare she come here seeking fodder for Alexandria's gossip mill, when all one had to do was take one look at Mariah to realize she was a gentlewoman caught in an embarrassing but temporary circumstance.

His father finally entered the fray. "Miss Harwood comes to us as a highly qualified tutoress as well as a gifted musician. We are most fortunate to have her in our household, and our daughters have already benefited from her accomplishments." He turned to her. "Perhaps later we might impose upon you to entertain us on the harpsichord with a musical rendition or two."

She gave him a grateful smile.

"I'm sure that would be most enjoyable." The minister peered across the table again at Mariah. "Still, as tutoress, I would hope you are including spiritual matters in the Barclay girls' education, as well, child."

"Indeed I am, sir." Mariah tucked her chin. "This is, after all, a Christian home."

"That is true." The reverend nodded in thought. "I've had many a spirited conversation with the dear lady of the house, since she comes from the land of the Puritans." He clasped his hands together. "Speaking of spirited, might I ask your thoughts on this morning's sermon?"

Mariah cut Colin a disturbed glance. The two of them had spent far more time merely enjoying sitting side by side than they had in paying attention to the man's dry discourse. She straightened her posture. "I believe your sermon centered on Psalm 139, did it not?"

"Quite. And what insights did you glean from King David's words?"

Colin attempted to stall for a few minutes. "We were discussing that on the way home, weren't we? It seemed each of us hit on a different point."

Mariah smiled at him and returned her attention to the clergyman. "I always find myself caught up in the beautiful lyrical wording. 'If I take the wings of the morning, and dwell in the uttermost parts of the sea. . . .' I do believe someone has set those very words to music in one of the pieces I've played."

"Ah, yes. Beautiful." Reverend Hopkins then spoke with more conviction. "But the meaning behind the Psalm has far more passion. 'O Lord, thou hast searched me, and known me. Thou knowest my downsitting and mine uprising, thou understandest my thought afar off. Thou compassest my path and my lying down, and art acquainted with all my ways. For there is not a word in my tongue, but, lo, O Lord, thou knowest it altogether.'"

Colin suddenly felt a twinge of guilt for having been less than truthful with the minister. Still, Mariah needed his help. "That scripture truly is powerful. Very powerful. To become aware that we have such an all-knowing and all-seeing God, One who cares enough to take particular interest in each and every one of us, that is an extremely profound truth. Is that not what we were talking about earlier, Miss Harwood?"

"Why, yes." She gave his wrist a secret squeeze under the table. "And you worded it most succinctly. Don't you agree, Reverend Hopkins?" She offered a smile that included his good wife. "And I want to add that I thank our Good Lord every night for bringing me to such a God-fearing family."

Delighting in her words, her voice, Colin wove his fingers through hers. Tomorrow. Tomorrow they'd be leaving his mother's ever-watchful eyes behind and spending the entire day together. And despite the nuisance of tattletale Amy's presence, he'd find a way to be alone with Mariah.

By hook or by crook.

Chapter 11

Colin prided himself for acting the perfect gentleman on the carriage ride to and from Alexandria. Positioning Amy and Heather on either side of him, he made sure his youngest sister would have nothing to tattle to their mother about when they returned home for the noon meal. He didn't want to cause the slightest trouble that could spoil plans for their afternoon outing—the horseback ride to the Great Falls.

It had taken him awhile to get used to the idea that Victoria was infatuated with Dennis Tucker. When they stopped by his friend's plantation to pick Tuck up on their return trip, she found the perfect spot for him—next to her. On her opposite side, Mariah appeared somewhat dull in comparison to Tori. As if in deference to the girl, she had chosen a frock far less fancy to allow Victoria to shine. Even her severe hairstyle lacked its usual bounce, while Victoria's golden curls and flowing ribbons danced on the breeze and reflected shards of sunlight as she chatted with Dennis. Colin began to see her with new eyes. . .the way any young buck might do. He found the concept unsettling.

When they reached the house and went inside for lunch, Colin followed the others, chuckling to himself that the business of courting could get so complicated. However, if Dennis happened to be Victoria's choice, he would do his utmost as her big brother to help her in her quest. After all, she could do far worse. Although Tuck often tended toward being on the footloose side and out for a good time, deep down he would invariably make the responsible decision.

The servants had yet to bring in the food, but delectable smells drifted in from the kitchen, promising a tasty meal. After the small group entered the dining room and found chairs, Mother joined them and took her customary place at the end of the long table.

Colin addressed her as he seated Mariah next to him in one of the side chairs. "Where's Pa? I thought he'd be eating with us."

"Down at the stables. He wanted to be sure the afternoon outing would be enjoyable for everyone, so he's selecting some gentle mounts for the girls."

"How thoughtful." Colin was relieved that his father would be preoccupied for a time. He had something to say that the older man would likely not approve of.

His mother directed her gaze to Victoria. "Were you girls able to find pretty fabrics and trims for your new gowns?"

As his sister opened her mouth to reply, Colin winced and held up a finger. "Before you ladies start talking ribbons and lace and other fripperies, I have a comment to make."

Just as he hoped, all eyes riveted on him.

"I think it's high time, Mother, for you to pay more attention to how Victoria dresses. The frock she has on today makes her seem much too—" He narrowed his eyes and stared at her. "Too grown up."

Victoria gasped, her mouth gaping in speechless shock.

The other young people exchanged puzzled glances but remained silent.

His mother appeared far from pleased herself as she spoke through tight lips. "Whatever do you mean, son?"

Not at all put off by her demanding tone, he cocked his head back and forth and straightened his spine. "It's like this. From the moment we reached Alexandria, it seemed every man in town began gawking at Victoria. Anyone with half a brain could tell what was on their minds. Then after I dropped the girls off at the seamstress's shop, I barely got half a block away before that upstart, Eddie Rochester, came running up to me, wanting to know if he could come calling on her this evening."

Mother's eyes grew wide as she swallowed the bait. The Rochesters were the wealthiest merchants along the quay. "Are you referring to Gilbert Rochester's eldest son?"

Colin smirked. "Quite. The one who's always tearing about the countryside in that fancy phaeton of his, kicking up all kinds of dust. Needless to say, I wasted no time in setting him straight."

"What did you say to him?" His mother clutched the arms of her chair.

"The truth. That Tori's just a child. Too young to start receiving callers."

Victoria paled and shrank in her seat in embarrassment.

"Too young!" Sinking back in her chair, Mother shook her head, her eyes ablaze. "This is not to be borne, Colin. You are turning out to be even worse than your father. I refused to tolerate his interference regarding our daughters, and I shall not abide such actions on your part either. Your sister is not a child. She will turn sixteen in less than a month, and she's a beautiful, blossoming young woman. As soon as you've eaten, I expect you to ride straight back into town and inform Edward he's more than welcome to call on Victoria at any time."

Colin had the sinking feeling he'd overplayed his hand a fraction.

"But Mama!" Amy lurched to her feet. "He's takin' us to the falls this afternoon. You promised." Folding her arms, she plopped back down onto her chair, her bottom lip protruding.

"I'll go first thing in the morning." Colin gave his mother a placating nod. "If you're absolutely sure you want that Rochester whelp hanging around here."

"He is a bit pushy," Victoria admitted in a subdued voice. "He's been tryin' to catch my attention at church for some time now. I've just ignored him."

Tori must have caught on to his attempt to whet Tuck's interest by injecting a little competition, real or imagined. Colin breathed a little easier. With any luck at all, having her and his friend otherwise occupied would give him some time alone with Mariah, which was the whole point of the outing.

"Darling." Mother spoke to Victoria in a more soothing maternal tone. "That's what young men do whenever a young miss catches their fancy. You really should be flattered. That particular gentleman would be quite the catch for any girl. Now, enough of this sort of talk. It's time to eat." Picking up a silver bell near her plate, she rang it.

Colin saw Tuck slide a glance to Victoria. One that lingered, as if seeing her for the first time.

Mariah must have noticed as well. She nudged Colin's foot with hers.

And now the rest of the day awaited them.

Mariah doubted there had ever been a more glorious summer day. The dreadful heat of the Sabbath had gradually dissipated during the night, and a milder, flawless morning dawned. Now a little past midday, luscious, billowy clouds floated across the bluest of skies, and birds of every hue and voice gave tribute to nature's perfection as the small group plodded their way over the rolling, wooded terrain toward the Great Falls.

Walking their long-legged Thoroughbreds beneath a shady canopy of trees to rest them, Mariah looked at Colin and chuckled as Heather and Amy sprang up into their saddles and galloped ahead in the wake of two young fawns sprinting through the forest. "At last. 'Tis a full week since you and I have been able to speak freely without someone reporting on our every word."

"Only a week?" A wry half smile twitched his lips as he tugged on Paladin's lead and drew him alongside her horse. A cool breeze from the river below ruffled the full white sleeves of his blouse and toyed with a lock of his hatless hair. "Seems more like a month." His dark eyes drifted to Mariah's and took their sweet time there before he so much as blinked.

"Before my sisters come back, I do want to apologize for not apprising you of something you may not know."

She tipped her head in question.

"I am but an heir to my family's wealth, still awaiting my inheritance. But my father assures me it won't be the case much longer. He's promised to deed over a portion of our land to me when I turn five and twenty—which is a mere seven months hence. At that time I'll have my own income to do with as I wish—and my own home, should I choose to build one."

He made it sound as if it was important for her to know those things, as if she would somehow be a part of it. But seven months. That was a long time to wait when one was forced to live under the thumb of his domineering mother. Still, so be it. Seven months or—heaven forbid—seven years, Colin was a man who was more than worth the wait. She moistened her lips and peered up at him through her lashes. "If it is not too bold of me to ask, do you so choose to build a home of your own?"

He flashed a sheepish smile. "Actually, until a week ago I hadn't given the matter much thought. But now the possibility seems to be growing more enticing all the time." He reached for her hand, his gaze still roving her face. "Mariah, we've known each other for such a short while, you and I, yet from the first moment I saw you, I knew you were incredibly special, and that proves to be truer by the moment. You must know you're all I think about every day, all I dream about at night. I don't think it was by some bizarre twist of fate that we met. I believe you came into my life for a reason."

Hearing the words she had hardly allowed herself to dream about, Mariah could scarcely draw breath over the throbbing of her heart. She'd never seen such a depth of feeling in Colin's expression before, and she was thankful that Victoria and Dennis weren't near enough to witness it, since they were riding a ways behind them.

Or were they?

Suddenly aware she could not detect the sound of the couple talking or the clop of their horses, Mariah turned and looked back along the trail. They were nowhere to be seen.

Colin scowled. "I can't believe this. A few subtle nudges on my part, and my pal absconds with my sister." He swung up onto Paladin and wheeled him around.

Mariah reached a hand up to stay him. "Wait a moment, Colin. Surely they'll be coming into view any second. Don't embarrass Victoria unnecessarily. She's been mooning after Dennis Tucker for so long, and he's finally beginning to show interest—thanks to you."

His expression darkened. "Indeed. Well, there's interest, and then there's interest."

Unable to resist such a perfect moment, Mariah gave him a coy smile. "And which kind of interest do you have in me, if you don't mind my asking?"

"Both!" Ramming his heels into Paladin's flanks, he sped off in the direction they'd come.

Both. Exactly what she'd hoped with all her heart to hear. She let out a slow breath and climbed aboard her mount. If only she hadn't discovered Victoria was missing. Perhaps there might even have been a proposal of marriage, had the moment lasted a bit longer. If she had ever doubted before, those doubts had just been put to rest, even though she could not imagine how things could ever work out toward that end. Particularly with Mrs. Barclay to consider.

Watching after Colin, she saw him rein his horse to a halt. Beyond him Victoria and Tuck rode slowly into view, laughing and absorbed in each other, completely oblivious to the fact that the protector of Victoria's honor awaited them. How amazing that this man who wouldn't give his sister a few measly minutes alone with her new beau had done nothing this entire week but think up plans to get Mariah alone.

Once the big brother made certain the couple took note of his meaningful glower, he came back to join Mariah. He shook his head while matching Paladin's gait to that of her mount, and his demeanor lightened noticeably. "I was hoping to distract Amy, particularly when we reach the falls, since she loves to play in the water there. But now this." He lofted a hand in the air in a helpless gesture. "My little sister will be the least of my concerns. It's my oldest one I'll have to keep a close eye on."

Mariah slanted him a smile. "Surely you can trust your best friend to be a gentleman."

"You jest." Scoffing, he tossed a glance of disbelief over his shoulder.

Surmising that the young man could be trusted about as much as she could trust Colin, given the right opportunity, Mariah stifled a giggle. "Well, kind sir, you did say the falls are very beautiful. There'll be other times for us, I'm sure."

He didn't respond immediately, just plodded along, a thoughtful tilt to his dark head. "The day of the race." He nodded with finality and relapsed back into his drawl. "I'll make certain of it then. That mother of mine has been runnin' my life far too long already, whether she's had reason to do so or not. It's time I put an end to her meddlin'."

Even though Mariah hoped with all her being that he spoke the truth, she couldn't ignore the twinge of uneasiness at the level of his determination. "You do remember her threat to sell me to some vile stranger," she murmured, as if voicing the thought aloud would bring the horrid prospect to reality.

A slow, smug grin moved across his lips. "Ah, but you forget one thing. Whose signature is on those papers?" He quirked a teasing brow. "Not hers. Mine."

Chapter 12

The next two weeks stretched on interminably. Mariah's thoughts insisted on reverting constantly to the horseback ride to the Great Falls. She'd come so close to securing a marriage proposal from Colin that afternoon. So close. But with him occupied in overseeing his sister's conduct during the remainder of the outing, there'd been no further mention of the possibility of a shared future for the two of them. Mariah now had no other recourse than to wait until the day of the upcoming race for another opportunity to be alone with him, and patience never had been her dominant virtue.

To be fair, Colin had tossed her a few meager crumbs of his affection now and then since their return—a private look, the occasional folding of her hand within his beneath the dining table. But sly little Amy managed to snag the chair between them most mealtimes, no doubt following her mother's instructions.

These days Colin and his father spent most of their hours out with the horses, since Mr. Barclay had decided to enter a second promising filly from their stables in the racing competition. Mariah filled the majority of her time with her teaching duties. Heather, the quiet middle daughter, showed amazing promise when it came to learning the violin, and Mariah truly enjoyed working with the talented young miss. Even if fate determined her stay here on the plantation to be cut short by marriage, she hoped to be permitted to keep helping Heather to master the instrument.

Increasingly, her dreams centered on taking her leave of this magnificent plantation and living with Colin in a fine home of their own. But since that all-important conversation on the way to the falls had been aborted, there hadn't been a single moment for them to be alone long enough to formulate any plans. Their very first day back, he'd been forced to make good on his lie to his mother by returning to Alexandria and convincing Edward Rochester he was welcome to come and call on Victoria. In turn, that young man's almost daily presence spurred Tuck to drop by most evenings as well.

Fanning herself while her charges composed essays regarding their jaunt to the falls, Mariah switched her attention out the small window, staring unseeing at a summer sky fragmented by the branches of a maple tree just outside.

Victoria obviously relished having wealthy and handsome young bachelors devoting endless evenings to showering her with attention. Mariah couldn't help but envy the girl as she watched from the sidelines, playing the harpsichord while Tori and the others danced and sang. Observing Colin coaxing shy Heather to dance with him did bring a smile, however. He was by far richer and better looking than either of the two young swains. He was sure to be a gentle father to his and Mariah's children. If. . .

She sighed and averted her focus to the music before her. The someday of her dreams could prove to be a long way off.

Race day arrived at last with a flurry of activity. Amid excited giggles and complaints, every hair on every head had to be in proper order, and every new garment had to accentuate the girls' slender bodies perfectly, especially Victoria's. "After all," Mistress Barclay had declared the day before, "we must all be at our best. We cannot look like paupers before our neighbors."

But no one looked forward to the day in Alexandria with more anticipation than Mariah as she floated down the stairs in her own most stylish summer gown. In daffodil lawn, its full skirt was drawn up on either side in a soft apron effect to reveal ruffled petticoats, and a broad sash of emerald satin formed a flowing bow in back. Around her neck she wore a delicate cameo on an emerald ribbon, a prized treasure that once belonged to her mother. She hoped to dazzle Colin enough today that she would become a betrothed woman before the sun set. Of course, the event would likely have to be kept secret until his inheritance had been secured, because under no circumstance—even considering her indenturement—would she go to his home or his bed without a proper certificate of marriage.

Her imaginings were interrupted when Amy bumped past her on the stairs. "Do hurry. Mama said I could bring Patches along with us. After the race and the picnic, she said I can ride around on him with the rest of the kids."

"I'm sure that will be—" Mariah stopped midsentence as Amy bolted away, the leather soles of the child's slippers echoing across the marble floor of the foyer and out the open door. *It'll be most enjoyable for Colin and me*, she added mentally with a wry smile. Having the youngster occupied was vital to the plan.

Reaching the bottom landing, Mariah strolled toward the entrance, her closed parasol tapping beside her like a stylish cane. *Dear Lord, I know You want what's best for me. . .and for my sisters*, she added for good measure. *Once I'm wed to Colin, I shall be able to buy their bond papers and perhaps even send Rose and Lily back to Papa in England. He'd like that, I'm sure. So whatever I must say or do today, I just know You'll agree will be for the best. Thank You.* Gratified that she'd remembered to pray, she stepped out into a glorious, dew-kissed morning.

The landau would be used again today. Jericho, the driver, stood resplendent in a crisp black uniform as he waited beside the open carriage door to assist everyone into the conveyance. Choosing a seat facing the rear so Mistress Barclay would be able to face forward, Mariah wagged her head and smiled at the sight of Amy. The child was turned to the rear and on her knees, facing her little spotted gelding.

"You get to come with us, Patch. We're gonna have so much fun!"

"You'd better turn around," Mariah urged the girl. "I hear your mother coming, and you're crushing that lovely new skirt."

Amy flipped around and smoothed her rose taffeta frock as her sisters preceded their mother out the door.

Heather, attired in ruffled peach, and Victoria in a soft blue the identical hue of her eyes, looked especially fetching as they approached the carriage. But though the new day gowns were lovely on the girls, nothing could compare to Victoria's breathless smile at having not only one beau but two!

Mariah squelched a smug smile. Today her parents would be there to chaperone their budding daughter. With any luck at all, the elder Barclays would be so busy watching Tori, they'd have no chance to oversee Colin and her. *Yes, Lord, this truly will be a wonderful day.*

Once the women were settled with their parasols safely stored and the driver had climbed up to his seat, the mistress cleared her throat. "Jericho, you may proceed now."

"Yes, Miss'tus." With a snap of Jericho's whip, the carriage lurched into motion.

"I wish Papa were here to see our new frocks," Heather lamented. "And my new parasol. It's ever so pretty."

"So do I, dear." Her mother looked across at Heather, who sat beside Mariah. "But you know he and your brother needed to take the horses into town yesterday so the animals would be completely rested for today's race."

"I know. But he's never seen me in anything this pretty. It makes me look grown up, does it not?"

Mistress Barclay offered a warm smile. "Yes. Ever so grown up. But your father always thinks you're beautiful, no matter what you wear."

Mariah couldn't keep from chiming in. "And I think that all of you look as marvelous as any stylish London family traveling to Bath on holiday."

"Do you really think so?" A faint pink tinge rose over Victoria's fine cheekbones as she reached up to touch the intricate cluster of curls Lizzie had fashioned for her.

"Absolutely. 'Tis an honor to be riding with you."

Her flattering words didn't seem to faze the lady of the family. Unsmiling, she swung her gaze to the passing countryside. "I do hope both horses fare well in the race today. Should that be the case, Eldon believes it would entice more of the gentry to buy locally, rather than import their Thoroughbreds from England."

Mariah gave her a polite nod. *Splendid! Another concern to keep the Barclays' time filled. Yes, this was going to be a very good day.*

⟞⟝

"I never expected so many people!" Mariah turned in her seat to peer over her shoulder as the landau crunched along the graveled road toward Alexandria. Even with the town buildings some ways off, crowds already milled about, blocking the road. In the distance, canopies of different sizes and shapes edged a long, narrow clearing, and men stood at each one, buying and selling. Others hollered above the noise, hawking their wares. Oblivious to the melee, children darted among the throng, rolling hoops and skipping arm in arm.

Along each side of what Mariah surmised was the racecourse, colorful groups had already gathered in the shaded areas beneath the trees and laid out blankets and quilts for their picnics. All this for a simple horse race! She shook her head in wonder.

Amy suddenly sprang to her feet and leaned over the edge of the carriage. "I thought so! A parade of musicians is comin'! With two drummer boys in front!" She swung her attention to Mariah. "Please, can I play a drum instead of that ol' violin? I hate those screechy strings, and a drum would be so much more fun."

Mistress Barclay reached out and tugged her daughter back to her seat. "Do try to be a young lady, child. . .at least until we get situated. And no, you may not have a drum to pound on. Drums are for announcing special events or beating out a cadence for soldiers to march by, definitely not for making parlor music."

The girl slumped down with a morose expression and crossed her arms with a huff.

"We're so sorry." Mariah hoped her soothing tone would placate the little imp. " 'Tis just one of those small disappointments we young ladies must face because we were born as daughters and not sons. But as you get older, I'm sure you'll learn to appreciate all the things you'll get to do that boys cannot."

Amy's dangling foot gave an angry kick to the padded leather seat board. "You mean like spending hours and hours in front of a mirror having your hair yanked and pulled? Ha! I'd rather gig frogs."

Her sisters, on either side of Mariah, burst out laughing, and she could do no less.

Even the lady of the family lost some of her starch by chuckling behind her gloved hand. "Mercy me, Amy-child. You are the gray hairs on my head."

The slightly off-key assembly of drummers and fifers marched off the road and continued on until they reached the edge of the racecourse, where their piercing ruckus ceased.

Mariah smiled at Heather. "When your flute arrives—a proper flute, mind you—you'll learn to make the sweetest sort of music, not at all like that annoying noise."

The girl's expression turned dreamy. "Indeed. I once heard a street musician in Charles Town playing a flute. His music was ever so enchanting and sweet."

"Yes, dear, I'm sure it was." Mistress Barclay smiled and reached over to give her daughter an empathetic pat, then called up to the driver. "Jericho, turn off here and drive us to that sprawling oak down near the far end."

"Yes'm. Y'all sure ya wants to go that far away?"

"Quite. I prefer to be away from the dust and racket."

As he reined the matched team dutifully off the road and headed for the spot she'd indicated, the mistress gave Mariah a nod. "We'll actually be able to see the finish line much better from there."

Amy again hopped to her feet. "Look, here comes Colin and Tuck—and that Eddie Rochester of Tori's, of course."

Victoria craned around to see them, but Mariah caught her arm and shook her head. " 'Tis best not to act too eager."

"Somebody else is with them. He looks quite tall." Amy frowned and leaned out so far over the edge Mariah feared she might topple off. "I don't know who it is. Do you, Mama?"

The matron glanced in the direction of the approaching young men and gave a half smile. "I do believe it's that young Washington lad, George, if I'm not mistaken. So sad about his brother dying of smallpox. I heard he's inherited Mount Vernon."

"You don't say." Victoria's blue eyes grew brighter.

"Don't waste a second thought on him, daughter," her mother cajoled. "Little money came with the inheritance. I doubt he'll amount to much."

"Well, he sure sits a horse fine." Victoria maintained her interest as the men drew up alongside.

Dennis Tucker swept his tricornered hat off his sandy head in a grand gesture and beamed, centering his hazel-eyed gaze on Victoria. "Good morning, ladies. What a pleasure to see such a bounty of beauty in a single carriage."

Not to be outdone, lanky, freckle-faced Edward gave a wry smirk. "A veritable bouquet of Fairfax County's loveliest blossoms, to be sure."

"Why, thank you." Mistress Barclay tilted her head to one side, and the wispy plume on her summer bonnet dipped delicately with the motion.

Mariah took the opportunity to admire Colin, attired in black racing pants and tall boots, a full-sleeved white blouse, and a gray-striped vest. He looked incredibly handsome.

And he was filling his dark eyes with her, his look conveying all the desire for her she knew he kept hidden inside.

Lest his mother notice their locked gazes, Mariah smiled politely at him. "Mr. Barclay, I don't believe I've met your friend."

Colin blinked, then regained his composure. "Ah, yes. Quite right.

George Washington, I'd be pleased to introduce you to Miss Harwood. She's the tutoress to my sisters that Tuck mentioned. I believe you've met my family."

The serious-faced young man tipped his hat and gave a polite bow of his head. "How do you do, miss." He offered only the hint of a smile as his blue eyes took in the whole group. He nodded to Colin's mother. "Mistress Barclay. A pleasure to see you again."

"Are you racing today with the others?" Mariah asked, noting the well-muscled gray he rode.

"Yes, but only for the sport. My horse is more accustomed to climbing mountains than running about a track."

"Aye." Colin placed a hand on the young man's shoulder. "George has been appointed by the governor, no less, to survey the backcountry."

"My." Mariah studied the serious newcomer. "For one so young, I'm sure that must be quite an honor." Just as she'd suspected, opportunities in this new country truly did abound. She scanned the other riders. "I wish you all good luck. May the best horse win." *And may I win my prize as well—the one awaiting a few short hours from now.*

Nice going, dunderhead. Colin clenched his teeth so hard his jaw ached as he called himself every foul name he could think of. He'd had that race in the bag. But after being in the lead for nearly the entire time, a flash of yellow distracted him as Mariah cheered him on from the sidelines, and the horse on his flank sped on by over the finish line, along with one of the others. Colin came in third. Why did she have to choose that all-important moment to look so breathtakingly beautiful that he'd lost his focus and eased up on Paladin? Well, nothing could be done about it now. Time to join the family and pretend he still had an appetite.

Striding up to the green plaid blanket where Mariah was busy helping his mother set out food for the picnic lunch, he let his gaze linger on the English beauty. The yellow gown gracing her enticing form made her look like a delicate spring daffodil waiting to adorn someone's elegant table. It was a wonder that the other competitors in the race hadn't been distracted as he'd been.

At least Pa's filly, Queen's Lace, had been the victor. Colin couldn't help but smile. The poor young thing was so frightened by all the horses chasing her, she'd practically killed herself trying to get away from them.

But there was another filly Colin didn't plan to allow to get away. Not today. He eased down onto the wool blanket beside Mariah.

He sensed her awareness of him as she casually brushed a brown-black curl from her shoulder without acknowledging his presence.

"I couldn't be more proud of Queenie today," Father gushed as he sat down beside Mother. "I truly believe our Thoroughbred business will begin to pay for itself in the very near future."

"I do hope so, Eldon." She gave his arm a gentle squeeze. "This enterprise has been quite expensive. And we'll need a considerable amount of money in the next few years." She tipped her head meaningfully in Victoria's direction, where her daughter sat with a beau on either side.

Colin knew his mother referred to the cash money that would be required to pay for his three sisters' dowries once they were married off to merchant heirs like Edward Rochester. She was determined that Colin's own marriage would bring more land to the family. Mother was also resolute to see him wed to one of the local plantation belles. Preferably one from a neighboring farm, like prissy Constance Montclair.

Suddenly aware that his pa was pronouncing the blessing over the food, Colin bowed his head. He was so torn. The fact was, he did want to bring property to his family, just not at the expense of his happiness. And he'd never known such incredible joy as had been his good fortune since Mariah came into his life.

He swept her a sidelong glance. Her head was bowed in prayer, and parted curls revealed a tempting, slender neck. He let his eyes rove the alluring curve. A lot of men managed to have both: a proper marriage and a mistress on the side. They seemed to fare well. Why couldn't that work for him?

"Amen." His pa finished, bringing a swift end to Colin's musings. Before the man could tack on the encouragement to eat, everyone began helping themselves to the fried chicken and summer salad. Father just grinned. "Your mother and I have been invited to visit the Lawrences after we finish eating. Harold Lawrence expressed an interest in buying our young winner."

A pleased murmur made the rounds.

" 'Twould be my honor to attend Victoria while y'all are occupied with business," Tuck offered with fork in hand as he flaunted one of his charming grins.

Mother met his gaze. "That's most thoughtful of you, Dennis. I gladly leave Victoria and Heather in yours and Edward's care. My daughters are to remain together at all times."

Colin squelched a smug grin. He should've known she was much too astute to be fooled by Tuck. Inhaling deeply of Mariah's lemon verbena perfume, he took a healthy bite of his drumstick.

"Oh, and Colin." Mother dabbed her lips with a napkin. "Do see that Amy and her pony don't get into any mischief while we're discussing things with the Lawrences."

"Mama!" Bread crumbs flew from Amy's mouth as she lurched to her knees. "You said I could ride around with the other kids. You promised."

"And you may, darling." She bestowed an indulgent look on her daughter as she spoke in her calmly superior voice. "Your brother will just be there to see you don't get too exuberant."

Not this time I won't. Pretending not to be disturbed in the least, Colin took a sip of his lemonade. Today, the little snitch was as eager to be rid of him as he was of her. He tipped his head at his mother. "This has been a delectable spread, Mother. Truly superb, as always."

Chapter 13

Idly twirling her lacy parasol, Mariah stood in the shade of a hickory tree not far from the entrance of the livery barn. Colin had gone inside to saddle Amy's pony, and from the significant look he'd given her on his way past, she knew he had no intention of remaining in the child's company for long.

She glanced around while she waited, noting that the crowd had thinned a bit. Some folks had left for their homes, while many continued to lounge at their picnic spots under the trees. A number of people still browsed the wares of the peddlers, and others loitered in front of a nearby tavern. A few passing men had sent Mariah suggestive grins, but she pretended not to notice as she admired the scenery. There couldn't have been a more perfect summer day.

Just how long does it take to saddle a little horse? She tapped her foot impatiently in the grass for several seconds, then left the protection of the tree and started toward the open barn doors. In the darkened interior, she saw Colin talking seriously to Amy as the girl sat astride her pony. From his unflinching stance, Mariah could only guess at the instructions he was giving her, since he intended for his sister to go riding on her own without him.

"I promise! I promise!" Pouting her displeasure, Amy rammed her heels into Patches's sides, and the pony lurched forward into a trot, barely missing Colin's booted feet as it charged out of the barn and past Mariah. "See you later!" The girl's joyous shout trailed off as she bounced away, long blond waves whipping behind her.

Watching after her young charge, a sudden uneasiness gnawed at Mariah's conscience. Amy was, after all, only eight. A very reckless eight. Anything could happen to her.

Colin strode out into the light at last, and he, too, wore a dubious expression as he joined Mariah.

She continued to watch down the road until Amy brought her pony to a halt alongside three other youngsters on ponies; then she glanced up at Colin. "Do you think she'll be all right?"

He shrugged a shoulder, as if Amy were the least of his concerns. "The squirt's been riding since she was two. I'm sure she'll be fine." Turning his attention from his sister to her, he tucked Mariah's hand into the crook of his arm.

"I suppose you're right." She somehow managed a confident smile, assuring herself that nothing should distract her from her own goal this day.

"The air's still filled with dust from so many people milling about." Colin's voice was low and promising. "Why don't we leave all the hubbub behind and take a stroll in the woods behind the livery?"

"That sounds most refreshing." Mariah smiled demurely up at him and allowed him to guide her along the side of the paddocks. But she couldn't help fighting a giggle at his calling the cacophony of sounds here "hubbub." Had he ever been to Bristol on market day, he'd know what real noise was.

He continued to lead her away, out of the sight of curious eyes as they meandered toward the seclusion of the trees. "Did you enjoy the race?"

"Oh, yes," she teased, "particularly when you were willing to risk it just to acknowledge my presence."

He chuckled. "Not only did I risk the race, it was that mind-stealing beauty of yours that cost me the victory. I now understand how the face of Helen of Troy could sink a thousand ships. I'm sure she had nothin' on you."

Truly flattered, it was Mariah's turn to laugh lightly. "Are we women that dangerous, milord?"

"Indeed you are. I'm afraid I'm in jeopardy of losing not only my heart but my very soul to you." The mirth in his face vanished as his demeanor turned serious.

Mariah's heart skipped a beat. "Good sir, please don't think me so terribly dangerous. All I ask of you is your heart. Your soul I must leave to God."

He cocked a dark eyebrow as he continued to study her. "Are you quite sure of that? Because you've completely bewitched me."

Reaching up a tentative hand, Mariah palmed his cheek, lightly stubbled with a dark afternoon shadow. "I do believe 'tis quite the other way round." She tilted her chin and smiled into his compelling brown eyes. "You have been my greatest temptation from the moment I first caught sight of you."

A chuckle rumbled from deep in his chest. "And you think you didn't tempt me? As you must have deduced by now, my family had no need of a bond servant, yet I went so far as to part with my father's good money to purchase you."

"You did indeed." She continued to drink in his handsome face. "And that makes you my hero."

He didn't respond immediately but let his gaze envelop her as his smile faded and his other hand covered her fingers on his arm. "I want to be more than just a hero to you, my dear Mariah. Much more." Then, as if suddenly remembering where they were, he turned and checked over his shoulder.

Mariah did the same. She could see no one watching them. In a few more steps they reached the cloister of deep shade beneath boughs and tangled vines. She closed her eyes as a cool breeze ruffled the ferns and shade grasses, brushing gently across her face and neck. It was quiet in the woods, as if they'd entered another world, just the two of them.

Colin drew her to him and lowered his mouth to capture hers.

Stunned at first, she felt a thrill spiral through her being all the way down to her toes. His mouth was so seeking. . . .

After an eternal moment wrapped in his powerful embrace, feeling his heart throbbing along with hers, she regained her senses. Easing out of his arms, she thrust him away and raised trembling hands to ward him off. "Mr. Barclay!" It had not been prudent to let him take her so far from the safety of other people. This definitely was not how their private interlude was supposed to play out.

"I. . .don't understand." Stricken, he just stared at her, uncertainty clouding his face.

Whether his frown signified confusion or anger at her rebuff, Mariah could not tell. She only knew she needed to proceed with care. "Kind sir, if I gave you the impression that I was someone with whom you could dally, I beg your forgiveness most ardently. My feelings for you are honest, sincere. . .and quite pure." Spinning on her heel, she straightened the lace ruching on her bodice, hoping to dredge up a convincing tear or two.

"Mariah." His quiet voice was very near. "Forgive me. It's just that I. . ." He released a shuddering breath.

The sigh did it. Her eyes swam. She turned back to him and took his hands in hers, tears trembling on her lashes as she gazed up at him. "I know, Colin. Truly, I do. Pushing away from you was the hardest thing I've ever done in my life. My whole body is aquiver from your touch. But I cannot help but believe 'twould be best if you do as your mother wanted from the start."

"What are you saying?"

"You must sell me off. Otherwise, I fear you'll be the ruin of me. Rose, Lily, my Papa. . . I could never bring such awful shame to my family. I just couldn't."

Gazing deeply into her eyes as his hands tightened around hers, he hiked his chin. "And you shan't." With his thumb, he wiped the pearl of moisture that had finally started its journey down her cheek. "No more tears, my love. The very moment my father signs over the southwest section to me as he promised, I'll announce our intention to marry." He pulled her close again, ever so gently, and lifted her chin with the edge of his finger. "If that's agreeable to you, of course."

"You would marry me? Are you sure? You know I come with no dowry." She gazed longingly into his eyes, vitally needing this binding commitment from him. "I'm certain that once my father has recouped his losses, he'll take it upon himself to send me something. I fear 'twould only be money, however, nothing compared to the land your mother expects you to bring to your family when you marry."

He grunted in disgust. "Mother. She's much too ambitious for her own good. Your love and your sweetness are all the dowry I shall ever desire, Mariah. I just regret that we must keep our betrothal a secret until January, and that you must continue on under her thumb until then."

Mariah gave an insignificant shrug. "She isn't so bad, truly she isn't. She merely wants the best for her family, as would any mother. I pray I will love my children as deeply as she does hers."

"Children." A slow smile spread across his lips. "I suspect you'll be the most beautiful mother who ever lived, and I hope someday we'll have daughters who look exactly like you."

"And sons," she said lightly, "who look just like you." In a burst of enthusiasm, she wrapped her arms around his neck. "Oh, Colin, dearest Colin, this is the happiest day of my life."

⚮

Unable to contain his own happiness, Colin laughed as he caught Mariah's luscious form to him and swung her around. He wanted to shout to the world that this beautiful creature had agreed to be his, his forever.

She laughed, too, throwing her head back in joy. "Yes, yes, I'll marry you."

"Let's go tell everyone! I cannot keep this to myself." Setting her down and tucking her against his side, he started back toward the clearing. Then he slowed and turned to her. "That is what I'd like to do. But we can't, of course. I know that all too well." He cupped her soft face in his hands and absorbed its stunning beauty. "January seems an eternity away. It will be difficult to keep my distance from you and act as if nothing has changed between us."

"I know. We shall have to keep ourselves incredibly busy until then." She offered him a saucy grin. "Have I told you what a wonderful talent Heather has for music? I do believe she'll be playing duets with me in no time at all. Would it not be wonderful if she could play at our wedding?" Her violet eyes glowed as she spoke, adding even more to her allure. "Yes, that's what I'll do. I'll spend my lonely hours working with Heather until she has mastered the violin. Have you a favorite piece you'd like me to teach her for the ceremony, perchance?"

Absorbed in her voice, Colin felt it was all the music he would ever need.

"Do you?" She stared up at him questioningly.

He smiled, realizing she expected a response of some sort. "Anything that pleases you will please me."

Mariah tilted her flirty face up to him, a teasing glint in her eyes. "I shall remind you of that years from now when you're being obstinate."

"Years from now. I like the sound of that." Taking her hand in his, he began walking again, matching his stride to hers as he cast a glance around. "Why can't it be spring? I would love to pick a huge bouquet of wildflowers for you as a remembrance of this day."

She reached over with her free hand and gave his elbow a squeeze. "I need no token to remember this lovely day. Not as long as you keep looking at me the way you are right now."

Colin raised her hand to his mouth and pressed a kiss to it as he stared longingly at her tender lips.

"But I do think we ought to get back and check on Amy, don't you?"

Realizing Mariah must have read the desire in his gaze, Colin began walking again. "Quite right. The squirt can get into trouble faster than a pair of barn kittens at milking time."

Emerging into the slanting afternoon light behind the livery, Mariah opened her parasol against the sun's bright rays and moved a few respectable steps away from him. "I do hope no one has missed us."

He scoffed. "I can't think of anyone who would."

The words were scarcely out of his mouth when a high, shrill voice called out his name.

Mariah stiffened with fear. "Who could that be? I pray 'tis not your mother."

"Of course it isn't." He'd spoken with more confidence than he actually felt. As he picked up the pace, growing apprehension pricked at him. "They're visiting the Lawrences, remember? Dickering over the price of the filly."

When they rounded the front of the barn, Colin spied Heather and Victoria searching the road into Alexandria and waved his arm at them. "We're over here, girls!"

Both spun around and picked up their skirts as they ran to him.

"Where are Tuck and Edward?" Mariah asked, scanning the area and seeing neither young man.

Panting from the run, Heather flashed a sly grin. "Hiding out, no doubt."

Colin, however, tensed, his rage rising. "Where are those bounders? They were supposed to stay with you."

"I'd forget about them if I were you," Victoria announced, looking from him to Mariah and back. "Mother's not in high dudgeon over those two. She wants you. Now."

Chapter 14

Amy stood with her parents and the Widow Doolittle in front of the woman's cottage on the far end of town. Frantic and on the verge of tears, the child wrenched free of Mother and ran toward Colin and Mariah as they approached. "Tell Mama it wasn't me! Tell her it was Henry Jay and Walter that did it. Not me."

Taking stock of the dour expressions on the faces of his parents and the widow as Amy flew toward him, Colin let out an exasperated huff. How long had the girl been on her own? Ten, fifteen minutes? More? This was not good.

The adults stood stock-still, glaring, their scowls aimed right at him.

He caught Amy by the shoulders as she barreled into him. "What's going on?"

"Henry Jay and Walter," Amy sputtered, out of breath. "They rode their horses straight through Mistress Doolittle's vegetable garden. But I didn't. I was careful and rode around it. Cross my heart and hope to die." She turned her beseeching eyes up to Mariah. "You believe me, don't you?"

Mariah reached out and brushed a strand of hair from Amy's sweaty face and tucked it behind her ear. "Yes, sweetheart, I do. You must try to calm down while we see to the matter. Surely there'll be some compensation that will satisfy the woman."

Watching Mariah as she settled Amy down with such tenderness, Colin's love for her doubled. She would be—

He glanced down the road and cringed at his parents' heated glowers. Picking Amy up, he trudged toward them with dread, knowing that in all likelihood their anger would be directed entirely at him. They would never think of being short with their youngest child. He had, after all, been ordered to keep an eye on her.

His mother's discerning gaze oscillated between him and Mariah.

Beside him, Mariah's steps grew hesitant. Just as well. She shouldn't be the one to catch the brunt of Mother's rage. Pausing, Colin glanced down at her and saw that her face had lost all color. "My dear Mariah, you'd best go and stay with Tori and Heather. They're under that old oak tree watching. From afar." He pointed in their direction. "I shouldn't be long."

"Are you quite sure?" she whispered.

"Of course. And here." He set Amy down. "Take her with you. I'll handle this."

Mariah clutched his hand. "Do be careful." Her eyes were clouded with fright, making her appear so vulnerable it cinched his heart.

"Don't worry." Starting back toward his parents, he drew a steadying breath and let it all out in a whoosh. "Time I became a man and stood up for myself." Though muttered to himself, the words bolstered him.

He barely reached the somber threesome before his mother opened her mouth in preparation for one of her tirades. Giving her no chance to lay into him, he spoke out from several steps away. "I understand there's been quite a disturbance here." He offered the tiny, birdlike widow his most sympathetic smile. "Having boys galloping roughshod through your garden, churning up your neat plants, must have been most frightening, to say nothing of the cost."

The little lady's thin lips gaped open. "Indeed. And—"

Colin cut in, overriding her. "Even though my sister did not happen to be one of the children who destroyed your vegetables, I was the one who gave her permission to ride with those boys, so I feel partly responsible for the destruction. More than partly, to be honest." It never hurt to add a little something for effect. "That is why for the remainder of the growing season I shall personally see that you have fresh vegetables every week for your table. Enough for preserving for your winter stores, as well."

During that pronouncement, he felt his parents' stares of displeasure boring into him as he attempted to smooth the widow's ruffled feathers. And the woman herself had yet to look mollified.

He reached into the pocket of his vest and withdrew several coins. "For all your trouble, Mistress Doolittle. Please allow me to put a smile on that handsome face of yours." He placed the money in her palm. "I want you to stroll right down to Miss Raeford's millinery this minute and buy yourself the fanciest bonnet she has in her shop."

A wary smile did tremble on her lips as the taut lines in her weathered face softened. "Mercy, Mr. Barclay, I couldn't be takin' your money."

"Nonsense." He closed her bony fingers over the coins. "I'll expect to see you sporting that new bonnet at church next Sabbath. By the by," he added casually, "while you're gone, would you mind if my parents and I step into your parlor for a moment? We have some private business to discuss."

"I don't mind a'tall." Her smile remaining in place, she turned to his mother. "You an' yer mister make yerselfs right to home, Mistress Barclay."

It seemed no easy task, but Mother finally pulled her glare off Colin and pasted on an answering smile for the Widow Doolittle. Colin wondered if the little woman realized it was as starched as a Sunday collar. "Thank you." With a significant look at his father, Mother turned and marched up the stone pathway to the older woman's porch steps.

Pa elbowed Colin in the ribs as they followed her. "Try to make your mother happy," he whispered. "If she's not happy, I surely won't be."

What about my happiness? It took considerable restraint not to shout the question, but Colin knew better than to voice it aloud.

Once inside the cramped little home Widow Doolittle occupied,

Colin noticed how worn the upholstery was on the settee, how dreary and faded the furnishings all appeared. "Before we start, do you think we could see about having the poor woman's furniture refurbished? This place is little more than a hovel. Surely someone of her age and all alone deserves better."

Mother's head snapped around. "What?" Then she glanced at her surroundings, her gaze falling on the frayed cushions. "Yes. That's quite thoughtful of you, Colin." Her soft tone turned hard. "However, it won't lessen the fact that you broke our agreement."

"I beg to differ." He hiked his chin. "Not once did I actually say I'd stay with Amy while she went riding with the other children. I was afoot, if you recall. How could I be expected to keep up with a trotting pony?"

"Don't play the fool with me. And don't think for one moment that I'm unaware of things that go on behind my back." Her slitted eyes flashed fire as she stepped closer. "I made the conditions for Mariah remaining in our service abundantly clear from the start. Yet the first chance you get, you choose to defy me and break our agreement."

"Your agreement. Your dictate." Colin hurled the words back at her with equal force.

She stiffened, arching a brow. "And my consequences. This very day I shall find some other fool willing to buy Miss Harwood's papers. It shouldn't be too difficult. I saw more than a few men ogling her today."

Colin held his ground. "And just how do you intend to sell someone you do not own? It's my signature on her papers, not yours. Legally I'm the person in charge of her fate." He stepped within a foot of her, satisfied that he'd played his trump card.

To his dismay, she did not budge. "That may very well be. But I'm sure the wench is not worth the cost of your home and inheritance. For all we know, your oh-so-proper tutoress could be a common thief or even a—a prostitute."

At the urge to push that vile accusation back down her throat, Colin stepped away and inhaled a calming breath. She was his mother, he reminded himself, and deserved his respect. He swallowed and took another tack. "Mother, you and Pa married for love. You told me that yourself more than once, and I know the two of you have been happy together all these years. How could you want less for me, your son? Or even poor, moonstruck Tori. She's wildly infatuated with Tuck. But he's from a mere plantation, and you will do your utmost to prevent her from marrying him because it won't fit in with your own selfish plans. She'll be kept from her happiness, too."

"Pshaw." His mother fluttered a hand, as if the news was of no significance. "Victoria's just a silly child. She has no idea what she wants. And you, Colin. Do you think that generations from now, your grandchildren will be gratified to know that our land was parceled off for the sake of your sister's puppy love? Or worse, that you would give up everything for some nameless, penniless pretty face—though I seriously doubt she'd marry you if you were the penniless one."

"Now that's quite enough!" Fists balled with fury, Colin turned away before he did something he would regret. "For all I care, you can take my inheritance and—"

His father caught his arm. "Stop! Both of you. Stop makin' ultimatums you may later regret." Having bellowed the order without bothering to conceal the light Virginia drawl he knew his wife detested, he lowered his voice and continued. "Son, you and your mother both need time to consider the ramifications of what you're saying." He wrapped one arm around Colin and the other around Mother. "I have a better idea. Let me tell you about it."

Both solemn faces swung their gazes to him in silence, neither ready to give an inch.

He spoke calmly and precisely, gazing from one of them to the other. "The meeting with Harold Lawrence didn't go quite as well as I'd hoped. The offer he made for Queen's Lace was less than fair, so I didn't accept it. We all know that filly's worth considerably more than he was willing to pay. So I've formulated a plan that might rectify the situation."

Regarding the confidence in his father's face, Colin held his breath, waiting to hear what the patriarch was about to say.

"Here's my thought. I propose that you, Colin, take Queenie and

Paladin on a packet north to Philadelphia and New York, then on to Boston. Set up races in those cities to show both of them off. They're the best in our stables. See if you can garner better offers for our Thoroughbreds."

That sounded feasible. . .

"Then, after they're sold, I want you to take that money and sail to England."

Colin's heart slammed to a stop. *He can't be serious!*

"Go to a few of the best horse farms in Britain and purchase a good stud. We'll need to introduce some new blood in our line to stay ahead of the competition here."

"But—that'll take months." Having finally found his voice, Colin tucked his chin. How could he consider going away, being parted from Mariah for some indefinite period—especially now that they had grown beyond mere attraction and wanted to share a future together?

His father nodded, gravely serious. "That's the point, son. I suspect you believe you have feelings for Miss Harwood. One would have to be blind not to see the sparks that fly whenever you two are in close proximity to each other. If those feelings truly are serious, the time apart will make that clear."

So speechless he could hardly think straight, Colin mulled his pa's idea over in his mind. It wasn't anything like he'd hoped or expected to hear. But the more he thought about it, the more he realized that perhaps his father was right. The plan would calm the waters for now. It would also guarantee Mariah's safe harbor until he returned—and to ensure that safety, he would take her papers along with him. Unwelcome or not, Pa's suggestion just might turn out to be the best for all of them right now. He glanced over at his mother.

"If I actually agree to this and sail to England, I'll travel to Bath while I'm in the country and bring proof that Mariah is who she says she is. You'll see she's been telling the truth." He then turned to his father. "And while I'm gone, I expect Mariah to be treated with Christian charity."

"You have my word." Pa gave a nod.

"And yours, Mother?"

She didn't respond for several seconds. Finally she inhaled a deep breath and slowly released the air. "She shall be treated with Christian charity."

Her reluctant promise put Colin only partially at ease. He could only hope that "Christian charity" meant the same thing to her as it did to him.

Chapter 15

Colin shook his head in amazement at the unbelievable agreement he'd just made with his father. Leave here, leave Mariah, for who knew how many months? Yet, all things considered, he couldn't get past the logic that it really was the best course to take. And the sooner he left, the sooner he'd return.

Still in the widow's shabby parlor, he darted a thoughtful look at his father. "Well, if I'm going to do this, I suppose there's no time like the present. Since both horses are already in town, I see no reason to take them all the way back to the plantation. The day is only partially spent. I'll go down to the quay and book passage on the next northbound packet." He kept his tone even and businesslike to prevent Mother from interfering or interrupting.

His father nodded. "There should be at least two packets at the docks as we speak. They brought people in for the race. I believe at least one of them is set to embark tomorrow at first light."

"Good. Then if Mother would be kind enough to pack some of my things," he went on without looking at her, "you can have them sent to me this evening, along with whatever traveling funds you expect I'll need. I'll secure a room at the inn and handle the boarding of the horses for the night." He paused, hating to delve into the next subject. "I do have one personal request, though, Pa." He leveled a serious gaze at him. "I'd like you to send Mariah's papers to me along with my luggage. I put them inside last year's ledger for safekeeping."

"Of course. I'll take care of everything."

A small sound came from his mother, one Colin surmised heralded her disapproval. But neither she nor her granite expression said a word. She did, however, glance toward the door, indicating her wish to leave this place.

Since he could say or do nothing at this point to win her approval, he sought his father once more. "I'd like a few moments alone with Mariah before y'all leave town. I need to assure her she'll continue on as tutoress for the girls and that she'll be treated with the respect and kindness due her position while I'm away." Turning on his heel, he headed for the entry before his mother could issue a protest.

At the door he stopped and turned back. "Perhaps while I'm speaking with Mariah, the two of you could go and see about having Mistress Doolittle's furniture re-covered."

Mother merely stared in her steady, aloof way, but Pa nodded in assent. "Of course. Otherwise we might forget."

"Also, I promised to make certain she's kept in vegetables. Since I won't be around to see to that, I'd appreciate it if you would make those arrangements also." That said, he opened the door and stepped out.

"There, Cora, my dear," he overheard his father say in a soothing voice. "You see? He's still the same thoughtful son he always was."

Colin paused, listening for his mother's response.

"Hmph. He was until that hussy stole his senses," she snapped, her stubborn anger as strong as ever.

Disappointed, he closed the door quietly after himself and crossed the small porch to the steps, wondering if the decision to leave immediately—or at all—really was for the best.

Waiting in the shade of the sprawling oak tree with Colin's three sisters, Mariah did her best not to appear anxious, though she would have given anything to know what was going on inside the little clapboard house. Tuck and Edward had come to join her and the girls now that Mistress Barclay was no longer in sight, and sitting on either side of Victoria in the shade, they kept Tori enthralled with their tales of derring-do. Amy had climbed onto a low-hanging branch and perched there with her legs dangling as she kept vigil on the widow's cottage, watching for the rest of her family to emerge.

Heather gravitated to Mariah's side. "Is this flute not the grandest thing ever?" She held out the shiny silver instrument her father had picked up in town and presented to her a short while before Colin met up with her parents.

"Yes, dear. It's lovely. But you'd better keep it in its case so it won't get dusty from the breeze, don't you think?" She gave the girl an encouraging smile.

"I want to try it first. Then I'll put it away." Holding it to her lips, she blew into the tiny hole, trying unsuccessfully to make a pure sound—or any sound at all. She scrunched up her face. "How do you make it work, Miss Harwood? Please show me."

At the moment, with her fate being warred over by the girl's family, giving a flute lesson was the last thing on Mariah's mind. Nevertheless, she took the long, thin tube from Heather and did her best to look happy to do so. "This is how you hold it." Showing her the proper angle, she placed her fingers along the keys. " 'Tis important to hold the flute parallel to your lips so you can blow into the headjoint, like this." She demonstrated the process, raising her fingers up and down on the keys to make a trilling sound.

"Oh, that is so pretty, like the sound of a robin's song." Heather's blue eyes glowed with anticipation. "I cannot wait until I can make pretty music."

"You will, in no time at all, if you practice faithfully. I promise. Now, come here." Gesturing for the twelve-year-old to come and try again, she placed the flute in the girl's hands and positioned her fingers just so on the proper stops and her left thumb on the lever. Then, lifting Heather's elbows, she helped her to hold the flute snugly against her mouth. "Now flatten your lips and blow."

As the girl followed her instructions, Mariah turned the flute slightly to catch the air just right, and a pure tone emerged.

"I did it! I actually did it!" A grin spread from ear to ear, making Heather's eyes sparkle. She thrust the instrument to Mariah. "Please play something for us, Miss Harwood. I want to hear how it should sound."

Mariah gaped at her. "Here? Now?" She glanced around, her gaze landing on the widow's cottage. *Whatever would Mistress Barclay think of my playing a flute in public?*

"Yes, miss. Please do." Tuck came up from behind them, followed by the others, who all nodded in agreement.

"Mercy me. I hardly think it would be ladylike to make a spectacle of myself."

"We'll all crowd around you then." Heather motioned to the small group for them to form a ring around Mariah. "No one will be able to see who's playing."

"Oh, very well." Mariah sighed as the young people circled around her. Being careful to stand where she could peek past Tori's two suitors and keep the gate of the widow's house in sight, she hesitantly accepted the flute from Heather. If Mistress Barclay appeared, she'd stop playing immediately.

Lifting the instrument to her lips, she played a familiar lilting tune.

Tuck grinned with recognition and started singing the lyrics to "Greensleeves," and one by one, the others joined in. Except for Amy. The child kept craning her neck to look up the street. Suddenly her mouth popped open and her eyes grew wide. "It's Colin."

Glancing beyond Victoria's beaus, Mariah saw the child's brother striding swiftly toward them.

He was not smiling.

A sickening feeling churned her insides. She lowered the flute and handed it to Heather. "Please excuse me." Breathless, she shoved past the young men and headed, heart pounding, toward Colin.

They met in the middle of the street. Mariah searched his face, trying to discern what might have taken place, but he took her arm without speaking and turned her toward the racecourse, where the family's landau remained parked in the shade of a tree.

Had his parents convinced him to retract his proposal? "What is it, Colin?"

He hurried her along. "We need a little more privacy."

Footsteps sounded from behind as little Amy caught up with them, her face pale with panic. "Am I in big trouble, Colin? What are they gonna do to me?"

He stopped and knelt before his sister and took her by the shoulders. "Everything's fine, squirt. Nobody's mad at you. Just go back to your sisters, will you? I need to speak to Miss Harwood alone." A light nudge sent her on her way.

Mariah's blood seemed to drain away, and a chill ran through her. It must be worse than she thought. They must be going to sell her off. What would become of her then?

Once she and Colin reached the tree sheltering the carriage, he stopped. With a tight smile, he took her hands in his.

Seeing no real hope in his expression, she could wait no longer to hear her fate. "What is it? Do tell me."

He cocked his head. "Nothing has changed between us, my love. You and I will marry, with or without my family's blessing."

Sensing a *but* coming, Mariah held her breath.

"But I'm afraid it won't be for a while. Something *has* changed, and that centers around where I'm going to be for the next few months."

Colin was to be sent away? Frowning in confusion, Mariah waited for him to explain.

"To appease my mother and to further our Thoroughbred enterprise, my father has requested that I travel to several cities here in the colonies. Afterward, I must take a quick trip. . .to England."

She nearly choked. "Quick trip, you say! When it takes six weeks to sail to England and six back? You'll be gone for ages!"

Catching her hands again in his, Colin smiled gently. "I meant that

I don't plan to spend more than a few days in Britain at most. I'm going solely to purchase a new stud for breeding purposes."

"But. . .England." An unexpected bout of homesickness swamped her. To think that Colin would be sailing to her homeland, and she would remain behind made unbidden tears sting her eyes. Still, the thought came to her that there might be a personal benefit to his crossing the ocean. "Perhaps you could visit my family, see how they're faring— should you travel anywhere near Bath, of course."

"I intend to do just that, sweetheart. I plan to book passage on the ship heading for the Bristol port. I hear there's a fine horse farm between there and Bath. It will be my honor to call on your father while I'm in the area."

"Oh, I'm sure Papa will be glad to meet you, to have news of my sisters and me and know that we arrived here safe and well. I should have already posted a letter to him. And to my sisters, really. I've been so busy I just haven't. . ." Realizing she was babbling, her vision of him blurred behind a sheen of moisture. "Oh, Colin, whatever will I do without you?" Only sheer determination and unwillingness to make the situation harder for him kept her from bursting into tears.

He lifted her hands to his mouth and brushed his lips across her fingers. "You'll concentrate on the fact that I'm coming back as soon as I possibly can. I was able to extract a solemn promise from my mother that you will be treated properly in my absence."

A lump formed in Mariah's throat. "She knows we're betrothed?"

He offered a sheepish smile. "I didn't exactly say the words. I reckoned it would make living here harder for you if I wasn't around. But I know she suspects we have feelings for each other. So I've decided to take your bond papers with me. She can't do anything without them. You'll be all right until I come back. I promise."

Despite her own sadness, he looked so concerned that Mariah mustered a smile and reached up to brush aside a lock of dark hair that had fallen across his furrowed brow. "Well, we'll have to make the most of it, somehow. I don't want you to worry about me in the least. As long as I know I have your love, I vow I shall do all that is in my power to gain your mother's goodwill."

He grinned, crinkling the corners of his eyes. "My sweet Mariah, you are far more than a man could ever dream of. I feel incredibly fortunate that you came into my life. But alas, it is my sad duty to bid you farewell now. I must hasten down to the quay to book passage for the morrow. I shan't be returning home with you this eve."

Her mouth dropped open in dismay. "You won't? Not even for a night?" Gripped by panic, she clutched at his vest, as if by holding on to him she could make him stay.

With a look of intense longing, he gave a somber shake of the head. "It's for the best, my love. I can't bear the thought of a long good-bye. It would only cause both of us more pain." Gently he removed her hands and kissed them. Then he looked deep into her eyes and pressed the softest of kisses to her trembling lips. "I must go now." Releasing his hold, he turned on his heel. "Don't forget: I love you, Mariah. I'll come back as soon as I can."

Mariah was utterly devastated as she watched her handsome betrothed walk away, leaving her behind to an uncertain fate. He'd made so many promises this day, even declared his love. But now he was leaving her for a raft of exciting cities—cities filled with beautiful women. He'd fallen so quickly for her beauty. Might he be as easily captivated by someone else? A woman with wealth and breeding who'd be acceptable to his family? Or even worse, would he be tempted by a whole flock of young, unattached maidens and forget her entirely? A small cloud drifted across the sun just then, dimming its bright light. Mariah felt as if it had drifted across her heart, blocking the only security she'd known since her arrival at the Barclay plantation.

Then a truly frightening thought twisted her insides. What of Mistress Barclay? The woman was so adamantly opposed to a union between her son and a bond servant. What clever form would her retribution take?

Chapter 16

On the ride home from Alexandria, Mariah studiously avoided looking at Colin's parents. The couple sat in pregnant silence on the opposite seat of the carriage, and both wore churlish expressions. Next to them, Victoria kept turning around to cast longing glances back toward town, obviously disappointed that she'd had to leave her two beaus so soon. Her dream-filled eyes gave no clue as to which young man she actually preferred. Mariah suspected that the sudden attention being showered upon her by both Dennis and Edward was too heady an experience for Tori not to take full advantage of it. She was, after all, barely on the brink of womanhood.

Lost in her thoughts, she felt Amy's small hand search through the mass of ruffled skirts to find hers. The child held tight, a tremor revealing her trepidation that her parents' wrath would soon crash down on her. But Mariah had no doubt who the real target would be. Herself. And there was nowhere to run to escape her fate.

Thank Providence for Heather, sweet Heather. Thrilled with her new flute and completely oblivious to the tension in the air, the girl wore a bright smile as if this day had been the finest of her entire life. She removed the instrument from its case and held it reverently in her hands. "Show me again where to put my fingers, Miss Harwood." She gazed expectantly up at Mariah.

Wishing the twelve-year-old had not drawn the unwelcome attention to her, Mariah did not dare a glance across to the elder Barclays but drew a nervous breath and took the silver tube from Heather. "Like this." She raised it and positioned each of her fingers slowly and deliberately on the proper keys, one at a time, and held them for Heather to study. Then, forcing a small smile, she handed the instrument back.

Heather did her best to do as she'd been shown and nearly got it right.

"Splendid. You've almost got it." More than aware the Barclays were watching, she struggled to ignore the pair as she gently adjusted Heather's little finger. She spoke as quietly as possible over the creaking and crunching of the landau as it rolled along. "Practice lifting up from each key one at a time until the movement feels natural."

Glad for the chance to divert her attention away from the older couple for a bit, she watched Heather work on her fingering. But when the girl raised the flute to her lips and took a breath, Mariah quickly stayed her with a hand. "I think 'twould be best if you just practice moving your fingers. We'll work on tones at home."

Mistress Barclay broke the stilted silence. "Yes, daughter. I cannot abide unnecessary noise. I have a beastly headache."

Knowing the woman's last comment was directed at her, Mariah cringed as a dreadful sense of foreboding chilled her whole being. *This is what Colin had left me to: his vengeful mother. How could someone who had avowed his deep love forsake me like this?*

꙳

For several days after their arrival at home, Mariah was ill at ease, waiting for Colin's mother to lash out at her, pile on extra chores, deprive her of privileges, or administer some form of punishment. But to her utter amazement, Mistress Barclay's veiled innuendo on the homeward ride from Alexandria never amounted to anything. As the next couple of weeks passed, the woman seemed quite relaxed, and though not overtly friendly toward Mariah, she acted as if nothing were amiss. At first Mariah thought the woman's courteous attitude was the result of her own extra efforts to be especially helpful and polite. It finally dawned on her that with Colin separated from her, there was nothing for his mother to find fault with.

She continued her duties as tutoress, instructing the girls in academics and all the female arts, plus giving them their music lessons. Of course, she often found herself obligated to ride with Amy as bribery for practicing the violin. Though Mariah begrudged the time spent riding horseback, she discovered that chasing after Colin's youngest sister was helping her to become a rather accomplished horsewoman. He would surely be surprised to discover her new skill when he returned. If he returned.

But no matter how busy her daytime hours were, the solitary nights were hard to endure, when she was alone in her tiny room and thoughts of Colin held free rein in her mind. She missed him so and wished desperately that he would send word to let her know she was still in his thoughts, especially since she'd heard that the most stylish young ladies in the colonies resided in Philadelphia and New York. He'd given his father three pounds to give to Mariah for pin money, and though she appreciated his thoughtfulness and generosity, she would have much preferred a letter from him.

To her knowledge, no correspondence had arrived for his parents either, unless Mistress Barclay had kept silent about hearing from her son and had seen to it that any missive to Mariah was destroyed. The woman did seem to have a certain smugness in her demeanor. Mariah wondered if his mother was still concocting secret plans that would keep Colin from returning to the plantation for a very long time.

Pleasant weather and calm seas had enabled the coastal packet to make good time as it carried Colin and his horses around the peninsula and up to Philadelphia. Aware that all types of business was conducted on the wharves, he was gratified by the considerable interest Paladin and Queen's Lace drew during their boarding in Alexandria and disembarking at the "red brick city." No sooner had he brought them down the gangplank, when two wealthy Philadelphia merchants approached him and agreed to arrange a horse race to take place within the month.

Colin spent the following three weeks ensconced in a nicely appointed guest room in the elegant brick manse of his uncle Matthew Lewis, a prominent lawyer. The bed with its jewel-toned coverlet was more comfortable than his bed at the plantation, and the rich furnishings were the best money could buy, but it wasn't like home.

Uncle Matt and Aunt Harriet loved to give and attend all kinds of dinners and extravagant events, and this evening the family was invited to a summer party at the home of one of Uncle Matthew's colleagues. Colin would have preferred another quiet evening to himself but knew it would be impolite to expect his relatives to go to the affair without him. Even if he begged off, they'd want an explanation, and he wasn't ready to provide any personal details.

Buttoning his burgundy silk waistcoat, he moved to the wooden mirror stand and checked his reflection in the long, oval looking glass to make sure his attire had been pressed neatly and fit well. He let out a deep, slow breath. Nothing fit as well as Mariah did when she was on his arm. How empty his days seemed now that he could no longer see her stunning face, hear her lyrical voice. The past weeks seemed an eternity, and time still stretched out before him like an unending road.

A knock sounded on the door, and his cousin Paul barged in without waiting for an invitation. Tall and slim, at twenty-six he retained a boyishness about him that glinted in his smoke-colored eyes and lopsided grin. "Do hurry, old man. We're going to be late. I want to get my bid in for as many minuets as possible with Evangeline O'Hara. Eve's sure to be the prettiest girl there."

"Is that right?" Colin made an effort to sound interested.

"Rather. So do me a favor and don't turn on your charms around her. You have my blessing when it comes to any of the other belles. Just leave Evangeline to me." He leaned to peer into the looking glass and ran fingers through his already neat light brown hair.

Colin gave him a pat on the shoulder and lapsed into the drawl he

MARIAH'S QUEST

was trying hard to overcome. "Fear not, cousin-mine. My romancin' days have come to an end. I've already found the one girl for me. She happens to be the most beautiful woman in the entire world."

"Surely not." Paul guffawed. "How would you even know that until you've seen them all?"

The words were like cold water splashed in Colin's face. He had to admit Paul was right. There must be any number of young misses as delectable as Mariah—ones with sufficient wealth to satisfy even his mother. Was his attraction to the English lass merely because she was the always-tempting forbidden fruit? He cut a speculative glance up at his cousin. "You make a good point, old chap. What are we waiting for? Let's go and see what the fair city of Philadelphia has to offer."

Six weeks. Six long weeks, and still no word from Colin. Was he alive or dead? Had she the slightest idea where to write, Mariah would have gladly put quill to paper if only to let him know what a thoughtless, cavalier blackguard he was. He wouldn't have had to extol his undying love for her in a letter were he concerned his mother might read it. But surely he could send a word or two—anything to let Mariah know he still thought about her.

Such morose, frustrating thoughts assailed her as she and Victoria stood on the veranda watching the girl's two beaus riding up the lane. In anticipation of the late afternoon ride, Tori had donned a gown of delicate blue lawn that accented the hue of her eyes. Mariah, on the other hand, continued to play down her own appearance by wearing her dull teacher's gray and capturing her curls in a tight bun. She didn't want to draw attention from the young belle.

Amy was already down at the stables. She'd hiked her skirts and sprinted to tell Old Samuel to saddle their mounts the moment Tuck and Edward came into view. She never missed an opportunity to go riding, whether her young presence was welcome or not. But then, her mother considered the child as suitable a chaperone as Mariah, probably even more so.

137

Peering again down the tree-shaded lane, Mariah cast a more assessing gander at the young men. It would only take her a little cunning look here, a bit of flattery there, to whisk one of them away from Victoria. Like Colin, Tuck was heir to his plantation, not the head of the household. . .not as promising as Mariah would like, while Edward was the son of a wealthy merchant and often bragged about his family's eight cargo ships. As Mistress Barclay said, ships could sink, taking with them an abundance of goods. But a rich family like the Rochesters could easily replace a lost vessel. Were Mariah to be presented to Edward's parents properly, without mention of that bothersome bond, she just might be accepted by the family. . . .

Beside her, Victoria raised her arm in a jaunty wave. Then, completely dismissing everything Mariah had taught her, she bounded down the steps and out to the curved drive to greet her callers before they even reined their mounts to a stop.

Mariah rolled her eyes and glided out with practiced grace to meet the men. Sorely tempted to pick one of them, she figured it might be best to concentrate on Edward, since he wasn't such a close friend of Colin and his family.

However, as both suitors dismounted in haste, vying to be the first to reach Victoria, the girl's happy laughter tore through Mariah. Tempting as it might be to lure one of the young men away, she knew she couldn't do it. Tori had been such a shy, lovesick lass when Mariah first arrived. It would be unbearable to watch her crawl back into that sad state again—especially after so many hours had been spent teaching her the art of courtship.

"Good afternoon." She offered a polite nod as she reached the lively threesome. "Amy and I will be tagging along on today's ride, but we shouldn't bother you."

Tuck flashed his usual flirty grin. "Rest assured, your company never bothers us."

"Nevertheless—" She slanted an assuring look to Tori as they started for the stables. "I shall spend the greater portion of the ride chasing after our adventurous Amy, in all likelihood, so I'll trust that Victoria will be safe with you two."

Edward's freckled hand went to his chest. "But of course. I, for one, wouldn't dream of allowing the smallest mishap to befall the lovely lass."

"Splendid." Mariah lengthened her steps to go ahead of the others. Suddenly she realized she was turning into Rose, her responsible older sister. *The spinster.*

Shocked by the idea, Mariah scoffed inwardly. Why, had she not just finished writing out a number of invitations to a horse and phaeton race the family planned to host on the first Saturday in September? Surely there would be an abundance of young men there to participate in the event. Before that day was over, she might possibly find another suitor for herself. One Mistress Barclay would approve of—and perhaps even help her to secure!

Mariah glanced over her shoulder at Amy, who lagged behind. The child always dawdled when coming home after a run on her horse, but then, the girl was permitted to straddle her pony rather than sit on a rib-jouncing sidesaddle. Mariah frowned at her. "Do hurry!"

The eight-year-old gave a sullen shrug and heeled Patches into a trot to catch up.

Victoria and her beaus had returned to the stables a good ten minutes ago. Mariah knew if she and Amy didn't make haste, there wouldn't be time enough for them to wash off the horse smell and change for supper.

"There's Mr. Scott." Reining her pony alongside Mariah's Thorough-bred mare, Amy shouted and waved at him. "We're comin', Mr. Scott."

Helping Samuel rub down the horse Victoria had ridden, the trainer paused and waved back, and Mariah suddenly wondered if the man had a wife. No one had ever mentioned one.

She maneuvered her mount closer to Amy's as they rode along the path between two plowed-under tobacco fields. "I'm curious. Mr. Scott has never said anything about having a wife living here. Does he have one, perchance?"

"Huh-uh. I think he had one, but she died or somethin'. If he wanted one, though, he could get one real easy."

SALLY LAITY AND DIANNA CRAWFORD

"Why do you say that?"

" 'Cuz I heard some of the widows at church talkin' about what a good catch he'd be, what with him makin' so much money, and all."

"What do you mean?"

Amy cut her a flippant look. "Oh, that's right. You wasn't here last spring when ol' Mr. Dumfries came ridin' in here big as you please. He offered Mr. Scott twice what Poppy was payin' him to come work for him. Mr. Scott's the best horse trainer in the whole blamed colony. Maybe even all the colonies."

How interesting. "I see. Offered so much money, I'm surprised he didn't take the position."

"He prob'ly would'a, but I ran up to the house and told Poppy what was goin' on. He came down an' offered Mr. Scott the same money if he'd stay here."

"La, he must be a highly valued man." Mariah nudged her mare forward again, viewing the redheaded trainer through more enlightened eyes.

As they approached the stables, Mr. Scott laid aside the curry brush he'd been using and strode over to help Mariah dismount. When he reached up to her, she offered her brightest smile as she came down into his arms. "Thank you," she gushed in her most pleasant voice. "I do hope we haven't kept you and Samuel from your meals."

"Not at all. Pansy doesn't bring our meals until after the family has been served."

"Oh, I didn't know that." It dawned on her that she knew very little about the workings of the plantation because she spent the bulk of her days in the upstairs schoolroom. "Speaking of supper, Amy, dear, run to the house and wash up, and I'll be along shortly."

Mr. Scott moved to the mare's neck and patted it as he gathered the reins.

"She's a fine riding horse, is she not?" Mariah ventured. "But watching the gentle way you work with all the stock, getting them to do your bidding, 'tis no wonder."

His green eyes swerved from the animal to her. "That's the trick, young lady. Firm but gentle handling, and a lot of patience, of course."

For a split second, she thought the man was going to smile. And though he did not, she kept hers from faltering. "I know just what you mean. Amy, too, needs lots and lots of patience, plus a firm but gentle hand."

He gazed after the girl as she ran toward the house, and his eyes crinkled at the corners as a slight grin softened his guileless features. Mariah wouldn't have described him as handsome, exactly, with that long face and slightly mocking mouth. Yet there seemed a compelling quality about him and an honesty not to be overlooked. "She's a corker, all right." His smile faded as he turned back to Mariah. "You're a teacher, Miss Harwood. What did you think of the sermon on 1 Peter chapter 3 last Sunday?"

"Oh, that." Mariah's smile evaporated. "Obviously some husband must have lodged a complaint about his wife."

The normally serious-mannered man burst out with a belly laugh. "Actually I was referring to the promise the passage contained: 'For the eyes of the Lord are over the righteous, and his ears are open unto their prayers.' "

A rush of warmth rose over her cheeks. "Mercy me. I mostly remembered the part where wives aren't supposed to dress pretty but let their inner beauty shine out. Oh, and let us not forget the part about being in subjection to their husbands." She grimaced.

Mr. Scott's lips broadened into a cordial smile, and a spark of humor in his eye added a certain degree of appeal that changed her mind about his not being handsome. "You must not have heard the command where the husband is to give honor to his wife and treat her gently because she's the weaker vessel, and how they're heirs together in the grace of life."

"I'm afraid I missed that part. The third chapter of 1 Peter, you say? I shall read it again this eve before I retire." She took a step backward. "I'd best go now and make sure Amy doesn't get into any more mischief before supper."

He chuckled. "Good luck."

On her way up the path to the manse, Mariah couldn't dismiss the trainer from her mind. Was he in his own quiet way hinting that he desired her? Perhaps even wanted her for his wife? If not, why had he brought up that business about husbands and wives being heirs together in. . .what was it? Oh yes, heirs together in the grace of life.

Curious to see if he was watching her walk away, she glanced back toward the stable. He was gone.

Just as well, she told herself. But still. . .

Chapter 17

Asoft September breeze stirred the lace underpanels on the open windows, and the sweet scent of late-blooming roses from the garden floated across the dining room.

"How sad," Amy mused, loading a huge amount of scrambled egg onto her fork. "Colin won't be here to race his phaeton. Poppy will have to drive it, and he drives as slow as a turtle. We'll lose for sure." Shoving the egg into her mouth, she spewed out another whining complaint from around the food. "And it's our race."

"Amy, really!" Victoria shook her head in disgust. "You managed to splatter egg all over the tablecloth."

Witnessing the exchange between the sisters at the dining table, Mariah hid her grin behind her napkin. The little imp was forever being taken to task for one thing or another. But nothing could dampen Mariah's spirits this day. After all, she'd lived the greater part of her life at the resort of Bath, where public balls or plays were scheduled for almost every evening during the season. Compared to her existence back home, life on a plantation in the colonies was decidedly more dull. Except today.

Today every family of consequence within twenty miles would be coming for the races. A dinner would follow, and later in the evening, a ball. The kitchen slaves had been cooking and baking for days, filling the house with marvelous, mouthwatering aromas. The Barclays had even hired a string quartet from Baltimore to perform throughout the afternoon and evening. It was certain to be a lively event.

On a shopping excursion into Alexandria with the womenfolk, Mariah had purchased an exquisite silk lace fan from France to go with her violet satin evening gown, and she had every intention of using that fan to its best flirting advantage. Smiling to herself, she picked up her cup of tea and took a sip. After all, it was Colin's fault for not having deigned to write a single line to her since his departure weeks ago. In essence, he himself had abandoned her to her fate.

"Mariah?"

Glad that the mistress had given the girls permission to use her Christian name at last, she met Heather's eyes across the table. "Yes?"

"Mother said me and Tori could play that piece you taught us durin' the dinner hour. I do hope we don't make any mistakes."

"*Tori and I*, dear." All this harping on drawls and proper grammar. Would it ever make a difference? "You've played that number flawlessly several times. Just pretend I'm the only one listening to you, and you'll both be fine."

Victoria released a sigh. "I do hope you're right. I don't want to make a fool of myself in front of Tuck. Or anyone else, for that matter, but especially Tuck."

As Mariah had suspected, Victoria was more interested in Dennis Tucker than she was in the merchant's son. If the mistress of the household knew that for certain, she surely wouldn't be happy. But considering the number of guests due to arrive today, perhaps Tori's interest would shift to someone entirely different. At her age, anything was possible, and the strawberry-pink gown of ruffled lawn she'd be wearing this evening would set off her feminine assets to perfection. A whole raft of young men might be drawn to her side.

Mariah swept a glance over her three charges as she forked the remaining egg on her plate. "We'd better finish eating so we can go upstairs and dress for the day. People will likely begin to arrive within the hour."

Amy tucked her chin and peered at Mariah through her silky lashes. "You must know if I get prettied up this early, I'll just be all dirty and mussed up by noon."

As if she'd been hovering out of sight eavesdropping on their conversation, Mistress Barclay chose that moment to amble in from the butlery. "I beg to differ, young lady. You won't be getting dirty at all, because I absolutely forbid you to go anywhere near the stables today. You'll act like a proper young lady and remain either inside the house or out on the lawn until race time, conducting yourself accordingly."

"But Mama." The child sank back against her chair with a miserable groan.

Her mother maintained her meaningful glare. "No buts. I already have more trouble than I can handle today. Speaking of which—" She switched her attention to Mariah. "I've been told that Lizzie, Celie, and Pansy woke up this morning, of all mornings, covered with red spots. From what Benjamin says, slaves from the Murray plantation just up the road have come down with the measles, and it would appear they have spread the malady to our people. I've told my husband time and again to stop allowing our slaves to mix with that Murray bunch on Saturday nights. His people appear less than well cared for, you know. But Eldon refuses to stop our slaves from mingling."

"Mercy me." Mariah wagged her head. "Measles. And today of all days. How unfortunate." She bit into her buttered biscuit.

"Quite. Needless to say, I cannot expose our guests to disease. The slaves will remain far from the premises until they recover. Some of our overnight guests will be bringing their personal servants with them, but there's no time this morning to train any of our field hands to help with serving the food. Besides the scheduled dinner for forty-five we'll be hosting, refreshments will be served during the ball afterward." A slight pause, and she let the cannon ball fly. "I'm sorry, but the duty must fall upon you, Mariah. I've no other recourse. You're simply going to have to help Eloise and Benjamin. I believe Ivy has not yet shown evidence of the illness, so unless she suddenly acquires the rash, she'll be able to assist as well."

Gasping, Mariah choked on her biscuit and started to cough.

The mistress shrugged a shoulder. "It can't be helped." That said, she took her leave.

Mariah glanced wildly around at the girls and saw that their mouths were also gaping. Surely this was just a nightmare. Yes, that's what it was. Any minute now she'd wake up.

Dressed in one of Pansy's extra uniforms—in hideous black—Mariah clenched her teeth together so hard her jaw felt like it would disintegrate. Her back ached, her feet ached, and she most likely reeked of kitchen grease and lye soap. Having been unable to snatch more than a minute here and there throughout the endless day to rest, she could barely keep her tears from breaking through the floodgates in back of her eyes and exploding forth in a torrent. This was to have been the most special of days. She should be flitting among the throng of visitors in a glamorous violet gown, fluttering the lacy fan demurely at dozens of handsome bachelors and catching their interest.

Instead, she'd been relegated to household slave, all but invisible in the shapeless black uniform and white apron. With a little more force than necessary, she plunked a heavy food tray on one of the three side tables now lining a wall in the dining room and removed a bowl of cut fruit and a platter of assorted cold meats and cheeses, setting them onto one of the remaining tables. If these fine people only knew that she, Mariah Harwood—lately arrived from the glorious resort of Bath, England, and now secretly betrothed to the son and heir of this very plantation—had been tripping about serving refreshments on the lawn all afternoon for everyone to gawk at! It was utterly humiliating and not to be borne.

Some guests, a number of them people she'd met at church and in the town shops, began gathering on the terrace just beyond the open glass-paned doors, chatting and laughing and enjoying themselves.

Savagely, she rubbed telltale moisture from her eyes, then rammed a stray strand of hair into the ruffled mobcap—*mobcap!*—Mistress Barclay insisted would keep most of the kitchen odors and smoke from seeping into her curls. She peered down at the latest white apron she'd put on over Pansy's uniform less than an hour ago. Already there were splatters here and there.

Dejected, she let out a huff. What difference did it make? Any of it? She'd never be considered worthy by any of these people ever again. She picked up the empty tray and started back toward the kitchen.

The patter of rapid footsteps came from the front of the house as Amy ran to her side. "Mariah, can I help?"

Mariah's eyes rounded as she beheld the youngest member of the household, golden ringlets straggling, hair ribbon askew, face and hands smeared with dirt, and several inches of her skirt pulled loose from the bodice. "What in heaven's name happened to you? Look at your hair. Your skirt. You look horrid!"

"Oh, this." Amy smirked, tugging at the gaping section. "It wasn't my fault, I promise. It was that Henry Jay again." Her lips pressed together in anger. "I was winnin' the footrace, and he just couldn't stand losin' to a girl. He jerked me back by my skirt, and I fell on the ground, and he fell on top of me."

"Amy, Amy. . ." Mariah just looked at her. "Supper will be served in just a few minutes. You cannot appear at the table in this frightful condition. Run upstairs as fast as you can and get presentable."

"But Lizzie's sick. There's nobody to fix my hair."

"Perhaps Victoria or Heather may still be up there. Tell them I said to do something with it. They're both getting quite good at fancying each other up."

"Tori always pulls my hair, and it hurts." The child's lower lip poked forward.

Mariah would have none of it. "Go! Now!" She pointed toward the staircase. "Catch your sister before she comes down. I not only want you to look as pretty as the other girls, I want you to look prettier. Do you understand? Now, off with you!"

"Yes, Mother!" With a toss of her wayward curls, the imp marched straight up the stairs with nary a backward glance.

Despite her weariness, Mariah couldn't restrain a smile as she watched after the disaster-prone child and shook her head.

"Thank you." Mistress Barclay stood in the butlery doorway. "For reprimanding Amy and sending her up for repairs." Then the bane of Mariah's hope strolled past her with her superior grace and rounded the long dining table as she headed for the terrace.

Mariah would gladly have chased after her and throttled her, only she was far too tired to do so.

The older woman whirled around.

For a moment Mariah feared that Cora Barclay had read her murderous thoughts.

The mistress tilted her head and met her gaze. "I know this has been a very hard and trying day for you." No emotion colored her features as she spoke the kind-sounding words. But having uttered them, she simply turned back again and walked out the door to join her guests.

"*Thank you, Mariah, for putting aside your fanciful dreams for the day and lowering yourself to be a doormat,*" Mariah muttered bitterly under her breath, her hands on her hips. "*I can never repay you for the great sacrifice you made for me.*" Hmph. A crumb of gratitude might have been nice. . . .

Then a more terrible thought surfaced. Even if Colin did still harbor the hope to marry her, would he honor their betrothal after he learned how she had been shamed this day before everyone he knew?

Once the morbid mental assaults started, others rushed in upon them. Colin's mother had been entirely too pleasant since her son had been forced to leave. Had this been her plan all along? The moment the devious woman had been waiting for to destroy her once and for all? Mistress Barclay, the ever-so-righteous Christian?

And what of those allegedly sick servants? Did they truly have the measles?

One way or another, Mariah planned to find out.

Mariah blinked awake, then closed her eyes against a bright ray of sunshine. *Sunshine!* She must have overslept. It had to be close to noon!

Throwing off her sheet, Mariah sprang to her feet. . .and groaned. Her legs were stiff, her back hurt, and her shoulders and arms ached from carrying so many heavy trays yesterday. She'd never labored so hard in her life. And poor Eloise! Mariah had never seen the plump, older slave looking so worn out as she'd been by the time all the dishes from the party had been washed and put away. Young Ivy had helped a little, at first. But she was a mere slip of a thing, and by midday she began to feel ill and took to her bed, leaving the bulk of the responsibilities to Eloise and Mariah.

Further remembrance of the day before brought a rush of humiliation that weighted down Mariah's chest. She'd never be able to dismiss the memory of staring eyes, the sneering remarks whispered behind fans. How would she ever rise above the shame? She most certainly wouldn't, not in this neighborhood, around those guests.

Oh no! We still have houseguests! Limping over to her washstand, she wondered why she hadn't been awakened and summoned to the kitchen. After pouring the contents of the pitcher into the bowl, she snatched a washcloth from its hook and placed it into the water.

The door swung open. "You're awake. Finally." Dressed for the day, Amy came skipping in. "Mama said not to bother you till you woke up. Heather got up a little while ago, but Tori's still sleeping. She stayed up till the very end, so Mama says."

Mariah squeezed moisture from the washing cloth and pressed it to her face, then turned to the girl. "Why was I not to be awakened? Surely Eloise wasn't expected to handle breakfast all by herself."

Amy shrugged a shoulder. "Tuck sent over two of their servants first thing this morning. They're down in the kitchen now, helpin' out."

"Thank heavens." With a sigh of relief, Mariah replaced the cloth on its hook and hobbled to her bed to lie down again.

"Oh, I almost forgot." Amy whirled around and dashed to her

adjoining bedchamber then returned just as swiftly. "Here." She held out a piece of correspondence. "Storekeeper Gladdings must've brought mail with him when he delivered supplies yesterday. Nobody noticed it layin' on the—"

Mariah didn't hear any more of Amy's ramblings. At last! A missive from Colin! She snatched the letter from the child and tore open the wax seal. Unfolding the paper, she scanned quickly to the bottom to check the signature.

Her heart sank. It was from Rose.

"Who's it from?" Coming closer, Amy angled her head, trying to peek at it.

Mariah took a second to control her disappointment. " 'Tis from my sister Rose."

"The one who got took away by the smelly man?"

She gave a weary nod.

"Read it to me, please. I never get mail."

"Very well." Feeling a headache coming on, Mariah patted the spot next to her on the bed. "But afterward you must promise to go and occupy yourself elsewhere for a few hours. I'd like to get a little more sleep." *And perhaps have a good cry.*

Only half paying attention to the written words herself, Mariah read the rather vague missive from Rose aloud, before shooing Amy out. Then she lay down on the feather pillow and reread it more slowly. She felt a niggle of guilt for not having given either Rose or Lily much thought since her arrival at the plantation, but she drew comfort from learning about her older sister's situation. It was hard to imagine Rose living in some remote village with few amenities, but hearing that her employer had turned out to be a kind man after all was welcome news.

Mariah wished she could say the same about Mistress Barclay. Suddenly filled with righteous ire, she eased to her feet, completed her toilette, and donned a gray linen dress. Then she went into the schoolroom to answer her sister's letter. Rose would be shocked to hear just how badly she was abused here at the Barclays'.

As she put quill to paper, she paused. She had no qualms about telling Rose all about Mistress Barclay's mistreatment of her, but she'd refrain from saying anything unkind about Colin—at least until she knew for certain that he'd abandoned her. She wouldn't mention the secret betrothal or write that he planned to visit Papa in England, either. She wasn't sure he'd keep his word and actually visit the family in Bath. It would be terrible to end up having to eat her words. Yesterday she'd eaten about as much humble pie as she cared to eat. *Ever.*

Salutations Rose. She began her response with as much dignity as she could muster. *I was quite surprised to hear from you. . . .*

Chapter 18

The weak February dawn offered only pale light as a cold, damp breeze blew wisps of morning mist about. Mariah snuggled deeper into her woolen wrapper as she stood by the carriage to bid the Barclays farewell. She had mixed feelings about choosing to stay behind, but after her day of servanthood at the gala held by the family on race day, there was no way she could face attending a Valentine's Day wedding in Baltimore with some of the same people. More's the pity. She might have met some rich gentleman there who wouldn't learn of her circumstance until she'd completely bewitched him. But on the other hand, with the Barclays away, she'd have an entire week of freedom. . .freedom to set another plan in motion, even if it did happen to be somewhat less appealing than her original one.

It piqued her that Colin had never written. How was she to know if he even intended to come back?

Victoria leaned out the window of the now hooded landau and touched Mariah on the shoulder. "I wish I didn't have to go. I'd rather stay here with you."

Knowing that Tori reveled in having three attentive young men dropping by to visit her several times a week now, it came as no surprise that the girl disliked having to leave her beaus behind. She took Victoria's outstretched hand and gave it a squeeze. "Dearest, think of all the other young gentlemen you would disappoint if you didn't go to Baltimore."

"What gentlemen?" Tori's face clouded over. "I don't know a soul there."

"You will, sweetheart, trust me. And you shall have the most marvelous time if you just allow yourself to do so. Besides, think of how you would disappoint your cousin if you failed to arrive, particularly since you agreed to be her maid of honor."

"You're right." Withdrawing her gloved hand from Mariah's grasp, she settled back against the leather cushion once again, only slightly mollified.

Out the back opening, Mistress Barclay mouthed a thank-you to Mariah as her husband tapped his metal-knobbed cane on the frame of the carriage bonnet, signaling their driver to start the team.

The landau lunged away down the lane, with young hands reaching out from both sides, waving good-bye. Mariah found herself a bit bereft already. The girls had truly captured her heart. The big house would seem empty without them.

With a sigh, she turned to glance down at the stables. Mr. Scott would be out working one horse or another soon. Perhaps she'd meander down there. After all, she had only a week to entice the redhead's affections enough that he'd purchase her bond. Still, she shouldn't be too pushy, look too desperate. He had to be the one to make the advances. Or at least *think* that.

She would take her time. She turned back to the house, intending to dress in an appealing, but not overly adorned, gown, and fashion her hair in a simpler, refined style. It would make her appear older and more serious. Perhaps she'd even look up a verse or two from the Bible to discuss, giving her a purpose he'd appreciate for her going down there. She smiled. Yes, that's what she'd do. After all, being married to a respected man like him would restore her own respectability. . .and with any luck at all, he might even turn out to be a pleasant husband. And generous, as well.

But as she mounted the steps to the manse, beguiling thoughts of Colin—handsome, charming Colin—slowed her down. Could she truly settle for Geoffrey Scott after him?

Mariah paused on the top step and gazed longingly down the lane. The trees were barren now, like her dreams, and reached uselessly up at the uncertain sky as if pleading for warmth. Surely Colin would return within the month, and remote as it seemed at this moment, he might still intend to marry her. But in case he'd changed his mind, she needed to have another plan in place, because she certainly would not remain in that house if he cast her aside like an old horse blanket.

Just then her stomach rumbled, reminding her that she hadn't awakened early enough to join the family at breakfast. She headed for the dining room, where the warm glow from wall sconces helped chase away the dreariness of the day.

Eloise and Lizzie looked up on her approach as they began removing trays of food from the sideboard.

Mariah held up a hand. "Just a moment, please. Let me fill a plate before you take everything away."

"Sho' 'nough, missy." The older slave handed her a clean plate. "Ah reckoned y'all already ate."

"I'm sorry, no. I've been out bidding the Barclays farewell. By the by, since it'll just be me here this week, I'll take my meals in the kitchen with you all. No sense going to extra fuss for one person. That is, if you don't mind."

Eloise smiled her apple-dumpling smile, white teeth bright against her dark brown skin. "Ah be hopin' you say dat. Dat ways we all can get us a li'l holiday."

Mariah returned her smile and gave sweet Lizzie a nod. "Yes, a Valentine's Day present for us while the family's away."

Sitting down at the table with her plate of food, Mariah realized she'd included herself with the slaves. Not a good way to be thinking if she wanted to better herself. But as she watched Eloise carry out a heavily laden tray, she couldn't help but sympathize with the older woman. She knew firsthand how hard slaves worked, ever since she'd been forced to help out for a day.

~

A couple of hours later, Mariah put a warm shawl around her shoulders and made her way to the stables, having found a scripture verse and put it to memory. She hoped to launch a spirited—and hopefully prolonged— discussion with Mr. Scott. Small puffs of her breath crystallized in the damp air, and she knew the chilly temperature would add a touch of color to her cheeks. She opened the door and stepped inside.

The sound of tapping drifted from the lamplit tack room, where she found the trainer working alone, hammering a metal brad into a halter.

"Good morning," she called out cheerily, appreciating the warmth coming from a round black stove.

Startled, he turned. "Oh, it's you, miss. I thought you would've left with the family."

She shook her head. "No. I no longer feel comfortable accompanying them to social events."

His sympathetic nod indicated that he understood. "Did you want me to saddle a horse for you?"

"No, thank you." She made an effort to convey a touch of sadness in her smile. "It's just a treat to be able to take a walk whenever I choose to. Normally my hours are all planned out for me ahead of time."

"I thought you enjoyed your work." Averting his gaze, he picked up the small hammer again. "I've noticed quite a nice change in the girls. Heather, especially, has blossomed since you've been here."

"Hasn't she, though?" Mariah moved a few steps closer. "That little dear has a true gift for music, and it's helping her to overcome her shyness. However, I do wish tutoring the girls had been my choice and not a duty pressed on me because of that awful bond."

He glanced up at her, his expression serious, and spoke quietly. "Have a seat." He indicated a nearby stool as he pulled another out from under the workbench for himself. The lamplight cast a golden glow over his coppery hair with his movements.

An invitation to sit down. . .a definite bit of progress.

"A scripture comes to mind that you might find helpful." He reached for a worn black book lying on the end of the workbench.

Mariah squelched a sigh and the impulse to roll her eyes. If the worst came to pass, could she really put up with a man who preached at her day after day? Watching him leaf through the pages, she recalled that both Papa and Rose had often quoted scripture, yet she hadn't loved them any less for it. She propped up a smile and tried to appear interested.

"Ah yes, here it is." He glanced up at her then returned his attention to the passage before him. "In the sixth chapter of Ephesians. 'Servants, be obedient to them that are your masters according to the flesh, with fear and trembling, in singleness of your heart, as unto Christ; not with eyeservice, as menpleasers; but as the servants of Christ, doing the will of God from the heart.' And let me see. . ." He tilted the Bible closer to the light. "Yes, here it is. 'Knowing that whatsoever good thing any man doeth, the same shall he receive of the Lord, whether he be bond or free.' So you see, in the end, being bond or free matters very little. Most people have to labor at something all their lives, be they master, servant, or slave. We simply must set our hearts and minds on pleasing the Lord, since He gives us so many blessings."

Mariah focused on his compelling green eyes. "Now that I see things through that perspective, I feel so much better." Surely that response would please the man. For goodness' sake, all one had to do was look at the ragged field slaves living here to see that nothing they had could possibly begin to compare with the Barclays' wealth. She needed to take control of the conversation. "Speaking of scriptures, I have—"

Mr. Scott got up rather rudely and crossed to the door, opening it to a rush of cold air. "A roan?" He shook his head. "His father will not be pleased with that one."

His father?

Mariah sprang to her feet and flew to the doorway.

A horse and rider trotted toward them on the lane.

The rider snatched off his three-cornered hat and waved it back and forth.

Colin! He'd come back at last! But remembering how she'd been humiliated while he'd been away, and considering that he'd never bothered to write, Mariah doubted he would still want to marry her.

Then another sudden realization caused all the breath to leave her lungs and make her knees go weak. The two of them would be in the house together.

Alone.

For a whole week.

———

"Mariah!" Colin knew she probably couldn't hear him over the distance separating them, but he waved his hat in a wide arc and heeled Russet Knight into a gallop. No woman he'd seen in all his travels had remotely sparked his interest, not when he had the most beautiful one in the world waiting for him.

Nearing the stables, he noticed that her welcoming smile wilted, then disappeared as her lips parted and she took some backward steps.

Her reaction baffled Colin. Throughout his absence, all he'd dreamed of was leaping off his horse, taking Mariah into his arms, and kissing her—her face, her eyes, her mouth. Why did she appear stunned? He reined in directly in front of her and Geoffrey Scott and dismounted.

The trainer moved close to the animal. "I assume you know your father's not going to be happy that you brought back a roan." He ran his hands down the stallion's foreleg.

"He'll change his mind when he sees Russet Knight run. The horse will sire some great champions." Colin's eyes gravitated to Mariah. Why was she standing so far away? They were betrothed, were they not?

Geoffrey continued to study the animal, then gave an assenting nod. "He does have fine lines; I'll say that."

Would the man never stop talking about the blasted horse? Reluctantly, Colin shifted his attention back to the trainer. "He'll look even better once he's had a few days' exercise. He's just spent the last seven weeks aboard ship." He looked again at Mariah, who stood frozen in place, then at Scott, and his suspicions came to the fore. The two of them had just been together—unchaparoned—for how long? "How've you been, my love?"

Her attempt at a smile fell flat. "Fine. And I assume you met with success in your venture. We didn't expect you to return for several more weeks." She flicked a glance toward the mansion.

"I was successful, yes, and in as short a time as possible. I bypassed the trip to Boston." He paused, eyeing Mariah. "Isn't it a rather odd time of day to be visiting the stables?"

Geoffrey Scott stood and straightened his posture. "I assure you, Colin, nothing is amiss here. Miss Harwood merely came here to ask me a theological question." He turned his attention to her. "You hardly had time enough to voice it. But never mind. You can ask me another time. Colin's back." With what appeared to be a genuine grin, he slapped Colin on the shoulder blades. "Glad to have you home again."

Somewhat relieved to have the matter concerning Mariah and the trainer cleared up, Colin cut a glance to her, still puzzled that she seemed so standoffish. He'd find out why once they had some privacy. Offering his elbow, he tucked her arm in his. "Geoff, would you mind seeing to the horse?"

"Of course. It'll give Red and me a chance to get acquainted."

Leading Mariah away from the stable, Colin started up the pathway toward the house. Strange that the rest of the family hadn't noticed his return. He guided her toward the gazebo so they could speak privately before going inside. He needed some answers.

～

"Why are we going to the gazebo, Colin?" Mariah felt fully aware of his suspicions about her and Mr. Scott, and since they were entirely correct, she wondered what she could say in her defense. There were no slaves out working in the dreary weather, but she didn't want to take a chance on one of them overhearing the conversation and bandying it hither and yon. She pulled her shawl closer. " 'Tis quite cold out here. Shouldn't we—"

He continued walking. "I want a moment alone with you before we go inside."

She huffed out a vapory breath. She might as well tell him, he'd find out in a few minutes anyway. "Your family is not at home. They left this morning for a wedding at the Spencers'. Your cousin Susan is getting married."

"You don't say." His dark eyes gravitated to the house as a slow smile spread from ear to ear. He changed direction so quickly, Mariah nearly lost her balance.

" 'Tis true. And I can see your reaction to the situation is far different from mine. What will people say when they learn we've spent the week by ourselves in the house, with none of your family around?"

"Is that why you haven't given me a proper greeting?" His steps never slowed.

"Colin. You're not taking this seriously."

He cut her a half smile. "You are so wrong, my dear Mariah. I can't imagine a more perfect homecoming. Do stop balking, or I won't tell you about my visit with your family."

He had actually gone to Bath, just as he'd promised! He must still want to marry her! Exuberant beyond words, she pulled free. "Race you to the house!" Hiking her skirts, she sprinted away.

With a burst of laughter, he started after her. He reached her just as she got to the porch steps and caught her around the waist, twirling her around.

Mariah squealed with delight and threw her arms around him as he scooped her up into his arms and bounded up the steps. Once inside, he lowered her to the tiled floor, all humor gone from his eyes.

His ardent gaze drew her to him, and he captured her lips in a breathtakingly sweet kiss she never wanted to end. Her heart sang. Colin had come back to her, and he really and truly was hers.

"Ahem." A heartbeat of silence. *"Ahem!"*

Mariah dragged her lips from Colin's, and they both turned to see Eloise glaring at them, her fists planted on her wide hips.

"Why, Mammy Eloise," Colin gushed. "You're a sight for sore eyes." He tucked Mariah close to his side and tugged her along as he went to wrap his other arm around the slave's generous girth. He gave her a peck on the cheek. "I missed you and your delicious meals so much. By any chance, have you got a little somethin' to tide me over until mealtime?"

Not cracking a smile, she arched her scant brows. "I does iff'n you unwraps yo'self from dat chil.'"

Colin laughed and stepped a small pace away from Mariah. "I was just showin' her how much I missed her—missed all of you."

Staring hard at him, Eloise smirked. "Well, now dat we got da happy homecomin' outta da way, keep yo hands to yo'self."

He held up the guilty culprits without erasing his grin. "Now can I have somethin' to eat?"

"Go set yo'self down in da dinin' room. Ah'll bring y'all out somethin' directly."

The cook's interruption had brought both disappointment and relief to Mariah. She'd truly enjoyed being so thoroughly kissed. Her lips still tingled, wanting more. "May I have a cup of tea, as well?" she called after the slave.

Colin seated Mariah near the head of the table and bent to tickle her neck with the brush of his lips, sending yet another delicious chill through her. Then he sighed and took his father's chair. He took her hand and raised it to his mouth, kissing her palm.

Her heart drummed a staccato beat. It was so good to have her Colin back. She leaned closer to him.

"I've missed you so much," he murmured, his gaze holding hers. "You were all I thought about all the time I was away."

"And I you," she managed to whisper. "I was so worried you'd find someone more appealing."

"That's not possible." He cupped her face in his hand. "You are everything I—"

"Masta Colin! I said keep yo' hands to yo'self." Eloise paused in the doorway.

Chuckling, he straightened. "Yes, ma'am."

Mariah giggled behind her hand and turned to the cook as the woman neared the table. "From now on, we promise to be good."

"I don't know, Mammy." Colin wagged his head soberly. "That's gonna be a hard promise to keep."

The cook slammed a tray down between them, rattling the dishes. "Jes' don't yo forget who be da mammy aroun' here." She placed the food pointedly before him, then set out a cup for each of them. She stared him squarely in the eye. "Ah will be back. . .with da tea."

As the slave stormed out with a huff, Colin tilted his head at Mariah. "You'll have to excuse her. She's been motherin' me for as long as I can remember."

"You don't need to explain. I personally know what a fine woman she is. Why, if it hadn't been for her, I don't know how I would have—" Realizing she'd said too much already, Mariah clamped her lips together.

His grin disappeared. "What do you mean?"

Inhaling a shuddering breath, she released it in a whoosh of air. "I hadn't planned to go into that just yet. We were having such a lovely time. But I suppose you'll find out soon enough."

He leaned back in his chair with a frown while Mariah spoke in a rush.

"The house slaves came down with the measles the day of the phaeton races, so I was pressed into service. I had to help Eloise prepare and serve food and refreshments to the guests throughout that day. Thank goodness your friend Tuck sent two of their slaves over to relieve me the next morning."

Colin's expression turned granite hard. "Mother was responsible for this. She deliberately humiliated you."

Reaching for his fisted hand, Mariah smoothed her palm over it. "What's done is done, dearest. My question for you is, since all your neighbors and business associates saw me in that shameful position, is it possible you would still want to marry me?"

A muscle worked in his jaw as he gazed steadily at her. "So that's why you didn't accompany the family to Baltimore. Mother saw to it that you were no longer considered fit for gentle society."

He now fully understood the extent of the damage his devious mother had done. Mariah held her breath.

He reached over and caressed her cheek with the backs of his fingers as his demeanor softened, then took a brighter turn. "Perhaps Mother did me a favor without knowing it. She single-handedly kept all my

161

competition away while I was gone."

Mariah relaxed and leaned into his comforting touch. "You were gone such a long time. But if you missed me so much, why did you not write to me?"

"Write!" He hiked a brow. "You knew where I was going and what I was doing. There was nothing to report until I went to see your father. And by that time, I knew I'd beat any post home."

"Papa! You did go to see him!" Mariah swept up from her seat and planted a kiss on his cheek.

Colin caught her to him with an eager laugh.

Mariah realized her mistake. Eloise would return with the tea at any second. She eased away and retook her seat.

It took several seconds for him to glance from her to the chicken and dumplings on his plate. Finally he picked up his fork and took a sample.

"How did Papa look?"

Swallowing his mouthful, he nodded. "Fine. He sends his love to you and your sisters. I found him most welcoming and liked him at once. That younger brother of yours, though, is a corker. He'd make a good match for our little Amy. He managed to wheedle a pony out of me."

"Surely not!"

"It's quite true." Colin chuckled. "I almost felt like I was home again. And the little beast did make a fine Christmas gift for him."

"A gift for the rascal, and not even a Christmas greeting to me?"

Colin's humor died. "I'm so sorry. That was terribly thoughtless of me." A guilty smile curved his lips, and he changed the subject. "By the way, I was able to persuade your father to seek a barrister's assistance regarding that financial problem. Both he and your father were hesitant to take an influential aristocrat to court, but I convinced them it was quite proper to do so."

Tears pooled in Mariah's eyes, clouding her view of this man who had come to the rescue yet again. "You truly are the most wonderful man," she choked out.

He took her hand in his once more. "And I have an entire *uninterrupted week* to show you just how wonderful I can be."

Chapter 19

Y ou know, the more I think about it, the more I have to admit you're right, sweetheart." Colin forked the last bit of his remaining dumpling into his mouth and washed it down with a gulp of tea as he and Mariah sat at the table.

Mariah tried unsuccessfully to read his expression as she set down her own cup. "About what?"

"We will need to be very discreet, not only after my parents return from Baltimore, but during this week, as well. Perhaps *especially* during this week. Our people here are loyal to a fault, but they also love to gossip. Word of our relationship could easily get back to my father and mother. I'll speak to Eloise and Geoffrey and ask them not to mention any of my lustful intentions toward you they happened to witness."

"Lustful intentions?" Mariah didn't like the sound of that at all. No wedding band graced her finger as yet, and she was not about to allow Colin liberties to which he was only entitled by marriage.

Colin chuckled and angled his head at her. "My lustful intention is to marry you, my dear Mariah. . .if you'll still have me, of course."

A huge smile curved her lips. "Yes! Oh, yes." Supremely grateful to hear him say those all-important words she'd longed so to hear, she reached over to give his arm a squeeze, but he warded her off with a raised hand.

"In that case—" He reached into his breast pocket and withdrew something in his closed hand. With a tentative smile, he opened his fingers to display an exquisite ring. "Your father assured me this would fit. Shall we try it?"

Mariah's heart tripped over itself at the sight of a beautiful amethyst surrounded by tiny diamonds. "You bought it from Papa?" Her eyes roved Colin's wondrous face as she nibbled her lower lip and held out her left hand.

"I did." Light from the wall sconces sparkled over the cut gems as he slipped it on her finger. "He wanted to give it to me without cost, since it was for you, but I insisted on paying. And look. He knows you well. It fits perfectly." He raised her hand to admire it more closely. "I chose this one because it reminded me of those incredible violet eyes of yours."

Mariah blinked back happy tears. "Oh, Colin, 'tis ever so lovely. I couldn't have asked for anything more beautiful."

"I'm so glad you like it." His lips spread into a satisfied smile. Then he grew serious. "Of course, you know that once the family returns, we'll need to keep the ring out of sight until I secure the land I've been promised. Only a few days more, my darling. I'll request it as soon as they get home from the wedding. The anniversary of my birth came and went while I was aboard ship. So I am now of age to take ownership."

Still admiring her ring of promise, Mariah raised her gaze to his and offered a melancholy smile. "Your birthday. Another celebration we weren't able to share."

"Don't worry, my love." Colin cupped her chin with his palm. "We'll have a lifetime of events to celebrate together."

"I hope you're right." Despite his brave words, Mariah couldn't prevent doubts from creeping in. "What if your father will only sign the land over to you if you agree not to wed me? Surely you know your mother especially will fight you on this. As her husband, he will have to give in to keep the peace."

He shrugged a shoulder. "They can protest all they want to. But after being separated from you for these unbearably long months, I'll not allow them to stop us from marrying. After all, I'm not without a few assets of my own. Last spring, Tuck and I both bought land between the ridges to the west of here. Do you remember that tall young gentleman I introduced you to at the race in Alexandria?"

"George Washington, I believe?"

"Right. Well, he's been working as a surveyor for the colony, measuring and marking off parcels of virgin land along the distant branches of the Potomac. The land out there is cheap, and George has been purchasing choice parcels for himself out of his earnings. He recommended some fine pieces of land for us to buy. I bought a picturesque little valley that has the South Fork of the Potomac running through it."

"La, your own valley." Mariah tried to insert some enthusiasm into her response, but as wonderful as that sounded on the surface, the thought of living so far from any sort of society was daunting. What about the Indians? Weren't they a concern?

Colin puffed out his chest, obviously proud of his investment. "Our land spreads between the Blue Ridge and Allegheny Mountains. Tuck and I canoed upstream to see our parcels last May. We traveled for miles past the last settlement. Can you imagine? We're the first people ever to hold title to that valley. If all goes well here, I'll take you there to see it next summer. Maybe sooner. Barclay Valley."

The place was so remote Colin could name the valley after himself! Mariah knew she wasn't anything like Rose. She'd never grow accustomed to living in such an isolated spot. She had a hard time concentrating on what he was saying as he continued on with enthusiasm.

"Don't look dismayed, my dear Mariah. It's an easy float downriver anytime we have a desire to visit the family. Also, I may not have mentioned this before, but I happen to own three fine brood mares of my own, plus their foals. All we would need is a good stud to start our own horse farm, if need be. So you see, darling girl, nothing shall keep us apart."

He rose from the table. "Come with me to the library. I'll show you on the map exactly where our land is—yours and mine."

"Yes," she managed as he pulled back her chair. "I'd love to see it." It was probably rather silly of her to conjure up all those stupid fears. As long as she was with Colin, he would continue to take care of her as he always had.

Surely he would.

As Colin opened one of the double doors to the library for Mariah, a loud pounding rattled the front door. Who could be calling at this time of the morning? None of the plantation workers used the front entrance.

He turned and crossed the foyer. While grasping the door handle, he heard Benjamin coming from the butlery. "It's all right, Benjamin. I'll get it."

"Yessuh." With a bow of his snowy head, the African flashed a friendly smile. "Glad to see y'all finally made it home, Masta Colin. We sho' did miss you."

"I missed all of you, too." Interrupted once more by the second round of knocks, he opened the door.

Dennis Tucker leaned a hand against the doorjamb, breathing hard. At the bottom of the steps, his mount also blew puffs of air and pranced nervously, its reins dangling loose on the ground.

Colin frowned. "Tuck! What's the big rush? Is your place on fire?"

"No." He panted, trying to catch his breath. "But I've come on urgent business. My kid brother saw you ride past our place awhile ago, but he didn't mention it right away, or I'd have intercepted you before you made it all the way home."

Colin glanced around at Mariah, who stood listening to the exchange with a puzzled expression. Exhaling, he stepped back to let Tuck in. "So what's got you all afire?"

"You haven't heard, then." He swept off his hat but held it in his hands.

"Heard what?"

"We're goin' to war!" His eyes flared wide with excitement.

Mariah gasped and hastened to join them. She pushed past Colin and faced Tuck, her hands on her hips. "Whatever are you talking about? At war with whom? You've been calling on Victoria at least three times every week, and I never heard one word from your mouth about any conflict."

"There's a very good reason for that," he shot back, hiking his chin. "Womenfolk always get hysterical anytime the word *war* is mentioned. Trouble's been brewin' for some time."

She pressed her lips together and released a breath. "That's absurd. If there was the least bit of danger, Mr. Barclay would never have blithely ridden off to a wedding in Baltimore."

Colin couldn't help but grin at her spunk. He looked from her to his friend. "She does have a point."

With a wary eye on Mariah, Tuck switched his attention to Colin. "I need to speak to you alone. Shall we adjourn to your father's library?" Without waiting for an answer, he strode across to the door Colin had opened moments before.

Colin turned to Mariah and took her by the shoulders. "Sweetheart, I'll be just a few minutes, I promise. And I also promise to tell you everything we discuss. So please go into the parlor and wait for me. I won't be long. You and I have plenty of our own business to take care of later." With a meaningful smile, he swung on his heel and followed his friend into the library, closing the door behind them. "So, what's this all about?"

Tuck met his curious gaze straight on. "Governor Dinwiddie received word back from England to call our militias to arms. He sent William Trent, an Ohio Valley trader, to Augusta County to lead their militia. He also sent George Washington upriver to Fredrick City to bring fifty men back with him to Alexandria for training and to be equipped. Dinwiddie instructed them to travel to the upper forks of the Ohio to build a fort."

Colin tucked his chin. "While it's still snowing? That hardly makes sense."

"This is serious, Colin. The French have to be stopped before they send more men down from Canada in the spring. George and the men

SALLY LAITY AND DIANNA CRAWFORD

from Fredrick City rode past our place just two days ago on their way to Alexandria. George told me that if you and I want to make sure the French are stopped before they turn their greedy eyes toward the backcountry where we bought property, we need to get ourselves down there to join him. We do happen to be part of the local militia, you know."

"But I only just got home. I haven't even unpacked."

"All the better. I spent all of yesterday convincin' Father it was my duty to go. I'm packed and was just waitin' for some food to be cooked for the journey. So don't worry about food. I'll share mine with you."

Colin was still trying to process the information Dennis had related. "But I—"

"What's the hesitation, Colin? With your family away, you won't have to waste your time arguin' with them."

"That's true, but still—"

Tuck barely paused as he rushed on. "By the way, Washington is already a hero. The whole colony is talkin' about him. Dinwiddie dispatched him to one of those Indian villages the French had taken over—one with an English trading post—to ask them politely to leave. I thought that was a foolhardy mission, myself, and it turns out George barely escaped with his life. He and his guide ended up comin' back across the mountains in winter *on foot*, with only scant supplies. Of course he's chompin' at the bit to get back there, this time with force."

Shaking his head, Colin kneaded his chin. "I know we're both signed on with the militia, but this is too sudden."

"Oh, and by the by," Tuck interrupted over his objections again. "Our friend George is now in command. He's been made a lieutenant colonel. I'm sure we can distinguish ourselves every bit as well as he has, if not better. How does Colonel Tucker or Colonel Barclay sound to you?"

"Fine. Fine. But as it happens, I have some rather urgent business here at home that needs to be taken care of."

Tuck rolled his eyes and let out a huff of breath. "Look, Colin, old man. Your family is gone for at least a week, if not more. I'm sure that once we ride into the Ohio Valley, we'll run those interlopers right off. We'll be back in no time at all. Even if we hadn't bought land on the frontier, it's

168

still our duty to go. Our militia has been ordered to Alexandria."

Trying to dispel the tightness in his chest, Colin breathed out a troubled breath and gave a reluctant nod. "You're right. It is our duty." But why did it have to be now? Why, when everything he'd spent endless months longing for was within his grasp?

He glanced toward the door. How would he explain this to Mariah?

Chapter 20

After agreeing to meet Tuck at his plantation in an hour, Colin quietly closed the door behind his friend. He needed a moment or two—or better still, a day or two—to formulate words that would pacify Mariah.

That was not to be.

The library door swung open within seconds. "I saw Tuck charge down the steps to his horse and—" Mariah stopped speaking and crossed the room, her intent gaze searching Colin's expression. "I don't relish the look on your face. What did Dennis say that has you so upset?"

Colin exhaled a slow breath, still trying to gather his thoughts. "Let's go into the parlor, my love." He gestured for her to precede him.

She didn't move. She stood regarding him with a puzzled frown. "Whatever for? You were going to show me the location of the land you purchased."

"Forgive me, but that will have to wait. An urgent matter has arisen. Please. . ." He motioned again toward the door. From her confused demeanor, he knew this was not going to be easy.

With some hesitation, she finally turned and did as bidden. Once in the parlor she took a seat on the damask settee and sat with her hands in her lap.

Colin gave fleeting consideration to taking a chair as far from her as possible but summoned his courage and sat beside her. He took her hands in his.

"Well?" Her dark curls graced her shoulder as she tipped her head in question.

"There's no easy way to say this."

"To say what?"

"I. . .I'm afraid I must leave again."

"Leave!" Her slender brows dipped toward each other. "When?"

Colin swallowed. "Now. Our local militia has been ordered to report to Alexandria at once."

"What are you saying, Colin? Surely they can't mean you. You're not a soldier. You're a plantation owner. A horse breeder."

Hating the look of pain in her eyes, he stroked his thumbs across the backs of her small hands. "This isn't England, sweetheart. Here in Virginia we don't have a standing army. Able-bodied men normally meet every month or so for drills. And when trouble arises, we're obligated to serve."

"But—" Mariah averted her gaze for a heartbeat, then returned it to him. "If what you're saying is true, why would your father go off to Baltimore as if nothing were amiss?"

"The orders were issued only a few days ago. With me away in England, he probably saw no reason to alarm all of you, especially since the trouble with the French is on the other side of the mountains. But even at that distance it's still in Virginia's territory and therefore must be defended."

"But if no one knows you've returned. . ." She gave a little shrug, a pleading look of hope.

"People do know. I disembarked at Alexandria. Folks saw me when I rode through town. I'm honor bound to go. It's my duty."

"Honor bound!" With a gasp, Mariah tore her hands from his. "What about your honor to me? You made promises to me, too. Not ten minutes ago you assured me we'd be married. Soon! Yet now you say you're going to ride off for who knows how long, leaving me here to languish again, and still as an indentured servant."

"Mariah, my love, the important thing is that you'll be here under my family's protection till I return. I don't believe this venture will take us more than a month or two to put to rights. Once we arrive in force, the French are sure to hightail it back up to Canada. The Indians in the area are loyal to us. They've been quite happy trading with the Ohio and Virginia Company for several years now. They'll side with us. You've nothing to fear."

"The Ohio and Virginia Company." She drew her lips inward in thought then relaxed them. "My sister is with one of their traders, is she not? Do you think Rose could be in danger?"

Colin cocked his head. "I seriously doubt she would've been taken into Indian Territory." He took her hands in his again. "It would be unseemly to take a gentlewoman into such a primitive area."

"But you don't know that for certain, do you? If you must go to join the militia at Alexandria, I beg you to find out exactly where Rose is. She was bought by that man Eustice. . .Eustice something. Smith, I believe it was. Eustice Smith. Please, Colin, would you do that for me?"

He smiled. "First thing, my love. I'll go to their headquarters again before I report for duty. Surely they know where she is by now."

At the despair evident in her expression, Colin drew her to him and held her close. "I'm so sorry. I love you so very, very much. Leaving you—even the thought of it—is like tearing my heart out."

"Mine, too," she murmured against his neck, her lips soft and moist.

He raised her beautiful sad face up and took possession of those luscious lips in a deep, wrenching kiss. How would he ever make himself walk out that door? But reality brought him back to earth. One thing that could never be bought was a man's honor. He had to go.

~~

Mariah paced the parlor floor, pausing every few minutes to look out the windows. Rain again. Would it never stop? It seemed the sky was weeping the tears she no longer possessed.

Two dreary, drizzly weeks had passed since the Barclays and Colin had left her in this big empty house alone. The family was to have been back in a week, but the foul weather must have delayed them. And Colin. . . Mr. Scott had expressed doubts that the militia would leave for the wilderness until the worst of the mountain snows had subsided. Small comfort, since wherever Colin was, he'd be out marching and drilling in this horrid weather. He could come down with lung fever and die. She shied away from the dreadful thought, unable to imagine an existence without him. At the same time, a tiny, shameful part of her worried on her own account. With Colin gone, her indenturement papers would belong to his parents, would they not? What would become of her then?

A gradual lessening of the heavy skies caused the room to lighten a bit, and Mariah moved to the window. Shafts of sunlight slanted through the clouds in the west. The storm must be coming to an end at last. She smiled. Perhaps she'd ride into Alexandria and check on Colin, make sure he was still in good health. He might have been able to learn something of Rose's whereabouts. Surely the rain would stop by the time she had a horse saddled. And she'd take some of Eloise's tastiest cooking along for him, as well.

Colin would be thrilled to see her; she was certain of that. She reached into the lace tucker in her bodice for the proof of his love and drew out the ring she wore hidden on a chain around her neck in case his family returned unexpectedly.

Turning from the window, she caught sight of a rider on the edge of her vision coming up the lane. Colin? *Please let it be him.* Perhaps he'd decided not to go with the militia after all. She tucked her ring back out of sight again.

But as the rider neared, she could tell it was someone else. With his hat pulled low against the rain, she couldn't make out the man's face. Dread cinched her heart. Was he the bearer of bad news?

She didn't wait for him to come to the door but snatched her cloak from the hall peg and tossed it about her shoulders as she hurried outside and down the steps. Before he even dismounted, she questioned him. "Have you come bearing news?"

"Actually, I have." He gave a nod. "I've some mail from Colin."

"You've seen him?" Hope sprang anew inside her being.

"Aye, at the militia encampment south of Alexandria. He's there with my son."

Suddenly Mariah remembered her manners. "La, please forgive me. Would you care to come inside out of the rain and have something warm to drink? You look drenched."

"That I am, miss." Swinging down to the ground, he shook rain from his slicker before following her up to the veranda. "I don't believe we've been introduced. I'm Albert Tucker, Dennis's father."

Now that she took a closer look, Mariah remembered seeing him at the gala on race day. Though considerably more heavy than his son, he did share the same hazel eyes and a smile reminiscent of Tuck's. "So pleased to meet you, sir. I'm Mariah Harwood, tutoress to Colin's sisters."

"Yes, I reckoned that. Dennis has often spoken kindly of you and how your tutorage has benefited the girls." He followed her inside.

"We find your son a very entertaining young gentleman," Mariah said, taking his rain slicker. "Do have a seat in the parlor. I'll go tell the cook we'll be needing refreshments."

Moments later, she found Mr. Tucker comfortably settled in a wing chair near the fire. He looked up with a smile as she approached. "Actually, I've come with several pieces of correspondence. Colin asked me to collect all the Barclay mail." He drew the items from an inside pocket of his frock coat.

"How kind of you." Mariah accepted the proffered missives and laid them on the side table, then took a seat across from him. Despite being intensely curious about the letters, she forced herself to give full attention to the visitor. "I assume Colin and Dennis are both well. I've been sorely tempted to ride into the city and check on them myself."

Mr. Tucker chuckled, then broke into full-blown laughter as he rested his hands on the full girth bulging at the buttons of his coat.

Mariah smiled politely while she waited for his humor to subside.

As his laughter died away, he wiped away some tears and took a shuddering breath. "My apologies, miss. It's just that every time I think of my son sloggin' through the mud, marchin' back and forth, back and forth, I can't help but laugh. He expected to be ridin' off on his trusty steed like some modern-day Lancelot to right all wrongs. It never dawned on him that in carryin' out his noble cause he might get dirty." He chuckled lightly again, then stifled it. "But the boy'll learn. My hope is that he'll come back a man ready to take up his responsibilities."

Mariah mulled over his words. "Did they, perchance, give you any idea of how long they'll be gone?"

"I'm afraid the boys don't know much at this point. But from what I gathered from a merchant friend of mine, most of the supplies the militia's been waitin' for have come in. I imagine they'll be leavin' soon."

"How long do you suppose they'll be out there?" Fearing the answer, she held her breath.

"That's hard to tell. Depends on how deeply entrenched the French have got themselves."

Mariah's spirits sank. "Are you saying they might be gone more than a month or two?" That was the amount of time Colin had figured the trouble would last.

He shrugged his shoulders and grimaced. "Don't be gettin' yourself all worked up, missy. The French are a long way down from Canada, and with a force of at least a thousand strung out for a couple hundred miles, that puts 'em a fair distance from their supplies. They should be runnin' out about now. It shouldn't take much to send 'em packin'."

Much as Mariah would have liked to believe that, doubts assailed her. "But wouldn't the Indians give them—"

Mr. Tucker wagged his graying head, his leather-bound queue brushing across his back. "We've got trade agreements with most of the Indians. They won't help the French. Now, stop your frettin'. And tell little Tori not to worry either. Worry causes lines in pretty faces."

Mariah detested being treated like a brainless twit. Nevertheless, she smiled while waiting for Pansy to bring in the tea tray. The sooner the man was served, the sooner he'd leave, and she'd be able to read the letter from Colin.

Another long, uncertain week crept by after reading Colin's disturbing note. According to him, Rose truly was deep in Indian country, but doing fine. . .or so the fur company proprietors had assured Colin, who considered the information further reason to remain with the militia. He vowed to rescue her sister if she was in danger. Mariah let out a weary sigh. Dear, brave Colin. Ever the hero.

Detecting a sound from outside, she rose from picking out a nonsensical tune on the harpsichord and meandered to the front window, where she spied the family's landau coming up the lane! "Thank heavens!" She slapped her hands together.

Then reality returned, and she wasn't sure whether to be glad or distressed. Having been in Baltimore these past weeks, they wouldn't know that Colin had come and gone. . .along with Victoria's Dennis Tucker. Possibly even Edward Rochester and the Fairchild lad who'd been coming to call. Hopefully someone along the road had informed the family of the trouble with the French so she wouldn't have to be the bearer of the unwelcome news.

She headed for the foyer to retrieve her cloak.

Benjamin came from the kitchen just then, wearing a happy grin. "Ah hears da carriage a-comin'. It's about time. We been lonesome aroun' here."

Always amazed at how much the slaves liked their masters—despite being owned by them—Mariah recalled that Geoffrey Scott had informed her that these slaves were Christians. Free in Christ, at least. She supposed that did take a measure of the sting away from being in bondage.

The tall African swung the door wide and stepped out to greet the arriving family and assist the women.

Mariah decided she could do no less.

Amy emerged first out the carriage door. "Mariah! We're home!"

She couldn't help laughing. "And so you are."

Victoria stepped down next. "Has my brother gotten home yet? Has Tuck come by asking for me? Or maybe Steven Fairchild?" She cast a furtive glance back at her mother, as if the third young man's name had been added to appease the woman.

Dread engulfed Mariah. The family knew nothing about the events taking place in the territory. "Let's get inside out of the cold, and I'll relay the latest happenings. First I'll go and tell Eloise you've come home."

"Yes, do that." Assisted by the butler, Mistress Barclay stepped gracefully down from the carriage. "If possible, we'd like an early supper. It's been a long and tiring day. Tell Eloise nothing special. Whatever's handy will do."

"Oh, and welcome home," Mariah remembered to say. "We've missed you." As she ran up the steps, she realized she actually meant those words. She truly had missed them—all of them—even the regal lady of the manor.

By the time she and Lizzie returned with a tea tray and a platter of small tea cakes and cookies, they found the weary family lounging in the parlor while Benjamin and the driver carted the luggage into the foyer. There was no sense of alarm among the group, so obviously Benjamin hadn't mentioned anything about Colin while she'd been in the kitchen.

Lizzie set the tea tray on the table and quietly took her leave. Mariah placed the cookies and cakes alongside. "Shall I pour?"

"Yes, please do." The mistress fanned herself with a handkerchief. "It's been a long, bumpy ride."

"Has there been word as yet from Colin?" Mr. Barclay sat down next to his wife. "Since we were delayed so long in Baltimore, we surmised he'd be here by now to greet us."

Just about to take her seat near the tea service, Mariah opted to remain standing. "Your son did, in fact, return home, sir. Three weeks ago. However, I'm sorry to report he was summoned to report for militia duty that same day."

"You're not serious!" His dark brows hiked high.

Mariah nodded. "Mr. Scott rode into Alexandria yesterday to check on them, and he was told the militia left for the Ohio Valley the previous day."

"They did what?" Teacups rattled on the tray as Colin's mother lunged forward. "Are you telling us that Colin left with the militia?"

"I'm afraid so, madam. He said he was duty bound to go with the militia and rout the French out of Virginia's western territory."

Mistress Barclay swung to her husband, a frantic expression contorting her face. "Eldon, you must go and fetch him home. He could get killed."

"Colin's gonna get killed?" Amy sprang to her feet.

Her mother turned toward the girls. "Go upstairs and change for dinner. At once."

"But Mama!" Victoria protested.

"Now." The mistress flicked a hand toward the door. "We'll talk later, after we've heard all the details and have sorted them out."

Watching the trio as they obeyed their mother, Mariah wished with every fiber of her being that she was going with them.

"Eldon, you must do something." Twisting her handkerchief into a tight, untidy knot, Mistress Barclay swung her troubled gaze back to him.

"There's nothing to be done, Cora, my dear. Colin has been on the militia roster since he turned sixteen. Surely you know that."

"But it never meant anything," she countered. "Just a bunch of young men strutting around the parade ground. Not leaving home and going off to start a war."

He let out an exasperated breath. "Well, it means something now, I'm afraid. We've heard the reports about the French moving into English territory. It was only a matter of time until something had to be done about it. Call the girls back, and let's have our tea. Mariah, would you pour now?"

"Surely, sir." The worst was over. Emitting a tiny whoosh of relief, Mariah sat down and picked up the teapot.

Suddenly Colin's mother shot a glare her way. "Why didn't you stop him?" She grabbed Mariah's hand. "You're such a clever girl, and he's so taken with you. I'm sure you could have used your feminine wiles to stop him from leaving."

Stung by the woman's vile insinuation, Mariah barely managed to set the hot china pot down before dropping it. "I tried, Mistress Barclay. I begged him not to go. Truly I did. But he insisted he had to go, that he was obligated. He would not be dissuaded."

The woman came to her feet and loomed over Mariah, her face

twisted, her hand raised, poised for a resounding slap. "You could have stopped him. You know you could have. If he gets killed it will be on your head. On your head! I want you out of my sight. Now!" She jabbed a manicured finger toward the door.

Chapter 21

Mariah's stomach roiled. She stared at the supper Pansy sent up to her room that evening after Cora Barclay's callous outburst. To think that after being so happy to have the family back home at last, she had been treated with such viciousness by her mistress. The woman had all but snarled as she berated Mariah for not preventing Colin from reporting to the militia. Why, a person would think she'd encouraged him to leave, when in truth, she'd begged him to stay.

Even more disturbing, his mother actually insinuated that Mariah should have used her womanly charms to induce him to remain at home—to sacrifice her greatest asset, her innocence. Highly unchristian of Mistress Barclay, indeed. Mariah grimaced.

Neither had the tirade been characteristic of the woman. Because of the grand hopes she held for her son, she had not been thrilled by an outsider's sudden presence in the household. Nevertheless, the mistress had heretofore treated Mariah with courtesy during her stay. She'd never been mean-spirited. Leaving the tray of food untouched, Mariah changed into her night shift and climbed into bed, even though she knew she'd face a restless night with little sleep.

Rising early the next morning, Mariah tiptoed through Amy's room without disturbing the sleeping child. Steeling herself to face her mistress—hopefully without an audience—she descended quietly. But inside she wondered if she was to be tossed out into the cold with no place to go until Colin returned.

At the bottom landing, she ran her fingers across her hidden amethyst ring. Perhaps if worse came to worse, and she was left to fend for herself, she might be able to sell a day gown or two to tide her over for a while. She still had more than two pounds sterling in her possession. Only as a last resort would she consider selling the beautiful ring.

She scarcely noticed the heat from the blazing fire while she traversed the parlor on her way to confront Colin's mother. The slight clatter of china drifted to her ears from the dining room. Upon entering, she saw to her dismay that both elder Barclays sat at breakfast.

Mr. Barclay stood to his feet at once, wiping his mouth with his napkin. "Good morning, child. I'd love to stay and chat, but alas, I have a full day ahead of me after having been gone so long." Then, coward that he was, he made a hasty retreat before Mariah had the presence of mind to answer.

She held her breath and flicked a swift glance at his wife.

"Do fill your plate and come sit down. I have something to say." The woman's tone was suspiciously pleasant, but Mariah wasn't sure if she'd caught a hint of warmth in those sable eyes.

About what? Mariah was sorely tempted to rail at her. *That shrewish mouth of yours?* But she refused to allow herself to act in a manner as unladylike as the uppity woman had displayed last night.

Despite not having eaten the previous evening, Mariah had little appetite. She chose a small serving of fruit and a buttered biscuit, then poured some tea and carried the items to the table, making certain an empty chair separated her from Mistress Barclay. She made a point of folding her hands and bowing her head in silent prayer. *Father in heaven, help me to swallow down this food, and help me not to let her get the best of me. In Jesus' name. Amen.* She raised her head.

Colin's mother set down her teacup. "Mariah, dear, I am. . .dreadfully sorry for my outburst yesterday. It was thoughtless and cruel. I should never have uttered such unkind words. I was overtired from our journey and not prepared to hear that we'd missed our son's arrival and departure. Nevertheless, I should not have taken it out on you. I hope you can find it in your heart to forgive me."

Realizing her mouth had fallen open, Mariah closed it and raised her tea to her lips, hoping to block some of her surprise.

The mistress continued. "Colin has always been extremely stubborn when he believes he's right. And as his father reminded me repeatedly, our son truly was obligated to report for duty." She smiled and reached across the space between them, catching Mariah's hand. "I beg you to forgive me for my ghastly behavior. . .please."

Something about the way her ladyship looked at her combined with that tender touch of her hand brought sudden moisture to Mariah's eyes. Until this moment she hadn't realized how starved she'd been for a bit of motherly affection. "I—I—" Her throat closed up as she fought against an emotional display. But try as she might, she was powerless to stop the unexpected rush of tears. "I'm—Excuse me," she blubbered between gasps as she blindly lurched up from her seat. "I—"

Mistress Barclay got up just as quickly. Coming to her side she drew Mariah close and patted her back. "No, dear. I'm the sorry one. I've been so obsessed with the notion of you spoiling my plans for my son, I haven't considered you and all you've gone through since leaving your home in England." She leaned back slightly and brushed aside a lock of hair from Mariah's face. "You truly are a beautiful and talented young lady, and from now on, I plan to make more of an effort to see that you're treated as such."

Desperately trying to get her embarrassing sobs under control, Mariah couldn't believe what she was hearing. Had Colin's mother implied she would champion her? Inhaling a ragged breath, she stepped back, wiping her eyes as she attempted a grateful smile. "I'm better now. I don't know what came over me." With a small, self-conscious shrug, she returned to her seat, and the mistress did the same.

A quiet moment passed while Mariah fortified herself with a sip of tea. Setting down her cup, she met the older woman's eyes. "Colin told me he was able to visit Bath while he was in England, and he brought me news of my family. I suppose it made me a bit lonesome for them, and a little homesick. I miss their gestures of affection. When you took my hand, I—" Another wave of feeling swamped her, and she drew another breath and fought off a new onslaught of tears. "Anyway, Colin accompanied my father to see a barrister about recovering the large sum he's owed. He feels quite confident that Papa will be reimbursed."

"I'm very pleased for you and your family." Though spoken kindly, some of the warmth was missing from Mistress Barclay's expression. "Colin went to call on your father, you say."

Mariah sensed that the woman's suspicions had again been aroused. "He did it as a favor for my sisters and me. I asked him to check on the welfare of my family if he happened to travel in the vicinity. My father was so very distressed when we departed last spring, I feared for his health."

The mistress gave a thoughtful nod. "Of course, that son of ours would do no less, I'm sure." She paused and her smile returned. "Speaking of being distressed, I suppose Dennis Tucker also went off with the militia."

"Yes, madam, he did. In fact, he's the one who came for Colin after Colin had barely arrived."

"Well, I can't say I'm sad that Dennis won't be around to turn Victoria's head for a while. Perhaps Edward will have a better chance now of charming her. Or did he report, as well?"

"I'm afraid that's something I do not know. But Victoria will likely be upset, regardless. She's so enjoyed all the attention the young men have paid her these past months." Mariah nibbled a bit of her biscuit.

"She has, hasn't she?" The woman's lips slid into an easy motherly grin as she took another sip from her cup. "My sweet baby girl is growing up. And Mariah, dear, I must not forget you. You've been doing such a wonderful job tutoring her and our other daughters also. Even Amy is beginning to act like a proper girl on occasion."

Mariah had to smile. "Thank you. Those girls are such dears that—"

"That's it!" Mistress Barclay clapped her hands together. "I have a wonderful idea. You deserve a special treat. And since our young men have traipsed off on their grand adventure, we should go on an adventure of our own. We'll take a coastal packet down to Williamsburg to see a play or two. That's sure to give Victoria something to think about other than her beaus. Besides—" She quirked a brow. "They have the most marvelous shops there."

Mariah was astounded that Colin's mother could act so nonchalant today after her violent reaction the previous evening. "But. . .shouldn't we wait here for news from the militia?"

Cora Barclay sent her a motherly look. "Not to worry, my dear. Eldon has assured me that the men won't even attempt to contact the French until after the spring thaw. For now they shall merely be getting into position and fortifying things. We've plenty of time."

My, how her fortune had changed since she arose this morning. Mariah glanced at her plate and noticed how much more appealing the food looked. She realized she was ravenously hungry. She picked up her spoon and dipped into the fruit. "Victoria has told me that Williamsburg is a lovely, genteel city. I would be thrilled to go on this little adventure with you."

From the deck railing of the coastal packet, Mariah gazed ashore at the busy wharf with its large warehouses and beyond to the higher ground that housed the sprawling settlement of Williamsburg. She turned to offer Mistress Barclay and the two older girls an excited grin. They'd arrived at last.

Though they'd all been eager to embark on the jaunt to the capital, three long weeks of bad weather had delayed their departure—stormy weeks that Colin had likely spent traveling into the backcountry. But as his mother had remarked often enough, her son had made the choice himself to go with the militia in the winter. Perhaps a bit of hardship would bring him home all the sooner. At least she could hope for that.

Refusing to dwell on the fact that Colin had once again left her to fend for herself, Mariah returned her attention to the activity on the waterfront, watching the burly dockworkers loading and unloading cargo from various vessels in the port.

Victoria moved up beside her mother as the gangplank was lowered to the dock. "Why can't we visit a few shops and show Mariah around town before we go to the Everards' house? You and Mistress Everard will spend hours and hours catching up on the latest happenings while we're forced to entertain those little girls of hers. That will be as tiresome as having Amy along, especially when Heather, Mariah, and I could be truly enjoying ourselves strolling about the shops."

Ambling toward the ship's gate, the older woman shot her daughter a stern glower. "And just what would my friend Diana think when our luggage arrived without us? I wouldn't think of being so rude, and neither should you. Besides, I've been wanting to see her and Thomas's new home since they moved in."

Heather, on her other side, spoke up. "You're absolutely right, Mama. I can't wait to surprise Francis and Martha with how well I've learned to play the flute and violin in a mere nine months."

Nine months! Had it really been that long? Following behind the threesome, Mariah sighed. Nine months since she'd come to live with the Barclays, and she had yet to wed Colin. The better part of a year as a bond servant, and she could see no end in sight. Yet her sister who'd been sent deep into the wilderness had managed not only to return to civilization a free woman, but marry. *Rose, married!* Mariah couldn't help but fight tears every time she recalled her sister's words in the letter that had arrived last week. Her rather plain, spinster sister had wed before *she*—the beauty of the family. And all because Colin cared more about promoting his honor than he cared about her.

Victoria slowed to join Mariah as her mother and sister strolled down the gangplank. She leaned close. "It's been two whole months since Tuck and Edward left to train with the militia, too," she murmured softly, then raised her voice to a normal level. "One thing is certain. If I happen to meet some handsome gentlemen who desire to spend time in my company, I shall not discourage them. In fact, I'd welcome thoughtful young men who refrain from leaving their ladies behind so they can go

SALLY LAITY AND DIANNA CRAWFORD

off to shoot at Frenchmen. What a useless pursuit."

Mariah had to smile. Perhaps Tori had the right idea. In this port no one knew Mariah was a bond servant. How tempting it would be to allow her own gaze to wander a little. Just then, a breeze off the water toyed with her light cloak. As she gathered the edges together, her hand brushed over the amethyst hidden on the chain beneath her lace tucker, proof of Colin's offer of marriage. She might not have the ring on her finger yet, but Colin was a far more desirable catch than that poor, woodsy frontiersman Rose had wed. Mayhap it would be best to wait a little longer. After all, he did happen to be the proverbial bird in the hand, if he'd only stop flying off all the time.

"Bolts of fabric from Paris!" a hawker shouted, dodging a loaded wagon and team rumbling across the wharf toward the business district. "Unloaded today! See them at the millinery shop!"

"Did you hear that, Mama?" Victoria all but ran down the gangplank. "Paris fabrics!"

Tucking her chin and elevating her brows, her mother caught hold of Tori's arm and drew her alongside. "Do remember you're a lady, Victoria. As soon as I hire a conveyance to take us, along with Lizzie and our luggage to the Everards', we shall be the gracious guests I know we can be. There will be ample time for shopping later."

"And lots of time to go to the theater, too." Heather's blue eyes sparkled.

Mariah understood the girl's reasoning. Musicians would be there to accompany the players. Just thinking about the possibilities ahead, her own excitement stirred. Why should she not enjoy herself while she visited the city with this wealthy family? Although she'd lived in Bath as a tradesman's daughter, most of the glamour and excitement of the resort had been reserved for members of the aristocracy. Here in Williamsburg with the Barclays, she could move in the best circles of the fledgling society—as long as no one found out she was a servant. For this week, at least, she truly belonged in the family. She threaded her arm through Victoria's as they approached a carriage for hire.

A gentle breeze stirred through trees just beginning to bud and leaf out on this gloriously mild day of April's second week. Overhead, in a sky of brilliant blue, puffy clouds floated lazily across the broad expanse. As the aged horse pulling the carriage clopped along Williamsburg's wide, packed-clay streets, Mariah turned her head this way and that, admiring the town's neat weatherboard houses with their broad-based chimneys. Many larger residences were made of brick and sat amid formal gardens that soon would burst forth in full glory. Surely that would be a sight to behold. Already the season's first brave flowers peeked out of the dark ground here and there, bobbing their bright yellow, white, and purple heads.

Beside her, Victoria sat in speechless anticipation, ogling every display window in the array of shops they passed. It would be hard to keep up with the girl once Mistress Barclay turned her loose. Smiling to herself, Mariah filled her lungs with the fresh breath of spring. This truly would be a grand adventure.

Chapter 22

Who'd have thought George Washington would have the audacity to order the military to travel in this miserable weather?" Tuck shook his head, and rain dripped from all three corners of his cocked hat. "It's takin' weeks."

Riding beside his friend as they headed for the Wills Creek Station, the first in a string of trading posts stretching all the way to the Ohio Valley, Colin chuckled and tugged his heavy wool cape closer. "Just be glad we're not walkin' in this muck like most of the other boys." He glanced back at the nearly three hundred men trudging up a trail heavily wooded on either side. Two loaded wagons lumbered slowly along, spitting mud at the grim-faced militiamen slogging along behind. A small herd of cattle churned through at the rear.

At least they were moving. Several times on the trip, the teams of horses had been unable to pull the wagons up a steep hill, and the men had to unload the crates and sacks and lug the supplies up through the slick mire themselves. With heavy rain and sleet hindering their progress, the group was making very poor time in reaching a post less than 150 miles from Alexandria.

Colin looked ahead, where George Washington rode at the front of the column. George expected his men to arrive at the trading post within the hour and rest there for a few days. Thank heaven.

Tuck edged his chestnut mount closer to Colin's and muttered a comment he'd made at least half a dozen times already. "The French enjoy their creature comforts far too much to be out in this freezing mess, you know." He exhaled a frosty breath. "I don't think George should've been put in charge of this expedition. He's too young, and we both know it."

Colin gave a nonchalant shrug. "Perhaps. But he does have some experience, at least. He's been comin' out here for the last three or four years surveyin'. If nothin' else, he knows the area. We don't. He also knows where the French are. He's even parlayed with 'em."

"And let us not forget," Tuck grumbled, "he's a particular friend of Lord Fairfax—"

"Who has Governor Dinwiddie's ear." Colin checked to make sure the men behind them weren't eavesdropping, then turned forward again.

"So." Tuck swiped a droplet off his nose. "He gets to decide that the rest of us catch our death out here in the elements. I should've stayed home. With everybody else gone, I would've had a clear field with lovely little Tori."

Colin narrowed his gaze. "No, you wouldn't. You wouldn't be alone with her. I'd be there to keep an eye on you."

"Ha! Like your mother watched you when you were sniffin' around your Mariah?"

My Mariah. So easily Colin's mind filled with thoughts of his English beauty, recalling the expressive violet eyes that stole his breath, the sound of her soothing voice. . . .

Tuck snorted. "You're far worse than me, old man. When it comes to a winsome belle, you end up talkin' out of both sides of your mouth."

"You're right." Colin couldn't help the sappy grin that quirked his lips. "But then, you were no better when it came to your older sister Trudie, as I recall."

Tuck's laugh met a swift end as he stopped and stared toward the front of the line.

A rider approached.

"I wonder who that could be." Colin heeled his mottled gray horse, Storm, forward and veered around the few rows of militia separating him from the front.

Tuck followed suit.

The burly rider reached Washington at the same time Colin and Tuck did. Soaked and muddy as his panting horse, he rendered a sloppy salute. "Sir, thank God you've come. The last of our men are just now stragglin' into Wills Creek Station."

"What men?" Washington's pocked face was stone rigid. "I was told the British regulars wouldn't arrive for another week or so."

"I don't know nothin' about that, sir. I'm with Lieutenant Trent. We was overrun by the French."

"I assume you're speaking of William Trent, are you not?" Frowning, George guided his mount closer to the newcomer.

"Yessir, I am. But he wasn't there when they come upon us. The first lieutenant left to get more supplies. Ensign Ward was in charge."

"And you say the French attacked you. Where was that, exactly?"

The man shook his head. "They *didn't* attack us, exactly. They come from upriver. Hundreds of 'em, in bateaux and canoes. And they brung cannons. I counted eighteen, myself. They had 'em all lined up, pointin' right at us."

Colin exchanged glances with Tuck. The French weren't holed up taking it easy during the winter weather after all. They'd gone down an ice-cluttered river, ready for battle. With cannons, no less. Definitely not good news.

"Sir," the bearded messenger continued, "there was only forty-one of us, an' our fort weren't near finished. Anyways, them Frenchies told us they wouldn't do us no harm iffen we'd leave and never come back. So you see, sir, we didn't have no choice."

Appearing to mull the information over briefly, Washington nodded with a calmness that surprised Colin. "Has Lieutenant Trent rejoined you?"

"Yessir. We met up on the trail. A good thing, too, 'cause we was gettin' a mite hungry, us bein' short of food, an' all."

Washington gave him another polite nod. "Well, thank you for informing me of the situation. Ride on back and inform your superiors we will be there shortly."

As the hefty militiaman snapped a salute and rode away, George turned to Colin, looking every inch the confident leader. "The French have taken the fort Lieutenant Trent was building where the Allegheny from the north and the Monongahela from the south join and become the Ohio River." He frowned and shook his head. "It's the most strategic location on the frontier. Whoever controls that spot controls all the waterways. It's vital that we take it back."

"Thomas Everard is a gentleman of standing here in Williamsburg," Mrs. Barclay remarked as the carriage drew up before a wood-framed townhome somewhat more modest, but no less charming, than some of the elegant mansions they'd passed. "He's the clerk of the General Court, you know."

Captivated momentarily by the sight of the Governor's Palace sitting like a jewel at the northern end of the broad street, Mariah nodded politely and returned her attention to the gable-roofed dwelling kitty-corner to it where they'd be staying during their visit. In all likelihood, it would contain furnishings as fine as any possessed by the Barclay family and their other affluent friends. She followed the family up the brick walkway to the front door, while Lizzie remained with the luggage.

The fashionably attired matron of the house rushed forth the moment the servant ushered the party inside. Tall and slender of bearing, she looked to be several years younger than Mistress Barclay. "Cora, Cora. I am so glad you've arrived. I've been on tenterhooks awaiting your visit ever since I received your letter."

As the women gushed their greetings to each other, Mariah's eyes drank in the richness of the central hall with its wainscoting and a fine staircase with elaborately turned balusters and sweeping handrails. The step brackets were richly ornamented with intricate carvings. Large urns positioned on cherrywood pedestals overflowed with fresh flowers emitting a heady fragrance into the air.

"Why, you're as beautiful as ever, I vow," Mistress Everard breathed. "And this can't be little Victoria, all grown up and so pretty." She released Mistress Barclay and took Tori's hands then reached for Heather. "And you, my dear, must have grown at least five inches since last we saw you."

"I can play the flute and violin now, too." Heather never missed an opportunity to mention her new talent.

"Oh my." The mistress placed a hand to her bosom. "How wonderful. You must play something for us later."

Just as the woman was about to turn to Mariah, what sounded like a herd of horses on the floor above came galloping toward the staircase. Down came two young girls, ruffles and lace billowing and bouncing, their sausage curls flying out. "Amy! Heather!" one of them called.

"Girls! Do calm yourselves!" A bit flustered, their mother turned back to her guests with a puzzled expression on her exquisite features. "Where is our darling Amy? I don't see her."

"I'm afraid Amy wasn't up to traveling aboard the packet, Diana," Mistress Barclay explained. "She's been having trouble with an upset stomach of late."

Mariah darted a glance to Tori and Heather to make sure they didn't blurt out the truth—that their little sister would rather sleep out in the stable with the horses than go shopping and attend plays, much less put up with what she considered silly, giggly, little girls.

The lady of the house shook her elegantly coifed head, her shining dark curls reflecting light from wall sconces. "How unfortunate. Francis and Martha were so looking forward to seeing her."

The joy on the faces of the young sisters wilted, and the older one, who appeared about seven, let out a whine. "Amy's not here? But I drew her a really pretty picture."

Her mother cupped her chin. "Darling, I'm sure Victoria and Heather would love to see your picture."

The youngest one, possibly five years of age, piped up. "Mine, too."

"Of course, sweetheart." Mistress Everard turned to the Barclay girls. "Would you mind going upstairs with my daughters? They've been working on a surprise for you girls since we received word you were coming."

"Of course not." Victoria's enthusiastic tone did not match her frozen smile as she cut a sidelong glance at her sister. "We'd love to, wouldn't we, Heather?" Snatching her sister's hand, she headed for the staircase and trailed up the steps after the giggling youngsters.

As the noisy group took their leave, the mistress turned back to Mariah. "And who is this attractive young lady you've brought with you, Cora?"

"La, forgive me, Diana. I should have introduced you." Mistress Barclay smiled at Mariah. "She's our private tutoress. We wanted someone a touch more educated and sophisticated for our girls than was offered at Miss Bridgestone's Academy. I'm most pleased to introduce Miss Mariah Harwood, from Bath, England. She's not only a wonderful instructress in all the womanly arts, but she's also an accomplished musician—much to our Heather's delight."

"Oh my." The young matron dropped into a quick curtsy. "I'm so pleased to meet you."

Mariah returned the curtsy. "And I you." If she didn't know better, she'd think wealthy Mistress Barclay was putting on airs for the wife of a clerk, bestowing such lavish compliments. But from the look of this fine home, especially in this colony, it was natural that a man in the governor's employ would be held in high esteem. Now, it seemed, so was she—so long as there was no mention of her being a bondwoman. Mariah highly doubted her mistress would divulge that. A smile tickled the corners of her lips.

"Oh dear, do forgive my lack of manners. Please join me in the parlor for refreshments." The hostess swept a graceful hand toward an open doorway, then turned to the uniformed slave who had let them in. "Gladden, would you see that tea is served right away?"

As they ambled into another front room with paneled wainscoting, Mistress Everard came to Mariah's side. "I've always longed to visit

England. My husband is from London, and he's promised to take me there one day. And I do so want to visit Bath while we're there. But before I ask you a thousand questions, I must catch my dear Cora up on the latest." She turned to her. "Cora, you are simply not going to believe this. . . ."

━━

If Mariah had been acquainted with any of the individuals mentioned in an animated stream of who did this, who went where, and with whom, perhaps listening to the two matrons seated together on a burgundy-and-ivory-striped settee wouldn't have been so tedious. She'd all but memorized the delicate porcelain figurines on the walnut mantel, the gold-framed mirror above, and the red window hangings that appeared to be some sort of rich wool.

A sudden burst of flute playing came from the stairwell, evidence that the luggage must have been taken to the upper floor. But the music ceased as suddenly as it began, as if a door had opened and then closed. Then hurried footsteps came down the stairs and tapped across the floor of the great hall. Perhaps the women would stop their infernal gossiping as if Mariah weren't even there.

Victoria swept through the parlor entrance. "Excuse me, Mother, but you absolutely must let me go to the shops to find another pair of gloves. The ones that go with my sapphire evening gown are not among my things."

Her mother sent her a condescending look. "Dearest girl, I'm sure you're mistaken. You took such great pains in laying out all your accessories."

"I know." Her expression turned woeful. "I can't imagine how I forgot them. Please, Mama. I simply cannot wear mismatched gloves."

Since she'd seen Tori place those gloves into her trunk, Mariah knew the girl was not being truthful. But she wasn't about to say anything that would cause strife between herself and the sister of her betrothed.

Mistress Barclay drew a deep breath. "You are quite certain you didn't bring them?"

"Yes. I looked and looked."

"But we've only just arrived, dear. Diana and I are having such a nice chat."

"No need to interrupt your visit. Mariah could go with me." Victoria swung a hopeful glance to where Mariah sat across from the matrons. "You wouldn't mind terribly, would you?"

"No, not at all." She rose. "A walk would be refreshing after that long journey aboard ship."

Her mother swung a slightly suspicious glance between the two of them. "Very well. But be back in plenty of time to dress for dinner. We shouldn't want to look shoddy for the secretary to the governor, now, should we?"

"Of course not, Mother." Tori reached for Mariah's hand.

"Do you have enough money with you?"

"Yes, Mother. Thank you." She tugged Mariah toward the entrance.

"That girl," Mariah overheard the mistress comment as Victoria ushered her to the front door. "She may think she's matured, but she acts the silly, thoughtless child at times."

Moonstruck would be more like it, Mariah reasoned as she accompanied Tori out into the lovely spring afternoon.

They set a fast pace in the direction of Market Square.

"Thank you for rescuing me."

Victoria laughed. "Rescuing both of us. What with Heather's shrill flute playing and the little girls' screaming, I just had to get out of there." She caught Mariah's hand and slowed her pace as she leaned close. "Look ahead. Two handsome young men are peering into that apothecary window." Straightening her shoulders, she toyed with a curl dangling by her ear and hiked her chin as if she planned to ignore them.

Mariah knew it was merely a ploy to get their attention. She'd taught Tori that trick herself.

And of course it worked. Before the two of them reached the finely attired young men, they'd turned to stare.

The bolder of the two, slim, with light brown hair and eyes, grinned and tipped his cocked hat as he stepped into Victoria's path. "Good afternoon, lovely ladies. Or should I say, the loveliest young maidens ever to grace our fair city."

Completely disregarding all that Mariah had taught her, Tori giggled and extended a hand. "Why, what a gallant thing to say."

"But quite true." The other young man, lanky and somewhat taller, with russet hair and green eyes, bowed before Mariah and reached for her hand.

"Excuse me. I don't believe we've been properly introduced." Though said as a proper chaperone should, her smile betrayed her good intentions.

The first fellow, still holding Victoria's hand, spoke up. "If you two are attending the play tomorrow evening, I'm sure I can arrange a proper introduction then. In the meantime, for convenience's sake, I'm Willard Dunn, son of Dr. Arliss Dunn, physician to our honorable governor. And my friend is Ronnie—"

"Ronald Sedley," his pal corrected, puffing out his chest. "My father is in shipping, out of Yorktown."

"How lovely." Victoria practically meowed. "I'm afraid our family merely farms and raises Thoroughbred horses. I'm Victoria Barclay, of Barclay Bay Plantation, near Alexandria. Perhaps you've heard of it? Oh, and this is our Mariah."

The words *plantation* and *Thoroughbred* seemed to impress them.

As both men again bowed, Mariah realized that Victoria had included her in the family. She decided not to correct her. "We're very pleased to meet you, but we really must be on our way. We have some purchases to make for the play tomorrow evening." She withdrew her hand as the pair continued to stare. "We'll be most pleased for a proper introduction then." She took Victoria's arm and prodded her onward.

The girl glanced back and waved. "Tomorrow eve. . ."

After they'd gotten far enough away, Tori turned to her. "Why did you do that? They were so handsome and—"

"I agree. However, we know nothing about them, and a small bit of encouragement is sufficient until we do."

"But they just told us—"

"And everything they said could have been lies. That is why a proper introduction is always vital. They know it just as well as we do."

"Fine!" With a huff, Tori jerked her arm free. "Well, what I do know is that those attentive gentlemen saw no need to go riding out into the wilderness, leaving me with nothing to do but twiddle my thumbs."

The last words struck hard. Mariah hadn't been twiddling her thumbs for a mere few weeks. Colin had been gone for months, only to return for less than an hour before he was off again.

"I'm gonna flirt with every good-lookin' bachelor I see while we're here," Victoria drawled as she increased the pace. "Mayhap I'll find a beau or two willin' to come visit me at the plantation. Isn't Mother always wantin' me to marry a merchant's son? Well, I just might give that Mr. Sedley some extra attention."

The girl was proving to be quite headstrong. Thank goodness, Mistress Barclay would accompany them to the play. Mariah changed the subject. "There's that millinery shop the hawker at the wharf said had a shipment of fabrics. They might have gloves as well." She pointed to a tidy wooden building just ahead that held a display of feminine accessories in its window.

"You know very well that I don't need gloves."

"True. But we'd better not return without some. I, for one, wish to remain in your mother's good graces."

Never had she uttered truer words. Mistress Barclay could very well become her mother-in-law before the end of summer. And though Mariah had never been known for her patience, she had to remain true to Colin while she awaited his return. *Please, Lord, bring Colin home soon.*

Mariah wasn't sure how much longer her patience would stay her. Those obviously prosperous young men were entirely too tempting.

Chapter 23

Rubbing the stubble on his face, Colin promised himself he would shave in the morning. He wagged his head with a smile. If his mother could only see how lax he'd become with his grooming. He'd managed but a quick wash before supper with nothing more than a small piece of soap. Considering he still wore the same clothing he'd had on when they slogged through all the mud on their way here, no less than a full bath and a change of attire would make him feel human again.

Colin rose from where he'd stooped at the upper end of a small brook that sliced through the large, oval-shaped meadow. He could easily see why the Indians had named it Great Meadows. A gentle evening breeze feathered across his face as he left the small spring behind, reminding him how grateful he was that the weather had finally turned warm. Starting toward the large ring of campfires and makeshift tents, he viewed the setting sun as it crowned the surrounding pines with gold. Not a single dreary cloud in sight.

He calculated that it must be sometime past the middle of May. Surely by now, Mariah had received the letter he'd left at Wills Creek

Station. It would have been sent out with the first dispatch rider going back to civilization. As so many times before, Colin was overwhelmed once again with a deep yearning. *Mariah. My beautiful Mariah. We've had so little time together. So little. . .*

He heaved a woeful sigh as he passed by the herd of horses, hobbled and quietly grazing. Finding Storm among them, he was pleased that the Thoroughbred he'd ridden from home had managed the rigors of the rugged wilderness so well, especially since the mottled gray was a more delicately boned breed of horse. But then, Paladin, whom he'd sold on his trip, had more than proved the breed's stamina that marvelous day Colin had held Mariah close all the way home from Baltimore—the day he'd fallen hopelessly, helplessly in love. Even after all this time, echoes of her delightful, sparkling laughter rang in his memory. How he wished he could hear it now, on this waning, lonely evening. He missed her so much, his insides ached.

A number of the horses jerked their heads up from the grass. Ears flicking, the herd turned their necks in the direction of the dark woods to the west. Several cows just beyond them mooed low.

Closing his hand around his revolver and drawing the weapon from its holster, Colin tried to peer past the animals. He wheeled to face the camp and raised the firearm high, waving it back and forth until he caught the attention of several of the men.

His heart pounded as he crouched and moved swiftly toward the animals, his only cover in this open space. Waiting and listening, he hoped the other men had remembered to prime their flashpans, then breathed easier, recalling that everyone kept their weapons loaded and ready since Trent's men had met them at Wills Creek Station.

No unusual sound came to his ears, but several of the horses remained alert and uneasy. Something—or someone—was out there. Bear, mountain cat. . .or the French?

Movement in the deep shadows produced an Indian wearing only a loincloth and leather leggings that reached halfway up his thighs. A musket dangled from his hand as, glistening with sweat and breathing heavily, he jogged past the horses.

A minute passed. Then two. No other Indians appeared. Not ready to trust that the man was alone, Colin remained hidden, his gun propped on the back of a sturdy quarter horse and aimed in the direction from which the Indian had come. When no other sounds came from the woods, Colin noticed the horses grazed placidly once again. He glanced back at the encampment and spotted the Indian walking with Washington toward the colonel's tent. Obviously the ruddy man had come with a message.

Colin holstered his pistol and ran across the field for the tent, his curiosity piqued. Was the news good? Or bad?

Approaching the command tent, he noticed a number of enlisted militia milling about outside. Obviously they were as curious as he to learn why the Indian brave had arrived with such haste. Upon entering the sailcloth enclosure, Colin saw that Tuck and the other officers had all gathered inside. The Indian stood next to the colonel.

Washington spied Colin and addressed him in his usual formal manner. "Lieutenant Barclay. Thank you for your vigilance."

Colin nodded acknowledgment of the compliment, though he was more interested in what the Indian had come to report.

"Gentlemen." Washington swept a glance around at the officers. "Our visitor comes from our good ally, the great Chief Monakaduto of the Seneca people. Some of you might know him as Half King. I shall allow his messenger to speak the words of Chief Monakaduto."

He then nodded to the sinewy brown-skinned man. Fully armed with a knife and hatchet tucked in belted and beaded sheaths, the Indian held his musket like a staff. His head was shaved except for a braided hank of top hair adorned with beads similar to the numerous ones decorating his moccasins, an armband, and earrings. The man made a striking picture.

"I come from great Chief Monakaduto," he spoke in halting English. "He say French warriors come. They come quiet like the fox. This many." He spread his fingers and thrust them forth three times, then held up four fingers. Thirty-four. "Chief Monakaduto say you come. Chief and Seneca warriors take you. Make war on enemy."

Dennis Tucker gave a huff under his breath. "Thirty-four. That ain't so many. Surely they don't plan on takin' on all of us."

Washington pierced him with a withering glare. "Most likely they've been sent to spy on us, discover the size of our force and what weaponry we have."

Compared to the strength of the French force that took the fort from Trent's men, Colin knew their militia made up a rather pitiful adversary. However, they were supposed to be joined any day by a Colonel Fry, with a regiment of regular British soldiers and a few pieces of field artillery. So far there'd been no word from them.

"It's vital we intercept this party before they reach our camp." Washington swept a gaze over his officers. "Each of you pick ten of your best men to accompany me. Captain Trent, I'm putting you in charge here while I'm gone."

Trent, a seasoned frontiersman, grunted. "You sure, Colonel?"

"Yes. You'll know what to do."

Colin considered that oblique statement a touch ominous, but he also knew Trent would take extra care after having lost the Ohio River fort to the French.

"Barclay." Washington turned his pockmarked face to Colin, his eyes serious. "You shall come with me as my second-in-command."

The men who would accompany Washington had a bite to eat and gathered their supplies, but it wasn't until after ten that night that they left camp. Colin noted with disgust that not a star was visible. Heavy clouds again blanketed the sky, casting the party into thick darkness that grew even blacker as they entered the woods behind the Indian guide. Not a single torch would be permitted this night.

The Seneca, who called himself something like Sequahee, set a fast pace, forcing the men to jog in order to keep up with him on a trace so narrow and overgrown they had to travel single file in silence, with no torches, and no mounts for the officers.

Running behind Washington, Colin noticed within minutes that the men in back of him had begun to slow. He paused to let his winded friend Tuck catch up, then whispered to him. "Keep up. Pass it on." Then breaking into a full run to rejoin Washington and the Indian, Colin sent a prayer heavenward that the others would do the same. *While I'm at it, Lord, keep us all safe. And if it's Your will, give us a swift victory.*

He tried to ignore the cutting straps of his jostling pack and the burning in his chest, along with the aching of his feet. The best way to do that was to allow his mind to fly home to Mariah. He was running headlong into danger for the first time. He could get killed. What would happen to her if he wasn't there to protect her? He and the bond papers in his breast pocket had been all that kept his mother from selling the girl into some other man's hands. If he died, the document, along with his other belongings, would be returned to his parents.

The thought distressed him. He should have signed off on the papers before he left, freeing Mariah. If he survived this engagement with the French, he would take care of that matter as soon as he got back to ink and quill at Great Meadows. He would dispatch the papers to her by the first courier.

A stickery branch caught the sleeve of his woolen frock coat. Without slowing, he gave a quick jerk to free himself, then resumed devising his plan. He'd send a letter along, informing Mariah she needn't tell Mother she was free. She should stay within the family's protection until he returned.

If he returned.

His chest tightened as a sharp pain gripped his side. But he refused to stop until George did. He couldn't let the younger man beat him.

About the time Colin was ready to give up, long-legged Washington stumbled to a halt, completely out of breath.

Colin nearly ran into his barely visible leader in the moonless night. Clutching his sides, he bent slightly until his own breathing slowed.

"That brave—is still—running." Washington gasped, gulping air between words.

"I know." Colin shook his head in wonder as the man behind him bumped into him. "But he's not loaded down as we are."

Others caught up, panting hard. Tuck and some of the others coughed.

"Take two minutes to rest," Washington ordered. "Pass the word down the line that I'll be setting a slower pace."

Colin's relief was short lived. The new pace might have been slower than the Indian's, but with Washington's ground-covering stride, their tall commander was still hard to keep up with except when the trail narrowed so that he had to stop and feel around, searching for the path. Worse, as the hours passed in pitch darkness, up and down hills, crossing streams, Colin sensed the men lagging farther and farther behind.

Panting, he trotted up to Washington and tapped him on the shoulder. "Sir, I think we need to stop," he whispered. "Take a head count."

"They've fallen behind?" the commander's quiet tone matched his own.

"I believe so."

After waiting for several minutes, the count was still seven short.

Washington straightened his broad shoulders and spoke only loud enough for them to hear in the still night. "Men, we can wait no longer. We'll pick up the stragglers on the way back—if they haven't already returned to camp."

Shrouded in heavy rain clouds, the fragile hint of dawn was making an effort to illuminate the forest floor when Colin spotted more light up ahead. A clearing. As he drew closer, he noticed a longhouse with wickiups circled around it. A couple of cook fires already blazed. They'd arrived!

A village dog sensed their presence and began barking, and others joined in, announcing the arrival of the militia.

Washington paused before emerging from the line of trees and turned back to the trailing men. "Straighten yourselves. Look smart as we march in."

Beyond exhaustion, Colin couldn't help but grin as he pulled off his hat and tucked any stray hairs back into his queue before replacing it squarely on his head. George Washington truly was a most seriously proper gentleman.

Seneca warriors poured out of their dwellings, hatchets and rifles in hand.

Although Colin was so tired he wanted nothing more than to fall to the ground and sleep for a week, he knew he had to appear fit, show no fear to the villagers as well as be an example for his own men.

From an immense longhouse in the village emerged an Indian in his prime, perhaps forty years of age, powerful looking and heavily adorned with beads and feathers. Already tall, his elaborately quilled headpiece gave him an extra foot in height. Small wonder he was called Half King.

Washington flashed a broad smile and walked immediately to the Indian, his arm outstretched. Grasping the tribal leader's hand with both of his, he gave a hearty shake. "Great Chief Monakaduto, I bring you greetings from Governor Dinwiddie."

Half King stared stony faced for a moment. "Wash-ton." Then gradually, his expression transformed into an enthusiastic grin. "Welcome." Spreading wide a tattooed arm, he invited the commander into his council house.

George turned to Colin. "Have the men partake of their victuals now. We will be leaving shortly."

"Yes, sir." Although Colin would rather have questioned his superior's judgment, he heeled around to the weary company of militiamen. A portending drop of rain pelted his nose. With a sigh, he met Tuck's bleary eyes and slowly shook his head. What sort of fighting force could these sagging, bedraggled men possibly make?

Chapter 24

Mariah smiled to herself as she filled her plate with scrambled eggs, biscuits, bacon, and sliced peaches at the dining-room sideboard. She hadn't been in such a cheerful mood since Colin proposed marriage and presented her with the lovely ring—those few precious moments before he abruptly deserted her yet again. Now she had a letter from him resting this very moment in the pocket of her skirt—and he'd written not to his family but to her personally, which absolutely proved his commitment to her.

Mr. Barclay had ridden in from Alexandria last night, just as the women were about to retire, and he had brought two letters with him. One for Mariah and the other to his wife from her friend Diana in Williamsburg. As Mariah blithely returned to her bedchamber with her own unopened missive, she felt Mistress Barclay's vexed stare following her every step.

Thinking back on the grand moment, Mariah turned with her plate for the open doorway to the terrace. Now that the days had grown pleasantly warm, the family breakfasted outside in the open air, already perfumed with the scent of flowers. She found the elder Barclays and Heather seated at the round terrace table.

The lady of the house looked up and smiled as Mariah approached, but her eyes held no warm spark. "Good morning, dear. I trust you slept well."

"I did, thank you." Knowing the woman itched to know the contents of Colin's letter imbued Mariah with a new sense of power as she took a chair and breathed in the balmy breeze wafting from the river. " 'Tis such a lovely morning, is it not? The tobacco fields are quickly becoming quite lush and green."

Heather turned a questioning expression to her. "So, Mariah, what did my brother have to say in your letter? Is he on his way home—or will he be coming soon?"

Before Mariah had a chance to respond, Amy charged out of the doorway, her full plate tilting precariously in her small hand. "Don't even ask. She wouldn't read it to me last night. She said it could wait till morning, but I don't see why."

"Be careful you don't spill your porridge, brat." Following after her youngest sister, Victoria rolled her eyes.

Their mother leveled them both with a glare as they took seats. "Don't be impolite, child. It's most discourteous to pry into someone's private correspondence."

"Why, 'tisn't prying at all." Mariah, enjoying the moment to the fullest, favored them all with her sweetest smile. "I merely thought 'twould be more expedient if I read Colin's letter to everyone at once. In fact, I've brought it with me." She derived a measure of gratification from knowing he'd had foresight enough not to include anything of an intimate nature in it.

"Splendid." Mr. Barclay gestured to his two daughters. "Settle down, girls. After I give the blessing, Mariah can read her letter to us, if she so wishes."

What a dear man. Colin was a lot like him. Mariah bowed her head.

She heard little of the man's prayer, however, as her thoughts returned to his son. Colin was by far more handsome than any of the fine gentlemen she'd met in Williamsburg—and much more of a stalwart hero. How sad that at this very moment he was somewhere in the wilds, risking life and limb for his family, his colony, and most particularly, for *his Mariah*, as he called her. She forced her attention back to his father's prayer.

"And Father," he continued, "we pray that You will find it in Your will to bring our son safely home to us. Soon."

"Amen." Having blurted the word out unintentionally, Mariah felt warmth tinting her cheeks. But Colin had left in mid-February, after all, and it was now the end of May. They all were anxious for his return.

"Yes. Amen." Mr. Barclay's voice contained a smile.

Amy spoke up immediately. "Read the letter now. Please."

Enjoying the experience of being the belle of the moment, for a change, Mariah grinned and withdrew the folded paper from her pocket. Slowly she spread it and lifted it up, aware that every eye around the table focused on her. "The letter is dated April twenty-first."

"That's over a month old!" The mistress frowned.

"Yes, it is. He writes: '*My dearest Mariah, I miss you and my family very much. When I left I had hoped to be home again long before now, but alas, that was not to be. When we arrived at Wills Creek Station, we were met by militiamen under Lieutenant Trent. They had been sent ahead of us to build a fort on the Ohio River, our destination. A large force of Frenchmen came from upriver and took it from them. We are now awaiting a regiment of regulars to join us.*' "

"What are regulars?" Amy scrunched up her face.

"British soldiers, my dear," her father explained.

"Surely that cannot be all he wrote. Do continue," Mistress Barclay urged.

Mariah returned her gaze to the lines penned by Colin's hand. " '*We will proceed to Great Meadows in Indian Territory and wait for them there before engaging the enemy. Pray for the rain to stop. Tell my family I miss them all. Most sincerely yours, C. Barclay.*' "

Before anyone could speak, she held up a finger. "He added a postscript: '*Tuck sends Tori his most ardent regards.*' "

Pinkening delicately, Victoria lowered her lashes and tried to contain her smile. It quickly wilted into a pout. "Tuck should've written a letter to me himself."

Heather sent her a sidelong glance tinged with a teasing grin. "Especially now that Tori's learned the truth about those other ardent admirers of hers in Williamsburg."

"What's this about?" Mr. Barclay looked from one of them to the other.

His wife shook her head. "Nothing at all, Eldon. Really. Diana Everard wrote a snippet of news about two young men who'd demonstrated an interest in Victoria while we were in their city. It's not of import."

Not to be put off, the older man narrowed his eyes. "What sort of demonstrating, if I might ask?" He pierced his oldest daughter with a speculative look.

Mariah hid her smile behind her napkin. The man was ever the devoted husband and father. Rather like her own papa, to be truthful. The thought was oddly comforting.

"It's nothing to fret about, dear." The mistress fluttered a hand. "Diana reported that Dr. Dunn's son, Willard, would inherit very little because his father is quite lax in collecting payment for his services. And the other young man's father—whom the lad alleged was in shipping— merely owns a ropewalk in Yorktown."

"What's a ropewalk?" Amy tipped her head to one side.

Her mother gave the child's hand a pat. "It's a place where men braid long strands of hemp into thick ropes for the ships."

"Well, it would appear then," Heather piped in, her sly grin broadening, "that Ronald Sedley's father truly is in shipping. Just not the very profitable merchant kind." She snickered at her little jab.

With a withering sneer at her sister, Victoria pursed her lips. "It means little to me. Neither of them was even a fraction as handsome or charming as Tuck, anyway."

"Or Edward Rochester," her mother added. "The son of the richest merchant in Alexandria is not to be discounted." She glanced around the table. "I vow, that's quite enough talking. Your food is getting cold. I'm sure Mariah wishes to finish with your lessons before the day grows uncomfortably warm."

Mr. Barclay drained the remainder of his tea and set down his cup. "I'm more concerned by the storm clouds hovering over the mountains, myself. I hope it doesn't rain too hard. The tobacco leaves are at such a delicate stage just now."

"Oh, la." Leaving her chair, his wife stepped to the rear edge of the terrace and peered past the house to the west. She turned back with a frown. "At this very moment, our Colin must be in a miserable downpour." Returning to her chair, she took the hand of a daughter on either side of her. "Everyone join hands. Our Father in heaven, I fervently pray that our son has a dry place to wait out the storm."

"And if not," Mariah added, "please enfold him within Your merciful warmth and comfort."

Colin released a disappointed whoosh of air. He'd hoped Washington's meeting with Chief Monakaduto would last a bit longer so he and the other men could rest from the fast-paced trek to Great Meadows. But less than half an hour found them on their way again, with the Seneca chief and two of his braves leading the way. Thankfully, these Indians set a slower pace than Monakaduto's messenger had last night.

As the misty rain turned to sprinkles, Colin restrapped his haversack inside his cloak, then stepped to the side of the elusive mountain path and whispered to each passing man. "Protect your powder. Keep it dry."

Every face held a grim expression, and Colin detected undisguised fear in more than a few eyes. This would be the first time any of them except Washington had ever faced a deadly enemy, and they were heading straight for the heavily armed French encampment.

The sprinkles turned to rain that fell straight and hard despite the thick forest growth. Large dollops pelted Colin's hat and frock coat and began to soak through to his skin. In no time at all, he was sure he couldn't have been more drenched if he'd gone swimming. His boots slipped and slid along on muddy, dead leaves as he stumbled over roots and stones on the trail.

Tuck moved up beside him, his tricorn drooping pitifully, his sword all but dragging on the ground. "If I survive this campaign," he muttered through chattering teeth, "and if I ever show up at your door askin' you to come play soldier again, you have my permission to shoot me. Right there on the spot."

Colin laughed aloud, the sound blasting into quiet broken only by the rush of falling rain. As Washington glanced back at him with a scowl, Colin slapped a gloved hand over his mouth.

Tuck immediately fell into line behind him.

Washington turned and raised a hand, halting the militia. He strode to Colin, swiping water from the leather haversack that held his paper cartridges as he walked.

Colin swallowed, fully expecting the leader to reprimand him in front of the men.

"Lieutenant Barclay," the colonel said quietly, "send an order down the line to fix bayonets. I doubt our weapons will fire in this rain."

Fix bayonets? A niggle of fear chilled Colin's blood. Hand-to-hand combat. As an officer, he'd been issued a pistol and a sword and had practice-fought alongside the enlisted men with their swordlike musket attachments. But the thought of actually slashing and stabbing other human beings had never seemed quite real. Until now. He steeled himself to sound confident before giving the order.

About a quarter of an hour later, Monakaduto stopped and pointed ahead.

The downpour had lessened to light sprinkles again. Without that cover of rain, Colin suddenly felt vulnerable.

Washington gestured for Colin and Tuck to join him and the chief. Silently, pistols drawn, they moved forward from tree to tree. Praying all the while that the powder was still dry, Colin peered ahead. He could make out some men huddled beneath an outcropping of boulders in a stone cliff.

Washington motioned for them to ease back. Ever so carefully, lest they be spotted, they backed away until they reached their party.

"Order the men to spread out in a semicircle," Washington said under his breath. "Have them move into firing position and await my order to fire. Lieutenant Barclay, take half the men to the right. Tucker, take yours to the left. Caution them against making any noise. With the element of surprise, a quick victory shall be ours. May the Lord keep and protect us."

As Colin positioned his men along the line, he felt compelled to whisper the leader's plea to each of them. "May the Lord keep and protect you." He knew this could very well be the last morning any of them might see.

Taking his own position behind a tree, Colin aimed his pistol at one of the French soldiers crowded within the shallow cave. The thought of ending that unsuspecting man's life disturbed him mightily, though he knew he had a duty to carry out. The safety of their own encampment at Great Meadows depended on it.

Suddenly Washington sprang into the open and gave a shout. "Fire!"

Colin squeezed his pistol's trigger and fired, but he heard only a dozen or so of the other weapons discharge.

An instant later, Washington shouted through the swirling gunsmoke. "Charge!" Then their commander raced forth, his sword in one hand, a pistol in the other.

Colin could do no less. Only a few sporadic shots came from the French, whose powder had become as damp as the militia's.

All was frenzy and fury, shouts and screams as Colin and the others swarmed the French, slicing and slashing in a violent rage.

Reason caught hold of Colin when a Frenchman tossed his knife to the ground, raised his hands high, and shouted something in his language. The man was surrendering!

About to slice down the fellow's shoulder, Colin stayed his arm. Heaving for breath, he looked around and saw that the rest of the enemy still standing had done the same.

The battle was over.

Surveying the area, he saw blood splattered all around him, on him, and on his sword. Nine Frenchmen lay dead. A wounded enemy soldier sat propped against a rock trying to staunch the flow of blood from his side. Others, bleeding from various areas of the body, remained on their feet. Assessing the scene, the realization that he'd been a part of that carnage sank like a rock inside Colin.

Chief Monakaduto let out an ear-piercing scream of victory as he thrust a bloodied scalp high into the air.

Horrified and sickened by the gruesome sight, Colin knew he must not show his revulsion. He strode stiffly over to where a granite-faced

Washington stood and forced himself to appear as calm as his commander while they watched the three Indians scalp the rest of the dead. His stomach roiled as he cut a glance at the prisoners. The stark fright clouding their eyes was palpable, as if they feared the possibility of suffering the same horrendous fate.

Once the last dead man had been scalped, Monakaduto stepped across a body with the unfortunate victim's scalp dangling from his hand. "Ensign Jumonville." He thrust the bloody thing toward Washington.

To Colin's amazement, Washington calmly took the offering and met the chief's eyes as he spoke. "This is a great honor that the great warrior chief of the Seneca gives me. You and your people will always be welcome in our camp, and we will help you in whatever way we can. This scalp that you have given to me I now give back into your care and ask that it now be carried to the Delawares who, I am told, have begun to cling to the French. Tell them this will soon be the fate of all Frenchmen in this territory."

The chief gladly accepted the return of the trophy.

Colin realized as never before why George Washington had been chosen to lead this expedition. Not only did he know the landscape and the customs of the local tribes, but with his straight posture and imposing height, the quiet young officer naturally commanded respect. He unquestionably had earned Colin's.

Indeed, Washington had grown into a true leader. And having survived this first bloody battle under the commander, Colin vowed he'd gladly follow Colonel Washington anywhere the man led.

Chapter 25

Mariah opened the window of the mansion's second-floor classroom to take advantage of the breeze, then turned to her students. "During this hour, girls, you may write invitations to as many of your friends as you wish to invite. However," she hurried to add in the face of the young ladies' excitement, "only those that have been scribed with the best of penmanship will you be allowed to hand out at church on the Sabbath."

Seated at her writing desk, Amy crossed her arms and stuck out her bottom lip. "That's not fair. I can't write as good as those two." She darted glances at both of her older sisters.

Mariah moved to the young girl's side and placed a reassuring hand on her thin shoulder. "I'll be judging each of you according to your age, and that is fair."

"Well, I think planning a quoits tournament is stupid and sounds medieval." With a disapproving wrinkle of her nose, Heather dipped her quill into her inkwell. "Especially if we're going to have other games as well, like graces and shuttlecock."

Victoria paused in her writing. "Really, Heather. The lads consider graces to be a silly girls' game and a shuttlecock tournament simply doesn't have a dignified ring to it. We have to include quoits."

Recalling similar foolish tiffs she and her own sisters had endured back in England, Mariah slowly shook her head. "Whatever you write, just make your strokes graceful and—"

A voice from the doorway interrupted her. "Missy Harwood."

Mariah turned to the downstairs maid. "Yes, Pansy. What is it?"

"Y'all has visitahs down in de parlor. Mist'ess Barclay says fo' y'all to come right quick."

Visitors! Mariah startled. Who would possibly be calling on her? Had Colin returned at long last? Glad that she'd donned her lavender muslin day gown rather than drab gray this morning, she reached up to see that the combs adorning the sides of her hair remained in place. "Who is it, pray?"

But her words failed to reach Pansy, who had already left for the servants' staircase.

All three girls laid aside their quills and sprang from their desks, curiosity lighting their expressions.

Tori started toward the doorway. "Mayhap Colin and Tuck are back!"

"Or someone's brought the viola Papa ordered," Heather suggested brightly.

"Well, whoever it is, I'm gonna be first to find out." With that, Amy bolted past them all.

"Wait! Stop!" Mariah almost had to holler to slow them down.

Thankfully, they complied seconds before they reached the grand staircase.

Mariah elevated a brow as she joined them. "We shall proceed to the parlor in a ladylike manner, as our guests—and your mother—would expect."

She had to remind them again halfway down. "Slowly, girls. Slowly." Finally, maintaining a calm appearance, they all strolled into the room.

A tall, magnificent-looking stranger turned toward them as they entered. He held a towheaded girl-child propped on his arm, and stepping from behind him, Rose—blessed Rose!—flew to Mariah, her arms outstretched.

Rendered momentarily speechless, Mariah barely managed a gasp as she grabbed hold of her sister and held on tight. Unexpected tears flooded her eyes.

After a long, hard hug, Rose eased back. "Let me have a look at you, dearest."

Not quite ready to relinquish the sister she'd missed more than she realized, Mariah dabbed at the moisture blurring her vision with one hand while clutching Rose's with the other.

Rose smiled and angled her head in assessment. "I must say, you're looking quite well. The Lord has truly answered my prayers. And Mistress Barclay tells me you've done wonders with her daughters."

Mistress Barclay! Peering past her sister, Mariah noticed the lady of the house, dressed to perfection as always, in emerald-striped dimity. She sat before a tea service, waiting for them all to join her. Mariah latched on to her manners and turned to the girls. "Rose, I'd like you to meet my charges. Victoria, Heather, and Amanda." She indicated each with a nod of her head.

The girls curtsied, bright smiles accenting their appealing charm.

"Can we stay?" Amy nibbled her lower lip, her eyes wide with hope.

"Yes, my dears." Her mother gestured toward chairs dotted about the spacious room. "If you sit quietly."

Mariah watched after them, then returned her attention to the tall, muscular man holding the toddler. The embroidered brocade frock coat he wore looked oddly out of place on his manly frame. A strip of leather held his dark, wavy hair in a queue.

"Mercy." Rose laughed lightly. "I was so thrilled to see you, my manners took flight. Mariah, dear, this is my handsome husband, Nathaniel Kinyon and our sweet baby, Jenny Ann."

"Your baby?" Mariah's mouth gaped for a second. "Oh. Your husband is a widower, then."

"Not at all." Rose bestowed a loving glance and gentle smile on her dear ones. "Jenny is our adopted child. Her parents died rather tragically, and her grandparents were ill prepared to care for her. They blessed Nate and me with that honor. We praise the Dear Lord for His goodness."

"She's very pretty, isn't she?" Having spoken her thoughts aloud, Victoria blushed.

Amy took advantage of the moment. "And her hair is so curly. It's almost white. Like an angel's halo."

Mistress Barclay sent them a remember-to-be-quiet look. "My sentiments exactly. But be mindful of your manners."

"Yes, Mama," they chorused.

Amy quickly scooted back in her chair and folded her hands like the little lady her mother wished she would become.

Still drinking in the sight of honey-haired Rose in her fashionable day gown of copper taffeta, Mariah barely caught Mistress Barclay's movement on the edge of her vision as the older woman reached across the small table.

"Mr. Kinyon, from whence do you hail?" The mistress handed him a cup and saucer.

He met her gaze and spoke, his voice low and somewhat commanding. "I'd say as the crow flies, madam, about eighty miles from here. Comin' downriver as we did, though, you could purt' near double that."

"Yes. Thank you." Rose accepted her proffered tea. "Even in one of those swift canoes we spent three days on the water—except, of course, whenever we had to portage around some rapids. But all in all, we had a safe, pleasant trip. And then to be greeted so graciously here by the lady of the manor. . ." She favored Mistress Barclay with a sweet smile.

"I could do no less for our Mariah. She's been an invaluable help to us." The woman paused. "You must stay with us a few days. We've plenty of room."

"Oh yes, Rose. Please do." Mariah searched her sister's blue-gray eyes. " 'Tis so marvelous to see you, and you must tell me everything. This is your final destination, I hope, or must you travel on?"

Rose tilted her head. "Actually, we had planned to travel up the Susquehanna River to visit Lily after we leave here. But we heard a bit of news in Georgetown last eve and. . ." She turned sad eyes to her husband.

He cleared his throat. "I'd planned on waitin' to join up with the militia till after Rose had a chance to visit both her sisters. But I hear tell things is startin' to get hot again betwixt us an' them Frenchies. So, soon as I take my li'l family back home, me an' my partner'll be headin' out to join up with the other boys."

"What do you mean, exactly, by 'getting hot'?" Mariah clenched her hands together in her lap. "Colin and Tuck are with Colonel Washington even as we speak."

"Colin is my son," the mistress explained. "Dennis Tucker is his friend from a neighboring plantation. Do tell us what it is you've heard."

Gently bouncing Jenny on his knee, Mr. Kinyon eased back against the Queen Anne chair that looked far too inadequate for his large frame. He'd drained the tea in one gulp, and the delicate china cup he held all but disappeared within his calloused hands as he set it on the lamp table beside him. "Well, it seems Washington an' some of his boys surprised a party of Frenchies a few days ago. What they didn't kill, they took prisoner. It's only natural that the French'll retaliate first chance they get."

"What about our men?" Mariah swallowed her angst. "Were any of them killed?"

"From what I hear, only one of our boys passed on to glory. A couple others got a scrape here an' there."

"The name," Mariah choked out. "Do you know the name of the deceased?"

He shrugged a massive shoulder. "Don't say as I rightly recall. But he was from up along the Shenandoah, I know that. You folks prob'ly wouldn't know him."

Mariah added her relieved sigh to that of the mistress and the girls.

The older woman leaned forward. "Nonetheless, we shall add his grieving family to our daily prayers. And I thank the Lord my son is safe. For now, at least." She paused again, then continued. "Mr. Kinyon, Mariah informs me you are an experienced frontiersman. I'd be most grateful if you would keep a watchful eye on my son when you join the militia. I fear he can be a touch reckless at times."

"My brother Colin's the bravest—" Amy slapped a hand over her mouth and cut a worried glance in her mother's direction.

Rose's husband shot the child a quirky grin, then looked back at the hostess. "I'd be glad to, ma'am. Colin Barclay. I'll look him up."

"Thank you. Lieutenant Colin Barclay." She gave him a grateful smile.

He tipped his head politely. "Me an' my wife want to thank you for takin' such good, watchful care of our Mariah. I know Rose'll sleep a whole lot easier now that she's met you."

Having spent a good deal of the visit looking from him to Rose and back, Mariah had to admit that for such a commoner, the frontiersman was incredibly charming and handsome. Still, she had a difficult time reconciling the thought of marriage between him and her sister. They seemed so at odds, so different, from totally different worlds. How on earth had prim and proper Rose ever attracted a rover like him?

As Mistress Barclay passed around plates of tea cakes, Mariah swept a reassessing look at Rose. Her older sister's experience in the wilds of this fledgling country had softened and polished her like a priceless gem and brought out an inner beauty that glowed from her eyes. Hair the color of warm honey and fastened in a cluster of long, silky curls secured at the crown, sparkled in the filtered light streaming through the tall windows. And her fine, copper day gown complemented her coloring and adorned her willowy frame perfectly. At long last, Rose had blossomed.

Amy, sitting straight and holding her cup just so, directed a question to her mother in a quiet voice. "Mama, may I say something?"

No one could refuse the sweet voice. "Yes, darling. You may."

"I think Mr. Kinyon is gonna get as bored as me sitting here with all the women talking. May I please take him to the stables and show him our beautiful horses?"

"I'd be glad to hold the baby," Victoria offered.

"Sounds good to me." He smiled at the girls. "Hear tell you got a fine-lookin' string." He relinquished Jenny to Tori's willing attention and took Amy's hand.

"Thank you, child," Mistress Barclay said, then met his jovial hazel eyes. "My husband, Eldon, should be home in an hour or so, and I know he'll enjoy getting to know you. In the meantime, however, I am absolutely dying to learn how a gentlewoman such as your lovely wife survived so beautifully the adventure of being taken deep into Indian country."

"I'll leave the tellin' of that to her." Chuckling, he escorted his little guide outside.

"Yes. Do tell us about it." Heather's eyes sparkled as she leaned forward in eager anticipation.

Mariah was equally interested in hearing about her sister's new life. After the frontiersman left the room, she also knew Rose would be able to talk more openly about what sort of husband she had married.

Then her heart jolted. Out in the stables Mr. Kinyon would meet Geoffrey Scott. Of course, with Mr. Scott's consuming interest in the Bible, he could easily bring up the fact that Mariah had taken quite an interest in things spiritual. In turn, Mr. Kinyon might share with the trainer all kinds of tidbits Rose had told him about her proud, now spiritual and headstrong sister. And heaven forbid, if Geoffrey Scott should mention all the time she'd spent trying to endear herself to him on the off chance that Colin didn't return. That would be dreadful. Dreadful indeed, since the frontiersman would be joining her betrothed soon.

"Mariah." Rose touched her arm and peered closely at her. "Is something amiss?"

Trying to slough off her fears, Mariah propped up a smile. "Of course not. Do tell us your experiences since we parted in Baltimore—and how it was you came to acquire that darling little girl."

For the next half hour, it seemed Rose spared no details as she regaled the Barclay ladies with a lightly humorous version of her wilderness experiences. Mariah's respect for her older sister rose several notches as she slowly shook her head in admiration. "Well, that husband of yours should return from the stables shortly. While we wait, I should like to show you our lovely gardens."

Rose smiled. "Why, that would be marvelous."

"May I go along?" Heather asked, her eyes on Tori, who gently steered the toddler clear of any mischief in a room full of "pretties."

Mistress Barclay intervened. "I think the two sisters would like a moment alone, dear. They've much to catch up on, I'm sure."

Surprised at the older woman's thoughtfulness, Mariah stood to her feet. "Then if you will excuse us. . ." She gestured to Rose, and the two took their leave.

Outside, Rose linked elbows with Mariah as they strolled amid the lush display of flowers and trimmed hedges in the waning afternoon sun. "I believe I've done quite enough talking this day. I'd like to hear how the Lord has taken such wondrous care of you, and how you have fared in this new land. You seem to have a rather comfortable relationship with these plantation owners."

Mariah hardly knew where to begin. "It wasn't always so, I must confess." Beginning with her arrival and the initial cool reception, she condensed the past months as best she could as she brought Rose up to date. "And now they treat me as one of the family, almost."

Rose searched her face. "Is there any hope of your actually becoming one of the family? I remember you made some rather reckless statements in your letters."

It was no use trying to hide anything from that astute gaze. Mariah reached into her lace tucker and drew out the amethyst ring. "Colin has asked me to marry him, but we feel it's best to keep it a secret for now. He assures me the family will come around, in time. First he must return from serving in the militia. I pray he comes to no harm." She tucked the ring back out of sight.

Rose nodded. "Little sister, surely you're aware that secrets have a way of coming home to roost. Nevertheless, I shall join my prayers with yours, dearest. If the two of you truly love each other, I'm sure the Lord will work out His perfect will for you both."

Approaching footsteps drifted to their ears, and they looked up to see Nate and Amy coming hand in hand.

A proud smile lit Amy's eyes. "He loves the horses. We're hungry now. I think it's time to go inside and ask when supper'll be ready."

Mariah smiled and fell into step with the others, but a persistent concern plagued her mind. *Had Geoffrey Scott and Mr. Kinyon been too forthcoming with one another?*

Chapter 26

As Colin and Tuck led their horses on the second return trek to Great Meadows in the last three weeks, Tuck emitted a labored rush of breath. "This June has to be the worst month of my life, bar none."

"Quite." Too weary to laugh, Colin raised an arm and wiped sweat from his brow on his grimy shirtsleeve. "We'd have to go a far stretch to come up with a worse one."

Tuck grimaced. "Unfortunately, next month will probably be a match, if we survive, what with every Frenchman in the territory and every Indian from up north on their way to kill us."

"It's gonna get interestin', that's for sure. If nothin' else, I hope it at least stays dry." Colin couldn't help wondering if the Indians accompanying the militia would stick with them or disappear into the night, the way the Delawares had a week ago. Fortunately, Chief Monakaduto had remained loyal. He and a Seneca squaw chief, Queen Alequippa, had added forty warriors to the ranks—far fewer than Washington had expected to join after the resounding victory over the French the militia had experienced in May. But as beneficial as it was to have additional warriors, the fact that they brought their families with them rapidly exhausted the food supplies. For the past several days, this motley army had nothing but fresh beef to eat.

The horses were in even worse shape. Without a daily ration of grain, the mountain grass was not sufficient to sustain them, and they were deteriorating by the day. That necessitated leaving the supply wagons behind at the Ohio Company's Redstone Storehouse—empty though it was. With the animals too weak to bear any sort of burden, the militiamen were forced to haul the remainder of the equipment on their backs. Watching them struggle against the weight of the swivel cannons and their trunk-thick posts, Colin couldn't help but feel sorry for them—especially since the regular soldiers Captain McKay had brought up from South Carolina were exempted from that duty.

Behind him, Storm stumbled on the uneven trail. Colin glanced back at the Thoroughbred as it plodded along, sagging and dirty, its head drooping low. He gave the animal's muscled neck an encouraging pat as he thought of the emergency stores left at Great Meadows, where a small garrison of militia guarded prisoners that had been captured. Hopefully sufficient grain would be available there to restore the herd.

Colin cast a disparaging look ahead at McKay's scarlet-clad soldiers and ground his teeth. The king's officer refused to order his redcoats to do any physical labor unless they received extra pay, and Washington had no extra resources. So the British soldiers packed none of the equipment, nor had they lifted a pick, shovel, or axe to dig defensive trenches, build fortifications, or help cut trees when the trail needed widening for passage of the wagons.

Morale in the Virginia militia sagged, and the men were on the verge of forgetting about the conflict with the French and taking on McKay and his regulars instead. At the root of the dissention was the fact that Captain McKay insisted he outranked Lieutenant Colonel Washington because he was older and his commission came from the king, not a colonial governor.

A disgusted huff from Tuck interrupted Colin's murderous thoughts. "Know what Sergeant Emmons said this mornin'?"

"No. What?"

"He said if the Frenchies do find us, they'll have nothin' to shoot at but movin' targets, 'cause we ain't done nothin' but move hither and yon since we left Alexandria."

Colin grunted. "He might have a point. This is the third time we're headed for Great Meadows, after all. But remember, one of those treks was taken just to separate us from McKay's men."

"And here we all are, back together again." Tuck scoffed. "Beat's everything, huh?"

"All I've got to say is that high-and-mighty McKay better start takin' our situation seriously. According to Chief Monakaduto's scouts, the French have added great numbers to their ranks, along with the hundreds of Indians they already had with them."

"A pity these redcoats have never seen the way Indians fight." Tuck gave an exaggerated shudder. "If they had, they'd all be totin' and diggin for all they're worth. They'd have trenches dug clear down to China."

Colin and Tuck trudged on in silence, punctuated now and then by a weary huff or a disbelieving shake of the head as they backtracked over terrain they'd covered before.

An hour later, the blessed sight of Great Meadows finally came into view. Banks created by knee-deep trenches that had been dug a few weeks ago now surrounded the encampment. Colin knew those fortifications would have to be greatly beefed up if they had any hope of surviving the imminent assault.

As they started across the swaying grasses, two men came riding out to meet their column. They headed straight for Washington and McKay at the front.

Colin nudged Tuck. "Might as well go find out what they have to report." He forced his bone-weary legs into a faster pace to pass the column of redcoats.

Tuck panted as he caught up. "Wouldn't it be marvelous if they came with orders sendin' us back to Alexandria?"

Colin didn't bother to respond to that far-fetched notion.

As the riders reached the commanders, one of them, a tall man in frontier attire, dismounted with a leather pouch in his hand. "I have a dispatch for Colonel Washington. From Governor Dinwiddie."

Washington took the pouch, his astute eyes never wavering from the man. "You aren't one of our regular dispatch riders." He shifted his gaze toward the one still mounted, including him in the assertion.

"Nay, we're not. Me an' my partner was on our way out here to see if we could help out, when we run across your man at Wills Creek."

"Sicker'n a dog, he was," his pal inserted.

Studying the pair, Colin noted that one of them had dark complexion and black hair, indicating the possibility of Indian blood. His own suspicions rose. Were they really who they said they were?

Lieutenant Trent, a former trader with the Virginia and Ohio Company, strode to the front, his head cocked as he peered at the newcomers. "Kinyon? That you?" A huge grin broadened his bewhiskered face.

"Aye. Me an' Black Horse Bob. We figgered you boys might need an extra hand."

"You thought right." The trader grasped the frontiersman's hand.

"Do you know these men, Trent?" Washington asked.

"I surely do. The Frenchies chased this pair outta their Muskingum store down on the Ohio last fall."

Washington broke into a rare smile and extended a hand. "I recall hearing about that. Was it true that you brought a white woman and a babe out with you?"

Shaking the commander's hand, Kinyon nodded. "Aye. We did. The gal's my sweet bonny wife now."

Forgetting his lower rank, Tuck edged forward. "What's in the dispatch, sir?"

"Yes." Captain McKay gave an arrogant tilt of his head. "It might be of consequence to us all."

"Of course." Washington's smile vanished. Opening the flap, he pulled out the stamped document and broke the wax seal. Unfolding it, he quickly scanned the paper, then looked up. "Considering our present circumstance, this is of little consequence."

"Well, what does it say?" McKay demanded.

Washington handed him the paper. "Governor Dinwiddie writes to commend all the men who were part of our last encounter with the French."

"You forgot to add the rest." McKay's face reddened with rage. "You've been promoted to full colonel."

The commander replied with equal force. "As I said, it's of little consequence at the moment." Retaking the paper, he folded and pocketed it.

"I brought two other letters with me." Kinyon withdrew them from the neck of his belted hunting shirt.

All eyes shifted toward him in the growing tension.

"A coupl'a letters for a Lieutenant Barclay." He scanned the group.

Colin's heart skipped a beat. *Mariah!*

"Letters!" Tuck piped in as Colin reached out his grimy hand toward Mr. Kinyon. "Are there any others?"

"No, 'fraid not." The frontiersman's negative shake of the head generated a number of grumbles from the gathering. He offered the onlookers a half smile as he handed Colin the two missives. "The Barclays asked me to deliver these when my wife an' I visited 'em a few weeks back."

"Thank you." Assessing the man and his Indian-looking friend, Colin wondered how this man and his woman happened to call at the plantation. They weren't the typical sort of visitors his family entertained.

"Give the order to march." Washington's command reminded Colin that the militia still had a number of rods to go before reaching the encampment—rods to cover before he'd find a private place to open his mail. The letters would have to wait.

The company hefted their gear and set out once again. Unfortunately, however, the instant they reached their destination, Washington called everyone to attention before they had chance enough for even a brief rest. "Men, we have not a second to waste. All those not tending the stock or preparing food, grab axes and shovels. We must start constructing a fort immediately." He eyed Captain McKay pointedly, as if challenging the man to order his regulars to help.

When McKay grudgingly acquiesced, Colin wasn't certain if he'd done so because the newly awarded full colonel had ordered the work or because the need was so dire.

While the various work parties began chopping down young trees, stripping off branches, and cutting pointed poles to size, Colin set his men to digging holes for the upright fort poles. During the frenzy of hard labor, the Indians inside the camp merely watched the action and talked among themselves. Not a good sign.

Colin noticed that Kinyon and his partner weren't among the slackers. Both took their turn digging holes beside Colin's already exhausted men. Curious about the frontiersman, Colin strode down the line to where the man worked, shirtless and sweating as he swung a pick. When Kinyon moved back to make way for a fellow with a shovel, Colin handed him a flask of water.

Smiling his thanks, the frontiersman raised the vessel and took a sizable gulp, then handed it back.

"Would you mind stepping aside with me for a moment?"

"Glad to." The big man handed off the pick and strode several feet away with Colin.

"You say you and your wife visited our plantation. Might I ask why?"

A deep chuckle rumbled from Kinyon's chest. "Kinda figgered that'd spark your interest. My wife is your betrothed's sister."

Colin blanched. "You know about our betrothal?" *Stupid question. Of course Mariah would tell her sister.* "Does my family know as well?"

He shook his head. "Mariah thinks it's your place to tell your kin. But my Rose was plumb pleased to see how well your folks are takin' care of her sister. She was more concerned for Mariah's—shall we say, welfare— than her little sister Lily's."

Colin had to laugh, remembering his encounter with prim and proper Rose Harwood. "I've no doubt of that. She wasn't too thrilled to see her sister ride off with a total stranger, one who was wholly attracted to Mariah's beauty. Would you believe she made me vow to deliver Mariah to my mother before the sun set, and also to see to her religious instruction?"

It was Kinyon's turn to laugh. "Sounds just like my Rose. She wouldn't have a lick to do with the likes of me till after I rededicated myself to the Lord." He turned serious. "I'm glad of that now. If not for God's protection, we never would'a escaped them Frenchies an' their Indian trackers." He nodded toward the gathering. "Speakin' of Indians, them Senecas ain't lookin' none too happy over there."

Colin followed his gaze. "I agree. Maybe they'd have been in a better frame of mind if they hadn't brought their families along. I wouldn't want to have mine here right now."

Kinyon glanced around and gave a wry grimace. "I'm startin' to wonder why I came. I don't see how we'll ever stand off the number of French and Indians that're marchin' this way."

"I'm sure Washington will have a dispatcher ride out for reinforcements. Our job will be to hold 'em off till then."

"Hmph. I sure hope you're right." Kinyon helped himself to the flask again and took another swallow before returning it. "Better get back to work. Rose wouldn't appreciate me losin' all this purty hair."

Having witnessed a few gory scalpings, Colin ambled over to another worker and handed him the flask. "Take a breather. I'll take over for a while."

The long afternoon dragged on. Not until a couple of hours after dark did Colin finally find a chance to retire to his tent and read his letters by wavering lantern light—with Tuck staring from a cot opposite him, desperate for word from Tori.

"I'll read the one from my father to you first." Colin smirked. "I'll not be readin' the one from Mariah out loud."

"But what if she—"

"If she says somethin' about Victoria, I'll let you know." He broke the seal and opened the first one:

My dear son,

I trust all is going well with you and the militia. I have heard disturbing news about the number of Frenchmen coming down from Canada. If at any time you wish to relinquish your

SALLY LAITY AND DIANNA CRAWFORD

commission and come home, I am certain I can pay another to take your place. In the meantime, be extremely careful. Your mother, especially, is most worried.

The girls send their love, as does Mariah and all our people.

Your loving father

Post Script: Tori is nagging at me to send Dennis her warmest regards.

Tuck reached for the letter. "Did she send Rochester her 'warmest regards,' too?"

"See for yourself." Colin relinquished the missive, hoping it would hold his friend's attention long enough for him to read the one from Mariah. He quickly broke the seal and spread the letter to catch the light from the hanging lantern:

My dear, dear Colin,

I miss you so. I pray each night that the Lord will send you back to me soon. We are all so worried about you. Your mother is convinced you will come down with some dreaded disease even before the Indians have a chance to kill you. I try to be more optimistic, because I know what a valiant hero you are. I am sure God would not take someone as worthy as you. Do come back to me soon.

With my deepest, dearest regards,
Your Mariah

His heart contracting, Colin smiled. *My Mariah.* How he wished he was with her at this moment, inhaling the fragrance that was hers alone, devouring the sight of her beauty, tasting those luscious lips. . . . Folding the treasured missive, he tucked it inside his shirt, next to his heart, then stretched his weary body out on the canvas cot and closed his eyes.

"Well, did she say anything about Victoria?"

"No." Utterly spent, Colin let out a deep breath. "Blow out the light and get some sleep."

But for Colin, sleep refused to come. The thought that he might not return to Mariah kept him awake. An army ten—maybe twenty times their number was marching toward them, intent on taking their lives. He and everyone else here could be dead within the next few days.

Dead. . .and he had yet to make peace with his Maker.

Listening for Tuck's breathing to even out in slumber, Colin slipped off his cot and sank to his knees.

Father in heaven, "hallowed be Thy name. Thy kingdom come, Thy will be done on earth as it is in heaven. Give us this day our daily bread—"

Yes, Father, the cook says we have only enough flour and meal for one more day, and we've already done without for days. The men won't have the strength to finish the fort if we don't receive more food.

And Lord, forgive me anyone I've trespassed upon. I cannot think of anyone lately, unless it's my parents. You know I proposed marriage to Mariah without their approval. But You also know their disapproval was only because of her lack of a dowry. Aren't we supposed to be storing our treasure in heaven?

He shifted his weight from one knee to the other. *All right. I guess I'm trying to justify my dishonoring of my parents with a lie by omission. Now, where did I leave off? Oh yes, there's a huge enemy army heading this way to trespass all over us. I know You want me to forgive them, but I'd much rather have them change their mind and go back to Canada. I'd sure appreciate You putting them in the mind to do that.*

What comes next? "Lead us not into temptation." *Well, Father, You know I have no access to that at the moment. But delivering us from evil is uppermost right now. Please deliver us, and I promise from this day forth I shall always pray for Your guidance first, instead of jumping into things like a stupid fool. And if You bless me and Mariah with children, I'll teach them to honor You and follow You all the days of their lives. Bless and keep all of us who are here at Fort Necessity, as George Washington dubbed this pathetic, half-finished place. And please give the commander the wisdom he needs to bring us through.*

I ask this in the precious name of our Lord Jesus. For Thine is the kingdom and the power and the glory forever. Amen.

Rising from his knees, Colin lay down again on his cot, and for the first time in months, a restful sense of peace washed over him. Moisture filled his eyes. God had heard his prayer.

Chapter 27

Bone weary, Colin felt as if every muscle in his body protested as he strained to assist a couple of his men struggling to heft a heavy log with a swivel cannon mounted on it. "Easy. . .easy. . ." He grunted as they positioned the unwieldy weapon over the gaping hole that would hold it steady, then dropped the post in with a thud. Colin straightened and stretched his back. What on earth was he still doing here? Monakaduto and the Indians had sneaked out three nights ago, leaving the depleted ranks to fend for themselves. He should have deserted last night as so many of the smarter militia had done.

Small wonder they'd all cut out. He glanced behind him to the pitiful fortification they'd managed to build. Spindly spikes a mere seven feet tall surrounded their tents and the tiny hut where their meager stock of powder and other supplies were stored. If they had enough black powder for even two shots at each of the French and Indians in the force coming against them, Colin would be mightily surprised. And if the gunpowder stayed dry once the rain started up, it would be nothing less than a miracle.

He turned to a pair of young men nearby. "Bring out your cannonballs and fixin's. Then you two stay out here to man the swivel. The scouts say the enemy will be here within the hour."

"Just us two out here in the meadow, sir?" Private Walker's Adam's apple bobbed as he cast a timorous look back at the stockade.

The lad had every right to be afraid. Colin clapped him on the shoulder, hoping to instill a measure of courage. "For now it'll be you and the other artillery men. When the time comes, the rest of us'll join you."

As Colin turned to go and check the progress of the other eight swivel cannons being put into position, he spotted Nate Kinyon coming toward him from the fort, so he moved out of earshot of the two privates.

The frontiersman glared up at the ominous clouds in the sky and wagged his head as he reached Colin. "Man, I sure wish you would'a snuck out with them other boys last night. You're gonna be mighty hard to protect once the shootin' starts."

"If I'd have done that, I wouldn't be much of an officer and a gentleman, would I?"

"No, I reckon not. But leastways you'd'a been alive to see tomorrow come."

Colin shot a quick glance back at the privates to make sure they hadn't heard Kinyon's words. "If you think it's that bad, why are you still here?"

"Two reasons. First, I made a promise to that purty li'l gal of yours that I'd look out for you, an' second, the thought of them Frenchies comin' down here from Canada thinkin' they can run us all out sticks in my craw." He slammed a beefy fist into his palm. "Them Yorkers gotta know the French went down right past their back door. And what about Connecticut an' Pennsylvania? Where are their militias, I'd like to know."

Colin grimaced. "Governor Dinwiddie sent messages out to all the colonies and to our allied tribes. They were all informed of this threat." He released a ragged breath. "So we're it. That is, what's left of us. Almost a hundred men lit out during the night. Guess they figured they'd follow the Indians' example of three nights ago."

"Well, you can't blame Monakaduto and his bunch for takin' off. The chief tried to talk Washington into takin' a stand on top of a hill, 'stead of down here in the open. But even if we'd done that, the chief still wouldn't have hung around and risked his women an' young'uns. We're way too outnumbered." He paused. "Speakin' of young'uns, Rose's little sister is somewhere up off the Susequehanna. I'm hopin' if we thin Frenchy's ranks out enough, they won't head up thataway. One of the Senecas told me the French are low on powder and supplies, too."

Recalling Mariah's younger sister, Colin nodded. "As I recall, Lily's owner didn't pay all that much for her papers. I should've thought to send money enough to satisfy him and gotten her out of there months ago." He peered back over his shoulder at the makeshift circle of pointed poles. "If by some miracle I make it out of here, I'll do just that."

"Meanwhile, we'd best concentrate on the Twenty-third Psalm, that my Rose is fond of quotin'. 'Yea, though I walk through the valley of the shadow of death. . .' "

Colin glanced out to the dark, shadowy woods that appeared even more sinister under heavy clouds ready to burst at any moment. "David must have had a place like this in mind when he wrote that Psalm, that's for sure."

Kinyon chuckled. "He also wrote, 'I will fear no evil: for thou art with me.' "

Meeting his gaze, Colin forced as much of a smile as he could muster. "Thanks for the reminder, friend. I'll pass that on to the men." He extended a hand to Kinyon. "It's been good getting to know you. I'd best get back to my men now."

"I'll walk along with you."

Bloodcurdling screeches and howling war cries erupted from the far end of the meadow!

Colin wheeled toward the sound.

Painted Indians emerged from the forest!

Adding to the sinister sound of their frightful yowling, the Indians began firing their muskets sporadically. Out of range, the balls fell short of the artillery pieces positioned to fire in that direction.

Colin raced to the nearest swivel cannon. "Don't fire until they're within range!"

Militiamen streamed out of the stockade and formed a firing line, with Washington in front. They waited for the enemy to advance.

They did not. Instead, the Indians began dancing, waving their rifles and hatchets and screaming their blood-chilling cries.

Then firing burst forth from the trees bracketing the long meadow. Rather than marching out into the open field and facing the militia like gentlemen, the French had set up positions on the wooded hills barely fifty yards from the stockade and launched an attack from there.

Ammunition rained down from both directions in a deadly crossfire.

"Retreat to the stockade!" Washington hollered amid the deafening racket and flying musket balls.

Colin turned—

〜〜〜

Another hot and humid day like yesterday. Mariah had promised the girls she'd finish with their lessons early and take Amy riding before noon. Sipping a gloriously cooling, iced lemon drink on the veranda, she waited for her young charge to bring the horses up from the stable. As much as possible, Mariah had avoided going down there since Rose and Nate left last month. She didn't want to deal with the penetrating looks Geoffrey Scott had been giving her since then.

Not wanting to be noticed, she glanced out of the corner of her eye toward the stables, where Mr. Scott stood talking to Amy as Old Samuel saddled the horses. Was the trainer questioning the child about her? Wanting to know if Mariah said her prayers at night? Asking what she taught the girls in their Bible lessons?

She cringed at the thought, recalling a conversation she'd had with Mr. Scott two days after Rose and Nate took their leave:

"I'd appreciate your opinion," he'd said. "When our Lord says we're to pray always, what sort of things do you think we should pray for?"

"To keep us and those we love safe, of course." Mariah answered quickly, blithely, considering Colin was in a dangerous situation in the wilderness.

"Yes, but what else should our prayers concern?"

She was quite confident in her answer. "At the moment, there couldn't be anything of more concern than Colin's safety."

"Indeed." With a narrow-eyed perusal of her, he smirked and turned his back.

Mariah's confidence collapsed as he strode away. For once in her life, she wished she'd have been more like Rose and interested in spiritual matters so she could provide wise answers to his questions.

That evening, in her quest to learn the answer the trainer sought, Mariah asked equally religious Mistress Barclay the same question.

"That's a very good question," the older woman said. "Let's both study the scriptures on prayer, and we can discuss them next Sunday."

That had not turned out well at all. Although much of prayer was supposed to be for the welfare of other Christians, the mistress found three verses in the epistle of James and made them memory verses for the family. They were most disturbing:

"Ye ask, and receive not, because ye ask amiss, that ye may consume it upon your lusts." Mistress Barclay considered just about everything Mariah secretly prayed for lust. But then, the woman had everything—she could afford to do as the next verse she wanted memorized said: *"Humble yourselves in the sight of the Lord, and he shall lift you up."*

The mistress saved the worst for last: *"For that ye ought to say, If the Lord will, we shall live, and do this, or that."*

Mariah gave a huff. Surely the Lord didn't expect everyone to wait for God to tell them every move to make every single moment. Besides, it seemed only natural for folks to pray for their desires—wasn't there a verse somewhere in the Psalms to that effect? Otherwise there would be nothing to pray about but the poor and needy.

The unsettling memory was terminated as Amy started up the rise astride her pony and leading the other mount. Mariah smiled with relief. A ride along the river road would be most welcome about now. Placing her glass on a side table, she started for the steps.

Galloping hoofbeats thundered toward them from the other end of the lane. At this time of day?

She whirled around and entered the house. "A rider is coming! Fast!" she called out.

Questioning voices and footsteps came from various rooms.

As Mariah returned outside and flew down the steps, the man skidded his mount to a halt in front.

"Why the hurry?" Mr. Barclay asked from the top landing.

"The militia's comin.'" Panting and out of breath, he continued. "Comin' down the river road. Your boy was with the militia, wasn't he?"

"Aye, that he was." With that, Colin's father came down the steps two at a time.

Mariah's heart leaped. Her hands flew to her face. Colin was finally coming home!

Mistress Barclay lifted her skirts and started down with the girls. "Did you see our son, my good man?"

"No, ma'am. One looks pretty much like all the rest, they're so ragged and dirty and unshaven. Well, I'm off. Folks down the road'll be wantin' to know." Reining his horse around, he galloped away again as fast as he'd come.

"Hooray!" Amy clapped her hands. "Colin's comin' home!"

Mr. Barclay snatched the reins of the second horse from Amy's hand and leaped into the saddle. Without a word, he charged down the road, with Amy chasing him on her pony.

Wishing she'd thought of the horse first, Mariah ran a few steps after the pair, then stopped to watch. She felt Victoria move alongside her.

"They will let Colin leave the others and come home now, won't they?"

"I certainly hope so, dear." Her mother, coming up behind, wrapped both Mariah and Victoria in a hug. "Praise the Lord! They're back. Our Colin is finally coming home."

The day grew ever warmer and stickier as Mariah and the others moved up to the veranda to wait. No one spoke as they stood in tense silence, straining their eyes for a glimpse of their returning hero.

Mariah could scarcely breathe. The rest of her life depended on whether or not Colin still wanted to marry her. If, heaven forbid, he'd been—no, she refused to allow that thought to go further.

Mistress Barclay sank onto a veranda chair, but within seconds rose again to her feet, watching with the others the far end of the lane.

Watching.

Waiting.

Mariah considered running down to the river road but knew how foolish that would be in this beastly heat. She'd be all damp and drippy.

Where were they? What was taking so long?

Pansy brought a tray of cool drinks without being asked. Remembering the one she'd left on a table moments ago, Mariah picked up her glass and took a gulp. Tension made it hard to swallow.

The great clock in the entry hall bonged twelve times. She'd come out to go riding at half past eleven. Mr. Barclay and Amy had ridden away over half an hour ago.

Heather broke the long silence. "Do you think we'll recognize Colin? I've never seen him with a beard."

No one answered. More minutes ticked away.

At long last, two horses and a pony turned onto the tree-shaded lane. They were coming!

Mariah inhaled a nervous breath and took a sip of her now-warm lemonade.

One rider broke into a gallop, racing toward them.

Mariah's heart kept pace with every hoofbeat as she and the others hurried down the steps. Staring ahead more closely, she slowed. Halted. The man's beard was golden brown, not black. It was Dennis Tucker. Where was Colin? Icy fear clutched her insides.

"Tuck!" Victoria gasped, breathless, and ran to him.

He reined to a swift halt before her and leaped from his mount, grabbing her up and swinging her around.

They blocked Mariah's view. She moved past them, still staring into the distance.

As the other, slower-moving horses neared, she saw that Mr. Barclay's mount bore two people. Amy plodded along at her father's side.

"Thank You, dear Lord," Mistress Barclay whispered as she came up beside Mariah.

Amy suddenly kicked her pony's flanks into a gallop and sped ahead of the other horse, straight to her mother. Tears streamed down her face as she collapsed into the older woman's arms. "He's b–blind," she sobbed. "Colin's blind."

Blind!

From far away, Mariah heard a gasp, and realized it was hers. Colin couldn't be blind. He just couldn't be. She'd prayed. They'd *all* prayed for his safe return. Her reasons may have been a bit selfish, but his family's weren't. How could God do this to him, to her?

Yet there he was, hanging on behind his father, hatless, a dingy white bandage wrapped around his head, shrouding his eyes. As they came closer, Mariah saw an angry red scar slashed down his temple. They came to a stop in front of her. Colin's hair was pulled back in a dull, limp queue, his clothes torn and filthy. Worst of all was the look of defeat where there should have been a smile. Did he even know where he was?

Words were coming at her. Mistress Barclay grabbed her arm and gave it a shake. "Did you hear me, Mariah? I said run into the house and order a bath for Colin."

"Y–yes. Of course," she choked out.

Colin's head turned toward her.

"And food for you, Colin." She forced a brightness she didn't feel into her tone. "I know you must be famished for Eloise's good cooking."

Glad for the chance to escape, she grasped her skirts and raced up the steps, her mind a stunned whirl of confusion. Not all blindness was permanent, she reasoned. But as she reached the butlery door, a shocking thought surfaced. What if Colin *was*? What good would her beauty— her primary asset—be then? It would mean nothing at all to him—if he even remembered her. Men with head injuries were often left addled thereafter.

She entered the butlery, her thoughts still in turmoil. Even if he still possessed a competent mind, what would life be like married to a blind man, waiting on him, leading him around wherever they went? Could she deal with a challenge like that? For that matter, could he? It wasn't fair. This should not have happened.

A sudden surge of anger overtook her. Colin had no one to blame but himself. He should never have left here in the first place. Was that blasted honor of his worth his sight?

Worth her hopes?

Chapter 28

Entering the kitchen, Mariah found Eloise wringing her hands and muttering under her breath as she paced back and forth. "My po' boy. My po' boy."

Pansy sat at the worktable blindly peeling a turnip while tears coursed down her face.

The sight of the slaves' anguish nearly made Mariah break down, too, but she had to stay in control. She drew a calming breath. "This situation is most disturbing for us all. But we must try to be as brave as I know he was."

"Does y'all know somethin' 'bout Mastah Colin dat we don't?" Pansy swiped at her dark eyes with the edge of her work apron.

Aware that the maid had misunderstood, Mariah shook her head. "I simply know that Colin is incapable of doing anything that's not heroic. Eloise, would you please fix a plate of food for him right away, and start heating water for a bath?" Without waiting for a response, she started to leave, then turned back. "Oh, I forgot. Dennis Tucker is here. I'm sure he'd appreciate something to eat as well."

Walking back through the butlery, Mariah had another thought. If the militia was returning, where was Rose's husband? He'd promised to keep Colin safe, but obviously he hadn't done that. He was probably too ashamed to show his face here.

Voices drifted toward her when she opened the door to the foyer. Gripped again by a sudden urge to cry, she pulled the door almost closed, leaving only a crack to peek through.

With his head still swathed in bandages, Colin came through the front door, supported on either side by his parents. Was he so addled that it took both of them to guide him?

The girls and Tuck streamed into the house just behind Colin, and though Victoria still clung to Tuck, her worried gaze never left her brother. Nor did anyone else's.

Colin shrugged out of his parents' grasp and reached for the cloth covering his eyes, lowering it.

Although Mariah's first instinct was to turn away, she forced herself to leave the protection of the door and move closer to see how much damage had been done to his wonderful face. To her surprise, his eyes looked as velvety brown as ever. Only his black beard and the red scar slashing his temple marred his appearance. Perhaps he wasn't blind after all! *Please, God, don't let him be blind.*

"Sunlight hurts my eyes," Colin said, the first words Mariah had heard him utter. And they were sane words!

"Then you can see, darling!" Joy filled Mistress Barclay's expression as she took his hand.

"No, Mother. Only light and shadows."

"But it's something, at least. Perhaps it will improve with time."

He released a weary breath. "The physician who examined me at Fredrick Town said if I hadn't started improvin' by now, he doubts I'll get much better." The statement came out in a flat tone, as if he spoke of nothing more important than the weather.

Mariah felt tears forming. She blinked them away.

Looking every bit as devastated as Mariah felt, Colin's mother reached out a hand and gently touched his face.

He flinched.

"Whatever future lies before us, my darling, the Good Lord will see us through," the mistress murmured. "We're just so thrilled to have you home again."

"Thank you, Mother. But right now, would you mind just seein' me to my room? I'm really quite tired." His monotone words betrayed no more emotion than his face.

Mariah bit the inside corner of her lips. He hadn't once asked for her. Was the old Colin gone? Forever?

Sorrow filled her as she watched Colin's parents assisting him up the stairs. The fear she'd most dreaded turned into a reality. Her Colin was gone. When the others gravitated to the parlor, she followed, not knowing what else to do.

The girls, talking all at once, hurled questions at Dennis Tucker.

"How did Colin get hurt?"

"Do you think he'll get better?"

Tuck held up his hands. "Whoa. Sit down, and I'll tell you what happened."

Mariah, as desperately curious as the sisters, sought the nearest chair and sank onto it.

Dennis remained standing.

"Sit, please." Victoria scooted over on the settee and patted the cushion beside her.

"No, I'm far too dirty." He inhaled a deep breath as his gaze turned to Mariah.

She wondered if Colin had told his friend about their secret betrothal. Unsure, she lowered her gaze to her hands, not wanting him to see her pain. She slowly raised her lashes as he began to speak.

"Colin was outside the stockade helpin' his men set up some swivel cannons when the French attacked us. Out in the open like he was, he didn't have a chance. Nate Kinyon was also out there. As soon as Colin fell, Nate hoisted him up and hauled him back inside the stockade. A musket ball caught him in the leg, but that didn't stop him. Colin owes his life to that brave frontiersman."

"Then Nate did the best he could," Mariah said in a near whisper.

"Quite. And you should be grateful that Colin was unconscious for the next three days. He missed our shameful surrender of Fort Necessity and the Great Meadows. Our militia was far too outnumbered. From what I heard, there's not another live Englishman on the other side of the mountain now." Tuck's expression turned brittle, the muscles in his jaw twitching. "All because none of the other governors would lift a finger to help."

"How awful." Tori sprang to her feet and went to him. "But you're home now, safe and sound. Surely the other colonies will understand the seriousness of the French invasion after learning about this latest atrocity."

The tension left Dennis' shoulders as he took her hands in his and smiled. "I hope so, sweetheart. I certainly hope so."

"I'm surprised Nate Kinyon didn't accompany you here, Dennis," Mariah interjected. "Was he too badly injured?"

"No, miss. The musket shot grazed his leg, but the wound was patched up afterward. Nate was with us most of the way back, but he lives upstream from here. When we reached his settlement, he went on home to his Rose."

Benjamin leaned his black face into the doorway. "Mistah Tucker, we gots some food for you in da dinin' room."

"Sounds great. Thank you. I could use a quick bite, then I must be off. My folks will think I'm dead if the militia passes by our place and I'm not with 'em."

With the three sisters clustered around Dennis, the foursome left the parlor for the dining room.

Mariah chose another direction. Desperate for a few minutes alone, she ambled outside and down the veranda steps, heading for the gazebo.

As she reached the corner of the manse and the charming white-latticed structure came into view, the floodgates behind her eyes finally broke. Hardly able to see for the tears, she picked up her skirts and ran past the hedged garden to the octagonal summer building where she wouldn't be heard. Sobbing openly, she raced up the steps and into the gazebo's shade, where she gave full vent to her sorrow.

She covered her mouth with both hands and slumped down to a bench as heart-wrenching wails from deep inside shook her being. Her beautiful man, the one who had always gazed at her with such worshipful eyes, her Colin who had traveled to Bath to help her father with his financial plight. . .Colin who brought back a ring as proof of his troth, who said he loved her, wanted to marry her. . . That man was. . .was her one true love. She knew that now. It wasn't his wealth she wanted, it wasn't his fine position in life. It was the man himself. She vowed she would do whatever it took, how ever long it took, to be with him, to take care of him, to love him.

Why had she never realized how deep her feelings for Colin had grown? Yet he hadn't asked for her, hadn't so much as spoken her name. Why hadn't he? Did he even remember her? All her scheming and planning had caught up with her, just as Rose predicted, and now Colin was quite possibly lost to her forever. Oh, how it hurt to love him still.

After a time, Mariah's sobs died away, and she pondered who Colin was now, how much he must have changed. What would it be like to suddenly become blind? She couldn't imagine being deprived of sight. Not being able to see everything that now lay before her eyes—this lovely home, its furnishings, the gardens, her clothes, the sight of Colin's teasing grin. A lifetime of darkness lay ahead of him now. Surely blindness must be akin to being buried alive.

She emitted a shuddering sigh. Even if he did remember her, Colin couldn't possibly still be the man who had asked her to marry him. No. His days of coming to her rescue were over, and he'd always been too much the knight in shining armor to allow her to come to his aid.

Tears again threatened. Angrily she shook them away. She must think of herself now.

She glanced down toward the stables. Geoffrey Scott was at this moment leading two horses toward a pasture gate—the two she and Amy had planned to ride earlier today. The trainer was perhaps a decade older than she, but rather handsome in a quiet sort of way. Narrowing her eyes as she studied him, Mariah shuddered. No. She could never wed Geoffrey, knowing Colin was so close, wanting to be with him, wanting him to look at her as he used to. The very thought of him never seeing her again made her heart ache.

Nothing was left to her but to write to Rose and Nate and ask them to pay off her indenturement, since Papa would eventually reimburse them. Then she'd go and live with them until she learned to stop loving Colin, how ever long that would take.

But then what? Rose and her husband lived in the woods outside a primitive settlement. What chance for any kind of an advantageous marriage would she find there?

Mariah let out a long, slow breath and glanced across the fields where the slaves were carrying the last of the tobacco leaves to the drying sheds. Summer would be over soon. Winter—dreary winter—would soon be upon them. For Colin it had already arrived. How would they all survive such sorrow?

One of Rose's favorite sayings drifted to mind: *Take care of today, and leave tomorrow's worries with the Lord.*

Of course. She'd been running headlong ahead of herself. Again. She would leave tomorrow to the Lord. Rising to her feet, Mariah tugged a handkerchief from her skirt pocket and dabbed away the remains of her tears. What was needed right now was to get through the rest of this woeful day. And the first order of business was to get some cold water to splash on her face. Crying made her look simply dreadful.

⌒

Mariah's eyes weren't the only ones swollen and red that evening at supper. Even Mr. Barclay's face showed signs that he, too, had wept. Attempting to give a brief blessing over the food, his voice broke when he mentioned Colin's name. And that made Mariah want to start bawling again.

No one else spoke either, except to ask occasionally for the pitcher of lemonade to be passed. The fried chicken on their plates grew cold as everyone just pushed it around in silence. Now and then someone would flick a glance toward the staircase and the upper floor, where Colin had asked to be left alone to rest. He had yet to speak to her, Mariah, his betrothed.

Finally Mistress Barclay rose from the table. "Shall we adjourn to the parlor? I'd appreciate it, Mariah, if you'd play the harpsichord for us this evening. Something soft and soothing, if you will."

"Yes. Something soothing." Mariah nodded, almost afraid to meet the older woman's gaze and see the anguish that his mother's heart had to feel.

But the lady of the manor wasn't looking at her. She stared past Mariah out the terrace doors, tears welling in her eyes.

Mariah breathed deeply to keep her own from spilling forth.

Never before had an evening been so quiet. No one spoke as they sat absorbed in their own thoughts, tears quietly flowing as Mariah played soothing pieces by Bach and Haydn. Thankfully having memorized them, she had no need to read the music through her tears.

Amy stood to her feet before the sky had darkened enough for stars to appear. "I'm tired. I'm goin' to bed." That from a child who possessed boundless energy?

Soon after, Victoria also got up. "It's been a long day." As she passed Heather, her sister followed.

Mariah continued to play, hoping the elder Barclays would also retire. She wanted nothing more than for this dreadful day to end. But the pair sat motionless, appearing oblivious to the music.

Detecting footsteps padding across the foyer toward the parlor, Mariah looked up from the keys and dabbed her wet eyes on her sleeve.

Lizzie, who'd been asked to sit outside Colin's door in case he needed anything, stood in the doorway. "Ma'am? Mastah Colin, he askin' for Missy Harwood to come."

Mariah's pulse began to throb in her aching head. Her hands froze on the keys. Colin wanted to see her! He had remembered her after all! Noting that his parents' gazes were now riveted on her, she hoped they weren't angry that he'd sent for her instead of them.

"If you'll excuse me," she managed to croak. She rose on shaky legs and started for the foyer.

"Give him our love," Mistress Barclay murmured after her.

"Yes, do that." Her husband put an arm about his wife and hugged her close.

Mariah didn't remember ascending the grand staircase, but reaching Colin's chamber, she entered and closed the door behind her. The room lay in darkness, devoid of a single lamp's glow. But faint light came from the open balcony doors, where she saw slight movement. "Colin?"

"I'm outside." He spoke in the same emotionless tone she'd heard earlier. "Come join me. It's cooler out here."

She found his shadowy figure in a chair with an iced drink jingling in his hand—the only other sound besides those of the crickets, tree toads, and other night creatures. Colin smelled of the pleasant spiced soap Eloise always made.

"Have a seat." He gestured in no particular direction.

"Thank you." Swallowing against a lump forming in her throat, Mariah settled her skirts about her on a cushioned, scrolled-iron chair nearby and forced a cheerful note into her voice. "You're right. 'Tis quite a bit cooler out here."

"How are my parents faring?"

His quiet question was hard to answer. What should she say? Realizing he'd asked her because he wanted the truth, she spoke in all candor. "They sent their love. And I do believe I can tell you that everyone is—is—"

He raised a hand. "No need to say more." He inhaled a breath, audible since only a small table separated the two of them. "When I woke up and discovered I couldn't see, I found it hard to accept, myself."

Mariah turned toward him. "Oh, dearest Colin, how dreadful for you." She wished she could see his face clearly, make out his expression.

"Nate Kinyon and his partner, Black Horse Bob, were there," he cut in as if she hadn't spoken. "They helped me past the worst part. Quoted lots of scripture, gave me long talks about how much worse things could be and the fine life I still have ahead of me." He gave a small huff. "Speakin' of Nate, he's truly an exceptional man. Your sister is fortunate to have him for a husband."

"Yes. When they were here, they seemed very. . ." She almost said, *very much in love,* but changed her mind. "Very well suited."

"Rose must be quite the woman, then. You should've heard the way he went on about her."

Mariah felt the same twinge of jealousy she'd always felt as a child when her aunt and uncle or their clergyman would go on and on about what a treasure Papa had in Rose. She inhaled a cleansing breath. "I'm sure Nate would praise her. Rose is a woman of great virtue."

For the first time, Colin turned toward her. "I'm glad to hear you say that." Reaching to the small table at his side, he plucked something rectangular from it and held it out to her.

Mariah grasped it and saw it was a folded document.

"Your indenturement papers. I've signed your release."

He was giving her back her freedom?

"But—"

"Dearest Mariah, I've had weeks to think about this. A beautiful woman such as yourself needs a man who will appreciate being able to feast his eyes on that loveliness every day the two of you spend together. Needless to say, I no longer have that ability."

Her heart stopped. "You're rescinding your marriage proposal?"

"It's the only gentlemanly thing to do. I don't want you to be saddled with a blind man for the rest of your life. And I'm certain your father would agree with me."

"But. . .but. . .I love you, Colin. Truly I do."

"I thank you for that. It's wonderful to hear. It really is. But I'm no longer the same man you fell in love with. And I don't want to be that poor blind fellow his long-suffering wife has to lead around. I'll make arrangements for an escort for you to your sister's in the morning. I'd also like you to take a nice colt and two fillies with you as a thank-you to Nate for saving my life, such as it is."

"No." How dare he make this decision without her?

"They'll follow along quite nicely, I'm sure."

"Who will?"

"The horses. They won't be much trouble. I'll have Geoff choose some with good temperaments."

"That isn't what I meant. I'm not leaving."

"Mariah, my dear, weren't you listening? There's nothing here for you anymore."

She sprang to her feet. "You are here! You are not nothing!" Clutching her hands together to calm herself, she lowered her voice. "This has been a very long day. We can speak again in the morning."

"My decision won't change."

Mariah whirled away. "And neither will mine."

Chapter 29

Mariah awoke in the pale pink light of dawn with new resolve. She'd lain awake for a good hour or more during the night, her mind vacillating from one emotion to another until she formulated a plan, a foolproof plan to make Colin want her to stay.

With a determined smile, she rose quietly, not wanting to awaken Amy in the next room. She made her bed and took care of her morning toilette, dressing quickly. Her appearance was no longer of importance to Colin.

But something else did matter to him. If he was so taken by Nate's mere description of Rose, Mariah merely had to do and say exactly the kinds of things her sister would. There'd be nothing to it. Hadn't she watched long-suffering Rose her whole life? Always doing for others, quoting the appropriate scripture for any occasion—at her?

Well, perhaps she wouldn't be quite as long-suffering as Rose. Her older sister had a penchant for taking self-sacrifice to such an extreme that, had she not ended up the lone white woman in Indian Territory, she surely would have continued her dull journey into a life of spinsterhood.

Chuckling to herself, Mariah thought back on the scripture she'd read to the girls a few days before: *"Put on the whole armor of God."*

Suddenly she remembered her betrothal ring. Removing it from its chain, she slipped the amethyst onto the correct finger, and held out her hand to admire its rich beauty. Then, after a passing glance at her sensible hairstyle, she turned on her heel and headed for the door. Convinced she was fully armored, she marched out ready for battle, but catching sight of Amy in slumber, she quieted her steps. War was far better waged without that child's impetuous mouth getting in the way.

No sign of life came from the older girls' room as Mariah tiptoed down the hall. Good. Going into a man's private chamber at this hour simply was not done. Pausing at Colin's door, she decided against rapping, since even that light sound might be heard. She walked in quite brazenly and closed the door behind her without a sound.

But Colin wasn't in his walnut four-poster bed. She scanned the masculine room with its sturdy furnishings and multihued coverlet only to discover it empty. Had he perchance stayed outside on the balcony all night?

Crossing the room, she checked to see if he was outside, and when he was not, she surmised he must have gone downstairs ahead of her. She hurried out, hoping to catch him alone, before either of his parents awakened.

She was too late. As she entered the parlor, the drone of male voices drifted from the dining room. Passing through the doorway separating the two rooms, she spotted Colin and his father at the far end of the long table, talking in subdued voices, half-eaten plates of food on the table before them.

Mariah paused, taking a moment to compose herself. She also took that moment to gaze on her beloved's strong profile. With the angry scar out of view and his face now clean-shaven, a person happening upon the scene would never guess he was a tragic figure who'd suffered a grievous wound in battle.

Those interminable tears threatened again, but she willed them away and resumed a resolute pace. The last thing Colin wanted or needed was her pity.

"Good morning," she singsonged, striding into the room. "Anything especially tasty for breakfast today?"

Both men abruptly turned toward her.

"Good morning." Mr. Barclay's cheerful tone matched her own. She wondered if his good humor was as false as hers.

Colin spoke in the same flat manner he'd adopted since his return. "Glad to hear you're up before the others. Fill your plate and join us."

"Thank you. I'll do that." Mariah didn't realize how hungry she was until the delectable aroma of fresh biscuits and gravy, cold ham, and spiced apples in cream wafted to her nostrils. She selected portions of each and poured herself a cup of tea before taking her place across from Colin. "You look quite rested, Colin." Raising her cup to her lips, she took a sip.

"I slept well. And you?"

"Thank you, yes." She placed her napkin on her lap and straightened her shoulders. She could play the polite conversation game as well as he. Maybe better. "I enjoy rising early before the business of the day is upon us. I shall be testing the girls on their French lessons this week." She turned to his father. "By the way, Mr. Barclay, did you not say you had some letters you wanted me to write for you today?"

"Yes, I did. But—"

"What my father means," Colin interrupted, "is that there's no need for you to spend time on correspondence. You'll be busy packing for your trip on the morrow."

"I'm sorry," she said in a sugary-sweet voice, "you must have misunderstood me last evening. I've no plans of going anywhere."

He spoke more forcefully. "It's already been decided."

At least he was showing more life. But unfortunately for him, he had no idea what he was up against. Mariah directed her attention to his father and held out her left hand, allowing the amethyst to catch the light from the sconces and reflect its full violet radiance amid the sparkling diamonds circling it. "I don't believe you've seen the betrothal ring Colin gave me. Is it not just the prettiest thing?"

The older man's shocked expression rivaled his son's.

"Mariah." Colin shook his head. "You know—"

"What's that?" Mistress Barclay had entered the room unnoticed. "Did I hear correctly? You're betrothed to Mariah, Colin?"

Mariah spoke before he had a chance to respond. "Why, yes, Mistress Barclay." She lifted her hand to display the ring. "Colin bought this from Papa when he was in England and asked my father for my hand in marriage."

"That was before this happened," Colin grated through clenched teeth. He pounded the table with his fist, and scooting back his chair, lunged to his feet. "I've since given Mariah her indenturement papers, and I was arrangin' with Father for her transportation to her sister's when she. . .she. . ."

"I what?" Mariah shot up from her seat and planted her fists on her hips, wishing she were a foot taller as she eyed him, even though such an advantage would have been useless.

Both his hands had balled into fists as well, and she was very glad a large table separated them. Then slowly he unclenched his hands and turned toward his father. "Will you please handle the matter we discussed? I'm goin' to my room. Benjamin!" he called out. "I need you!"

"But, darling," his mother pleaded as the slave rushed in from the butlery.

"Let him go, Cora." Mr. Barclay met her gaze. "You can speak with him later."

As Mariah watched Colin leave on the African's arm, the enormity of what she'd just said and done began to dawn on her. Had it been not more than ten minutes ago she'd promised herself she would act just like Rose? Mortified, she dropped down to her seat again and picked up her teacup, wishing it made a larger shield. Her pulse throbbed in her throat so intently she feared it must be visible.

Mistress Barclay lowered her elegant self to the chair her son had just vacated and arched her brows. "What, may I ask, have I missed here this morning?"

"Quite a bit, my dear." Her husband tipped his head in amazement. "Your son and our tutoress were having a rather heated disagreement about her future. Seems they have differing views on how and where she should spend it." A most unexpected grin slid into place.

Speechless, Mariah could only stare.

The lady of the house hadn't been struck dumb, however. She leveled her gaze on Mariah. "You say you and our son are betrothed?"

Mariah breathed deeply, trying to still her pounding heart. "Yes, madam. Since February, when Colin returned from England."

The woman's glare hardened. "Why is it we are just now hearing about it?"

"Colin felt it would be best to wait until his return from duty with the militia. He thought it would be only a matter of weeks. But. . ." She gave a helpless shrug and raised her cup to her lips, swallowing a gulp of mint tea.

"Engaged all this time. And now that he's been blinded, you've suddenly lost interest, is that it? He's no longer worthy of your—"

Mr. Barclay interrupted. "You've got it backward, Cora." He reached for his wife's hand and enclosed it in his. "It's Colin who wants her to go."

"Oh." The mistress settled back in her chair and gazed across at Mariah, her dark eyes now soft with sympathy. "My son wishes to break off the engagement."

"Yes." Feeling emotion welling in her again, Mariah struggled to maintain her composure. "He thinks that just because he's blind I should stop loving him and find someone else. Well, I'm sorry, but I can't do that. I love him dearly, and I don't know how to stop loving him. I don't care about his blindness." Despite her best efforts, those blasted tears started again. Clutching at her napkin, she sprang from the table to escape before they noticed. "Please, excuse me."

"Wait!" Mistress Barclay also came to her feet. Circling the table, she approached Mariah and drew her into her arms.

Overcome by the unexpected tenderness when Colin's mother hugged her close and hard, Mariah's tears poured out in earnest. Sobbing uncontrollably, she melted into the older woman's comforting embrace.

Her tears stemmed from a mixture of joy and sadness, made even more intense when Colin's father came to join them and enfolded them both in his strong arms. For several moments, they wept together.

Finally, Mr. Barclay broke away and wiped his nose on his handkerchief. He spoke with emotions still quite raw. "Enough of this, ladies. God will help us all through this hard time, I'm sure. Colin included. Meanwhile, Cora, my love, dish yourself some breakfast, and the three of us will discuss the dilemma while we eat." He glanced warmly down at Mariah. "I've come to think of you as my daughter, Mariah, as part of our family, and your desire to stand by our son despite all that's happened means more to me than you will ever know."

Mariah stood in the doorway of the classroom, watching the girls ambling listlessly toward her for their morning lessons. She flashed a broad smile. "Good day, girls. I've a bit of news that might cheer you up."

Amy's expression brightened as she passed by on her way to her desk. "We can skip our lessons today?"

Mariah sent her a surely-you're-not-serious smirk. "I'm afraid not."

All three grumbled and took their places, obviously still weighted down by last night's gloom.

Reaching to close the door, Mariah spied Mr. Barclay at the top of the staircase at the other end of the long hall. He headed straight for Colin's room.

Her pulse picked up the pace. She backed into the schoolroom out of the man's view. How would Colin take his parents' decision concerning her? If only she could get the girls settled quickly and concentrating on their French verbs, she might be able to saunter down that way and overhear Colin's reaction.

She turned toward her unsmiling charges as they sat with their hands politely folded on their desks. "I know I promised to test you on your French first thing—"

"Promised?" Victoria scoffed, pursing her lips. "More like threatened."

"Yes, well, I'm aware that all our minds were too unsettled yesterday, so I've decided to give you some extra time to study." *While I sneak down to Colin's door and press my ear against it.*

Heather looked up, her azure eyes sad and troubled. "Oh, Mariah, havin' Colin come home blind is like havin' him come home dead."

It made no sense to correct the thirteen-year-old for dropping her Gs. This was not the time for a grammar lesson. The devastation felt by Colin's sisters was more than evident. Mariah crossed to Heather's desk and lifted the girl's chin. "That's simply not true, sweetheart. If you'd heard Colin bellowing his head off at breakfast this morning, you'd know he's nowhere near dead. He's very much alive."

Amy scrunched up her face. "Was he mad because Storm wasn't with him? He loves that horse almost as much as I do Patches. Almost as much as I love Storm. Did Colin say what happened to him?"

"I'm afraid not, dear." Mariah shrugged a shoulder. "The matter of his horse never came up. In fact, considering the mood your brother's in at the moment, I would suggest you wait a few days before mentioning the animal's whereabouts."

"But what if he got left behind someplace to starve?" Amy's chair screeched as she sprang from her seat. "He might be hurt. What if Storm's blind, too?"

Mariah moved to her and placed a hand on the child's shoulder, gently easing her back down to her seat. "Sweetheart, I'm sure nothing like that has happened. Most likely, another militiaman was riding him, since Colin wasn't well enough to be on horseback. Storm is probably stabled in Alexandria as we speak, waiting for someone to go and retrieve him."

"I'll do it. He knows me." Amy started to get up again.

Losing her patience, Mariah stopped her with a firm glare. "No one is going anywhere until after you've finished your lessons. I suggest you begin studying." She glanced at the other two sisters. "All of you."

It seemed to take forever for them to delve into their French vocabulary. But once they all were preoccupied and mouthing the verbs they'd been working on, Mariah knew she could leave. "I'll be right back, girls. I forgot something in my room."

It was the perfect excuse, really. If she happened by chance to overhear something along the way, no one could accuse her of eavesdropping. In fact, she'd keep to her side of the hall, in the event that Mr. Barclay—

or worse, Colin—should come out. Her stay in this house was quite conditional, after all. Everything she did for the next few days, at least, must appear above reproach. Then why was she out here now, with nothing but snooping on her mind?

Ignoring the twinge of conscience, she stopped directly across from Colin's room and craned her ear toward his door. Not a sound could be heard. Perhaps a step or two closer—

The chamber door swung inward! Mr. Barclay stood in the opening.

Mariah cringed at her bad timing. Surely the man could see her heart pounding beneath her bodice.

He stared at her briefly, then closed the door quietly behind himself. "Aren't you supposed to be with the girls?"

She prayed that the sudden warmth at her collar wouldn't rise to heat her cheeks. "Why yes. I just stepped out to retrieve a book from my room." Gratified that her response had come without hesitation, she breathed easier. "So, if you'll excuse me, I don't like to leave the girls unattended for long." She swept past him and headed for the door she shared with Amy. However, against her better judgement, she couldn't prevent herself from turning back. "Is all well with Colin?"

"As well as can be expected." No smile accompanied the statement. He strode past her and down the stairs, leaving her to speculate.

In case he paused on the steps for any reason, she continued on through Amy's room and into her own to fetch whatever book was most handy. But she wondered all the while what Colin's father had told him and how Colin had taken the news.

Mariah recalled that after breakfast, Mr. Barclay had decided to have Geoffrey Scott deliver the young horses Colin had mentioned to Nate— without Mariah. The decision thrilled her, even though that would give the trainer yet another encounter with Nate Kinyon. For whatever reason, Mr. Scott had been quite distant since his last conversation with her brother-in-law.

She let out a calming breath. The Barclays had decided to allow her to continue on as before, at least until the weather cooled. The mistress felt there was no need to make hasty decisions in such sweltering heat.

Mariah had the impression that Colin's mother was on her side, though the older lady never actually said the words. In all likelihood, there were very few local belles who would consider marriage to a blind man, no matter how rich and handsome he might be. Thank goodness for that. Given Colin's state of mind, Mariah wouldn't put it past him to propose to some other maiden just to rid himself of her.

But one truth remained. He loved her every bit as deeply as she loved him. He'd proved it to her over and over.

As she searched through the stack of books on the small stand beside her bed, the amethyst ring caught on the edge of one of the spines. She paused and let her gaze linger on the violet gem in its exquisite setting.

A smile played across her lips.

She'd do it. The more allies she had, the better. Scooping up the top book, she hurried back to the classroom.

Chapter 30

Returning to the classroom, Mariah assured herself she wouldn't be doing anything that should prick her conscience. Besides, this was nothing like trying to eavesdrop. Assured of her pure motives, she sauntered over to Victoria's desk and leaned down, placing her left hand strategically across the girl's French text. "Do you need any help with pronunciation?" Slowly she swept her hand across the page.

"No, I'm— Oh! What a beautiful ring." Tori caught Mariah's hand. "I've never seen you wear this before. What kind of stone is it?" Raising her lashes, she gazed up at Mariah, her sky-blue eyes wide, curious.

"Let me see." Heather rose and left her seat, with Amy traipsing after her as they came to look.

Amy leaned down to peer more closely. "Is it real?"

Mariah shrugged a shoulder. "I certainly hope so. Colin bought it for me when he visited my father. It's an amethyst."

"If it's from your poppy, it has to be real." Amy gave a confident nod.

Having returned her attention to the lovely ring, Victoria looked up again at Mariah. "But Colin returned home from England months ago.

Did he just now give it to you?"

"Actually, no. He gave it to me just before he left for the militia." Mariah's heart began to beat harder. "But since he had to go away again in haste after asking me to marry him"—all three girls gasped—"he suggested that we wait to tell your family until he came back home. So I've been wearing it on a chain around my neck."

"Oh, how romantic," Heather breathed, dreamy eyed.

Tori gazed down at the amethyst again, then at Mariah. "And Tuck was so happy to see me, I just know he'll propose soon, too." She twisted a finger around a golden curl near her ear.

About to remind the young lady that her mother would likely refuse her consent, Mariah chose not to burst Tori's bubble. She needed the three girls to be happy about her betrothal to their brother so they might help to further the cause.

"Hurrah!" Amy threw her arms about Mariah's waist. "I'm so happy! You're gonna be my big sister, and you won't ever have to leave us again." Abruptly letting go, she flew toward the door.

"Wait! Where are you going?" Mariah called after her.

The child didn't even slow down as she vaulted out the door. "To see Colin!"

"No! Wait!"

But her words had no effect. By the time Mariah reached the hall, Amy was charging into her brother's room.

Mariah dashed madly after her. What in the world had she been thinking? She should have thought things through before divulging news of her betrothal to that impulsive imp.

She hesitated only a second at Colin's open door, determined to catch Amy before she said anything. But stopping that girl was akin to stopping a waterfall.

Already the child's boundless energy had her jumping up and down in the middle of her brother's quarters. "I just heard the news!"

Mariah's heart sank. Too late. She closed her eyes.

"Why didn't you tell us?" Amy stopped and turned around, searching the room. "Where are you, Colin?"

Thank You, Lord. Mariah clutched her chest and tried to catch her breath. Colin wasn't in his room. She moved forward to collect his sister.

The door to the balcony swung open, and Colin came inside. "Is that you, Amy?"

Mariah halted in her tracks. She didn't want him to know she was there.

Amy had no such concern. "Yes. It's me. I'm real happy for you."

He tucked his chin and frowned. "Happy that I'm blind? Why would you be happy about that?"

"No, silly. I'm sad about that. I'm happy you're gonna marry Mariah."

Wincing, Mariah softly back-stepped toward the door. She had to get out of there.

But Amy gushed on with nary a breath. "That's the bestest thing I heard since. . .since you gave Patches to me. Isn't that so, Mariah?"

Mariah's heart stopped as she froze in place. She felt like a trapped rabbit and wanted nothing more than to escape and run.

His features hardening to granite, Colin raised his chin. "So my betrothed is here in the room with us."

"Uh-huh." Amy turned and pointed. "Right over there by the door."

A hole, Mariah thought. If only there was a rabbit hole to drop into. Still, she knew she had to stand firm. Too much was at stake. "I'm sorry Amy burst in on you unannounced, Colin. I know you asked to be left alone today. I'll take her back to the classroom." She took a step forward.

"No!" Amy stomped her foot and crossed her arms. "I want to talk to Colin. I want to tell him about me and Patches and all the things we did while he was away."

"Come, dear." Mariah tugged on the child's arm.

But Amy jerked free and turned a beseeching look up at her brother. "Colin, you were gone such a long time. Too long. Me and the horses missed you somethin' awful."

"Amy. . ." His demeanor softened a bit as he moved cautiously toward a wing chair to his right and ran a hand down its side, as if assuring himself it was positioned properly. Then he eased himself down to the cushioned seat. "I missed you a lot, too, squirt."

Hearing a gentleness in his tone that hadn't been there since his return, Mariah felt a ray of hope. Until he spoke again.

"Come give your brother a big hug, then run along. I'd like a private word with Mariah."

Amy glanced from him to Mariah and back and shrugged her thin shoulders. "Oh, sure." She ran into his open arms. After a sweet moment or two, she eased from his embrace and stepped back. "I reckon now you to want to hug and kiss and all that stuff, huh?"

He gave a small grunt and lightly swatted her bottom to hurry her on her way. "Somethin' like that. Oh, and Amy, please close the door on your way out."

She giggled and ran to do his bidding.

As the door slammed behind Amy, Mariah felt like a condemned person with a noose around her neck, waiting for the trapdoor to collapse.

Colin released a slow breath. "Seems you've been mighty busy this morning, haven't you?"

She cringed at the clipped syllables.

"Mighty busy." He wagged his head, a droll smirk tightening his mouth.

Moistening her dry lips, she shrugged a shoulder. "The girls noticed my ring." It was a lame excuse, and she knew it. For a second she had the impression that Colin could see, the way his glower bored into her.

He did not respond, just rubbed a hand across his chin.

Lowering her gaze from what she reminded herself was an unseeing stare, she noticed that both of her hands clutched handfuls of her skirt, crushing the muslin fabric. She tried for a casual tone. "Well, I really should get back to your sisters."

"Not so fast." He paused momentarily, as if gathering his thoughts. "Obviously I did not make myself clear when we spoke last night, so I'll repeat what I said. There will be no wedding, no matter how many members of my family you rally. Your brother-in-law told me you'd always been considered the clever one among your siblings, and I see you've proven him right."

Chagrined by the statement, Mariah did her best to sound appalled.

"The man has scarcely set eyes on me. He knows nothing about me."

Colin tipped his head. "It doesn't really matter." He stretched his long legs out before him and relaxed against the chair. "My decision wouldn't be any different if you were the queen of kindness itself. But if you will leave my home without any further protest, I'll give you a choice. If you don't wish to go live with your sister, I'll pay your passage back to England and give you a goodly sum to jingle in your purse, besides."

Mariah's hackles rose with each word. She could not believe he thought so little of her. Nevertheless, she composed herself and spoke evenly. "I understand that, at the moment, you believe your world has come to an end. But as time goes by, you'll come to realize life hasn't really changed so very much. And when that time comes, and you regain your senses, I plan to be here."

"My senses?" He scoffed. "All of them? Except, of course, for that particularly crucial one. . .my sight."

Mariah regretted her bad choice of words. She sought another tack. Oh yes, Rose. Say what Rose would say. "I can see I've upset you again. For that I am truly sorry." At a loss to say more, she backed toward the door, until her fingers grasped the handle. "I really must return to the girls. Perhaps we can talk again later."

"Wait!"

But Mariah whirled out the door and closed it behind her, ignoring his voice. She hurried away as fast as she could.

That had not gone well at all. She had to stop trying to manipulate the situation. If only she'd remembered her decision to act like her older sister before allowing herself to become so vexed. After all, when had anyone ever railed so vehemently at Rose—except for the night she informed the family she'd sold most of their prized possessions out from under them.

Slowing as she neared the schoolroom door, Mariah paused. The single reason the family had yelled at Rose was because, for once, she'd uncharacteristically taken matters into her own hands. She'd done the sort of rash thing Mariah might have done under those circumstances.

A grimace flattened Mariah's lips. Possibly she wouldn't have been quite as self-sacrificing as Rose had been, even selling herself. But for now, this situation required self-sacrifice. Colin needed that.

From now on, she'd stop trying to be clever, as Colin had so rudely put it. She would step inside Rose's very skin, martyr herself for the cause of Colin's ultimate happiness.

And hers.

Hearing the door to his chamber close and Mariah's footsteps receding down the hall, Colin closed his eyes in disgust. Some homecoming. He'd been positive that Mariah would gladly accept her release. Apparently, he'd underestimated her greed.

This added torment was more than anyone should have to endure. After weeks of travel in a bumpy wagon, listening hour after hour to the groans of other wounded men, he couldn't wait to leave the terrible defeat behind and return to familiar surroundings.

The defeat. The surrender. His only saving grace was that he'd been unconscious when Washington signed the surrender document and hadn't had to witness that humiliation. From the reports he'd heard, a heavy rain had started after he'd been shot and never ceased through the night. Because of their too hasty efforts to construct the fort, the gunpowder had little protection from the elements, and only a few able soldiers remained after the first barrage to fend off the surrounding horde of French and Indians. The situation had been hopeless from the start.

Nate said it was only by the grace of God that the French commander had even offered the militia the opportunity to surrender, and only then because one of his Indian scouts had reported hearing marching drums coming from the east.

Even now, Colin couldn't hold back a sarcastic chuckle. As if any of the other colonies would have come to their assistance. Knowing that their fellow English colonies refused to lift a finger to prevent the French from taking over their territories was indeed bitter medicine to swallow.

With a ragged sigh, he rose from the chair. Hands outstretched, he made his way to the bedstead, then edged around it to the night table for a drink of water. Soon, he vowed, he'd have this room memorized, then the rest of the house, and even down to the stables. He was determined not to stumble around much longer.

Finding the glass, Colin lifted it and took several swallows, enjoying the sensation of the cool liquid coursing down his throat. Somehow, with God's help, he'd survive being blind. His thirst sated, he set down the glass and sank onto the bed he could feel behind his legs. Yes, somehow he'd eke out a life for himself—just not the one he'd expected.

At that deflating thought, he lay back on the pillows and tried to blot from his mind the well-laid plans he'd always had for himself.

Sleep. He needed more sleep.

But as he lay there in the unending darkness, his anger refused to let go. Anger at the French, the heedless colonial governors, and a fate that would change a man's life forever. But mostly he was angry at that arrogant, selfish Englishwoman, Mariah Harwood.

Why had he never noticed her true nature before? In reality, the two of them had spent very little actual time together. Mostly he'd just thought about her, created in his mind the woman he believed her to be. . .and for no other reason than her beauty. She was the most beautiful, most alluring woman he'd ever seen in his life. The siren who lured sailors to their deaths on a jagged reef. The Delilah to his Samson. She was a liar.

Only after he told her to leave did she say she loved him. Not when it would have meant something, like the last time he'd feasted his eyes on her and held her in his arms and asked her to marry him. He might have believed her then.

But not now.

From what Nate Kinyon had told him, Mariah had not come to America with Rose out of a desire to help her sister or the rest of her family. She had come with all her superior ways with but one goal in mind—to catch a rich husband. And the mere fact that her catch ended up blind would not stand in the way of a fortune hunter like her. He frowned. Mother had seen through her from the very start. Oh, how he wished he'd listened to her.

A niggling thought crept in, and his gaze gravitated naturally toward the faint light streaming from the balcony's open door. If Mother had seen through Mariah to her devious, selfish nature, why had she so readily agreed with Father this morning to allow the pretender to stay?

Chapter 31

As time ticked slowly by, Colin found it difficult to get any much-needed rest. In his mind he could still hear the rush of heavy rains and recall slogging through the mud with the militia. The clatter of chopping trees for the fort echoed in his head, along with the roar of artillery and the sharp report of musket fire. And he could hear cries of the wounded, mournful and heartrending. The sounds never seemed to end. Perhaps in time, with any luck at all, they would.

But the darkness would be his lot forever. He might as well get used to it.

When he heard the girls leave their classrooom and go downstairs for the noon meal, he rose from his bed and began counting off steps to various spots in his room. Six steps to the balcony door, four steps from there to the wing chair, two more to the bed, five to the door to the hallway. With each successful journey around the chamber, his confidence lifted, and so did his mood. He wasn't even perturbed when he heard rapid running in the hall. It was to be expected in a house filled with lively sisters.

His door flew open.

"Colin!"

Glad to hear Amy's voice, he smiled. "Come sit down, little sis. Tell me all that's been happening. Is the horse from England faring well?"

"Oh, yes," she gushed. She hugged him, then flopped onto a matching chair, the scent of outdoors clinging to her like a shawl. "By the time Poppy even noticed him, Russet Knight was racing up the lane so fast Poppy didn't care what color he was." She paused for breath. "I couldn't wait any longer. I came to find out where Storm is, since he didn't come home with you. If he's someplace close, like Alexandria, I wanna go get him back."

Colin kneaded his chin. "I'd forgotten all about Storm. Thank you, squirt, for reminding me. Poor fellow, he's had a hard time of it. I'm sure he must be stabled somewhere near where the militia disbanded. Tell Pa to send someone after him."

"I will. And I'll tell Poppy you want me to go, too. Storm will be so glad to see me an' Patches. He's prob'ly real lonesome. I hope somebody took good care of him."

Colin chuckled as he heard her fling herself off the chair and dash away. He could just imagine the glee on her expressive face as she ran. The kid would turn herself into a horse if she could.

Settling back with a smile, he wondered if Amy would ever outgrow her fixation for horses. Being so much younger than her two sisters and never having been allowed to mix with the slave children, she'd had no one to play with except the horses. . .and him. Bless her heart, she was the only family member who didn't pussyfoot around him since he'd come home.

He stood and counted his way to the door. Time to start learning how many paces there were to the stairs.

On his third trip to the staircase and back, he heard someone coming up the servants' staircase. Probably Benjamin bringing his tray of food. He'd wait just inside his room and hold the door open for the slave.

But the footsteps didn't sound heavy like the butler's. They sounded light. Feminine. Had Mariah volunteered to bring his meal, hoping to get another chance at him? His lips flattened into a grim line.

"Why, thank you, dear," his mother said as she passed him. "I was wondering how I'd manage that. Where should I put your dinner?"

He sighed with relief and closed the door then turned toward her voice. "The table between the chairs will be fine."

"Let me help you to the chair."

"It's not necessary, Mother. I know where it is." He moved cautiously toward it and sat down.

"Oh. How wonderful. Your sight is improving after all. I've been—"

He shook his head. "No, it hasn't. But if you'd please have a seat for a moment, I have something to say."

"So do I, dear." Her skirts swished softly as she seated herself. "That's why I brought your meal myself. I wanted to talk to you."

"About what?"

"A few minutes ago, one of the Tucker family servants came with a message saying they'd like to drop by after supper. Of course, I sent a return invitation that they join us for our meal. From the way Dennis was hugging Victoria yesterday, I fear he intends to offer for her, and you know how I feel about that. I absolutely refuse to give up one acre of our land, and your father knows that all too well. I figure with the Tuckers at our supper table, we'll have the advantage. Particularly if you are present."

Having remained quiet out of respect as she prattled on, the anger building inside him boiled over. "With the poor blind son present, you mean."

She gasped. "Not at all. I meant no such thing. I just felt that having another adult on our side would help the cause."

"Let me get this straight. You still consider Tori as property to be bargained over—unlike me. Now that I'm damaged, you'll gladly pass me off to a lowly bond servant." He sniffed in disdain.

His mother took a sharp intake of breath. "Why, what an outrageous thing to say."

"I agree." But he didn't soften his tone.

"Concerning Victoria, she's a young, impressionable girl who will fall in and out of love probably a dozen times between now and next year. And yes, I'd prefer she marry advantageously. It's what I've always desired for all our children."

269

"Yet you don't think it an advantage for her to live close by, where she could still be part of our lives, and we could visit her whenever we please."

She didn't respond for a second. "That *is* a lovely sentiment, however—"

"But you don't mind sending her away to some far-off port city, while you invite a scheming bond servant to be your new daughter. Is that right?"

He heard her sink back in the chair. "My. You are being vicious today. But considering your recent trauma, I shall make allowance for that and let it pass." Her hand covered his.

He flinched and pulled away from her touch.

"Colin, dear," she began evenly, in her most patient tone. "I have spent many hours in prayer since your return. Many hours. And when I saw Mariah collapse into heart-wrenching tears after you so rudely rejected her, I had not the slightest doubt those tears were real. Her heart was shattered. I know she loves you very deeply."

Colin gave an inaudible huff but let her continue.

"Now, as for her being a schemer, I can only say that her service to us and her care for the girls has been above reproach and far outweighs any amount of money you paid for her. My only regret is that I was forced to order her to take on the duties of a kitchen maid when we were shorthanded the day of the race. For quite a spell after that humiliation, she was hesitant to join us whenever we had visitors."

He considered that information before answering. "If what you say is even remotely true, it's all the more reason she should leave this house. Being married to a blind man is decidedly not advantageous for such a talented and comely lass. She could do far better."

A weary sigh issued from his mother. "Son, I'm afraid you don't know the first thing about love: true, God-given love between a man and a woman, the selfless kind than overcomes any obstacle and endures regardless of adversity." The rustle of her skirts indicated she'd risen. "I apologize if I've upset you. I take into account that your feelings are all topsy-turvy right now. As for Mariah, we can discuss her another time.

But for this evening, I expect you to be a gentleman and, if nothing else, help entertain our guests. After all, Dennis is your best friend."

He felt the breeze from her wake as she started for the door.

"I'll send Benjamin up later to help you select your clothing." Without further word, she left, her light footsteps fading as she went down the hall.

"Hmph." Colin snorted, knowing that if he didn't join the party she'd probably bring every last one of those guests right up to his room. And the last thing he needed was to have this last small piece of sanctuary totally overrun.

Sanctuary. . .where people sought safety in the Middle Ages.

Sanctuary. . .

His mind drifted to England, a land of green hedgerows and charming hamlets. He recalled the magnificent cathedrals he'd seen there: cool, quiet places where one could almost feel the presence of God. He'd felt that same quiet peace the last night before Fort Necessity was attacked, when he'd knelt down to pray right after he'd made God a promise.

How quickly he'd forgotten.

A ragged breath came from deep inside, and his shoulders slumped. "Forgive me, Father. I know I was growling at Mother, when all she wants is what's best for us—even if she does happen to be wrong. From now on, Lord, I'll try to pray first before opening my big mouth. Please keep reminding me to do that. And please give me the calm to be the gentleman Mother wants this evening."

He wanted to add something about Mariah but didn't know where to begin.

⁓

"Shh!" Mariah put a finger to her lips as she and Victoria passed Colin's door on their way to the girls' room just beyond. "He might be asleep." And she certainly wasn't up to facing another bout with him at the moment. Reaching Tori's chamber, she ushered the girl inside.

A giggle bubbled forth from Victoria, who'd been flighty since hearing her beloved would be coming to supper. "I just know Tuck is gonna ask

Papa for my hand, so I must look absolutely perfect." She twirled happily in a swirl of sprigged muslin skirts as she danced toward the dressing table. Tugging the ribbon holding back her curls, she carelessly tossed it away, then lifted her golden tresses to the top of her head and arched her brows as she bent to gaze at her likeness in the looking glass. "You simply have to make me look spectacular, Mariah. Please."

Mariah couldn't help a light laugh. "Not too spectacular. You don't want to appear obvious, do you? How about perfectly pretty, instead?"

Victoria pursed her lips, and her blue eyes sparkled with joy. "I suppose perfectly pretty will do." Scooping her skirt to one side, she dropped down onto the dressing table stool. But her smile wilted as Mariah stepped up behind her and picked up the brush. "No matter how many times I've told Mother I love Tuck, I know she doesn't believe me. He's not the son of a wealthy merchant, you know. She's sure to try and stop us."

Mariah's first instinct was to urge Tori to get her father alone and extract a promise from him to say yes to a match between her and the young man from the next plantation. Mr. Barclay had such a soft heart when it came to his girls.

But what would Rose say? The twinge of conscience clanged into her thoughts as surely as if Rose were present. "I think we should pray about it, sweetheart."

Victoria's eyes popped wide, as if that was the last thing she'd expected to come from Mariah's mouth.

Nevertheless, Mariah persisted. "Let's bow our heads, shall we?" She waited for Tori to follow suit. "Dear heavenly Father, we know that You love us, and because You do, You gave us the commandment to honor our parents. Sometimes that is really hard to do. But we know that our parents also love us and want what's best for us."

Tori interrupted. "But, Lord, You said in Corinthians that it's better to marry than to burn, and I burn with love for Tuck."

That was too much for Mariah. She sputtered into laughter, and Victoria joined in. After a few moments, Mariah regained control and purpose. She wrapped her arms around her sweet charge and gave her a squeeze, then bowed her head once more. "Yes, Father, You certainly know Victoria's wish in the matter. We ask that You please soften Mistress Barclay's heart concerning Tori's deepest desire."

And Colin's, concerning my own. . . She released a pent-up sigh.

Chapter 32

After the butler helped him into clothing appropriate for the evening, Colin relaxed in his room. Or tried to relax. For the past two hours there'd been a steady cacophony of giggles, loud thumps, and slamming doors and drawers in the next chamber. The racket coming from Victoria's room seemed to have no end.

"From all the commotion, you'd think they were preparing for a coronation," he muttered. But then, for all he knew, that sort of nonsense went on all the time in the female world. He'd never before been confined to his room long enough to overhear the way his sisters conducted themselves when preparing for company. Truth was, the womenfolk in the family always emerged from their cocoons looking quite beautiful. . . especially Mariah. He called forth a vision of her in lavender ruffles that complemented her ebony curls and incredible eyes, then dismissed it with a scowl.

Someone rapped on his door and opened it.

"Mastah Colin, yo' folks wants you to go greet de guests now. I's to take y'all down."

"Thanks, Benjamin." Colin nodded and made a point of not hesitating as he crossed the room. "Don't take me down at such a slow pace that I look helpless."

"No, sah. We'll high-step it all de way."

Grinning at the mental image that conjured up, Colin took the butler's arm. "Have the Tuckers arrived yet?"

"Dey was jest turnin' on our lane when I come up fo' y'all."

"Good. Then I should reach the foyer before they knock."

"Dat's what de Missus say."

Colin grunted. For all her fine words, it appeared Mother didn't want him to be an embarrassment any more than he did himself.

As they started down the stairs, doors opened and closed behind him with a flurry of female whispers and the rapid patter of approaching slippers. The girls—and most likely Mariah—were coming in all their glory. They called out greetings as they raced past him.

"Hi, Colin."

"Love you, Colin."

Then he heard much more sedate footsteps. "Good evening, Mr. Barclay." Mariah matched her steps with his and the butler's as they continued down the wide staircase. "You look quite dashing this evening."

Colin reminded himself to be polite. Still, he didn't want her to attach herself to him. The Tuckers would be at the door any second. "Thank you. Your perfume smells nice."

His mother's voice drifted from the foyer as she instructed the girls to quiet down.

The brass door knocker tapped.

Colin's spirits sank. He had yet to reach the marble floor. How many steps remained to the bottom landing before the guests were admitted inside?

Mariah threaded her arm through his. "Benjamin, you may go answer the door. I'll allow Colin to escort me the rest of the way."

"Yes'm."

Before Colin could protest, the butler hurried away, leaving him at Mariah's mercy. He heard the door open.

"Last step," Mariah said softly. She moved with him toward the cluster of happy voices.

"Good evening, everyone," Dennis's mother gushed. "It was so nice of you to invite us. And Colin, it's great to see you up and about."

Mr. Tucker stepped closer and squeezed Colin's shoulder, speaking in his booming voice. "I second that, son."

"Yes, old man," Tuck piped in. "You're a far sight better lookin' than you were when we dragged you back here."

Colin nodded and smiled toward each voice. "We're glad you could come."

"And Mariah." Tuck spoke from right in front of her and Colin. "You look marvelous this evening."

"Thank you."

"I'm sure you look dashing as well, Tuck," Colin chided, "if Tori's sugary welcome was any indication."

"Colin! Please!" his sister gasped.

Mariah gave a quick yank to his sleeve.

"Only teasing, sis."

Mother finally came to the rescue. "Helen, Drew, it's such a warm evening I thought we might be more comfortable out on the terrace. Shall we?"

"Sounds delightful, Cora, my dear," Father said, taking charge.

"Heather?" Colin heard Tuck say, and he knew his friend would be escorting both sisters outside.

Colin grimaced, wishing he'd spoken sooner himself so he could walk with someone instead of scheming Mariah. "Amy?"

Mariah turned him to follow the others and spoke in a whisper. "Amy had supper earlier. Your mother thought it best, considering her, shall we say, indelicate way with words."

He emitted a low chuckle. "I'll bet she did."

"It's wonderful to see you in such high spirits, Colin," Dennis's mother said, walking ahead of him and Mariah. "You always were such a brave boy."

The pity in her tone made Colin want to retch.

Mariah, however, tightened her hold. "I understand that your son was also quite brave, Mistress Tucker. Victoria said he, too, was wounded."

"He was?" Her voice shook. "Dennis. Is it true? You were shot? Why didn't you tell me? You might've been killed."

Tuck quickly put her at ease. "A musket ball merely grazed my shoulder, Mom, that's all. Nothing to get upset about. It was all but healed by the time I got home."

As the woman questioned her son further, Colin felt compelled to express his appreciation to Mariah for steering the attention away from him. He leaned close to her scented warmth. "Thank you."

"No need."

A waft of cooler air brushed his face. They'd reached their destination, and he hadn't made a single misstep. He had Mariah to thank for that, too.

The chairs scraping around the table ceased quickly as everyone found seats. Colin managed to hold out Mariah's chair for her before taking his own. Her perfume so sweetened the air around him, he wondered if she'd applied the entire bottle.

Footsteps from behind preceded the aroma of roast pork, mashed potatoes, spiced applesauce, and collard greens, as the servants carried platters of food to the table and dished out portions to everyone. Colin appreciated having something besides perfume to inhale.

At the head of the group, Father eased his chair back and stood to offer the blessing. "Our most gracious heavenly Father, we thank You for this opportunity to fellowship with dear friends and enjoy the bounty You so faithfully provide. We ask Your blessing upon our food and our conversation. And we are most grateful for Your mercy in bringing our sons home to us again. May You watch over the colony of Virginia and the other colonies during this time of trial. Amen."

At least he didn't mention my personal trial. I'm thankful for that small mercy. Other sounds drifted to Colin's ears—the snapping of napkins to be placed on laps, the tap of forks against plates. He hoped he could manage the task of eating without looking foolish. While Mistress Tucker began expounding on Mother's lovely garden, Colin edged his fingers up from his lap to feel for his napkin.

Mariah's hand covered his and guided it to the cloth beneath his fork, then quickly slid her fingers away.

"Oh, yes," Mother said. "The star of jasmine cuttings I ordered last spring have done beautifully. Already they are climbing the railings and have such a sweet, heady, scent. Especially at eventide."

While everyone delved into the food, Colin nibbled on a buttered roll he'd felt on his plate.

Mariah cleared her throat. "Mistress Barclay, the pork is so deliciously tender, it falls apart at the touch of a fork."

Already having detected the meat from its aroma, Colin knew Mariah was trying to provide information for his benefit, and he appreciated her thoughtfulness. He managed to spear a piece of it and forked it to his lips.

"Why, thank you, dear. We are fortunate to have Eloise's skills. She's always been a wonderful cook."

"I agree, Cora," Tuck's mother said. "One of these days, I'd be most grateful if you'd send her over to teach our cook how to make those wonderful, flaky pastries she does so well. Hettie has never been able to master them."

Mother gave a throaty laugh. "I can send her, but I doubt she'll give up her secret recipes. They were passed down to her by a French Creole cook at her prior owner's."

"Speaking of the French," Father cut in, "when my daughter and I rode to Alexandria to retrieve Colin's horse this afternoon, I picked up a newspaper from Philadelphia. The publisher, a man named Benjamin Franklin, wrote a very interesting piece stating that if the colonies don't start cooperating with each other soon, the French could very easily concentrate their efforts, and with the help of their Indian allies, they could pick us off one by one."

"A pity he didn't write that before our valiant boys were forced to go to battle with too few men and insufficient supplies," Mr. Tucker said on a wry note. He set down his glass with a click.

"At least we Virginians put forth an effort," Tuck boasted. "And now, at long last, the House of Burgesses has agreed to spend twenty thousand pounds toward the cause."

Father chuckled. "Yes. And they finally got Governor Dinwiddie to sign it, including the rider abolishing that gold pistole fee on land patents. From what I heard, Dinwiddie was livid when he saw that proposed—again."

"Well," Mr. Tucker replied. "I, for one, am glad the rider was included. Gold is much too hard to come by in the colonies as it is, without shipping it over to England to fill their coffers."

"Getting back to that newspaper article," Father said, "there's a very-to-the-point picture in it. One of a snake being cut into several pieces, with the name of a colony on each section. Below it read, 'Join or Die.' Very apropos, wouldn't you say?"

Mother coughed lightly into her napkin. "I think discussing such a topic at the dinner table is definitely not apropos. Would you gentlemen mind saving this conversation for after our meal?"

"Quite right, Cora, my love. Till later, gentlemen."

Colin could almost see him raising his lemonade in a salute and tipping his head.

"Speaking of later," Mr. Tucker chimed in, "I have a bit of business I'd like to discuss with you and your son after supper."

Detecting an almost imperceptible titter from Victoria, Colin surmised she would be the topic. But why did his and Tuck's parents want him involved?

"I see." A curt note tinged Mother's voice. "Well, Eloise has made some delightful apple dumplings for our dessert. After we've had a chance to enjoy them, Helen and the rest of us ladies shall wait for you menfolk in the parlor. I do hope you won't be overlong. The girls have some lovely entertainment planned." She rang a silver bell to call for dessert.

Colin picked up his fork and made another stab at his plate. He still had some food to take care of. All in all, though, this promised to be a lively evening.

"Would you gentlemen care for a cigar?" Colin's father closed the library door for privacy.

"Don't mind if I do," Mr. Tucker responded.

Colin heard the humidor being opened and smelled the rich aroma of tobacco.

"I selected the best leaves myself," his father said, his inflection proud.

Not eager to handle something with one end on fire, Colin gave a negative wave of his hand. "Not just now, Pa."

"None for me either," Tuck said.

Colin stifled a smirk at the uncharacteristic hint of nervousness in his friend's voice. No doubt Tuck's palms were sweating, as well.

"Then let us be seated." Father spoke pleasantly. "We might as well be comfortable while we discuss our business."

Tuck took hold of Colin's arm and turned him a bit. "Come sit with me on the settee, old man." The slight tremble in his fingers on Colin's sleeve was more than evident. Obviously he needed moral support.

As they settled back against the damask upholstery, faint music drifted from the parlor across the way. Colin detected only the harpsichord and flute and figured Tori was too overwrought to play her violin. He figured she'd perched on whatever chair had the best view of the library doors.

Mr. Tucker cleared his throat. "I'm sure it's no surprise why we're here this evening. Our son Dennis has expressed a desire to wed your daughter Victoria. I've been told the only impediment to a marriage between the pair is the matter of a dowry acceptable to us both. Is that correct?"

Seated beside Colin, Tuck nudged Colin's shoe with his.

"Yes, that is true," Father answered. "Cora and I—well, the whole family, to be entirely correct—think very highly of Dennis. He more than proved his worth by not shirkin' his duty last winter."

No one spoke for a few seconds. Colin had expected his father to say more, to state the dowry he and Mother, especially, were willing to send with Tori—unless he was waiting to hear Mr. Tucker's proposal first.

Mr. Tucker shifted in his seat. "Since you and I both agree our farmland is worth far more than a mere sack of coin that is easily squandered, Dennis and I have come up with a simple solution. If Colin would concede to deed over his property on the South Fork of the Potomac, it would in no way diminish your fields. You could reimburse Colin the price of that land, plus a small profit, of course."

Caught off guard by the suggestion, Colin suddenly realized why the Tuckers had wanted him present. He hoped his expression hadn't betrayed the disappointment that sank in his heart like a rock. Not only had his own dreams been tied to that parcel, but it hurt to think they knew he'd never be able to fulfill those dreams now.

Obviously his father noticed his lack of response. "Tuck, what do you propose to bring to the marriage?"

"M–me? I. . .uh—"

Mr. Tucker cut in. "Eldon, you know Dennis is sole heir to all our properties."

"Quite. But I'd like to hear what his plans happen to be for my daughter."

"Plans?" Tuck finally managed. "I plan to love her and cherish her, sir. And the moment you agree to our marriage, I plan to start building a cottage for us." He turned slightly in his seat. "A cozy little honeymoon cottage near where the brook comes out of the woods in the west section. Our own private place."

The more his friend rattled on, so full of dreams for Tori and himself, the more dejected Colin became. If he hadn't lost his sight, he might've been discussing his marriage to Mariah this evening.

Father interrupted his thoughts. "Well. That would please Victoria, I'm sure. But as to the South Fork parcel, that is not my decision. It's for my son to decide."

Hoping to hide his melancholy, Colin sat up straighter and raised his chin. He forced himself to speak in a normal tone. "It sounds like a reasonable solution to me."

In a flash, Tuck grabbed him and hugged him, thumping him on the back. "Thank you, my friend. Thank you." He sprang to his feet. "I must go tell Tori."

"If you happen to see Benjamin in the foyer," Colin called after him, "tell him I need to speak to him." He lumbered to his feet and turned in the direction of his father. "I'm rather tired now. Would you give the ladies my regrets?"

Chapter 33

Mariah could scarcely concentrate on the classical pieces she'd chosen to play for the dinner guests. Though she rendered each one flawlessly, her attention remained focused across the way, her angst easily as keen as Victoria's. The girl sat forward in her chair, her gaze fixed on the library doors.

Hoping against hope that by some miracle Colin's desire to marry her would be rekindled as he listened to his friend's plea for Tori's hand, Mariah released a ragged sigh. Surely he'd noticed what an asset she'd been to him this evening. What an asset she would always be.

The library door swung open, and Mariah's fingers accidentally struck the wrong keys. Fortunately, no one seemed to notice as Dennis rushed across the hall to the parlor, grinning from ear to ear.

Mariah couldn't help smiling herself when Victoria jumped to her feet and flew into the young man's open arms.

Mistress Barclay, however, didn't appear so thrilled. The woman's grim expression revealed the realization that her lifelong plans for her daughter had been thwarted.

But Dennis Tucker's mother rushed to the couple and embraced them both. "Praise be! I have a new daughter."

"And I have a new brother!" Heather laughed and joined the celebrants.

Tuck drew Tori close to his side and strode to her mother, who remained seated and unsmiling. "I hope you will be happy for us. It won't be necessary for you to give up any of your land holdings."

She tilted her perfectly coiffed head. "I don't understand. Your father is willing to accept money instead?"

"Not exactly." He gave her a smug smile and hugged Victoria. "Colin has agreed to deed his land on the South Fork to me, and in turn, your husband will compensate him."

Stunned by that news, Mariah rose from the harpsichord stool. "Are you referring to the parcels you and he bought in the backcountry?" The land Colin had promised to take her to see.

"That's right." He turned back to Mistress Barclay.

Her demeanor changed to one of approval as she stood to her feet and took their hands in hers. "Why, what a perfect solution. I'd never have thought of it."

Tuck shrugged a shoulder. "Well, the property is in question at the moment because of the French. But I'm willing to gamble that the colonies will come together soon and push the French forces back to Canada, where they belong."

"I'm. . .so pleased for you." Mariah somehow managed weak congratulations as she started for the doorway. She could no longer bear to be around Victoria and Tuck and their overflowing joy.

Mr. Barclay and Colin emerged from the library at that moment. "I'll return shortly," the older man called over his shoulder as he and his son started up the staircase.

Mariah's spirits sank even further. So Colin also felt the need to escape. Obviously he didn't want to be near her after having just forfeited the land he promised would be theirs alone.

She clenched her teeth as rage overtook her despair, then composed herself and turned to the happy couple with a forced smile. "I'm truly thrilled for you both. But I'm afraid I have a bit of a headache, so if you'll please excuse me. . ." She hurried out of the parlor, almost crashing into Dennis's father as he came to join the lovebirds. "Forgive me," she blurted but kept going.

On her way up the stairs, she met Mr. Barclay descending, a huge grin broadening his mustache. She breezed past him with a polite nod.

Her anger continued to build. At the top landing, Mariah glared at Colin's door. It was high time she gave him a piece of her mind. Marching straight for his room, she reached for the handle. But her hand froze before touching the metal. Were she to barge in and start yelling at him, she'd end up crying. And the last thing she wanted to do was bawl in front of him over this latest all-too-evident rejection of her. She'd already been humiliated beyond belief.

Blinking back stinging tears, she continued on to her and Amy's door, only then remembering that the child was in the room. Her shoulders sagged. Taking a deep breath to fortify herself, she walked in.

Amy tossed a stuffed horse aside and jumped up from her bed. "Well? What did Poppy say?"

"He's agreed to allow them to marry." Surprised at her own flat tone, Mariah propped up a faint smile.

"Oh, goody. Tuck is always so much fun."

"Indeed. Why don't you go downstairs and congratulate them?"

The words had scarcely left her mouth before Amy charged out of the room and down the hall.

Thank goodness. Some peace at last. Without so much as a backward look, Mariah crossed to her chamber and the blessed darkness within, closing the door behind her. Hot tears streamed down her cheeks before she was halfway to her bed.

Her foot tangled in a carelessly discarded garment, and she stumbled to her knees, catching herself at the edge of the bed. She sobbed even harder. All was lost now.

Sagging against the mattress, her head drooped as she gave vent to her grief. Then she peered up through blurry eyes. "Why did this have to happen, Father? What have I done that was so bad You'd allow things to turn out this wrong? I haven't flirted with any of the men who come here—even though You know they stared at me. Nor did I go after those young swains in Williamsburg who were oh, so willing. I've been trying to be good like Rose." She searched the darkness. "Are You even there, Lord?"

Utterly bereft, Mariah collapsed in her sorrow. It was true. God didn't care about her at all.

From somewhere deep inside, Mariah sensed a voice telling her to open her Bible at the bookmark.

The bookmark. Where had Mistress Barclay left off last Sunday and instructed her to continue with the girls? She couldn't remember. Colin had come home then, and she'd simply forgotten the passage they'd been discussing.

Pulling herself up from the floor, she drew a handkerchief from her skirt pocket to wipe her eyes and nose, then lit her lamp. She rummaged through her stack of books till she found the leather-bound volume.

The protruding bookmark caught her eye, and she admired the delicate flowers Rose had embroidered all around its edges when she'd fashioned it as a Christmas gift years ago. *Oh, Rose, if only you were here with me to hold me and love me. I'm so alone.*

Dabbing at a new onslaught of tears, Mariah sank onto her bed and opened the Bible. A tiny smile tugged at the corners of her lips when it opened to the preachy book of James. Her gaze immediately was drawn to a verse in the fourth chapter:

"Humble yourselves in the sight of the Lord, and he shall lift you up."

"It always comes back to that, doesn't it, Father? Seems I'm always praying for what I want, working and trying to that end. And it always falls apart. I give up." A new river of tears flowed like rain on a windowpane. *I give up.* She'd never felt so defeated in her life. *Dear God, You say You want us to come humbly to You. Well then, here I am. This miserable mess I've made of my life and myself is Yours if You want it. From now on, whatever You want me to do or say or be, I'll obey You. From this day forth I'm Yours to do with as You wish.*

An indescribable warmth began to flow through her being, filling her, fuller and fuller, until there was no room left for pain. All pain, all angst, all her sorrow miraculously evaporated like dew in the sunshine.

God did love her after all. He loved her so much that He was hugging her from the inside out, making her new.

She picked up the Bible to read again. She wanted to know more. So much more. She flipped to the Gospel of John. Rose always said that was a good place to start.

~

Mariah didn't have the slightest concept of how long she'd been reading her Bible when the outer door burst open, and excited chatter and laughter spilled in as three giggly girls returned.

Without knocking, a glowing Victoria whirled into Mariah's chamber, followed by her sisters. "Isn't this the most marvelous day there ever was?" Flinging her arms wide, she closed her dreamy eyes and twirled in a circle.

"Yes, dear." Amazingly, Mariah meant it from the heart. "A most marvelous day, indeed."

The threesome sprawled onto Mariah's bed, all talking at once.

"Wait!" Laughing, she laid aside the Bible. "One at a time, please."

Victoria grinned. "Me first. After all, it's my wedding day we're talking about." She snagged Mariah's hand and held it to her bosom. "And you must, you absolutely must, come with me to the dressmaker to help me choose the loveliest satin and lace. My bridal gown must be the most perfect gown ever, the envy of every girl in the colony."

"Tell Mariah how Tuck talked Mama into having the wedding in just two months." Heather jabbed her sister with an elbow. "He really, really wants to marry Tori."

Mariah's mouth gaped. "Two months! That's an awfully short time to plan a wedding."

"Actually," Victoria said, "it'll be in ten weeks. That's when the leaves should start displaying their beautiful fall colors. Can't you just picture the guests coming up our lane with the trees all ablaze? And what do you think about weaving autumn branches into a wedding arbor?"

Not to be outdone, Heather inserted her intentions. "Of course, I'll be playing something airy on the flute to go with the wind rustling through the leaves. It'll be perfect."

Heather is turning into quite the romantic, Mariah thought with a smile.

Amy rose to her knees. "And Mama said I could go with Poppy to deliver invitations to all the neighbors."

"Oh, yes." Victoria tousled her kid sister's hair. "Those to Mother's family in Boston will have to go out in the post right away. Wouldn't it be wonderful if some of our relatives came from such a distance? Just for my wedding?"

Laughter bubbled out of Mariah as she drew Tori into a hug. "Yes, sweet girl. It would be wonderful. And you're quite right. This is a most marvelous day."

Chapter 34

Colin seethed as incessant plans for Victoria's wedding bombarded him from all directions at the breakfast table. Was there nothing else of worth in the world to discuss? The sole reason he'd come downstairs to eat with the family was to prove to them and himself that he could maneuver his way to the dining room without help. Now he regretted his stupidity.

"Mariah," Tori gushed, "what would you think of a rich brown chiffon threaded with gold? With my golden hair and the vibrant autumn leaves, brown would be truly stunning. Can't you just imagine?"

Mother spoke up. "Darling, we have such a short time to plan. There's no time for ordering special fabrics. I'm afraid you'll have to choose from the materials Mistress Henderson has available in her shop."

"Quite right." Mariah's teacup clinked against the saucer as she set it down. "I noticed some lovely silks from India when last we were there. But rest assured, Tuck is so eager to make you his bride, your gown won't matter. He won't see anything beyond the love in your eyes."

Pa harrumphed. "He's a bit too eager, if you ask me."

At this, all the women broke into laughter.

Et tu, Mariah? Colin grimaced and let out a disgusted breath. One would think she'd at least have the decency not to flaunt her lack of sorrow over their broken engagement in front of him.

As if oblivious to his displeasure, Mother and the girls continued parrying wedding ideas back and forth. Beside him, Mariah reached over and squeezed his hand.

He snatched it away and felt around for his fork. Picking it up, he shoveled food into his mouth, no longer caring how much fell to the table or dropped on his clothes. He just wanted to get out of there as soon as possible.

After a few quick bites—each one punctuated by a feminine titter or high-pitched shriek—he shoved back his chair and got up.

"Colin, dear," his mother said, "must you leave us so soon?"

He turned for the doorway and mentally tallied the eight paces it would take to get him there. "I have a headache."

"Another one? How dreadful. Eldon, perhaps you should ride for the doctor this morning. I'm sure he must have some powders that could help."

Colin shook his head. "It's not that kind of headache." He made a point of striding in the direction he fervently hoped would take him out of the room and not into a wall. After he managed to pass safely through the opening dividing the dining and parlor rooms, he heard Mariah's cheerful voice.

"Ladies, I think perhaps we should temper our exuberance whenever Colin is present so we don't upset him. Don't you agree, Mistress Barclay?"

He paused to hear his mother's answer. "Yes. We were quite thought-less, carrying on so. We should be more considerate."

Hmph. First insensitivity, and now pity? That enraged Colin all the more. He thrust a foot forward, only to realize he'd lost count and had no idea where he was. He had to resort to feeling his way the remainder of the distance to the foyer. After a few false starts, he finally felt the marble tiles beneath his shoe. Far enough. "Benjamin!"

The door to the butlery opened. "Yessuh?"

"Would you accompany me to my room? I'd like to speak to you."

"Yessuh." The African came to his side and clamped a big hand around Colin's elbow.

Colin began to relax as they walked toward the staircase, and some of his ire subsided. But not all. "Please inform Eloise I'll be taking all my meals in my room for the time being."

He felt a slight stiffening in Benjamin's touch. "But suh, the missus won't be happy 'bout dat."

"That may be, but things aren't always to our liking, are they?"

"No suh. Dat, fo' sure, is de truth."

Detecting an underlying sadness in the butler's voice, Colin realized that he, too, had just been insensitive. His blindness had cost him a good deal of his freedom, but Benjamin had never known any freedom, not from the day he was born. He gentled his tone. "Benjamin, you've been such a faithful servant my whole life, and I want you to know I appreciate it. If there is ever anything you want or need, don't hesitate to ask."

⌐⎯⌐

Thank goodness for Amy, Colin thought as the two of them headed down toward the stable—even if she did walk him into walls and ruts from time to time. But he was getting a bit better at navigating with the help of a cane. He just wished it was a few inches longer.

With all the preparations for the upcoming wedding, the past several days had been to his advantage. Everyone in the household was so busy rushing about, they'd pretty much left him to his own devices. After all, heaven forbid if a wedding were to take place when a speck of dust remained in the house, or a stray leaf should fall upon the perfect lawn.

His shin banged into something hard. "Oww!"

"Oops. Sorry." Amy squeezed his hand. "I didn't steer you over enough to pass the water trough."

He exhaled a disgruntled breath and reached down to rub the knot he could already feel forming.

"Amy, you always need to let Colin know what's ahead of him," Geoff reminded her.

Colin raised his chin in greeting. "I heard you were back from delivering the horses to the Kinyons." That was the main reason he'd come to the stable in the first place. He was eager to hear about the trip.

"Aye." The trainer took Colin's other elbow. "How about a cup of tea? We have a lot of catching up to do. And Amy, why don't you go help Old Samuel? I believe he's currying your pony right now."

On their way to the tack room, Colin inhaled the familiar, welcoming smells of leather and oils and smiled in appreciation.

Geoff guided him to a seat, then poured tea into two mugs and sat nearby. He immediately began rattling off details about the mares that had foaled recently, which horses had been sold, and the racing times of the three fastest ones. "By the way, I took a good look at Storm this morning. He should muscle up again within the next few weeks. I don't know yet if he'll ever be as fast as he was before. Looks like he took a real beating during the time you were involved with the militia."

Colin gave him a droll smile. "He's just lucky we got back before he was served up for dinner. Our food supply was down to nothin' by the time we reached the first settlement and could buy enough grain and meal to see us the rest of the way. But Storm has already proved himself. He'll make a great stud." Which brought him to the real reason he'd come to the stable. "How was your visit with the Kinyons?"

He heard Geoff stretch his legs out in front of him. "They were surprised and thrilled when I delivered the horses, but Nate Kinyon said you didn't owe him anything. He only accepted them because you were so bent on rewarding him."

"He's right." Colin nodded. "I was. It's important to me for Nate and Rose to have them." He paused. "What about his wife? What did you think of Rose?" He took another sip of tea.

"Hmm. I'd have to say she doesn't have Miss Harwood's striking beauty, but she's comely enough. Her kind of beauty comes from inside. A God-given goodness, you might say. It's hard not to look at her and admire her."

Colin cocked his head to one side. "I'm sure you're right. And to think I could've bid on her that day, instead of a—"

"Aye." Geoff took a last gulp of tea and set down his mug. "But Kinyon mentioned that his wife believed her sister had grown up a lot since she's been here with your family, considering she was a rather fickle, feckless girl in her younger days."

"More of an opportunist, I'd say," Colin said wryly. "Nevertheless, Mariah was actually quite put out when I ended our betrothal." For some reason, it was important that people knew it was he, not Mariah, who ended the engagement.

"I'd imagine it must be hard having her in the house with you now. You might consider solving that problem by giving her her freedom."

Colin grunted. "That's been done."

"You don't say. Then why is she still here?"

A smirk played across Colin's mouth. "I believe she thinks she'll eventually wear me down. But that's not gonna happen."

Geoffrey didn't respond right away. Colin could hear him toying with the empty cup. "Now that you mention it, I don't mind telling you I've had my own doubts about her sincerity. While you were away in England, she would glide herself down here in those expensive clothes of hers, asking me all manner of theological questions. But once you returned so eager to see her, she never again came flattering me with her sweet smile to ask my learned opinion about some Bible passage."

This information concerning his devious wench niggled at Colin, but he refused to be affected by it. After all, hadn't he made some promises to the Lord, of late? "I'd be interested in some friendly theological debates myself. I'll hog-tie Amy to keep her put long enough for her to read some scripture to me. What book would you suggest we start with?"

"Colin? You in there?" Tuck's voice floated toward him from outside.

"Yes. Come on in." He noticed the glow from the doorway darken with a shadowy specter as his friend entered the tack room.

"I brought Duchess." A furry head slid onto Colin's knee.

Having already detected the characteristic panting of the friendly dog, Colin scratched the collie behind her ears. "How ya doin', old girl?"

"Have a seat," Geoff offered.

"Thanks." The other end of the bench complained as Tuck sat down. "Mom an' me was laughin' last night about the way Duchess used to herd my little brother Sam away from the outside fires, horses an' carriages when he was little. That dog's always been a great natural herder. And the thought came to us she might be a sight better than Amy at walkin' with you, Col. You could keep Duchess on a short leash, right beside you."

Colin arched his brows, considering the offer. "It's worth a try. You sure you don't mind loanin' her to me?"

Tuck responded with a chuckle. "She'd probably be happy to escape Sammy. The kid's gettin' too big to ride her anymore, but he keeps tryin' anyway."

"Hi, Tuck. Hi, Duchess," Amy said out of the blue. Colin hadn't even heard her come in. "I heard what y'all were just talkin' about."

That didn't surprise Colin. She never missed anything—except telling him about that water trough, of course. His shin still throbbed.

"You mean about Sammy tryin' to ride the dog?" Tuck asked.

"Uh-huh. And I got a splendid idea. How about we swap my pony for Duchess?"

Colin tucked his chin. Were all girls fickle? "I thought you loved Patches."

"I do. I love him a whole lot. He's been the bestest. But I'm growin' up, and it's time I had a real horse, not just a pony."

All three men chuckled at the bodacious imp.

"So you think you're big enough now for a Thoroughbred, is that right?" Colin turned toward Geoffrey. "What do you think, Mr. Scott? Is Miss Amanda ready for a real horse?"

"Hmm. What one did you have in mind, missy?"

"Russet Knight."

Colin almost choked. "He's the fastest one in the stable. You'll start on Snowflake."

"*Snowflake!*" Amy moaned. "She's slow as molasses."

Tuck entered the mix. "Plenty fast enough for an eight-year-old."

"*Eight!* I'll have you know I'm nine and a half."

"Eight, nine, or ten," Colin said, "it's the pony or the mare. Take your choice."

She released a snort of defeat. "Oh, all right. Snowflake."

"And one more thing, little sis. Don't be in such a hurry to grow up. We'd all miss havin' you around. A lot." *Especially me,* Colin added silently. She'd brought the only little sparks of happiness he'd had in his life.

Chapter 35

U sing her very best penmanship as she wrote out wedding invitations, Mariah found it almost impossible to concentrate on the task. An hour ago, Colin, Amy, and that exceptionally intelligent dog had passed right by her on their way out to the stables. She couldn't help glancing up from the table on the terrace every so often and gazing toward the barn, but they were nowhere in sight.

She chided herself for being concerned. Far better to pay attention to the costly paper Mistress Barclay had been hesitant to risk at the hands of her daughters. Surely her fingers would stay steady long enough to pen this one last note.

The mistress and the two older girls would be home soon from yet another gown fitting. Then, thank heavens, they'd all sit down and help address the invitations. How could one family have so many acquaintances?

Mariah smiled, remembering how Amy had chattered incessantly about the morrow, when she and her father would ride into Alexandria with invitations needing to be sent out on north- and south-bound coastal packets. Then they would deliver the remainder personally to all their local friends. That would be the highlight of the entire affair for the girl. The child had spoken of little else for days. And most important, she'd sit proudly astride her new Thoroughbred, a handsome chestnut with a white star centered between its huge brown eyes.

As Mariah sprinkled silver dust on the last invitation to dry it, she caught movement on the edge of her vision. Colin and his sister were leaving the paddocks behind and heading toward the manse. Amazingly, instead of holding on to Colin, Amy was skipping backward ahead of him.

His whole demeanor had improved dramatically since the collie's arrival a couple of weeks ago. Colin now walked with assurance, appearing as tall and confident as when she'd first met him. He no longer squinted in the sunlight and had regained most of the weight lost during the militia's weeks of privation. Of course, the fancy cane he used added additional flair.

Duchess wagged her long, furry tail against Colin's leg as they walked, no doubt shedding hairs on his breeches. Though Mistress Barclay had allowed the animal to stay inside the house, she'd frown whenever she spied a hair on her son or the furniture. She kept the maids busy searching for each and every strand or tuft of rust-colored fur—even though the dog had been bathed twice and brushed daily since its arrival.

As Colin and Amy neared, Mariah's gaze lingered on his strong, handsome face. She rarely saw him for more than a few seconds here and there since he took his meals in his room and declined to spend evenings in the parlor with the family. As much as she longed to be near him, she suspected he stayed away because of her. She had finally reached the conclusion that for this family's peace and happiness to be restored, she would have to leave. And she would, once Victoria was married and on her way.

Besides, Rose was in the family way now, with her first baby due to be born in December. Mariah didn't want to miss the blessed event. Her hand moved to the letter in her pocket as it often had since she received the gladsome news yesterday.

Duchess started barking.

Looking to see what had drawn the dog's attention, Mariah spotted the Barclay landau coming up the lane. A second carriage followed.

The family was not expecting guests. Mariah stood for a better view. "Oh, dear." She recognized Mistress Engleside and her two rowdy sons, whose towheads bobbed up and down with the vehicle's movement.

Amy, however, let out an exuberant yelp and ran to meet her young friends. No doubt the boys' feet wouldn't hit the ground more than two seconds before the scuffling and chasing around would start.

Mariah glanced back to Colin. Though his sister had deserted him, his steps hadn't faltered. Still, perhaps she should go to him, in case he needed assistance navigating through the carriages and people. She doubted he'd appreciate help, especially from her, but she descended the veranda steps anyway as everyone converged amid happy chatter and the high-pitched greetings of the children.

Colin and Duchess halted just short of the first conveyance. "Good afternoon to you all," he said. "If you'll please excuse me, I was about to retire to my room."

"Colin, dear," his mother called after him, but he didn't turn back.

Mariah watched in amazement as he quickly found the steps with his cane and mounted them. He and the dog disappeared inside the house. She bit back her disappointment that he'd passed right by her again as if she didn't exist.

"Oh, blast!" Amy latched on to Mariah's arm as the chattering womenfolk started toward the house. "Would you do me a favor, Mariah? Please, please, please?"

Mariah eyed her. "What have you gotten yourself into now?" The boys, appearing none too clean, crowded close.

Amy tossed her blond head. "It's nothin' like that. I promised Colin I'd read to him as soon as we got back. And now I can't. I have company."

"But you know he doesn't want anyone but you to read to him."

The child fluttered a hand as if that was of little import. "Oh, he's not nearly so grumpy anymore, and you read so much better than me." She bobbed up to her tiptoes with a pleading look. "We're readin' some real interestin' stuff right now. Even Colin couldn't answer some of my questions."

"You don't say. And what were you reading?" Mariah stalled, warring against her desire to be near her beloved for a few minutes.

"About the apostle Philip and some man called a eunuch. Colin tried to 'splain somethin' about bulls and oxen, but I thought it was a *man* Philip was baptizin'. Maybe you can figure it out and let me know later. Will you do it? Please, please?"

"Very well." Mariah knew she shouldn't have agreed. *But, Lord, is it terribly selfish of me to want to be near him, speak with him, this one last time?*

"Thank you! Thank you!" Amy grabbed Mariah in a hug, then hitched up her skirts and took off for the stables with the boys.

Returning inside, Mariah cast a furtive glance at the staircase Colin had ascended moments before, and uncertainty slithered through her. He'd be most displeased. But perhaps after she let him know she'd be leaving they could have a pleasant chat. . . .

She took a deep breath, then bypassed the stairs and headed for the butlery door. She'd stop at the kitchen for a tray of refreshments, to give him time to get settled and allow her heart to stop its infernal pounding.

Duchess, lying at Colin's feet, gave a throaty bark as the chamber door opened.

He smirked. "I reckoned you'd run off to play with those other brats, Amy."

A moment of silence.

"It's not Amy. She asked me to come read to you in her place."

"Mariah." The woman never missed a chance. "That won't be necessary."

She moved closer. "Truly. 'Twould be my pleasure."

Colin inhaled, recognizing the fragrance that was hers alone. Why did she always have to smell so good? And why did her voice have to sound smooth and rich as warm honey?

"I brought some refreshments." Coming entirely too close, she placed the tray on the table.

He gave a resigned sigh. If she was going to insist on staying in this house with the blessing of every other member of the family, he might as well get used to it—for all the good it would do her. "As you wish."

He heard her fussing around, placing items on the table and removing the tray. "Eloise sent up a bit of her iced peach tea and some spice scones."

"Please thank her for me."

"I'll do that. Is it all right if I give Duchess a scone?"

"I reckon." He could tell from the rustle of skirts that she'd taken her seat, and he surmised she was probably wearing that shiny emerald gown that complemented her coloring so well. Strange how much stronger sounds and smells affected him now that he could no longer see.

"I have to tell you," Mariah said, "how much reading for you has improved Amy's reading skills."

He nodded. "She does seem to be getting better. She still needs to spell out big words, though."

Mariah gave a light laugh. "I still remember the first time I saw her. You were so right; she is a handful. But such a fun, happy one."

Chuckling, Colin found himself beginning to relax. "She's a corker, that's for sure." Perhaps things wouldn't go so badly, after all. He reached out a cautious hand and found the frosty glass.

"Where's your Bible?"

"On the bureau."

She swished quietly away. Even the sound of her soft steps enticed him. He couldn't help but remember her alluring curves. . .and those incredible violet-blue eyes. Too late he realized her being here was not such a good idea. He was on the verge of telling her so, when she spoke.

"I received the most wonderful news yesterday. Rose, my sister, is with child. She's due to give birth in December. So I thought I'd take a riverboat up there after the wedding and spend some time with her. If you don't mind."

If I don't mind? Was she joking? He'd been trying to rid himself of her since he returned—unless this was some kind of ploy to get him to beg her to stay. "You're free to come and go as you please. Give your sister and Nate my best wishes and sincere prayers for their child's safe entrance into the world."

A heartbeat's silence preceded her next words as she returned from fetching the book. "I will gladly do that." She settled into her chair again and opened the Bible. "Now, did you finish with Philip and the Ethiopian eunuch that Amy found of such interest?"

Colin couldn't stop his grin. "Absolutely. We're definitely finished with that."

"Then I'll begin with Acts, chapter nine: 'And Saul, yet breathing out threatenings and slaughter against the disciples of the Lord, went unto the high priest, and desired of him letters to Damascus to the synagogues, that if he found any of this way, whether they were men or women, he might bring them bound unto Jerusalem.' "

Even if the words were full of strife, the lilting music of Mariah's voice melted pleasurably into his ear. Colin took a sip of his cool drink and eased back to listen.

" 'And as he journeyed, he came near Damascus: and suddenly there shined round about him a light from heaven: and he fell to the earth, and heard a voice saying unto him, Saul, Saul, why persecutest thou me?

" 'And he said, Who art thou, Lord? And the Lord said, I am Jesus whom thou persecutest: it is hard for thee to kick against the pricks.

" 'And he trembling and astonished said, Lord, what wilt thou have me to do? And the Lord said unto him, Arise, and go into the city, and it shall be told thee what thou must do.

" 'And the men which journeyed with him stood speechless, hearing a voice, but seeing no man. And Saul arose from the earth; and when his eyes were opened, he saw no man: but they led him by the hand, and brought him into Damascus.' "

Blind! How dare she toy with him! Colin sprang to his feet. "That is not where we left off."

"I'm afraid it is." Sadness cloaked her gentle words.

He didn't want to believe her, yet there was a ring of truth in her voice.

"Chapter eight ends with, 'The eunuch saw him no more: and he went on his way rejoicing. But Philip—' "

"Right. I remember." Colin lowered himself with care, hoping he hadn't moved away from his chair. He despised looking helpless. Once in his seat, he silently thanked the Lord. "Read on. Let's get the blasted section over with."

"As you wish. 'And he was three days without sight, and neither did eat nor drink.' "

"That was me." He spoke in a flat tone. "They told me I'd been unconscious for three days. And when I woke up, I was blind."

"I can't imagine how you must have felt."

"Yes, well, go on. I'll have a word or two with Geoff later about picking this chapter."

She let out a hushed breath and continued. " 'And there was a certain disciple at Damascus, named Ananias; and to him said the Lord in a vision, Ananias. And he said, Behold, I am here, Lord. And the Lord said unto him, Arise, and go into the street which is called Straight, and enquire in the house of Judas for one called Saul, of Tarsus: for, behold, he prayeth, and hath seen in a vision a man named Ananias coming in, and putting his hand on him, that he might receive his sight.

" 'Then Ananias answered, Lord, I have heard by many of this man, how much evil he hath done to thy saints at Jerusalem: And here he hath authority from the chief priests to bind all that call on thy name.

" 'But the Lord said unto him, Go thy way: for he is a chosen vessel unto me, to bear my name before the Gentiles, and kings, and the children of Israel: For I will shew him how great things he must suffer for my name's sake.

" 'And Ana—Ana—' " Mariah's voice had grown increasingly hoarse. She stopped reading and drew a ragged breath.

Colin knew she'd started weeping, feeling sorry for him. It had been hard enough to endure hearing the passage without her pity. "Finish or leave," he said, not bothering to mellow his tone.

He could tell from her raspy breathing and sniffling that she was trying to regain control. If she didn't manage to recover her composure soon, she'd have him tearing up, too. He broke into the silence. "Unlike Paul, I was not given back my sight, but the Lord has made me see myself for the cocky, vain peacock I was."

"And me, as well." Emotion still clouded her words. "You saw me for the vain, selfish princess I was. What I didn't see in your eyes and hear in your voice, the Lord showed me. And believe me when I say it has not been pretty to look at—or live with. I've had to face what a hedonist I've always been, seeking my own pleasure, my own desires. It's been—a. . . hard lesson." Her voice broke.

Please don't cry. Didn't she know the sound of her weeping wounded him to the core?

She drew a deep breath. "But one lesson I shall never forget." She paused abruptly. "I'm sorry, but I don't think I can. . ." She gulped in more air. "I really must go."

"Wait." Without thinking, he reached across and snagged ahold of her skirt before she could rise. "I need to say something. To thank you, actually. I know it was rude of me to tell you to leave me alone. But you've been more than gracious about doing as I asked."

"No need to thank me. It was merely my feeble attempt to stop being so selfish and. . ." She swallowed. "So grasping."

"Grasping?" He frowned.

"Quite. You were right to cast me aside. Once you were unable to see the outer person, you beheld the ugliness that dwelled within me. You saw the real me, and I repelled you."

He tipped his head. "If that's what you thought, why did you stay?"

"I don't know. I just couldn't make myself leave. But I'm trying, Colin. Truly I am. If I can convince myself I'm merely going to Rose's for a short visit, I might actually go. And then, God willing, perhaps I'll find the fortitude to make myself stay there."

He considered her words, knowing how hard it must have been for her to be so openly honest with him. "Surely by now, Mariah, you have some idea of what life would be like married to a blind man."

She scoffed. "Perhaps if you'd stumble around more and act like a blind man, that would help. But oh, no. You must go around looking and acting more like my valiant hero every blasted day."

He felt her bump against the table and knew she'd gotten to her feet.

"So I really do need to leave this place now, or I'll never—"

Thrusting himself up, he reached for her and drew her into his arms, his heart throbbing in his chest. "Never what?" he managed to whisper as her scented warmth stole all other thought.

"Never stop loving you." Her trembling palm cupped his cheek.

He could not discount the sincerity in her voice, any more than he could ignore the love he still held for her. Maybe she still had flaws. Maybe they both did, but obviously the Lord was working in both their hearts. The last thread of his resistance unraveled. "My sweet, beautiful love. I have one more request. Please don't stay away for long." He lowered his head, and his yearning mouth found hers.

Chapter 36

"Thank goodness the rain last evening was light." Mariah threaded her arm through Colin's as they strolled out of their favorite place—the gazebo, where within its shadows, she always allowed him to kiss her. Her lips still tingled from his last kiss. "All our lovely autumn leaves might have come down."

Colin chuckled. "They wouldn't dare. Mother wouldn't allow it."

"I hope it stays nice for the wedding, day after tomorrow." She paused. "Oh, there's a dip coming up ahead."

"How many times do I have to tell you? I don't need your help unless I'm about to walk off a cliff or something equally hazardous."

"Well, I'm talking about a muddy bog from the rain. So you go right ahead and wade through it then. But I'm planning to walk around it." She started to pull away.

He caught her hand and tucked it back into place. "I do believe you're always gonna be a handful, my love."

"Only because you insist on being difficult over my slightest suggestions." She veered them to one side of the mushy spot on the lawn.

"You've been saving me over and over since the moment we met."

"Ah, yes, that was quite the moment—you standing up there all gorgeous in royal blue. I'm amazed I didn't have to bid a whole lot more than I did." He tipped his head and softened his voice. "Mmm, you smell good. Let's go back to the gazebo. I want to kiss that beautiful face some more."

"Certainly not." Mariah dodged as he tried to nuzzle her neck. "I'm sure half the plantation saw us as it is. Likely the only thing keeping your mother from taking a leisurely stroll out to the gazebo is the fact she's too busy keeping Tuck's hands off Victoria to wonder what you and I are up to."

He gave her waist a squeeze. "Well, she'll only wonder for two more days."

"Mmm. I can hardly believe we're actually going to be husband and wife."

"Aye. Then no one can say anything when I want to kiss you." He lowered his head to capture her mouth.

"Colin." She leaned away. He was getting much too eager. Time to change the subject. "It was sweet of Tori to allow us to share her day. The Lord has truly been with us, having you come to the auction at just the right moment, then bringing us together again at the right moment. His timing is perfect. I thank God every day that your mother and my sister never stopped praying for us."

He nodded in thought. "I'm really glad Rose and Nate are coming to our wedding. I'd like to get to know them both better."

They passed the arbor with its leafy branches already wound into a lovely arch where the double ceremony would take place. Mariah drew a tremulous breath. "I am so looking forward to seeing Rose. I hope the trip downriver isn't too strenuous for her, being with child. And I hope Mr. Scott reached Lily in time for her to come also. You did say it wouldn't take more than two weeks if he rode straight through. Of course, there would've been the matter of persuading her employer to let Mr. Scott buy back her papers."

"Leave your worries with the Lord. If possible, she'll get here on time."

"But we've only two more days—"

"I know, love." He stopped and took her face in his hands. "Two days, and I can finally have you all to myself."

"Me and your other girl, Duchess," she teased.

"I probably won't be needin' her for a while. She can spend more time with Amy."

Mariah turned. "Speaking of your sister, she's riding here fast, with the dog chasing after her. Oh, dear. She just galloped up on the lawn. Your mother will be furious."

Amy brought Snowflake to a turf-kicking halt. "Guess what!"

"You're in trouble again?" Colin grinned toward her voice. "You'd best get that horse off the lawn. You know every blade must be perfectly in order for the wedding."

The girl grimaced at him from her perch in the saddle. "In a minute. Guess what! Mariah's sister and husband and little one are walking up from the landing this very minute! And Rose is lookin' kinda fat. You know what that means."

Rose is here! Forgetting decorum, Mariah rose to tiptoe, wrapped her arms about Colin's neck, and kissed him right on the mouth while Amy gushed on.

"And Poppy took the carriage into town to meet the coastal packet. People are all startin' to come. Even Aunt Hester, all the way from Boston."

Laughing, Colin tightened his hold, keeping Mariah close. "Aye, squirt, they are. Now take that horse back to the stable. Quick!"

"And put on something pretty," Mariah added. "Maybe that'll make up for the trampled grass."

"Oh, all right." Pouting, Amy nudged the Thoroughbred into motion, and off she went.

Colin gave a playful tug to one of Mariah's curls. "Shall we go meet your family?"

~~

Colin wished he could actually view the joyous reunion as Mariah left his side to administer hugs one by one. But the laughter in their voices spoke volumes as greetings were batted back and forth. He was especially glad Nate was here.

"And of course you all remember Colin," Mariah said brightly. "Except for this little angel." She caught Colin's arm and stepped close again. "Darling, I'd like you to meet Jenny Ann."

Plump, damp fingers reached from Mariah's embrace and touched his face. He caught the tiny hand and nuzzled the little one's palm. She giggled.

"Jenny has the blondest hair you ever did see," Mariah supplied for him, "and huge blue eyes, clear as the sky. Isn't she the friendliest little thing?"

Detecting an undeniable odor wafting up to his nose, Colin smirked. "I believe little Jenny has brought an extra present with her—that might need attending."

"Quite right." Mariah stepped back from him. "Rose, why don't you and I take her and go freshen up a bit while the men get reacquainted?"

"Sounds wonderful." Rose's voice drifted back to Colin as the women started away. "I'd like to put my feet up for a while, too, if you don't mind."

"Nate, why don't we go sit on the veranda?" Colin turned in the direction of the women's departing footsteps. "Would you like tea or something stronger?"

"Tea'll do fine." Nate came alongside. "First, though, where should I put our luggage? Womenfolk sure do need a passel of stuff with 'em."

Colin laughed. "They certainly do. Just set the bags down by the front door, and I'll have Benjamin tote 'em up to your room."

"I must say, you sure look a sight better'n when I last saw you."

Colin's cane tapped the first step. "Quite. But then we were all a dirty, smelly bunch." His foot found the riser, and he started up. "By the way, how's that leg of yours comin' along?"

"It weren't much to holler about. The ball went clean through, an' I've got most of the strength back. I figger another month or so. . . ."

Someone hurried out the door and came toward them. "I heard you got here, Kinyon," Tuck said. "How've you been?"

"Good. Great to see you again."

"Tuck," Colin interrupted, "give Pansy a holler, would you? Have her bring us out a tea tray."

Once the men took seats around the table, Colin spoke. "So, Nate.

Did you get all your crops harvested? You were plannin' to paint your house, too, as I recall. I don't remember the color."

"Yellow. And once Rose saw the color of your front door, she wanted ours the same. I had to do a whole lot of mixin' before I got it just the right shade of dark blue, too." He sniffed. "Women always make a lot of work for a man. You two positive you wanna get hitched?"

Colin and Tuck both laughed. Then Colin cocked his head. "Considerin' my infirmity, I believe I'll get out of most of it. But Tuck, here, is already jumpin' through hoops. He's got men buildin' a honeymoon cottage as we speak. Ain't that right?"

"It was my idea," Tuck said in a defensive tone.

"Right." Colin smirked. "And what colors is she havin' you paint every room and every door?"

Nate guffawed. "Yeah. What shade of pink does she want in the bedroom?"

"Carry on, you two," Tuck said. "It doesn't matter what color the walls are after the lamps are snuffed. Speakin' of that, Colin, have you and Mariah decided whether or not you're goin' with us to Philadelphia for the honeymoon? We could have a lot of fun together."

Colin nodded. "We'll come on one condition. I want plenty—and I do mean plenty—of time alone with my wife."

"Trust me, old man," Tuck snickered. "That won't be a problem."

At that, they all burst out laughing.

The door opened, and footsteps approached. "I brung the tea, Mastah Colin. I be pourin' it fo' y'all." Pansy set the tray on the table and served the men before returning to the house.

His mind still lingering on enticing thoughts of the honeymoon ahead, Colin took a drink of the fragrant tea.

"Either of you heard anything new about them Frenchies takin' over the Ohio Valley?" Nate asked. "We're so far upriver, we're always the last to get any news."

"I drove into Alexandria for some bricks yesterday." Tuck's enthusiastic reply turned Colin's head toward him. "That's all anyone at the brickyard was talkin' about. They can't wait for next spring to take up arms and run those blighters clear back to France."

"What about England?" Nate probed. "Dinwiddie heard from the king yet?"

Colin chimed in. "No. But if nothin' else lights a fire under the British, the fact that the fur companies won't have any new pelts to ship next spring sure will. Added to last year's huge loss, that's a tidy amount of profit they won't be countin'."

"There was mention of somethin' else," Tuck said. "The governor of New York has called for a meeting with the Mohawks and any other Iroquois tribes that'll come."

Nate scoffed. "I doubt many chiefs'll show up. Most of 'em have gone over to the French. They're loyal to whoever brings in the trade goods." He crunched into a cookie and talked around it. "The Iroquois in the Mohawk Valley only listen to one white man—a large landowner up that way by the name of William Johnson. He learned their language an' knows what pleases 'em an' what sets 'em off. Even got hisself an Indian wife an' made a pile of money off tradin' with 'em. Problem is, the governor thought Johnson was gettin' too big for his britches an' fired him from the job of Indian agent. The Indians have refused to parlay ever since."

"This is not a time for personal squabbles," Colin mused. "Or pretty soon the French will have bought the loyalty of every Indian on both sides of the Appalachians."

Nate broke in again. "From what Tuck just said, I'm sure that New York governor's had enough pressure brought to bear that he's rehired Johnson. That must've stuck in his craw. But right now he needs to be concerned about the folks livin' out on the fringes. Folks like Rose's sister Lily."

"I'm quite sure we'll have Lily here with us very soon," Colin informed him. "I sent my horse trainer—you met him when he delivered those horses—"

"Aye. Fine fella, that Scott. And thank you again. What with the fur trade gone, those mares' foals will bring in a nice bit of extra jingle— enough to keep the women happy, at least. But what were you sayin' about Lily?"

"Six weeks ago, Geoffrey Scott left here for her place up off the Susquehanna. He took enough money with him to free her and get her back here. We're hopin' they make it in time for the weddings."

"Right." Tuck clamped a hand on Colin's shoulder. "Our weddings. Two more days, old man. Two more days."

Chapter 37

Returning from her own little haven, curling iron in hand, Mariah paused at the door to the older girls' chamber she and Amy now shared because of all the overnight guests. It was almost noon, and the room overflowed with life and laughter and females still in their dressing gowns. The upstairs maid, Lizzie, was assisting the Barclays and Rose in beautifying heads of hair for this afternoon's weddings.

"Tori, stop elbowing me!" Heather, sharing the bench in front of the looking glass with her sister, held up a palm full of hairpins for their mother.

"Then move over," Tori demanded. "I'm the one getting married today, you know. Ouch! Lizzie, you're pulling my hair."

"Den be still, missy, or you's gonna get burnt wi' dis hot iron."

Taking her curler to the brazier to heat it, Mariah smiled as she watched Rose attempting to catch all of wiggly Amy's hair up with a ribbon. How many times in past years had she watched Rose fixing Lily's hair in that same style. Now here she was, fussing over this restless imp with that same limitless patience. It was as if the Harwood sisters had never left home. Almost. If only Lily had arrived in time for the wedding. . .

"There, Heather. All finished." Mistress Barclay's own coif reflected the latest fashion as she turned to Mariah. "Come, dear, it's your turn."

Warmth for her new mother-in-law filled Mariah. Smiling at the older woman, she made her way to the dressing table. Mere months ago she couldn't have imagined Colin's mother approving of her, much less insisting on styling her hair for her wedding.

Mother Barclay gently brushed out the length. "Don't you find it interesting that you look more like me than any of my own daughters? Both of us with dark hair and identical complexions. Now when someone asks if you're mine, I can say, 'Yes, she's my oldest.'" Still holding the brush, she wrapped her arms around Mariah and gave her a hug. "Thank you for giving Colin back his smile. He had me quite concerned."

A sheen of moisture filled Mariah's eyes as she glanced at the older woman's reflection. "And I should like to thank you for being you. You kept me safe even when I wasn't certain I wanted you to."

Tears gathered in Mother Barclay's eyes, also.

"Oh, now, none of that," Rose cajoled from across the room as she tied a pink bow in Amy's tresses. "Red eyes will surely detract from all this finery."

Mariah and Colin's mother both dabbed at their eyes and joined the others in laughter.

A quick knock sounded at the door, and Pansy brought in a tray of food. "Eloise figgered y'all wouldn't be comin' down to eat, so we's bringin' it to y'all."

A person bearing a second tray came behind the maid, and as Pansy moved to the side, there with the widest grin stood Lily!

"Oh, Lily! You came!" Mariah leaped up and flew to her. Mother Barclay quickly whisked the tray out of the way as Mariah and Rose smothered their baby sister in kisses and hugs.

Mariah finally tore herself away enough to introduce the girl to the others in the room.

"I feel as if I already know all of you." Lily's face beamed. "Mr. Scott told me all about you on the trip here."

"We've heard much about you, too," Mother Barclay said. "However, I did expect you to be somewhat younger."

"You do look older," Mariah agreed, assessing the golden waves pinned high atop her sister's head. Loose tendrils framed her heart-shaped face. "Didn't the Waldons treat you well?"

"Of course they did." Lily gave her another hug. "They're fine, Christian people. I couldn't have asked for a kinder family."

Mariah touched Lily's shoulder. "Lily, why don't you come with Rose and me to my room for a few minutes so we can catch up while the others continue getting ready. We've a couple of hours before the ceremony."

"Indeed." Lily's gray eyes widened. "I had to thread my way through hordes of people down on the lawn. There must be at least a hundred guests milling about."

"Two hundred would be more like it," Victoria corrected as Lizzie put the finishing touches to her cluster of silky curls. "Isn't it exciting?"

"It surely is, and I'm so happy to be one of them," Lily answered over her shoulder as her sisters escorted her out the door.

Once the three young women were in Mariah's room across the hall, Mariah flipped her mass of loose black curls out of her eyes and pulled Lily down on the bed with her. "We've missed you so."

"I know just what you mean," she said. "I didn't know how I longed for you until I actually saw you. And you, too, Rose. You positively glow. Marriage and motherhood certainly agree with you."

Rose eased herself down onto the coverlet with a smile. "I must say, Mistress Barclay is correct. You've grown up a lot this past year."

Lily gave a light laugh. "I had to if I was going to emulate you. I had three young children and a baby to care for, not to mention a household to run."

Mariah shot her a questioning look. "So Mistress Waldon's health has not improved overmuch?"

"Some days she's better, but alas, those good days are getting farther and farther apart."

Rose gave an empathetic nod. "I don't understand why Mr. Waldon moved so far away from family and learned physicians."

"Actually, it was his wife, Susan, who insisted on the move," Lily told her. "They had already purchased the land, and John had spent weeks at a time away from the family building the house and barn and getting their first crop planted. Susan refused to let her capricious illness interfere with their plans. They'd already waited until the baby's birth, then months of useless doctor visits. She didn't want to wait any longer. She's quite the courageous lady."

"Still," Rose said with a shrug, "their going seems foolhardy. How long has she been ill?"

"Her joints began swelling a few weeks after the birth of baby David. And the fevers and rashes come and go. The physicians in Baltimore didn't know what to make of it. Mostly they wanted to apply leeches." Lily grimaced. "Susan didn't feel she had enough blood as it is, without those slimy creatures draining any more."

"I see." Rose caught Lily's hand and patted it. "Small wonder you appear so much older. You've had three children under eight, a baby, and a sick woman to look after. Thank heaven that's behind you now that you've come to us. Mariah and I both want you, so now your toughest decision will be whether to remain in this beautiful mansion with Mariah, or come to my more humble but very loving home and live with Nate and me."

Lily gently drew her hand from Rose's and stood, facing both sisters. "Those are both lovely, tempting offers, but—" She reached into the drawstring purse dangling from her waistband. "Mariah, please return these funds to Colin for me." She handed over a wad of banknotes.

"But—I don't understand." Mariah stared at the money, then gazed up at Lily.

"That's the money Colin sent to buy my papers. I refused to let Mr. Scott approach the Waldons about it. My place is there, with them."

"But, dearest," Rose protested. "With that amount of money, surely Mr. Waldon could easily hire someone else. Someone older, more experienced. . ."

"But not someone who cares for them as I do. I almost think of the children as my own. Rose, Mariah—" She reached for their hands.

"When Mr. Scott arrived with the offer to purchase my bond, I followed Rose's example. I got down on my knees and prayed until I was sure of the Lord's will for me. So when we left to come here, I made certain my return trip was already arranged."

"No!" Mariah sprang to her feet. "I've heard the men talking. By next spring the English are going to go to war with the French in earnest—and you live in a much too vulnerable area."

"Nate agrees," Rose said. "Why, our Jenny's mother and father both died at the hands of Indians who raided their farm not far from where you live."

Lily rolled her eyes. "Really, Rose. Those people lived at the very edge of civilization, west of the Susquehanna River. We have a blacksmith, a carpenter, a harnes maker, a metal worker, and even a pastor, of sorts."

"What about a fort, in case of attack?" Mariah challenged.

"Well, we don't have an actual fort of our own, as yet, but the men are planning to build one. The men of the cove go to Harris's Ferry once a month to train for the militia, just as they do everywhere else. And a group of Moravians has lived among the tribe to the north of us for years, and the Indians at Shamokin have all pledged their loyalty."

"I don't care about any of that." Mariah crossed her arms. "I want you with us. I'm sure Colin would gladly send two servants to replace you. Surely the Waldons would be better served that way than by a mere slip of a girl."

Lily met Mariah's concerned gaze. "As I said, I'm convinced that the Lord wants me there, and there I shall stay until He wishes me to go elsewhere."

"Oh, Lily," Mariah moaned as she drew her baby sister into a hug. "If the Lord truly wants you there, then I will try my hardest to be happy for you—even if I will still worry about you."

Rose grunted and shifted her unwieldy body off the bed. "Speaking of happy, we won't have a very happy groom if we don't finish getting you ready."

"Quite right!" Mariah pulled them both into another embrace. " 'Tis my wedding day!"

"Time to go, honey." Mariah gave a gentle push to Amy's back.

The child looked darling in a frilly taffeta gown of rose, a pink bow in her pale blond hair. She stepped out the front entrance on her hopefully graceful and slow parade down the veranda steps, past the many seated guests, to the wedding arbor just out of sight. From a basket on her arm, she scattered yellow and burgundy leaves along the path.

Lovely airy music drifted from Heather's flute up near the front as she provided accompaniment for her sisters along their way.

Victoria had a stranglehold on Mariah's hand. "I'm so nervous." Her face paled despite the touch of rouge on her cheeks. "Mayhap Mother was right. She said I was too young to get married."

Mariah smiled. "Darling, you'll do just fine, I promise. Dennis is probably shaking in his boots, too. Oh, that's your cue." She adjusted the stylish hat over the girl's golden tresses. "Start walking—and don't forget your bouquet by the door. And remember to take small steps."

Letting out a shaky breath, Tori reached for her nosegay of red roses, her hand visibly trembling. Then she put a slippered foot out the door and began her slow walk toward the arbor. Mariah watched after her, noting how fragile she looked in an exquisite gown of white lace. The full skirt trailed behind her with each hesitant step. She made a beautiful bride. She was young, that was true. But her whole life lay before her, waiting to be experienced with the young man of her dreams. And they would grow old together.

Recognizing her own musical cue, Mariah glanced at herself in the credenza mirror. She'd donned the taffeta gown she'd worn the day she first met Colin, and though it was elegant in its own way, it would by no means upstage Tori's. Besides, to Colin she'd always be the girl in the royal-blue gown, and this way, he would at least see her in his mind. She caught up her bouquet of white roses, then floated out the door and down the steps. The day was lovely—mild, with a mere whisper of a breeze, and fluffy white clouds scattered across a cerulean-blue sky.

Colin was so right when he said his mother wouldn't allow it to rain.

Her lips lifted at the thought, and the smile grew as she spied Rose seated near the front with Nate and Lily. Nate bounced an enthralled Jenny Ann on his knee. Immediately across from them were Mariah's new in-laws. They were all family now. *Father God, I am so richly blessed. . .thank You.*

Her gaze traveled to the colorful arbor where Victoria now stood gazing worshipfully up at a grinning Tuck, handsome in dove gray, then on to the black-robed minister. But she'd saved the best for last. Her eyes found God's precious gift to her.

Colin stood resplendent in an embroidered satin frock coat of *café au lait*, with black velvet breeches and white stockings. A ruffled cravat rested just below his chin. His unseeing dark brown eyes appeared full of joy as they searched out the sound of her footsteps.

Realizing she'd hurried her pace to reach him, she slowed it again to match the tempo of Heather's music.

At long last, she reached his side. When she took his hand, Colin smiled and folded hers within the crook of his elbow—always her protecting hero. He bent close, and his breath feathered her curls as he whispered in her ear. "I've been waiting here forever, my beautiful bride. What took you so long?"

"I guess I had a lot of growing up to do," she whispered back. "But I'm here now—and forevermore." And they turned to face the minister.

"Dearly beloved," the Reverend Mr. Hopkins began, "we are gathered here, in the presence of God and this company, to witness the joining of this man and this woman"—he nodded toward Dennis and Victoria—"and this man and this woman"—his head turned slightly to include Colin and Mariah—"in holy matrimony."

Mariah raised her lashes and gazed up at Colin. His melted-chocolate eyes were so soft with love, she almost felt he could see her. Her heart crimped with bittersweet joy, and she sent a silent prayer aloft. *Forgive me, Lord, for spending so much of my life in a quest for wealth above all else, when You were waiting to show me that the abiding love of a wonderful man is the true treasure beyond price.*

Discussion Questions

1. Mariah journeyed to the colonies with her sisters, but her motivation for the trip was completely self-serving. What factors in her life may have turned her focus inward rather than outward? Does she remind you of anyone you know?

2. Despite the advantage of having been raised in a Christian home all her life, Mariah's faith was shallow and only on the surface. Do you think God answers prayers that come from a selfish heart? Do you believe God really hears *all* of your prayers? If so, why?

3. Colin's mother was a thorn in Mariah's side, and she never really could relax around Cora Barclay. Have there been people in your life who required you to have an extra measure of grace? How did that turn around for you?

4. What kinds of things from Mariah's past actually helped her in her relationship with the Barclay family? What lessons in your past turned out to be valuable in your present life, and why?

5. Colin was attracted to Mariah from the moment he laid eyes on her. Does physical attraction alone make for a lasting relationship? What other things should a person consider? What is the most important requirement for a Christian in choosing a life partner?

6. Colin had also grown up in a strong spiritual environment, yet he rarely gave much thought to God until he found himself in a tough spot. Why do you suppose people so often wait for something bad to happen before they realize their need for the Lord? Do you think a person can run out of chances?

7. Was there a particular character in *Mariah's Quest* that you identified with? Why?

8. Mariah wasn't *all* bad. What were some of the characteristics in her life that were actually redeeming graces?

9. While Colin was off with the militia, Mariah and his family prayed daily for his protection and safety. Yet he received a permanent injury that changed his whole life. Why do you think God allows bad things to happen to good people? What "good" came out of Colin's blindness for Colin and Mariah?

10. When the future looked dark for Mariah and Colin, they found the peace that only comes from a heart that is completely surrendered to God. With their faith renewed, do you think they could have found happiness even if they hadn't been reunited? Is there a scriptural truth for that?

11. God sometimes works in roundabout ways to bring His purposes to pass. Why do you suppose that is? Can you pinpoint one of those mysterious miracles in your own life?

12. Mariah and Colin found their happy ending with each other. But that doesn't happen for everyone. How can we truly be sure God knows best?

SALLY LAITY has successfully written several novels, including a coauthored series for Tyndale, three Barbour novellas, and six Heartsong romance novels. Her favorite thing these days is counseling new authors via the Internet. Sally always loved to write, and after her four children were grown she took college writing courses and attended Christian writing conferences. She has written both historical and contemporary romances and considers it a joy to know that the Lord can touch other hearts through her stories. She makes her home in Bakersfield, California, with her husband and enjoys being a grandma.

DIANNA CRAWFORD is a California native. She has been published since the early 1990s and writes full-time. Her first inspirational novel was the premier of a six-book series for Tyndale that she coauthored with Sally Laity. Dianna is married and has four daughters and seven grandkids.